THE
FORBIDDEN
TEXT

To Mike,
You are a true gift
to The world. Thank
you for Being!
With Love & Light,
Dawn

THE FORBIDDEN TEXT

A TRANSFORMATIONAL THRILLER

DAWN CLARK

GREENLEAF
BOOK GROUP PRESS

Published by Greenleaf Book Group Press
Austin, Texas
www.gbgpress.com

Distributed by Greenleaf Book Group LLC

For ordering information or special discounts for bulk purchases, please contact Greenleaf Book Group LLC at PO Box 91869, Austin, TX 78709, 512.891.6100.

Design and composition by Greenleaf Book Group LLC
Cover design by Greenleaf Book Group LLC
Executive Editor: Clark Kocurek
Author photo by Jill Hunter, www.JillHunterPhotography.com

Publisher's Cataloging-In-Publication Data
(Prepared by The Donohue Group, Inc.)

Clark, Dawn E.
   The forbidden text : a transformational thriller / Dawn Clark. -- 1st ed.

   p. ; cm.

   1. Women psychiatrists--United States--Fiction. 2. Intelligence officers--United States--Fiction. 3. Terrorism investigation--United States--Fiction. I. Title.

PS3603.L27 F67 2012
813/.6   2012940050

ISBN 13: 978-1-60832-280-0

Part of the Tree Neutral® program, which offsets the number of trees consumed in the production and printing of this book by taking proactive steps, such as planting trees in direct proportion to the number of trees used: www.treeneutral.com

Printed in the United States of America on acid-free paper

TreeNeutral®

12 13 14 15 16 17   10 9 8 7 6 5 4 3 2 1

First Edition

In honoring memory of my father, James Clark,
who always taught me to follow my heart.

Dedicated to my children
Clark, Katherine, and Christopher

ACKNOWLEDGMENTS

"Hope is like a bird that senses the dawn
and carefully starts to sing while it is still dark."
—Anonymous

First and foremost, I'd like to thank my children. Without their love and support this work would surely never be. I owe a special debt of gratitude to Clark Kocurek for his contributions to the action-oriented parts of the story and for his editorial genius and patience throughout this process. A gifted writer in his own right, he stood by my side from beginning to end to help me better express my vision to the world. Katherine offered priceless perspective, inspiration and support, ultimately sourcing her own creative spirit to bring Eliza's journal to life. Christopher gifted me with insightful commentary, assisted with character development, and bridged gaps with his swift editorial pen.

I'm grateful to my mother Flora for generously sharing stories about my father and for always believing in me, and to her husband, Dietmar, for offering a shoulder of support and taking such good care of my mother. I am thankful for my sister, Desirée, for reading an early draft and offering kind words of encouragement.

I am grateful beyond words for the Brackman family. Bobby reminded me to follow my passion despite the demands of life, and Diana opened her heart and home, providing a sanctuary for the project's completion. Along the way, Diana and Bobby, and their children Adam and Lauren, have helped nurture my children, as well as my creative spark.

Eternal gratitude to Beth Beloff, who shared adventures, brainstormed ideas, and offered tireless hours of edits and moral support to help me emerge from my cocoon as a writer, and to both her and her husband, Marc Geller, for being such gracious hosts and opening their home to my family.

Joseph Meyer IV deserves a special thank-you for his big-picture perspective and his faith in my work. I am immensely grateful for his continued support, which helped minimize stress and facilitate the completion of this novel. Special thanks to Jim Bonnet for helping me transform a sixty-six-page treatment into a novel. His unflagging belief in my abilities was a godsend. I am grateful beyond words to John Burgos for his stalwart friendship, tireless encouragement, and for making me laugh on a daily basis; to Colin Finlay for his soulful friendship and generous contributions of photography; to Bobby Muller for his courageous spirit and for offering his support in helping me get this work out to the world; to Sir Michael Carlin for his openhearted friendship; to Mark Pellington for sharing the journey and for his superb advice and skill in the creation of my video content. His help has been invaluable. My heartfelt thanks to my old friend David Monroe, who has been a constant supporter since the beginning of my career as a writer. Thanks to Jerome Conlon for dialoguing about my experiences in the subtle realms and how these invisible fields of engagement relate to business and the world at large; and to Aarron Light for encouraging me to pursue the joys of fiction writing. Special thanks to Jennifer Godfrey, Beatriz Schriber, Tina Smith, Roger Fearon, and Kim Ribbans, who offered extra eyes for proofreading and encouragement along the way. And I really appreciate the heartfelt hospitality of my wonderful relatives in Germany and Switzerland, which made it possible for me to travel and write. A big thank-you to Doug Gobel for helping with initial cover design; to Jill Hunter for gifting her time and talent to capture the author photo; and to Lizette Mattes for her editorial genius. Thank you also to the team at Greenleaf Book Group for being so great to work with and to Sheila Parr for helping to bring the final cover design to life.

The Universe conspired to help me bring this book to you from my first jotting down the story on a flight from Greece to all the amazing souls who helped me bring it to fruition. It would be impossible to name everyone who has offered me a hand, but for each and every one of you, and you know who you are, my gratitude is eternal.

THE

FORBIDDEN

TEXT

1

SOVIET-OCCUPIED EASTERN EUROPE, 1988

Adrenaline pushed James Clark hard. Twenty-two minutes and three and a half miles of mountainous terrain behind him, a bright orange light briefly illuminated his path through the woods. Explosions erupted in the distance, shaking clumps of lingering snow from the trees. Heart pounding, chest heaving, he paused briefly to look back. Fire painted the night sky orange.

His mind flashed back to less than an hour before. He had infiltrated the secret Soviet compound to extract her before the airstrike hit. Startled awake, she had opened her mouth to scream, but Clark's hand had been faster, stifling her into silence. Black clothing veiled his tall, sinewy form, and in the dark confines of her room, her fear-filled eyes searched out his shadowed face.

"Hello, Eliza," he whispered, his breath falling warm against her face. Her eyes softened in recognition and he released her mouth.

"Get dressed," he urged her. "We don't have much time."

"I had given up. I thought you were dead!"

"I'm hard to kill," he replied as he pulled back the scratchy woolen blanket. Everything was going according to plan until he saw the newborn infant swaddled on her chest.

"What the hell?" he stammered.

"Her name is Alexia," Eliza offered in abbreviated response as she passed the sleeping baby to Clark, leaving unspoken questions unanswered.

Awkwardly, he accepted the tiny bundle and his stomach knotted. His plans hadn't included extra passengers.

Sensing his tension, the child began to stir in his arms.

Clark didn't know much about babies. A nuclear warhead would have been easier for him to handle—those he knew how to disarm.

Eliza scrambled to dress and began stuffing final items for her daughter into a well-worn, brown leather bag.

Seconds counted down inside Clark like a timer on a detonator. He didn't have to look at his watch. He could sense it—the airstrike was in motion. "Hurry!"

"We can't leave until I go to the lab!"

"There's no time for that! All you need is a coat."

The baby squirmed again, threatening to rouse.

Eliza hurriedly handed Clark the bag and slipped into a threadbare gray overcoat. "I've got to get the map. I can't leave it behind!" she said.

"Damn it, Eliza! Forget the map," Clark said, as he awkwardly jiggled the bundle to keep it quiet. "We have got to leave now!"

"I can't let them have it. The map leads to the Forbidden Text!"

"You're the real asset. You can re-create the fucking map!"

"It's not that simple," she argued. "It's cryptic—filled with symbols and ciphers."

Clark wanted to let her retrieve it, but every second spent at Blackheart's lair—Himmelshaus—was a second closer to death. Unceremoniously and without another word, he shoved the baby back into her arms, slung the satchel over his shoulder, and motioned toward the door. "We're moving out," he ordered, leaving no time for a reply.

With a frustrated sigh, Eliza complied, and they hurriedly retraced Clark's earlier footsteps through the hall and down the stairs, his weapon leading the way. Stopping short in a darkened stairwell, Clark paused to scout ahead with his senses. He had learned much from his Apache grandfather, Tsóyéé, during childhood; becoming 'one' with his surroundings had saved his life countless times.

He felt it before he heard it—a forewarning in his gut. Instinctively, he shoved Eliza flat up against the wall with an arm across her chest, as the fingers of his other hand wrapped silently around the handle of his carbonized dagger.

In Eliza's arms, the blanketed bundle stirred, threatening to cry. She kissed her daughter's forehead softly and began almost imperceptibly swaying from side to side, praying that her racing heart would not further alarm the child.

From down the hall, two long shadows approached, hurriedly making their way across the white tile. Clark couldn't see the shorter man's face but immediately recognized the taller of the pair as Nikolai Krueger, a high-ranking KGB official he'd code-named Cobra. The medium-built, slick-haired, pinch-faced Russian had the smile of a charlatan and a razor-like mind. Cunning, Krueger was determined to procure, to steal if he had to, the maximum personal gain from the system in which he lived. *What the hell was he doing here?* Clark wondered. *He was supposed to be dead!* Regardless, in a few short moments, the airstrike would introduce Krueger to his maker.

As the shadows passed, Clark grabbed Eliza's hand and sneaked them out an unmarked fire exit. Outside in the snow, they pressed into the dark shadow of the building. A crackling, cold Siberian wind bit Clark's face as he surveyed their escape route through the compound.

"Damn. The cloud cover's breaking," he muttered almost imperceptibly.

Intermittent rays of moonlight reflected brilliantly off smattered patches of icy snow. Their shroud was rapidly dwindling.

"Wait here," Eliza said as she thrust Alexia into his arms. "I'm not leaving without the map." The silk scarf wrapped around her head concealed all but a few golden tresses. Her sapphire eyes showed no fear, only determination.

Clark shot her a stern look. "My job is to get you out!" he snapped, shoving the child back at her. "It's too dangerous!"

Eliza understood his fear but ignored his warning. Meeting his gaze, she took his hand in hers and placed it on the brown satchel.

"Sewn inside the lining," she began, her voice low and earnest, "are my journals, along with notes about Blackheart's master plan. I can explain everything later, but right now I've got to get the map. The Forbidden Text can never be allowed to fall into *Father's* hands!"

"Just tell me where to look. I'll go."

"You'll never find it in time," she replied. The resolve in her voice left no doubt. She would be going with or without his permission.

"If you're not back in eight minutes, I'm coming after you."

She leaned in and placed a quick kiss on her daughter's cheek. Wisps of the baby's auburn hair glinted in the moonlight. She glanced at the timer on Clark's wristwatch—fourteen minutes until Himmelshaus would be leveled. Pausing only a second longer to press her lips against his, she turned to leave. Clark pulled her back, against his better judgment, and deepened the kiss. Despite himself, emotions—a counterintelligence agent's greatest weakness—flooded his being. For an instant he found himself lost, floating in that space of timelessness, until a roving searchlight descended out of the blackness and snapped them back to the bitter, cold reality at hand.

"I'll be right back," Eliza whispered. Turning, she darted through the shadows and disappeared into a neighboring building.

Clark crouched and carefully laid the sleeping infant down, tucking it out of harm's way. Silently, he threaded a suppressor onto the barrel of his custom .45 caliber Colt Commander. Six terrible minutes passed.

A shrill alarm sliced through the air.

The baby whimpered and burst into a wail just as Eliza came crashing, stumbling, out of a side door fifty yards away with guards in hot pursuit.

"Run!" Clark roared, drawing his gun up to aim.

Quickly regaining her footing, Eliza sprinted full-tilt in his direction.

The first guard from the door intercepted a muffled bullet from Clark's suppressed Colt with his temple, falling in a heap that the second guard nearly tripped over.

Clark, forced to aim close over Eliza's shoulder, fired two more rounds into the second man's chest.

As the second guard hit the ground, Eliza was closing the distance. But a third guard leapt sideways from the door, placing himself behind Eliza—Clark had no shot.

The soldier raised his rifle and squeezed off a round before Clark managed to jump to the side and land a bullet in the man's knee.

But, the guard's single shot had been enough.

Eliza staggered and careened to the ground. Her blood splattered red onto the snow and slowly pooled around her. Clark charged to protect her, emptying the rest of his magazine into her assailant before pulling out his knife, just as another guard emerged. With deadly accuracy, Clark hurled his dagger.

Spinning through the air, the blade slammed hilt-deep into the man's solar plexus, instantly dropping him to the wet stone.

Clark's world went into slow motion. Heart racing with adrenaline, he ejected the empty magazine from his pistol and clicked a second one into place as he knelt beside her, anxiously searching for signs of life.

Her eyes, light fading, locked on to his. Her breath came in short, ragged pulls. "The map . . . it's gone . . ." she said, her face growing ashen.

Clark felt her hand touch his. He looked down to see her fingers unfurl and reveal a bloodied, crumpled piece of paper inked with strange geometric shapes.

Taking the note, his eyes brimmed with unspoken emotion.

"Keep Alexia safe," she said.

"I promise," he choked out.

A faint smile graced Eliza's lips before death arrived to soften the pained expression on her face.

Clark kissed her mouth softly. The coppery taste of her blood mixed with the salt of his tears. He pressed her eyelids closed. His focus shifted onto escaping with the child. She was all he would have left of Eliza.

With his mind reeling, he raced back and scooped up the now mewling infant. Gun in hand, he carried the baby like a football and ran, escaping into the misty cover of the dark spruce forest.

Moments later, explosions cracked through the crisp night air. Clark glanced back. The sky glowed orange with fire. Himmelshaus—Blackheart's secret base of operations—was history. Struggling to catch his breath, he looked down into the infant's pale blue eyes and wondered, *How in the hell am I going to save this child?*

2

BOSTON, PRESENT DAY

D
r. Katrina Walker's pale blue eyes surveyed the clear Boston skyline as she walked toward the subway. She had just finished presenting to a packed auditorium at Harvard University. Prompted by concerns of terrorism, and in light of a recent study confirming that standard lie detection methods and polygraphs often fail, the National Academy of Sciences had demanded that new initiatives be explored, and Katrina was one of the experts whose advice they had sought.

Dr. Katrina Walker was highly regarded by her colleagues; her papers on the underlying superstructure of field engagement, along with its applications and fusion in biology, physics, and psychology, were considered next-generation thinking. Today, her leading-edge presentation offered alternatives for identifying spies and detecting threats to national security through the emerging field of bioenergetics.

At the nape of her neck, a loose bun concealed long, reddish locks and bespoke academia, adding an intellectual twist to her natural beauty. Walking alongside the Charles River, Katrina looked more like a student than a professor.

With the presentation over, she thought her tension would have eased, but the wind's breath confirmed something was definitely wrong. Once before, she had harbored a similar sensation of unrest. Two hours later, her mom had been airlifted to the hospital.

3

James Clark pressed the button on the side of his watch. The digits glowed pale green: 17:28. His senses were on high alert. Washington DC was home to more spies than anywhere else in the world. Even the pavement had eyes. Keeping to the shadows of the residential block, he pulled up the lapels on his black overcoat and walked briskly through the evening air. A few moments earlier a sedan with dark tinted windows had dropped Clark a mile from his final destination, and he was now making a distinctly unremarkable pedestrian approach to the Diamond Club—an upscale gentlemen's club boasting an immodest 23,000 square feet of adult entertainment.

As he walked inside, a scantily clad brunette with a generous smile and conspicuously large breasts purred, "May I take your coat?"

"Thank you," Clark replied as he slipped off his outer garment.

The saucy brunette smiled approvingly as she eyed his tall, well-toned physique.

Clark's eyes cut through the dimly lit, smoke-filled room assessing the menagerie that lay before him. The place was packed. Plush sofas and rich burgundy love seats sported intoxicated men draped with luscious silicone beauties. Five blocks from the White House, the upscale club offered table dancing and did a booming business with politicians, ambassadors, executives, and men anxious to deflate their bulging bank accounts. The club's interior was a stimulus overload—lights flashing through smoke, expensive décor, and exotic sultry women everywhere.

Clark made a beeline for the bar and ordered himself a single malt scotch, neat. Dressed in a black business suit, he blended in with the hundreds of other suits attempting to escape reality. Downstairs, two large stages featured an erotic extravaganza. Upstairs, a tribal beat pounded as a dark-skinned beauty seductively made love to a tall chrome pole and mesmerized the crowd.

Peering over his now half-empty glass, Clark spotted her. Black hair cascaded over her bare shoulders, accentuating an ample bosom pressed high by a tight black bustier. She prowled across the room, her emerald eyes fixed on his as she made her way through the sea of tables.

Arriving at his side, she wrapped a shapely, tan leg around one of his and stroked the side of his roguish face. "What can I do for you?" she vamped with a smile.

A faint smile crossed Clark's lips. She was striking. Silently they exchanged knowing hellos. Under different circumstances he would have revisited their past, but now was not the time. Vanessa had been an operative as long as he'd known her. At the Diamond Club, she was the gatekeeper.

"The usual," he replied amusedly, playing along.

"Let's go, handsome," she said, squeezing his right buttock firmly before taking him by the hand. For years, Vanessa had tried to set Clark's heart free from the invisible fortress that held it hostage, and although not yet successful, she hadn't given up.

Passing the VIP champagne rooms, Vanessa led Clark down a long hall and past the back rooms, where money could buy more than a man could, or perhaps should, ever wish to experience. Finally stopping in front of a door marked Private, she pulled a key out from between her generous breasts. Teasing him, she pressed her scantily clad form against him and kissed him deeply and slowly, silently hoping to stir him.

4

Successive explosions, moments apart, ravaged structures in Boston's Copley Square. The shock wave shattered windows three blocks away. Panic reigned; terrified people scurried to escape the danger zone. Survival instincts fueled a stampede of shoving and shouting, with little regard for life. The first explosion had ripped through the lobby of the Grand Hotel, a stone's throw from the Convention Center, disemboweling the meticulously renovated 180-year-old building. In the hollow orifices where antique glass panes once stood, smoke belched as flames hungrily lapped the red brick exteriors.

Miles away, Katrina squeezed through the subway doors to catch the inbound Red Line. The train lurched to a start. She found an empty seat and closed her eyes. The surrounding commuters' chatter blended with the whoosh of the train as Katrina's mind drifted into a light sleep.

In her half-dreams, a nightmare unfolded. Gurgled screams of terrified people accompanied wafts of burning flesh and painted grisly images in her mind.

The subway jerked to a halt and Katrina's eyes flew open. A deepening sense of disquietude crept through every fiber of her being. That had been the third such dream in as many days.

Glimpses of human tragedy etched in time had plagued her for years. To better understand the phenomena, she had consulted Russell Targ, the physicist who had formerly run the U.S. government's remote viewing program, Project Stargate. He had explained that she was tapping nonlocal reality—a field of information not limited by the realms of time and physical space—a field capable of being imprinted by intense emotion. Tragedy was what Katrina stumbled into most often when she connected, and she rarely knew if she was experiencing the past, an incident occurring in real time, or a premonition of things yet to come.

The subway doors slid wide open.

The conductor's voice boomed, "We are experiencing a temporary service interruption. All passengers must exit. The MBTA apologizes for any inconvenience."

Throngs disembarked into an already overcrowded underground where police officers searched commuters' bags at random, percolating fear. Pressed shoulder to shoulder, Katrina soon found herself wedged against the handrail of the towering up-escalator.

The moving staircase groaned under the weight of hundreds as it laboriously lifted its payload skyward. Midway to the surface, a deafening thunderclap rumbled, jarring the step beneath her feet.

The escalator creaked.

The lights flickered.

Riders held their breath.

Blackness overtook them.

With a final screech, the escalators clunked to a halt.

People, startled by the sudden darkness and faraway noises, began climbing over one another as they desperately sought the hallowed surface.

A second boom crashed through the darkened underground and rattled the narrow passageway.

Any remaining civility disintegrated as people began to scream and grapple with each other, panicking in their desperate attempt to claw skyward.

Instinctively, Katrina jumped the rail, opting for the stairs between the escalators. She knew her best chance of escaping the growing pandemonium was to break free from the crowd. Dozens followed suit.

Three grueling minutes later, Katrina surfaced into the dim, gray dusk. Boston's streets were congested. Somewhere in the distance, sirens wailed. Walking at an accelerated clip, Katrina headed for home through the chaos.

Horns honked.

Ahead, people crowded around the window of a nearby sports bar. Standing on her tiptoes, Katrina stopped to peer over their shoulders to see what was going on. The bar's televisions showed local news channels and camera crews reporting live from a wasteland of rubble and raging fire.

Katrina stared at the monitors in disbelief. Goose bumps rose along her arms and a chill washed over her. Her visions from moments before had been realized.

The television's emergency broadcast caption read, "An unexplained explosion at the Grand Hotel ruptured gas lines, causing secondary explosions in the subway system. Public transit is closed until further notice. Logan Airport is temporarily closed due to concerns that today's events may be the result of domestic terrorism. State police encourage residents to curtail travel until further notice. Casualties from the Copley Square blast are still being counted. Viewers are advised that the following images are extremely graphic and may not be suitable for children . . ."

The television continued its gruesome display—dozens of charred bodies curled up on the ground, their facial features petrified into charcoal masks. Seriously injured victims with second- and third-degree burns were forming queues for overtaxed medical assistance. Every ambulance within a one-hundred-mile radius of Boston was being deployed to the bomb site, and paramedics were in deadly short supply.

It seemed this time her vision had been in real time. Katrina's stomach churned sickeningly. Instinct told her there was more to come.

5

In the dim hallway of the Diamond Club, Clark fondly reciprocated Vanessa's advances. *Must keep up a good front for the cameras,* he thought, smiling to himself as he sensuously stroked her bare back and pulled her closer. The sultry vixen egged him on, and then, with a coy wink, she unlocked the door marked Private.

Once inside, Clark threw the deadbolt, and Vanessa quickly crossed to the mini-bar, where she pressed a granite tile on the backsplash. In response, a nearby mirror rose six inches to reveal a bioscanner and keypad. Moving to stand before the security panel, Vanessa's facial and retinal features were matched, the keypad lit up, and she typed in the access code.

A clicking sound in the wall signaled the latch had been released behind the full-length mirror that hung across the room. Without a word, Clark nodded a thank-you to Vanessa and disappeared into the dark crevice behind the looking glass that was, in reality, a hidden door to an antechamber behind the wall.

Inside, dim red lights from pinholes in the ceiling eerily illuminated the small cubicle. Clark listened with his body and felt the locks almost imperceptibly slide back into place. With the door sealed shut, the only way in or out was a stainless steel elevator, which, having no call buttons, was secured by more biometric sensors.

Clark glanced up at the security cameras, one in each corner. Unwelcome visitors, who might somehow have managed to get past Vanessa and the retinal scan, would at this point find themselves locked in a death chamber. Delta Force monitored the feed 24/7 and would arrive via the elevator, happy to provide uninvited guests with a one-way ride to nowhere.

Placing his right hand on the scanner, Clark submitted his body to the verification procedure, and the elevator doors slid silently apart. The elevator descended rapidly and slammed to an abrupt halt. No ping or chime greeted his arrival, just the barrels of two M-16s manned by vigilant marines.

"Stand down!" barked a burly, black-suited Secret Service agent. Pushing his way past the guards, he apologetically motioned to Clark, "This way, sir. He's expecting you."

Clark took the lead down the long, gray corridor. The agent stretched his stride to keep up. They were deep inside Stingray—a virtual honeycomb of underground tunnels that accessed a highly classified, close-in bunker system designed to take key officials out of the White House, or the Washington DC area, in the event of a terrorist strike. Built in the aftermath of 9/11, Stingray's construction had been easily masked with the renovation and re-urbanization of DC. Historically, The Greenbrier, a five-star resort some 250 miles from Washington, had served as an underground fortress, along with Site R and Mount Weather. But times had changed. Enemies had become harder to detect; faster exits were now imperative; new, state-of-the-art facilities were required. The Diamond Club was merely a front, one of several unlikely venues through which the top-secret subterranean labyrinth of Stingray could be accessed.

At the end of the hall, Clark passed through the final blast door, leaving the Secret Service agent behind. He had entered Halo Sector, a place few people ever saw. Ahead of him, behind a bullet-resistant door, waited the president. Despite all of the operations he had run, or possibly because of them, Clark felt a rush of adrenaline pumping anticipation through his body. His prior clandestine meetings with President Roberts had conditioned him to know that a crisis was looming. Today, it was the explosions in Boston.

As he opened the door, President Roberts' worried eyes greeted him from behind a desk adorned with the presidential seal.

He had wondered how this woman would handle the presidency compared to the men he had dealt with before. Many people had questioned whether her maternal instincts would make her weak when a strong hand was needed. It hadn't. President Lara Roberts, much to Clark's satisfaction, fared extremely well under pressure—even better than many of her male predecessors. At times, she served as a matronly figure to the nation, and at others, she could be as cold and calculating as the most Machiavellian politician.

Roberts motioned for Clark to take a seat in one of the two guest chairs. Lara appeared young for her fifty-six years of age, but today stress had etched new lines in her otherwise youthful face. Taking off her reading glasses, she locked gazes with Clark. "You're the secret-keeper on this one, Jim." Tension hung thick in her conspiratorial tone. "And we don't trust anyone."

"I understand." Clark nodded.

"Bill Sterling will be the public front, but it's going to be your job to puzzle it out." Sterling was head of the CIA bridge organization that pooled Homeland Security resources with those of the Company. Clark had known Sterling for years and understood the need for a front—a public point of contact for the press and overt investigations. Officially, Clark and his organization didn't exist.

The president pulled three sealed folders from a briefcase and pushed them slowly and smoothly, one at a time, across the polished hardwood table toward Clark.

With the first folder, she cleared her throat and said ominously, "This green one contains what we know." Pushing the second folder, her voice wavered. "This orange one is what we suspect, and this one," she said, pushing a red folder across the desk, "details our worst fears." Before he could comment on the contents of the folders, the president said, "We've run face recognition analysis on potential suspects for the Boston bombing—you're not going to like what we found." The president grimaced. "Once you've read the briefs, you'll understand why we are so concerned."

Clark had dedicated his life to shutting down dangers that most citizens remained blissfully ignorant of. Counterterrorism, deep cover infiltration, rescue missions, and bomb demolitions were all part of his repertoire. Crises typically evoked no fight-or-flight response in him. This time was different. Something deep within him, a danger signal of great magnitude, put him on high alert.

6

A screaming ambulance pushed its way through gridlocked traffic, and Katrina strained to hear as she answered her ringing cell phone.

"Hello . . . Dr. Walker?" said the anonymous voice.

"Yes, who's this?"

"I've got to see you right away!" pleaded the hysterical woman. "You're the only person who can help me."

"What's going on?"

The woman hesitated. "They say you're like a human lie detector. I need help," she begged. "I can't talk about it on the phone, but I'm afraid I might do something terrible!"

Katrina listened between the lines to see if she could discern any additional information from the caller's morphic field. But no mental pictures came, just the sudden knowing that she needed to see this woman immediately. They set a meeting for seven o'clock that evening.

Cold rain began to fall, but Katrina didn't notice; her mind was preoccupied with thoughts of her new client and the day's events. Arriving home, Katrina locked the door to her newly renovated brownstone behind her, turned on the TV, and headed to the kitchen to start some hot tea. The evening's regular programming had been replaced by emergency broadcasts, and she couldn't take her eyes from the flat screen.

In downtown Boston, the skeleton of the former landmark hotel, the Grand, smoldered quietly near the Copley Center. Worried reporters chronicled events. "This just in! Twenty-three confirmed dead, numerous missing. A suicide bomber is suspected, and several arrests have been made. The Department of Homeland Security encourages anyone with relevant information to come forward immediately!"

The sickening feeling in Katrina's stomach inched its way into her chest. She did not feel reassured by the arrests. It all resonated too close to the disturbing visions that had been haunting her. The whistle of the teakettle sliced through her thoughts.

On the counter next to the stove, an LCD picture frame offered comfort, displaying a photo of her and her former boyfriend, Marc Stevens. She missed him. They had decided to take a break when he accepted a position in Atlanta after graduating medical school, but neither had started dating again. Perhaps they were still more than friends. She picked up her cell phone and tried to call him, but the phone lines were overloaded.

Seven o'clock came and went. The mysterious caller still hadn't arrived.

7

The glow that emanated from a small window of St. Arnold's Catholic Church near Fifth Avenue warmed the chilly New York night, shining hope to the gloomy darkness outside. Within, tucked away inside his modest study, a ruggedly handsome, middle-aged priest pored over an aged, leather-bound Bible. Silently, he sat as his pen furiously channeled his impression of the divine, bringing forth the final kernels of inspiration needed for his sermon the following morning. The sole source of light, a desk lamp, illuminated particles of dust that hung suspended in the air.

The priest's name was Father Paul Burgess, and his fiery passion had brought new life to the church. By most, he was considered the up-and-coming spiritual leader of the diocese.

Bam, bam, bam. The unexpected knocking of an inadvertently heavy hand shattered the quiet and echoed through the chamber.

Burgess set down his pen and answered, "Come in."

"Hello, Father Burgess," Deacon Hill greeted him as he barged somewhat apologetically into the room, smiling broadly. "God's grace upon you this fine evening!"

"And upon you as well, my dear friend." Burgess's personable features were half obscured by shadow.

"I expect we'll have a full house tomorrow."

Burgess frowned. He picked up his pen and spun it with his left hand while adjusting his wire-rimmed spectacles with his right. "Yes, tragedy and fear tend to bring many lost sheep back into the fold." Always a good host, Burgess asked, "Won't you sit for a moment?"

"No, thank you," replied the deacon as he patted his generous belly, "I was on my way to supper and thought you might like to join me."

"I'm afraid not," Burgess replied. "I still have a bit of polishing to do on this sermon, and only . . ." He checked his watch, "My goodness, it's late. There is much to do yet, and I need to get some rest."

"I've always admired your desire for perfection—it definitely shows," replied the deacon. "I'll leave you now, but I'll be in attendance tomorrow and we can talk more afterward."

"I look forward to it," Burgess said and smiled. He was very fond of Deacon Hill and always enjoyed his company.

With that, the deacon left.

As the door clicked shut, Father Burgess checked his watch again and frowned. "Yes," he said to himself sighing deeply, "there is much to do." Then, eyeing the darkened corners of the room as if checking for specters, he slid open the drawer of his desk and produced a tarnished, antique brass key. With a faraway look, he tucked it into his pocket, crossed the room, and slowly cracked opened the door.

As the deacon's footsteps faded around a corner, Father Burgess slipped out of his office and trod silently down a side passage, where he descended the hewn stone stairs, ultimately arriving at an unlit entryway.

Black iron bands strapped the aged oak door.

Checking behind him to be sure he was alone, Father Burgess turned the key, opened the door, and ducked inside.

8

Forty-three minutes after meeting with the president, Jim Clark entered a twenty-two-story high-rise in Washington DC, which ostensibly housed extraneous federal offices. Below ground, unbeknownst to even those who worked there, it concealed Clark's special operations unit, AWOL, which handled an assortment of hand-chosen missions.

Originally constructed during the Cold War, the building's top-secret bunker had housed the unencrypted blueprints for the United States' ICBM platforms and was designed to withstand missile strikes, biological warfare, or even a nuclear blast. Buried deep below the surface in excavated bedrock, it featured three-feet-thick walls of steel-reinforced concrete, with airlocks that served as entry points. It came well equipped with life support systems, medical equipment, food supplies, and a weapons arsenal, in the event anyone ever needed to make a last stand or disappear below the surface. Today, after extensive upgrades, the top-secret bunker served as AWOL's state-of-the-art command center.

Clark was deep in thought as he entered the building. With the president's folders in hand, he held an internal dialogue with his long-deceased grandfather. *Is this what you had in mind, Tsóyéé?* "I doubt it, but it's the best I can do," Clark muttered to himself.

Jim Clark had been a lanky fourteen-year-old when his Apache grandfather had asked him to journey deep into the forest before daybreak to accompany him on his final days. It was late autumn, and his mother had allowed him to miss school because Tsóyéé had been the only consistent male figure in her young son's life, but she could never have imagined what Jim would be asked to do.

Nine days passed, and on that last starlit night, Clark sat by the fire with his grandfather, who had drawn a colorful blanket over his bony shoulders to keep out the cold. Without explanation, Tsóyéé reached into his weathered buckskin bag and produced a ceremonial pipe. His ancient eyes embraced his young protégé solemnly. "You are a man now," he said to the young, thin Jim. Bringing the pipe to life with a flaming stick, he puffed twice deliberately and passed it with both hands to seal the sacred rite of passage. "From this time on, I will call you Kwahu."

The air was cold. Moonlight shown on freshly fallen snow and illuminated a bright monochromatic world. An owl hooted nearby.

The boy squared his shoulders and sat up tall as he accepted the pipe and partook of it, unfazed by the harsh smoke. Jim knew the name Kwahu meant "Eagle" and that this was a great honor. By accepting the sacred pipe of his lineage, the wiry teen became a man.

The flames from the campfire illuminated his grandfather's weathered and wrinkled skin, as well as his clear, wise eyes. Tsóyéé was a seer, a shaman, and a guide.

"You have done well, Kwahu. You have learned the whispered spirit-talk of nature and the ways of the soul," the aged man said, beginning what would be his final lesson. "The end days of the world, as we know it, are upon us. A new world waits to be born; yet a great time of trouble lies before us. Prophecy speaks of this, as do the oldest of earth's religions."

Young Jim listened intently, and small shivers ran along his spine. He was awestruck at the old man's presence of mind and certainty.

"It is almost too late to clean up the mess we have made of our earth and to repair the damage to World Soul. We are all part of a universal brotherhood, but man has forgotten." Grandfather paused to receive the pipe. Closing his eyes, he inhaled deeply before returning the pipe to Kwahu and continuing in a somber voice. "The greatest war of all time is about to begin. The battle will be waged in the hearts and minds of men. Most are deceived into believing we are separate from each other, separate from nature. This is a false path that will end in destruction."

A deep-flowing spiritual bond ran between the aged shaman and the teenager. Jim thought back to all the teachings about shape shifting and veils of illusion, and he nodded. He understood the interrelationships between the interior landscape of a man's soul and his exterior experience; and he respected the shamanic realms where wars could be fought with equal, if not greater, relevance than wars waged in the realm man called reality.

Grandfather continued with knowing eyes as he drew a raspy breath and coughed.

"There is hope. In days long gone, Great Spirit breathed life into a Stone Tablet, embedding the rock with sacred knowledge that has the power to repair the fractured world. This tablet was then broken, its pieces hidden throughout the world for safekeeping. These pieces must be reunited to unlock its potential. Time runs short."

Over the years Jim had heard many of his grandfather's prophecies, but this one filled him with an unspoken sense of destiny.

"Humanity's greatest struggle will coincide near your final years." Tsóyéé's eyes grew grim as he gazed on Jim. "My grandson," he said slowly, "you are dear to me like none other. In my visions, I have seen that you have great power to tip the scales." Grandfather's face grew taut and haggard with despair. "If you choose the path of Darkness, you will be ultimately powerful and have almost any whim fulfilled. If you choose the path of Light, you shall be granted great love but be cursed with much torment." Grandfather wheezed and shuddered, drawing the blanket close around his shoulders. "I beg you, Kwahu, choose carefully. Without you, the world will have no chance," the aged man whispered, as he lay down on his bedroll to rest. "Trust your heart to guide the way."

The next morning Jim awoke to find that Grandfather's spirit had moved on. He sat numb for many minutes across from the lifeless corpse. Eventually, with a heavy heart, he set about the forest gathering dry wood; he built a funeral pyre and somberly laid his grandfather's body atop it. As Kwahu followed ancient tradition and he kindled the pyre, his tears mingled with the hot flames. Stoically, he focused on his admiration for Tsóyéé rather than on his grief.

The wind blew, rustling through the ceremonial feathers bound to the sticks that held the lean body up to the sky.

The flames grew.

Jim swallowed hard and stood back as an unrelenting blaze transformed his grandfather's physical form to smoke and ash. And as Tsóyéé became one with creation, the youth committed his soul to becoming a warrior of Light, as his grandfather had done before him.

But how? The question lingered long after the flames flickered and died.

9

At 7:55 p.m., almost an hour late, Katrina's new client, Susan Bradford, finally arrived. She was not what Katrina had expected. Calm and reserved, Susan stood under an oversized black umbrella. It was hard to believe that this was the same hysterical woman Katrina had spoken with on the phone.

Dressed in a tidy pink suit and matching shoes, with her brown hair pulled back in a bun, Susan took a seat on the edge of the sofa across from Katrina. She folded her hands neatly in her lap and stared intently at a knot in the hardwood floor.

"I'm sorry for asking you to meet me on such short notice," Susan began in a quiet and apologetic tone.

Katrina studied the woman who sat before her. Her voice was familiar from the phone, but the woman's composure was drastically different. Something was askew. Puzzled by the change, Katrina made small talk and scanned Susan's morphogenetic field for clues. Unlike the typical information profile found in most people's biofields, Katrina encountered dead air—a type of radio silence. The information in Susan's field was cloaked—heavily guarded and veiled.

Susan cut off Katrina's polite chitchat. "I'm feeling much better," she announced summarily and stood to head for the door.

"Didn't you say you might do something terrible?" Katrina called after her, concerned.

Susan stopped dead and turned to face Katrina. The question had hit a chord. A remembrance of some sort erupted like a plume in Susan's field. Below it spun a dark vortex with a long, black thread-like tail that disappeared below her shielded cover—the telltale marker of a deep core fracture. Confusion riddled Susan's eyes and desperation crucified her composure. Burying her face in her hands, Susan's reserved demeanor crumbled. She plopped unceremoniously back down on the couch.

This was the person Katrina had spoken to on the phone.

"Tell me what's going on," Katrina prodded gently, hoping to unlock the networked webs of information that lay hidden.

Susan looked up. Her eyes darted about the room, reminding Katrina of a cornered animal. Susan's tumultuous field trembled and offered glimpses of erratic substructures, similar to what Katrina experienced when working with clients suffering from posttraumatic stress and dissociative identity disorders.

"There's no one here. You're safe," Katrina assured her.

Susan's hands began knotting themselves in her lap as she whispered, "I'm so scared. I feel like I can't breathe . . . like I'm losing control." Tears began streaming as she shakily continued, "I've started to remember—filling in memory gaps from childhood." Susan paused and absentmindedly scratched the back of her left hand, as if an inner itch drove her mania. Fresh, bloody scrapes evidenced the hand's frequent use as a scratching post.

"Go on."

"It all started after my son was born three months ago—shocking, horrible, hideous memories. Things I've done," Susan admitted apprehensively, grinding to another unexpected halt.

The scratching resumed. Her field fell off-line, going silent along with her words.

"Are you married?" Katrina asked, trying to re-engage.

"No. I left him," Susan replied, visibly repulsed. "He made me sick. I hated having sex with him. He reminded me of . . . my father."

Katrina was intrigued; Susan was a complex case. The word *father* was uncharacteristically charged and created simultaneous, anomalous disruptions in her field.

"I really think I should leave now," Susan said as she nervously motioned to the door.

"Stay. Let me help you, for the sake of your son."

The mention of her son had once again caused Susan to falter. As she did, a green-colored trickle of energy seeped through her concealing armor. Katrina was certain that Susan's desire to seek help was rooted in her love for her child.

"I got pregnant the first time at fourteen," Susan began, hesitant to share, her eyes once again glued to the hardwoods. "The memories have been coming back so clearly lately. It was my father's child. I gave birth at home. I was in eighth grade. It was a girl." Her voice trembled. "Later that day, he forced me to take the baby out into the backyard . . . "

Susan raised her fear-stricken eyes, but upon meeting Katrina's steady gaze, she promptly cast them down again in shame, as her right hand unconsciously wandered back to her left and began slowly scratching. "He made me . . . smash her head in with a brick," she continued morosely. "I killed her and buried her in the backyard. No one ever knew."

Katrina listened to the fantastic story and remained neutral. The imprints in Susan's field didn't match her words, although deep trauma certainly existed.

"How can I trust myself with my new baby?" she sobbed. Then, as if seeking to share her pain and absolve herself from her reprehension, Susan purposefully locked gazes with Katrina and said, "I need you to uncover the truth about what happened to me."

Looking deeply into Susan's left pupil—the window to her soul—Katrina connected with a black abyss and tumbled into a chasm of cold terror. With a popping sound that only Katrina could hear, the death-defying freefall ended and Susan's energetic fingerprint snapped into focus, and a young version of Susan began to materialize in Katrina's mind's eye. Just as she was starting to make out some details, the opening to Susan's soul slammed shut. A blast of hot, foul-smelling air forcibly threw Katrina out. Katrina had been excommunicated from Susan's inner realms. Re-entry was denied.

Susan, anxious for feedback, asked, "So, what can you tell me? Can you see anything in my field?"

"Yes," Katrina replied honestly. "I can see that you love your son very much and that your heart connection with him has triggered a deep desire to heal your past. I can also see that today's explosions have somehow exacerbated some of these old, deeply buried traumas."

"Did you hear they think it was a suicide bomber?" she asked frantically. "What kind of a world is this for a baby?" Susan choked out before a ping inside her purse stole her attention. Excusing herself, she dried her tears, blew her nose, and then fished out the phone to read the text. No sooner had Susan's eyes glanced at the screen than her personality did a pendulum swing. Eerily, and in an instant, the distraught, disheveled shell of a woman morphed once again into the calm, detached person who had arrived at Katrina's door.

Standing up suddenly, Susan announced, "I must go now." After scheduling an appointment for the following week and an abbreviated farewell, the ultra-composed version of the pink-clad woman disappeared back into the dreary night.

Katrina locked the door behind Susan. Accustomed to using her enhanced perceptual abilities in her practice, Katrina was concerned by Susan's field. The information contained in bioenergetic imprints could not only facilitate lie detection but also, from the standpoint of therapy, could help identify the root causes of people's ailments. Heartbreak, trauma, and betrayal often created earthquake-like fault lines or fractures within a person's core matrix. Treating just the superficial collateral damage, whether physical or emotional, wasn't enough for complete recovery. People could be in therapy for years with no real resolution; and while this approach helped people cope with the symptoms, it did not fix the underlying instability. More quakes were destined to manifest if the core fracture was not repaired, and Susan was no exception.

Everyone had some kind of fracturing that needed repair—some worse than others. For Katrina, it was a deep sense of loneliness, as if something or someone was missing. The origin may have been rooted in Katrina being an only child, or perhaps in her father's death prior to her birth. Either way, she had always felt out of place, as if she didn't belong. At an early age, she had learned not to talk about her sensory abilities. Even her mother forbade Katrina to speak of what she perceived, because it made her uncomfortable.

Only once, when she was nine, did Katrina dare to share with classmates. A girl, who lived with her family in a restored Victorian home, had invited Katrina to a slumber party. They had all stayed up late watching movies and talking. Katrina thought nothing of it when she saw a man, dressed in dusty brown clothes, appear in the doorway to the room where they were playing. She also thought little of the fact that she could see through his body, which appeared semi-opaque.

Introducing himself as Mr. Brattle, the man explained that he had been waiting quite some time to deliver a message. Katrina agreed to help, but when she shared the message with her friends, they were astonished and terrified by what she had said, and she quickly found herself being sent home when the girl's parents realized the man's story correlated with the circumstances surrounding the previous owner's untimely death. While her classmates alienated her and whispered behind her back, she slowly came to terms with the idea that she'd been conversing with his ghost.

In school, Katrina learned prodigiously, had quickly accelerated two grades, and was ultimately admitted to Harvard at sixteen. This had made life even more socially challenging. To cope, Katrina focused on schoolwork. Then, one foggy evening, her mother was fatally injured in a car crash on the Massachusetts Turnpike, leaving her all alone.

With her mother gone and no friends to risk losing, Katrina no longer had a reason to hide her abilities. Harvard provided a forum for new ideas, edge physics gave a framework through which to express them, and her academic adviser provided moral support for her pioneering efforts in applied neurophysics and subtle field dynamics. Nonetheless, in the prime of her midtwenties, she still felt alone.

10

After his grandfather's death, Clark committed to being a force for good on the planet. Joining the army for a chance at college through the GI Bill, Clark soon found himself pulled from a standard tour of duty and assigned to the counterintelligence corps. In this new role he cross-trained extensively in black ops, encryption, unconventional warfare, special recon, counterterrorism, and guerrilla tactics.

Clark was then deployed to the front lines of an invisible war—literally dubbed the Invisible War—where a hotbed of weapons more insidious than nuclear bombs flourished. Silent and unstoppable, the new arsenals included biological and chemical warfare agents. World powers grappled to snag the brightest scientists—the critical brainpower that would devise weapons capable of selectively destroying mankind, yet leaving infrastructure in place as untarnished spoils for the victor.

The ultimate battleground of the Invisible War centered on the minds of men. Russian research in this sector dramatically outpaced Western powers. Ample funding and a willingness to delve into mind control, the paranormal, and other psi applications opened unseen doors and cracked the psyche, exposing possibilities previously thought unimaginable. Government propaganda from all sides kept the public in the dark, while the American government struggled to keep up. Counterintelligence became the order of the day, with the full realization that stopping these invisible weapons, once deployed, would be impossible.

To prepare for deep infiltration behind enemy lines, Clark was assigned to a specialized language school in Monterey, California, where full immersion scenarios sharpened students' life-and-death skills. Aliases were assigned, complete with cover stories; students were quizzed in foreign languages during sleep. Those who responded to their birth name, answered in their mother tongue, or defaulted to their authentic background failed. Clark had a keen sense of language. In less than a year, he became fluent in German, Polish, and Russian, and could get by in Mandarin, French, and Italian.

This, coupled with expertise born of his grandfather's teachings, soon earned Clark the highest security clearance—Cosmic Clearance— and he was ushered into a world known only to a select few, a world shrouded in unscrupulous duplicity where souls were sacrificed as a means to an end. Once inside, it was not long before Clark found himself at odds with certain CIA initiatives and realized that the actions of the government he served did not always align with his basic beliefs in human rights. Finally, in protest over a mission he believed unethical, Clark tendered his resignation.

An hour later he had been recruited again, this time by the president himself. They couldn't afford to lose him. Instead, the president offered him a special deal to retain his services. Remaining under Cosmic Clearance, Clark would operate off the books. In this new capacity, he would answer only to the president and have the right to reject any mission that fell outside his moral bounds. Clark agreed. His records were sanitized. Officially, Clark was now dead.

In his new discretionary role, Clark was a rogue for democracy; much to the dismay of the establishment, his first official act was to name his off-the-books task force AWOL—Absent Without Official Leave. And while this seemed fitting—Clark was indeed absent without leave, dead in fact, from an official standpoint—the acronym itself held a hidden meaning of which his grandfather would have approved: A Warrior of Light.

Geared to move rapidly in response to terrorism and modern-day threats, Clark's special unit was supported by "reprogrammed funds" and functioned outside traditional channels with a speed that circumvented bureaucracy. The scope of his unit's surreptitious missions far exceeded that of the CIA and ranged from deep reconnaissance to extractions and counterterrorism. Congress and the public had no idea Clark's team existed.

Now, in the late-night hours, a soldier stood guard in the lobby of Clark's building and nodded knowingly as Clark approached the metal detectors and emptied his pockets into the plastic bin. Reaching under his left armpit, he unholstered a compact SIG-Sauer P229 and passed it to the guard, before motioning to the black briefcase tucked under his arm that housed his new assignment. "I'll have to hold on to this, Chad," he said perfunctorily as he walked through the scanner.

"No problem, sir. Have a good night," the soldier replied, handing him back his loaded weapon, butt first.

Despite the late hour, the building buzzed with activity. Walking through the lobby, past the elevator banks, Clark traversed a long back hallway, finally arriving at an unmarked door. Pulling an access card from his pocket, he glanced back over his shoulder, swiped the card, and entered the lifeless foyer of his home—AWOL's underground hideout.

Instantly, a dozen infrared eyeball security cameras scanned him.

Nondescript and impersonal, the room was windowless and bare with the exception of a generic elevator shaft illuminated by fluorescent ceiling lights. After tapping a sixteen-digit code on the keypad near the elevator and submitting to the retinal scan, Clark entered the gateway to his secret citadel. Seconds later, after descending several stories, the elevator doors slid back to reveal the heartbeat of his organization: a high-tech, state-of-the-art operations center where his handpicked team busily monitored world events, tracked terrorist cells, and defused escalating crises.

Clark strode briskly toward his private library, his mind focused singularly on the current emergency. Halfway there, a bright, cheery voice said, "Hello, sir, I was just looking for you."

Sara Velasquez's short legs did double time to keep up with him. Sara, barely taller than five feet, had been dubbed "Sprite" by Clark, not only for her tiny stature, but also because of her boundless energy and seemingly magical genius in the fields of counterintelligence. She was mercury in action. With short, dark hair worn spiky, tipped in varying shades over the years, a butterfly tattooed on her neck, and an eyebrow piercing, most people wouldn't have recognized the gold that lay beneath.

"Can it wait?" Clark replied, his stride not slowing.

"Of course," Sprite answered.

"I need Bill Sterling down here in thirty minutes. It's urgent."

"Consider it done."

Once inside his private library, Clark secured the door and walked directly to one of the massive floor-to-ceiling bookshelves. Pulling a thick, leather-bound volume entitled *Criminal Identification and Investigation* from his set of reference books, he flipped open the pages to expose a cavity that housed three fingerprint identification pads. Pressing his fingers in place, part of the oak-paneled wall nearby slid open. He stepped inside the small, dark vestibule that was now exposed. The wall resealed behind him.

A flat screen monitor flickered to life, briefly illuminating the pitch black with an eerie green glow and flashed, "Enter Pass-Thought. Time: 6 . . . 5 . . . 4 . . ."

The most sophisticated security system in the world, the Brain Computer Interface utilized brainwave signatures as pass-thoughts in response to visual stimuli; and since such patterns were unique to each individual, it created the perfect, unhackable password.

Beeping a tone of approval to the thought Clark had projected, deadbolts slid back, offering him admittance to the climate-controlled underworld of the Crypt—America's most classified storage vault.

Housing a jungle of government secrets, the Crypt, like Clark's unit, did not officially exist. Row after row of incriminating evidence, undisclosable information, and hidden truths lay stuffed away in storage boxes and file cabinets. The Crypt contained secrets—American secrets, stolen secrets, and secrets that no one had lived to tell about. The truth about MK-Ultra, Roswell, the Kennedy assassination, the importation and utilization of Nazi war criminals, and even the circumstances behind Marilyn Monroe's death were all held in this underground vault— destined never to escape. Salvage from Area 51, along with records of UFO sightings and details of unofficial operations, also inhabited the darkened shelves. Uncataloged, the five-acre graveyard of buried intelligence was hallowed ground.

At this moment, none of the stored contents interested Clark. Today he came seeking the utmost privacy—a level of security only the small reading room inside the vault could provide. Modest by modern standards, the cramped quarters were not designed for comfort. Switching on the green-shaded banker's lamp, Clark sat down on the worn swivel chair behind the steel, military-issue desk. He disarmed his self-destructing security briefcase with a six-digit code and removed the three sealed folders. Donning seldom-worn reading glasses, he broke open the seal on the red folder.

The more he read, the more color drained from his face.

A ghost had returned to haunt him.

Reading another line, he was suddenly overcome by an unfamiliar sensation—fear.

11

In Boston, the storm outside Katrina's window escalated. The wind howled, and rain pelted the double-paned glass. Susan had left hours before, but Katrina couldn't get her client out of her mind. After tossing and turning for quite some time, Katrina finally fell into a restless sleep and ultimately into a strange and lifelike dream in which, wearing only her nightshirt, she shivered in the cold drizzle of a dismal twilight. Standing outside an old stone building, Katrina tiptoed through squishy mud to peer through a grimy window.

Hazy at first, the room inside came rapidly into focus. To her puzzlement, Katrina saw a blonde version of herself being forcibly restrained and made to watch as a man brutally tormented a young girl with a taser.

Two rows of children stood witness—all wearing identical uniforms.

Desperate to help the girl being tortured, Katrina tried to pry open the window, but the panes were sealed shut. She attempted to see the scene through the eyes of her doppelganger, a trick she usually managed in lucid dreams, but despite her best efforts, she remained locked out.

Limp, the child sprawled on the floor. Katrina hammered on the window with her fist and shouted as the middle-aged man in a lab coat picked the girl up to carry her away.

Stirring, the youngster fought back. Her cries could be heard at the window, and she caught sight of Katrina standing outside. "Help me!" the girl called.

Locking gazes, Katrina shivered as she found herself staring into the eyes of a young Susan Bradford.

Suddenly, a gaping void overtook Katrina's senses; she could discern no more about the terrors behind the dirty glass. This vacuum had no air, no sound, and no discernible temperature or texture. Katrina tried vainly to fill her lungs in the nothingness and awoke trembling and clammy.

The house was frigid and oddly still.

Rolling over, she glanced at her alarm. The numbers glowed 4:54 a.m.

Ill at ease, Katrina switched on the light and attempted to dispel the lingering nightmare. She never underestimated the value of dreams. Rethinking the visuals, she realized that she must have been processing encrypted imprints she had picked up from Susan during their session.

A flash of young Susan being hauled out of sight replayed in Katrina's mind, and an aftershock racked her body as she wondered what might have come next. She sensed that the root of Susan's traumas was part of something bigger, something so traumatic that her mind had repressed it. She needed help!

Katrina snatched up her cell phone and dialed Susan's number, heedless of the early hour.

12

In the bowels of the Crypt, a dark feeling crept through Clark's bones as he closed the president's final brief. A dangerous past he thought he'd laid to rest had just been resurrected. After securely locking all three briefs in the bottom desk drawer of the underground reading room, Clark pensively entered the adjacent labyrinth of subterranean corridors. Overhead lights flickered on and off in a motion-triggered dance as he navigated the five-acre maze of a vault.

In some areas, boxes stacked ceiling-high narrowed the walkway to less than shoulder width. Turning sideways, he slid past banks of locked steel closets, wooden crates marked Top Secret, and World War II-era filing cabinets crammed full of classified documents too incriminating to be digitized. Zigzagging through myriad interred truths that were never intended to see daylight, much less risk public excavation through the Freedom of Information Act, Clark finally arrived at a small, dusty, three-by-four-foot safe.

A deep ache filled the hollow of his chest as he spun the tumbler, dialing the memorized combination. After hearing a clunk, he somberly opened the door.

It had been a long time.

With a knot in his throat, he reached into the dark cavity and pulled out the brown leather satchel Eliza had given him on that fateful night more than two decades before. Swallowing hard, he tried to push down his emotions, but despite his best efforts, visions of Eliza infiltrated his mind: her warm breath, her soulful eyes, and her hand in his.

After her death, he had read her journals and understood why she had felt the map was worth risking her life for. Still, he couldn't help but wonder. *Was my judgment clouded because I loved her? Did that last kiss cost her her life? Could I have stopped her?* Similar inquisitions had put his soul on trial thousands of times. His absolution had finally come in a dream, in which Eliza had assured him it wasn't his fault.

His mind drifted back to the smell of her hair as she lay in his arms, their bodies spent and sweaty, floating in the sweet afterglow of lovemaking. He separated the fingers of her right hand with his and grasped them tight, curling against her. She had unlocked a part of him that defied logic—a connection that stretched beyond time. Officially, his mission had been to infiltrate Blackheart's organization and bring out critical intelligence that could end The Invisible War. That had been a success, but somewhere along the way, he had surrendered his heart to Eliza.

He pushed his burden of guilt deep into the recesses of his mind. He had to function. Based on what he'd read in the president's reports, this endgame was nothing short of apocalyptic. The stakes had never been higher. Eliza had entrusted him with her daughter; he couldn't afford another fatal miscalculation.

Inside the bag, he rummaged past a few odds and ends, tokens Eliza had packed that he couldn't bear to part with, until his hand found a stack of corded pressboard folders. Carefully selecting one labeled "Master Plan," he left the rest behind and sealed the vault. As the lock clicked into place, Clark stoically sequestered his emotions and exited the repository of secrets.

Upstairs in the situation room, three of Clark's team members sat at the long oval conference table along with Bill Sterling, the CIA's Liaison to Homeland Security, and Sterling's chief deputy, Lance Fleming. When Clark walked in, all eyes were turned to a flat screen blaring breaking news of an unexplained power outage in Chicago.

Clark glanced at the television, frowned, and turned it off.

"But, people are rioting . . . " Lance Fleming protested.

"And a state of emergency is about to be declared," Clark added. "Ignore it. From this point on, almost nothing released to the public will be true," he assured them all bluntly. "Traditional agencies are stumped, and until we figure this out, they'll be rounding up the usual suspects."

The room fell silent.

Clark made introductions. Bill Sterling acknowledged the AWOL team with a terse, silent nod as his pudgy fingers fidgeted with a pack of Marlboro Reds. Lance Fleming eyed Clark's group hawkishly. Tall, lean, and tense, his glance lingered momentarily on Sprite, whose brightly dyed hair and piercings were oddly incongruent with the surroundings and his expectations.

"Sprite," Clark introduced, "is a tactical infiltration specialist and all-around genius in the lab. Need a special potion, she can make it."

Lance Fleming's thin lips stretched into a smile. Clearly, something about that proposition intrigued him.

Clark then introduced Amjad Nguyen, a shy young man who had joined AWOL at age sixteen under unusual circumstances. "This is Shortcut, our computer-age information hound," Clark began. "Besides being able to beat the odds at craps and blackjack, he can hack, decipher, and program almost anything." The twinkle in Clark's eye conveyed his pride. Shortcut had come a long way from when Clark had first met the scrawny teen in a jail cell after he had been convicted for successfully hacking the databanks of the National Security Administration. Having an uncanny knack for computers coupled with a complete lack of supervision because of his being bounced through the foster care system, Amjad spelled trouble for authorities. Clark had recognized his potential and offered him a role in AWOL, where he saw to it that his young recruit had the education his precocious mind deserved, along with appropriate avenues for utilizing his talents. AWOL became the home Shortcut never had, and Clark became his mentor.

Shortcut extended a hand. Still somewhat introverted, he didn't speak; instead, he nodded from behind his round wire-rimmed glasses.

Last, Clark motioned to Derek Gray. "He does what I'm too old to do," Clark painted with a broad stroke. Derek leaned across the table and offered a firm handshake to both Sterling and Fleming, his piercing eyes making quick assessment of the CIA entourage.

Introductions complete, Clark cut to the chase. "We've got a damn serious situation on our hands. Chicago is a disaster. Newscasts are reporting a power outage due to a municipal computer failure. But, in reality, there is an epicenter where all electrical circuits are fried. Everything electronic—computers, microwave links, medical equipment, and traffic lights have all been fried. It will take weeks for systems to get repaired."

Shortcut's mouth fell open slightly. His eyes widened far beyond their almost imperceptible almond shape as the realization hit him. "An NNEMP attack?" he ventured.

"A non-nuclear electromagnetic pulse?" Fleming clarified, in disbelief.

"Looks that way," Clark confirmed ominously. "Mass chaos. All systems are down. Martial law is in place."

"You've got to be shitting me!" Sterling exclaimed.

Sprite piped in, "A suicide bombing in Boston and an EMP blast in Chicago, all in the same day? Has anyone claimed responsibility?"

"No," Clark replied. "But this much I can tell you—it's not an Islamic extremist cell."

"Well, who the hell is it?" Fleming blasted impatiently.

"No leads on the Chicago perpetrators yet. Forensics in Boston has surveillance videos and body parts, including some fingertips with prints. It appears our suicide bomber was a zero-risk civilian," Clark continued darkly. "A painfully normal American—he could have been your next-door neighbor."

"Damn," Sterling's mouth turned down as he grumbled, "What the hell's going on?"

Clark slid copies of a typed memo to all in attendance. "Here's the current official statement and basic tacticals. As I'm sure you can imagine, this is being run Code White on a strict need-to-know basis." Turning his attention to Sterling and Fleming, he added, "You two are the face of this op, our liaison to the public." And with that, Clark activated an interactive mapping system in the center of the table, transforming it with the click of a mouse to real-time 3-D holographic images of the affected urban terrain.

"So far, these have been the strike zones . . ." Clark gestured, "and I'm expecting more."

13

"Amen," rumbled the congregation as Father Paul Burgess finished leading the opening prayer in the cathedral of New York's St. Arnold's Church. He smiled, lowered his folded hands, and smoothed his page of notes on the pulpit. It was a full house. Worried people stood in the aisles hoping for answers from the church when none could be found elsewhere.

"Today's sermon," continued Father Burgess, "is about how God can help you understand and face your fears."

There was a general nod of approval from the front two rows.

Father Burgess sensed their warmth and smiled at the gathered flock.

"These are frightening times," the devout priest began, "but with the strength that God imparts to us, anything is possible. Moses, Noah, even our Savior Jesus Christ, all faced personal hardships. Yes! They sweat and they strove, they fought against the times, and they sacrificed their lives to the glory of our Father! And look at what each accomplished! It was their undying faith that allowed them to carry on against all odds with purpose and direction. Even now, by doing the work of our Father, these men are still remembered." Burgess cleared his throat, took a sip of water, and touched his side with his right hand as if suddenly feeling uncomfortable, before resuming with a quotation from Charles Dickens' *A Tale of Two Cities.*

"I see a beautiful city," he began with a tear gleaming in his eye, "and a brilliant people rising from this abyss; and, in their struggles to be truly free, in their triumphs and defeats, through long years to come, I see the evil of this time and of the previous time of which this is the natural birth, gradually making expiation for itself and wearing out."

He paused, his arms held out in a triumphant V. After a long, slow silence, members of the congregation were literally sitting on the edge of their pews to hear what was coming next. Father Paul Burgess slowly lowered his arms and continued with a steady voice. "It is a far, far better thing that I do, than I have ever done," he said in closing, tears streaming down his face. "It is a far, far better rest that I go to, than I have ever known."

As he said these final words, he slipped his right hand under his vestment.

🗒 🗋 ⓥ

Deacon Hill clattered down the cobblestone walkway. He had overslept, and for the first time in years, was late to Mass. As he hurried along Vincent Lane toward St. Arnold's, which was still two blocks away, he glanced up at the big clock on the church steeple. It was 10:19, and he felt ashamed.

As if in admonishment from God, a loud crack split the air. In horror, the deacon looked on as a violent rending explosion burst from the windows of the beautiful cathedral, launching shards of soot-blackened stained glass. The mammoth church began to collapse right in front of his eyes—slowly at first, then building momentum as the crumbling structure disintegrated; any possible survivors were buried under a crushing blanket of dust and stone.

14

Shortly after noon on Sunday, Susan Bradford wheeled her stroller and its precious sleeping cargo into the Coffee Bistro of the Galleria, a mega shopping mall in the outskirts of Washington DC. As she ordered a cup of coffee, the *Washington Post* headlines caught her eye: "The Reign of Terror Continues." Impulsively her scabbed hand grabbed the paper, and she searched for a seat.

The Galleria was crowded, and the coffee shop was no exception.

Finding a small table, Susan pulled the stroller up alongside it. Her eyes plowed past the headlines, and she consumed the article with dizzying speed. A deep sense of malignancy tormented her mind, and engrossed, she turned the page to read on.

Seemingly out of nowhere, a deep voice interrupted her thoughts.

"Do you mind if I sit down?"

Susan glanced up to see a well-dressed man in his sixties leaning on a cane.

"My hip—it's not so good, and the other tables are full," he explained politely.

"Please, take a seat," Susan replied.

Groaning slightly, the aged man eased himself into the chair and introduced himself as Gregory Malchek. Then, with the silver handle of his ebony walking stick, he motioned toward the newspaper photo of the rubble that once was the Grand Hotel. "Stressful times," he commented. "How are you holding up?"

Susan's shoulders slouched. Surprised and somewhat relieved by his asking, she confided, "Honestly, I just haven't been feeling quite myself lately."

"Who knows," he smiled with promise, "maybe you'll get lucky today. They're about to announce the winner of the SUV."

Susan looked up and cocked her head to the left. *How did he know I bought a raffle ticket for the SUV?*

Normally she avoided such schemes, but in recent recurring dreams she kept seeing herself driving the exact kind of car they were raffling off today. She had bought a ticket against her better judgment and her father's admonitions against gambling.

The man's ice-blue eyes mesmerized her from under bushy, snow-white eyebrows that stuck out in all directions. A brief and awkward silence filled the space between them.

Breaking the gaze, he reached into his pocket and retrieved a silver pocket watch. Flipping the lid open, he announced, apparently to himself, "High noon," despite the fact that the hands on the timepiece clearly indicated 12:23.

Momentarily disoriented, Susan blinked twice before snapping into action. "I've got to go!"

"Of course you do," Gregory Malchek replied with a satisfied smile to a now empty table.

Susan hastily threw her cup in the trash, excused herself, and careened the stroller toward Itsy Bitsy, a new upscale children's store in the mall. Taking possession of the newspaper Susan had left behind, Malchek tucked it under his arm and exited the mall, his gait impaired ever so slightly by a nagging limp.

Inside the children's store, Susan quickly found what she was looking for—an exceptionally plush teddy bear with chocolate-colored eyes that matched her's and her son's. Embedded in its chest was a heart-shaped picture frame. Rubbing the velvety nap of its fake fur against her cheek approvingly, she purchased the bear and rushed to a nearby photo

booth, where she held her son's face close to hers while the machine snapped a shot of them both. Satisfied, she slid the photo into the bear's heart-shaped frame, stuffed the cuddly toy inside her bag, and hurried toward the restroom near the food court.

The giant mall clock confirmed that time was running short.

She quickened her pace. Deftly maneuvering the stroller into the handicap stall, she locked the door behind her. Her frantic behavior paused, and she leaned in to pick up her child. Tenderly, she held him close. A tear rolled down her cheek as she whispered softly, "Mommy loves you," and rocked him back and forth. A moment later, after kissing him twice on each cheek, Susan returned her son to the stroller and swaddled him securely. Her shoe set the brake, locking the wheels, and she nestled the stuffed bear and its heart-shaped picture close to the baby.

As soon as she had positioned the bear to her liking, Susan's fingernails unconsciously scratched the back of her marred, now slightly scabbed, left hand. Her troubled eyes chronicled a raging inner war—remembered purpose dueled against the deep love born of motherhood. Rationalizing that she had found the only workable solution, Susan grabbed the diaper bag and left her tiny son behind.

With quick steps, she arrived at the opposite end of the mall where a large throng of people gathered in front of an Abercrombie & Fitch. A sigh of relief escaped her lips as the master of ceremony took the stage and started hyping the crowd. She'd made it in the nick of time.

Hopeful ticket holders prayed against all odds that theirs would be the winning raffle number for the new, fuel-efficient SUV with leather interior.

Wedging her way through the crowd, Susan knelt down near the speaker's platform and began groping inside her diaper bag.

"Lost your ticket?" someone asked.

Susan smiled at the question. Her blood-scratched hand had found what she so desperately sought.

The MC's voice boomed, "And the winning number is . . ."

Susan's eyes closed and she gratefully murmured, "Finally."

A split second later, the MC stopped mid-sentence as his eyes widened in shocked disbelief.

15

CNN news blared through the earbuds of Frank Davis's iPhone as he stepped off the Philadelphia subway. Earlier that morning, an unexplained explosion at a church in New York and a strange incident at a shopping mall outside Washington DC had further rattled the public's trust. Homeland Security had raised the nation's alert status to red, but that in no way deterred diehard fans like himself from flocking to the home turf of Frank's favorite football team, the Eagles. This afternoon the crowd at Lincoln Financial Field, or "the Link" as fans lovingly called it, churned with anticipation.

Frank glanced at his watch. Despite his busy morning, he had made it in plenty of time. With attaché case in hand, Frank's head bobbed above the crowd as he joined the hurried migration of thousands toward the stadium's entrance gates. He licked his right forefinger and held it high in the air to check the wind's direction. A smile broadened his face. "The wind is in our favor," he muttered out loud as he darted exuberantly out across Eleventh Street toward the Link's plaza. He never noticed the green Ford Taurus racing to snag an elusive parking spot.

A bone-chilling snap cracked through the air as his right leg gave way to the metal grill. Hurtled sideways, Frank's briefcase flew out of his hand and smashed against the concrete nearby.

Anti-lock brakes chattered.

The Taurus slammed to a stop.

Jumping out of his car, the driver ran to see if Frank was still alive. His apologies and guilt ended instantly when he nearly tripped over the open attaché a few feet away.

"What the hell?" screamed the driver, gesticulating toward the contraption inside.

A digital timer counted down.

The open-ended mouths of six metal tubes interfaced with the sides of the briefcase and connected aerosol canisters to the outside world. A trigger mechanism sat ready to release whatever noxious agent the metal cylinders housed.

"He's got a fucking bomb!"

Shocked, panicked fans ran in all directions to put distance between themselves and the ticking deathtrap. Mass chaos gave way to a stampede. Fleeing onlookers dialed 911, not for an ambulance, but for the bomb squad.

16

In the outskirts of Boston, FBI agents surrounded Susan Bradford's upscale apartment complex. Nearby residents stood gossiping as sixteen reels of yellow crime scene tape cordoned off the three largest buildings in the complex and an "entry specialist" unceremoniously picked the lock on Susan's apartment door. Badge-wielding agents took turns barraging neighbors with questions.

Bill Sterling arrived just as the scene was made secure. It had been a hell of a day. Clark had called it right. There had been more incidents, but none of it made sense.

Sterling flashed his credentials to the FBI agent standing guard outside. It had been a long night at Clark's facility, and a helluva day! Emotionally spent, he entered Susan's apartment, where five forensics specialists were combing through the residence. Surveying the scene, Sterling noticed the corner of a blue date book sticking out of the top drawer of Susan's desk. Barking at a nearby agent who was rifling through the trash, Sterling grumpily motioned to the book. "I'm going to need that ASAP."

The agent nodded. His latex-gloved fingers removed the day planner and dropped it in a plastic bag, which he sealed and handed to Sterling.

"Mr. Sterling, you'd better come look at this!" urged another FBI agent who pointed toward a closet.

Sterling stepped inside. Wire clippings littered the floor, and a partially intact hand-drawn circuitry diagram was pasted to the wall. "Shit!" he said, as he eyed the prescription for death scrawled on the inside of Susan's closet. Hitting the speed dial on his cell, he dialed Clark.

17

As the Black Hawk helicopter banked hard right to come in for a landing at the Link, Lance Fleming scanned the mayhem below. Parking lots on three sides of the stadium remained gridlocked with escaping evacuees. The remaining side, however, looked like a ghost town, except for one man, with his right leg twisted beneath him, sprawled in the middle of Eleventh Street.

Seventeen feet away, the timer on the deadly attaché counted down from 32:16.

Straggling spectators covered their ears as the Black Hawk dropped out of the sky. Although equipped for medical evacuation, the tactical helicopter also had externally mounted machine guns, striking further fear in onlookers. The copter's side door flew open before the skids kissed the pavement. Troopers wielding assault rifles hopped out and scanned the area as the bomb squad arrived on the scene, sirens wailing.

Lance Fleming unfolded his tall frame from the copter and headed straight for Frank's body.

The bomb squad captain did double-time to intercept Fleming and demanded, "Who the hell are you? This is a secure area!"

Fleming's eyes narrowed. Whipping out his badge, he quipped sardonically, "I'm the friendly ambulance service." With a forced smile, he added, "Don't worry—I'll leave the bomb disposal to you."

Taken aback, the captain frowned a bit uncertainly as he scrutinized Fleming's credentials. "The man needs medical attention, not the CIA!"

"This one's out of your jurisdiction," Fleming dismissed flatly.

The captain harrumphed. "Normally municipal paramedics would . . ." his voice trailed off as he caught sight of two bomb disposal engineers geared up in full protective suits signal ready to approach the target. Equipment was being unloaded at breakneck speed. "Just get him the hell out of here!" the captain said with the wave of a hand. "I've got more important things to worry about. I don't even know what kind of fucking bomb I'm dealing with—radioactive, biological, chemical, or just this asshole's idea of fun."

"Hopefully the latter," Fleming muttered. "Keep me posted." He handed the captain a business card and headed off to where the medics were preparing Frank for transport. Fleming squatted down beside Frank and pressed two fingers against Frank's carotid artery, feeling for a pulse.

Frank's eyelids fluttered and he moaned.

"My name is Lance Fleming. Can you hear me?"

A long pause brought a tortured expression to Frank's face. "Uh-huh," he finally croaked.

"Where does it hurt?"

"My leg. I can't move it," Frank managed, gasping a short, ragged breath.

"Oh yeah, I see that. It's pretty twisted up," Fleming responded smugly, "like a pretzel," he smiled.

Frank stared wide-eyed and silent at his apparent Florence Nightingale.

Fleming turned to the medics and barked, "Let's get him the hell out of here!"

"Morphine drip, sir?" the shorter medic asked.

"Hell no," Fleming retorted with venom in his voice, "I want this bastard to feel some pain."

18

Clark rubbed his tired eyes as he scrutinized the long list of bomb components from Susan's apartment. In the back of his mind, he registered a ringing phone.

A moment later, Sprite appeared at his side. "Bill Sterling's on the line—says it's urgent."

Clark scooped up the phone.

"Good news," Sterling reported excitedly. "We've got a lead. Susan Bradford, the mall perpetrator, saw a therapist the night before she pulled her stunt."

Clark's features brightened. "Are you serious?"

"I have Ms. Bradford's date book in my hand," Sterling confirmed, "and a phone message from her shrink trying to schedule an immediate follow-up."

"Let's bring the good doctor in. What's his name?"

"It's a her—a Dr. Katrina Walker, 11 Sagemont Street . . ."

"What?" Clark interrupted, stunned. "Dr. Katrina Walker? In Boston?"

"Do you know her?"

Clark skirted the question. "Damn it, Bill, she's in grave danger," he replied in a tight voice. "You can bet if we know Susan Bradford saw a therapist, then whoever's behind this knows too."

Sterling's boy-like enthusiasm wilted. "Let's hope we're not too late," he sputtered.

19

Breathing hard, Katrina sprinted the last hundred years toward home. She had hoped the evening sun would help her find that quiet place in her mind, the one that was triggered by a runner's high, but today, rather than gaining insights born of a running meditation, she remained edgy, her senses on high alert. She checked her voicemail. There was only one: it was from Marc calling to say that he would be out of pocket because he was pulling double shifts in the ER. There was still no return phone call from Susan Bradford.

Sweaty, Katrina headed upstairs to shower. She turned the faucet to its hottest setting and then cranked it back a quarter turn. Within seconds, steam began to fill the bathroom, and she slipped out of her clothes, letting them fall to the floor. She put her iPod onto the dock and pushed play before pulling back the translucent curtain and stepping in. Soothing melodies shared airspace with rolling waves of steam, and Katrina exhaled softly as the warm running water washed over her.

In the backyard of her townhome, crouched in the darkness behind the azalea bushes, a man in faded blue jeans and a black hooded sweatshirt squinted up at the bathroom window. Earlier, he had unscrewed the bulb on the exterior flood lamp, so now, in the dark, his approach to the back door went unnoticed.

He quickly raked the pins of the deadbolt, his fingers sensing the subtle nuances as each pin slipped into place. Nudging open the door, only several inches at first, he listened before slipping inside without a sound.

The shower water stopped.

Downstairs, the intruder froze.

Katrina climbed out of the shower, her moist skin steaming, and toweled off. The hot shower had eased her muscles but not her mind. A sense of paranoia had begun to seep through her, and her chest tightened with a new feeling of foreboding. She silenced the music and stopped breathing for a moment to listen for sounds.

Nothing—except for the plop of a drip from the showerhead.

Chiding herself for being jumpy, she cracked the bathroom door an inch to let out the steam and rubbed her towel across the foggy mirror.

The trespasser crept upstairs on silent feet, pausing just long enough to pull a black ski mask over his face.

Katrina's mind ran through the day's events. Maybe her uneasiness was merely a reflection of unresolved feelings from her nightmare about Susan. She turned on the faucet to brush her teeth.

With the toe of his boot, the masked man pushed open the bedroom door.

Katrina froze with her hand still on the faucet and listened again. *Maybe it was the water heater turning on?* Trying to calm her nerves, she dismissed her fear as a symptom of fatigue from a poor night's sleep and reached for the toothpaste.

His objective in sight, the intruder peeked through the crack in the bathroom door, admiring Katrina's reflection in the mirror. Firm and supple, her muscles were well toned, her breasts pert and round, her skin still moist and steamy.

Toothbrush in hand, a dagger of alarm resonated through Katrina's core, and she decided she'd better check to make sure the doors downstairs were locked.

Suddenly the bathroom door slammed open. Out of nowhere, strong arms grabbed her from behind.

Katrina opened her mouth to scream, but no sound came out.

A gloved hand covered her mouth. She chomped down hard on a finger and savagely kicked her attacker's shin, connecting her heel to his bone.

Surprised, the man released her.

Katrina spun out of his grasp and bolted out of the bathroom into the bedroom, diving for her nightstand, where she kept a canister of pepper spray.

He silently closed the distance. His eyes appreciated her naked beauty through the slits of his ski mask.

Wheeling around, she took aim, but it was too late. All she saw was the barrel of a gun pointed at her.

She heard a loud pop.

A sharp sting cut off her thoughts. In disbelief, she stared down at the dart embedded deep in her thigh, the bright red plume of which contrasted boldly against her cream-colored skin.

The room began to spin in slow motion.

Numbly, Katrina reached down, yanked it out, and stared uncomprehendingly at the needle's tip.

A warm, disconcerting sensation washed through her body.

Her vision grew soft and cloudy. The projectile's load had hit her brain.

Katrina's assailant closed the gap, ready to fire another round if she had any fight left in her.

She searched out his eyes through the holes of the mask, but his image doubled and his form blurred indistinguishably from the wall.

Blackness crept through her peripheral vision as her legs gave way beneath her.

The hardwood floor rushed to meet her face.

In the distance of her consciousness, she felt his arms against her bare skin, catching her before she hit the ground. Then, everything went black. Darkness folded over her.

20

Black Hole was an interrogation facility far beyond the reach of habeas corpus, the Fifth Amendment, and the most basic of human rights. Deep in the bowels of this dank cesspool, Frank Davis slowly opened his bloodshot eyes. The searing pain in his leg reminded his foggy brain that he was still alive. Bound to a chair, he sat slumped with his head resting on a table.

To his right, an expansive floor-to-ceiling mirror adorned the wall in the otherwise spartan room. Struggling to focus, Frank stared bleary-eyed at his reflection. The image of his crumpled leg saturated him with a strange mixture of confusion, repulsion, and shame. His pant leg had been cut wide open, and the limb, already swollen and deep purple, had been splinted but not cast. He tried to remember what had happened and how he got here, but the memory was a blur. All he knew was that he'd already been put through a battery of lie detection tests for some crime he couldn't remember committing.

Lance Fleming's voice boomed behind Frank as he flung the door open. "It's about damn time you came to!"

Frank jerked, startled.

Fleming barged into the room, circling the prisoner. His eyes pierced his target. "What kind of work do you do, Mr. Davis?" Fleming pressed.

"I . . . I'm a sales rep! I sell computer chips," Frank stammered and pulled against his restraints, unsuccessfully trying to keep Fleming in his sights.

"Let's see . . . we have a single mom, a priest, and now a salesman. What am I dealing with here, the Rotary Club?"

"What are you talking about? Where am I?" Frank stammered.

Fleming stopped pacing and leaned in toward his prey. Softly he cleared his throat; a thin smile cracked his rigid features. "You're in hell, Frank. You're in hell," he delivered in a low growl.

Frank Davis squirmed uncomfortably. His eyes widened with panic. "I don't understand. Untie me, please!" Begging, he yanked harder against his bindings.

Fleming, amused, glanced at the mirror, as if sharing a joke with someone on the other side. Redirecting his focus, he snapped, "Frank! Pay attention! Why were you carrying an attaché case into the stadium?"

"I had some files to go over before the game! For Christ's sake!" Frank pleaded, "Let me go."

"Jesus can't help you here," Fleming said with cold satisfaction. "Why would you want to exterminate so many fans at the Link? That's not very Christian of you."

"Exterminate? What are you talking about? I would never . . ."

"Cut the bullshit!" Fleming barked. "I personally had the pleasure of viewing your homemade deployment device—nice piece of work, I'll give you that. Now you better fucking tell me who put you up to this, or things are going to get very ugly here—I promise."

The sound of Lance Fleming's methodical footsteps pacing across the concrete floor rang insanely in Frank's ears. "Oh God, oh God, oh God," he started whimpering, "I don't know, I don't know what you're talking about. I don't even own a gun!"

"You don't know, huh? How about . . . now?" Fleming reached down and grabbed Frank's leg at the fracture. Eyes narrowing, he studied Frank's face for signs of weakness as he dug his thumb into the wounded bone. His reward, a high-pitched screech, echoed in the room long after he released his pressure.

Gasping violently, tears welled in Frank's brown eyes. "I don't know anything," he repeated, anguish contorting his sincere face. "I was just going to the game. I haven't missed one in two years."

"You're never going to see another if you don't start talking—now!" Fleming's fist pounded hard, rattling the table in front of Frank. "I'm on a tight schedule, and if you don't spill and tell me why you tried to kill thousands of your fellow fans . . ." he paused and whispered in Frank's ear, ". . . you're going to see a whole new world of pain."

Frantic and confused, Frank's eyes darted about the room. "Please, may I call my wife? Or a lawyer?"

"No, you can't." Fleming smiled calculatingly.

Frank looked at him with bewilderment. "But . . . why? I've got rights."

"Because, Frank—you're dead."

Frank Davis stared into Fleming's cold, diamond-hard eyes and blinked, speechless.

"See for yourself." Smiling, Fleming smacked the current *Philadelphia Inquirer* down on the table in front of him.

Frank stared at the front page in disbelief and read the headline: "Prank Bomber Dies En Route To Hospital." Beneath the text, a color picture showed his contorted body sprawled on the pavement near his attaché case, the bomb squad on the scene. Frank swallowed hard.

"I'm starting a scrapbook for you," Fleming heckled. "And if you ever want to come back to life, you'd better start telling me the fucking truth."

"My wife, please, I have to call her. I have kids. They depend on me. If they think I'm dead, they'll be devastated." Sobs racked his chest.

"First, you're gonna tell me who put you up to this!"

"Who put me up to what? I don't know what you're talking about. I haven't done anything wrong. I was just going to the game."

"I see how you want to play it, Frank. That's fine by me. Just get one thing straight: By the end of this magic hour, you will have told me the name of whatever sick religion or political vomit you subscribe to, along with the names of the people who inspired you to forfeit your meaningless life—do you get that?" Fleming poked him hard in the chest for emphasis.

Frank Davis recoiled submissively. "Please, I'm cooperating. Have pity on me. I'm innocent."

Fleming's patience evaporated and he exploded. "You were carrying a fucking bomb!—and you have the nerve to ask for my pity?" Fleming hocked phlegm from his throat and spat in Frank's face. "You're a fucking traitor. I should have shot you in the street like the dog you are; instead I have to pussyfoot around."

In shock, Frank blinked as warm milky spittle slid down his cheek. "I swear on the lives of my mother, my wife, and my son and daughter," he entreated earnestly. "I don't know how that thing got into my briefcase."

"And your whole family is dropping dead right now, you coward." Then, unexpectedly, Fleming spun and delivered a punch lightning-fast to Frank's jaw.

Frank reeled, wild-eyed in confusion. Blood oozed out of his mouth. "Why are you treating me like this? I need a doctor," he sputtered lamely.

"You're a mental case, Frank. You need a shrink—not an MD. Your leg will heal by itself . . . although it may be a little crooked," Fleming added. His voice had become cold and cruel. "But you're not really gonna need it. Are you?" Determined to get answers before there was another attack on the public, Fleming strode across the room to a dark corner. From experience, he knew that fear could be a far more effective motivator than physical pain itself.

Seconds later, a loud crackling noise emanated from the shadows near Fleming, accompanied by a shower of electric blue sparks.

A trickle of blood dripped down Frank Davis's chin and into his lap. He gasped for air and looked up helplessly to see Fleming smiling menacingly and wheeling out a small cart. On it was a car battery, jumper cables, pliers, a corkscrew attached to a drill, what looked like giant steel wool Q-tips, and a vat of water.

Moving close to Frank's bound form, Fleming tapped the ends of the jumper cables together six inches from his face.

A blue arc dazzled the air and made Frank's hair stand on end.

"Now, listen carefully," Fleming snarled. "You've met good cop—you're about to meet bad cop," he said. "Good cop is going to ask you nicely one more time: Who put you up to this?" As he spoke, he slowly waved the jumper cable clip ominously close to Frank's groin, "And if you don't give him a straight answer, bad cop's gonna clamp these babies right to your balls."

21

Katrina regained consciousness with a groan. The room was dark except for the light from a candle on the nightstand nearby. She was lying on a strange bed, clad only in a bathrobe. Groggily, she pulled back the unfamiliar robe to examine her thigh.

A dull ache and the bloodied, bruised puncture mark confirmed her hazy memories of the assault and snapped her fully back to consciousness.

Where am I?

Her eyes searched the dark recesses. Sensing someone in the shadows, she bolted upright, heart pounding.

The room instantly threatened to spin out of control.

"Take it easy, Dr. Walker," said a deep voice. A tall, well-built man with chiseled features stepped into the light.

Icy numbness filled Katrina's veins.

Her breath caught in her throat.

She tried desperately to scan his energy signature to confirm or deny him as her kidnapper, but the dart's drug still impaired her sensory abilities.

His eyes were hard and military, yet concerned. "You can relax," he informed her in a calm, steady voice. "You are safe now."

"Who are you? Where am I?" she demanded, steadying herself with her hands.

"My name is Derek Gray," he replied, turning on the light. "You're in a government facility. You were brought in for your own protection."

She stared back at him fiercely through the haze that still lingered in her mind. "Protection from what?" she challenged, her tone seeping with suspicion. Intuitively she sensed he was somehow involved with her abduction.

"I'm not at liberty to discuss that."

"Well, who the hell is?"

"I'll take you to him," Derek replied, extending a hand to help her gain her feet.

Rejecting his helpful gesture, she climbed down off the bed herself, only to have her robe fall half open, offering a generous glimpse of her body. Quickly cinching the bathrobe tight, Katrina caught the flicker of his smile before he averted his eyes.

Katrina warily eyed the handsome stranger as he walked her down a long corridor and into the fluorescent wash of a sophisticated control center—a labyrinth of satellite displays and floor-to-ceiling computerized global tracking maps. Thankfully, her surroundings had stopped spinning and she was able to search for clues to her whereabouts. People worked busily at computer stations. A few of them glanced up awkwardly as she passed.

Breaking the silence, Derek finally offered, "He's expecting you."

"Who?" she demanded, frustrated, not appreciating his secretive manner.

Derek ignored her question and picked up the pace until they left the windowless, high-tech jungle and arrived at an eclectic enclave populated by a comfortable, leather seating group, a richly crafted rug, and a coffee table laden with refreshments.

As she approached, a tall man in a slim-fitting, black sweater and khaki slacks stood to greet her.

22

"Good evening, Dr. Walker," Jim Clark said as he reached out in a warm gesture to shake Katrina's hand. "I'm sorry we have to meet under these circumstances," he added with a face that masked his anticipatory excitement.

"Who the hell do you think you are, abducting me?" Katrina challenged frostily as she refused his handshake.

"My organization rescued you from your abductors, Dr. Walker. Please, sit down." He gestured to the generously stuffed brown leather sofa. "We need to talk."

Katrina remained standing and squared her shoulders, dubiously eyeing her host. "Who are you? And where am I?" she demanded.

"I'm afraid I can't disclose your location—it's classified," he informed her. "But my name is Jim Clark," he continued with a friendly tone, "and for the moment, you'll have to trust me."

Trust was the last thing Katrina felt. Her leg still smarted from the dart, and her head swam.

Striving to allay her concerns, Clark produced a black leather-bound identification badge stamped with the presidential seal.

She scrutinized the photo, and taking inventory of the good-looking and athletically built man, read aloud, "James Clark—Cosmic

Clearance." Age-wise, he looked as if he might be in his early forties, but the wisdom in his eyes told her otherwise.

"That's me," Clark replied, matter-of-factly, and flipping the badge shut, he took a seat in an oversized chair.

Reluctantly, Katrina sat down stiffly across from him. Arms folded, her bare feet resting on the Oriental rug, she tried to make sense of her situation.

For Clark, the close proximity to Eliza's likeness was unsettling. Although he had provided for Katrina from the moment she was put in his charge as an infant, watched her from afar during her youth, made sure she had the best schooling and home environment possible, and even surreptitiously attended Katrina's lectures, he had never risked an in-person meeting for fear of compromising Eliza's daughter's new identity. He quickly redoubled his heart's armor to keep his emotions at bay; they were, after all, an operative's worst enemy. He'd already lost Eliza; he wasn't about to risk losing her daughter due to clouded judgment. "I would like to personally apologize for any inconvenience you may have experienced," he began politely. "I know that you are probably," he paused and searched for the right words, "uncomfortable right now."

Katrina's left eyebrow rose, mocking his understatement. "I've been shot with a tranquilizer dart, abducted from my home, and, regardless of your claims to innocence, Mr. Clark, I know your friend over there," she added, nodding toward Derek, "was somehow involved. I sense it. So, why would I be uncomfortable?"

Clark remained calm in the face of her sarcasm. "Derek didn't shoot you, Dr. Walker. They did."

Katrina glowered at him quizzically. "Who is 'they'?"

"That's something I was hoping you might be able to tell us," Clark remarked. "Derek arrived on the scene just as you were being loaded into an unmarked white van. You're lucky he got there when he did."

Katrina looked disbelievingly back and forth between the two men. She could tell Clark was holding something back but wasn't sure what.

Derek filled in, "There was a bit of a skirmish. The man who abducted you was badly injured but made it into the van. He and the driver got away. The van's plates were stolen, so that's a dead end."

"Do you know a woman named Susan Bradford?" Clark questioned bluntly, pointing to a nearby computer screen that displayed a driver's license picture.

Katrina hesitated. "Yes. She's a new client."

"Do you know what your client did earlier today?"

Katrina shook her head no.

"She killed herself along with seventeen others in a mall outside Washington DC."

"What? How's that possible?" Her mind struggled to connect the dots.

Clark pressed a button on a remote control. A large LCD screen flickered to life on a neighboring wall.

Katrina focused on the grainy video feed.

"This," Clark said as he fast-forwarded the footage, "is from the mall's security camera."

A knot wrenched in Katrina's belly as she watched the grainy image of Susan Bradford approach a sizeable crowd gathered around a stage where a master of ceremony stood with a microphone. In silent horror, Katrina witnessed the grisly scene unfold.

Susan fumbled with a diaper bag. Suddenly the MC stopped mid-sentence. Eyes wide, he gasped in disbelief before grabbing his left arm and collapsing. Audience members crumpled one by one: some cried out in pain, others clutched their chests, still others clawed at their heads in agony. Helplessly, the victims watched each other suffer. A few reached for cell phones, struggling to call for help or to reach loved ones before they died. Susan, too, succumbed, but without a fight. Holding the diaper bag tight to her chest as it exploded, flames engulfed Susan and destroyed the bag's mysterious contents.

Clark flicked the video off. "Based on the evidence found at Ms. Bradford's house, it seems she had built a directed-energy weapon that triggered heart attacks and brain hemorrhages."

Katrina swallowed hard and stared at him, eyes wide in shock. "I've never heard of such a thing," she finally managed.

Clark nodded. "Invisible warfare—it exists. Our military has developed EM pulse guns that can stop cars, but this is a rather sophisticated application." Clark's concerned eyes caught hers. "You're in extreme danger, Dr. Walker. If I was able to find out that Susan Bradford met with you hours before executing her kill, you can be sure that whoever she worked for knows about you too."

Katrina's head spun as she contemplated his remarks.

"They're the ones who infiltrated your home and drugged you," Clark explained, his voice low and serious. "They wanted you alive and well for questioning."

Her chest tightened.

"As soon as I learned of your involvement, I sent Derek to extract you. My hope was that he would get there before they did, but as it was, he got to you just in time. So, yes," Clark conceded, "Derek was involved, but he came along after you were unconscious. Besides," he added with a wry grin, "if we wanted to pay you a visit, we would have knocked on your door."

Katrina sat, momentarily struck silent. She was confused and could say little but, "Thank-you."

Clark smiled and was about to expound on his explanation when Sprite rushed over and interrupted. "President Roberts is on the line."

"Take Dr. Walker to get some clothes," Clark replied, as he put the phone to his ear.

23

With a quick nod, Sprite led Katrina back through the underground maze to the room in which she had awakened and flipped on the light. In the short time Katrina had been gone, the bed covers had been pulled smooth and the candle extinguished. But what Katrina noticed most was an acute lack of windows that someone had taken the care to offset with artwork.

"Clothes are on the chair," Sprite smiled. "By the time you're dressed, I'm sure Commander Clark will be ready to reconvene." Closing the door behind her, Sprite added, "Someone will be back to get you soon."

Katrina heard the deadbolt click. She walked over and checked the handle. The door had been locked from the outside. A tight spot of annoyance formed behind her temple. She didn't care how top secret this facility was. There was no excuse for imprisoning her. Mr. Clark had a lot to explain.

Slipping out of her robe, she hurried to dress. A size-four pair of khaki pants, a crisp white shirt, and tasteful undergarments awaited her, tags still in place. The outfit was smart and fit her uncannily well. At the foot of the bed, she found a pair of functional, stylish boots in size seven and a half. The brown leather was soft and supple, and the footwear fit her like a glove. As she tied the laces, a wary uneasiness crept through her. How did they know her sizes?

A knock at the door interrupted her speculative deliberation. "Ready, Dr. Walker?" asked Derek Gray's deep voice.

Hastily coaxing her fox-colored tresses into some semblance of order, Katrina answered, "Ready."

24

The deadbolt to her guest quarters slid back and the door swung open. Derek Gray looked her over twice and nodded approvingly. "Not bad," he said, cracking a smile.

Katrina looked at him flatly. "Why was the door locked? I thought you were supposed to be the good guys!" she quipped sardonically.

"It's a top-secret facility, Dr. Walker," Derek reminded her as he escorted her back toward AWOL's command center, "and you don't have clearance to be here."

From down the hall, she could see Clark, a phone to his ear, busily studying dual monitors in a large computer station. She walked faster.

Clark ended the call just as she arrived. "I trust you are more comfortable," he said, motioning for her to take a seat as Derek excused himself.

"Well, it's certainly an improvement," she conceded, "but . . ."

An assistant set a steaming cup of tea in front of her, which interrupted her impending complaint, and Clark began firing questions at Katrina.

"Dr. Walker, did you suspect that Ms. Bradford was involved with a terrorist organization?"

"No! Nor did she tell me that she planned to blow up a mall," Katrina added earnestly between sips of green tea, taking great comfort in the warmth of the cup between her hands.

"What *did* she tell you, then?"

Katrina hesitated, trying to get a read on Clark.

"Please, Dr. Walker, you don't know what I know, and, hell, you don't want to know," he began. "There is no doctor-patient confidentiality here. I need your cooperation. It's imperative that you tell me everything Susan Bradford told you."

"It was a very strange session," Katrina began cautiously. "Susan told me she had been raped repeatedly by her father and that she believed him to be involved with a cult."

Clark's otherwise unreadable face showed a slight curiosity when he raised one eyebrow.

"She had been experiencing escalating problems since her son's birth—panic attacks, paranoia, nightmares, and troubling remembrances. And although that resonated true," Katrina took a breath to choose her words carefully, "the specific memories haunting her were not verified by her field encryptions."

"Explain."

"That's a little difficult," Katrina warned.

Clark's jaw tensed. "Try me."

"In short, words carry a frequency signature. The same goes for memories and events stored in someone's morphic field. If someone's telling the truth, the frequency signature of their words matches the experiential data stored in their field. Lies, on the other hand, register anomalous inference patterns." She paused, expecting puzzlement.

"I'm aware of your recent lecture," Clark said, not disclosing that he had actually been in attendance. "I know you can perceive subtle field information and are developing applications for strategic defense." Katrina didn't try to hide her surprise. She would not have expected a man in his position to understand, much less place value in, her area of expertise.

"That's why I brought you here for protection. I need to know what you gleaned from Susan Bradford's field, not just what she said," he pressed, "and be specific."

"I've never seen a field like hers. It was shattered beyond belief," Katrina began quietly. "She had 'hot topics,' but the disturbances those caused in her field were quickly hidden. The stories she told about her biological father and the cult activity he forced on her did not register in her field as truthful."

"What kind of hot topics?"

"The bombing in Boston, for example, caused erratic outbursts in her field. But even more strange were the twisted imprints associated with the word *father*."

"So, what are you telling me? Was she or wasn't she molested by her father and involved with a cult?"

Katrina sensed that he was seeking confirmation of something he already suspected but wasn't willing to share. "Based on the lack of correlation with her field imprints, I don't think her emergent memories were based on real events," Katrina concluded. "I think they were pseudo-memories created by her subconscious to mask deeper traumas."

"I see," Clark replied contemplatively without surprise.

A silence fell over them as the last words settled. Clark opened his mouth to say something but closed it again.

Katrina waited, watching the gears shift in his head, compiling, organizing tidbits of information no one else had; yet he wrote nothing on his yellow legal pad. She softened her focus and surveyed his field, only to find his personal information sequestered behind an impenetrable shield of duty.

A buzz from Clark's cell phone broke the silence. He answered, "I'll be right there," and abruptly ended the call. Looking at Katrina with a penetrating gaze, he asked, "So what's the bottom line?"

"In essence," Katrina replied, "I believe Susan's giving birth to her son unlocked a deep desire within her to heal some repressed trauma," she continued, "and that the false memories she was experiencing reflected her mind's attempts to cope with a hidden truth that desperately sought to be unveiled."

25

It was nearly 3:00 a.m., and Bill Sterling sat waiting in the situation room resting his cheek on his right hand. A cigarette hung precariously from his left, unfurling a fluid stream of smoke. He was staring numbly at the surrounding data displays that chronicled real-time updates from the ongoing investigation when Clark walked in.

"What've you got, Bill?" Clark asked.

"Not a helluva lot," he replied, distraught. A gray skeleton of ashes from his cigarette fell on the table. Only a butt survived. Annoyed, Sterling squashed it forcefully into the ashtray. "I just don't get it!" he said, waving an exasperated hand in the direction of the screen that bore the names of the domestic terrorists. "They're all clean! None of 'em had so much as a friggin' parking ticket!"

Clark's eyes narrowed slightly. "Hiding in plain sight," he replied. "Have you got anything on their political and religious beliefs?"

"All different," Sterling summarized, "but not a zealot or fanatic in the bunch. The church was blown up by a priest, for Christ's sake!" He rubbed his temples to ease the headache that hadn't yet responded to the four ibuprofen that he'd popped with his coffee an hour before. "Father Burgess became a man of the cloth in his thirties and was the up-and-coming clergyman—smart, dedicated, and apparently extremely pious."

Clark scribbled a few notes on the legal pad he'd brought with him. "And there's no indication that any of them ever knew each other?"

"Nope. Nada. The details, for what they're worth, are all here in the sit-op report." Sterling pushed a thick manila folder, emblazoned with a CIA seal, across the table toward Clark. "They're all legitimate United States citizens." Sterling harrumphed and refilled his half-empty coffee cup. "Want some?"

"No, thanks," Clark replied.

Sterling collapsed back into his chair. It groaned, as if protesting his weight.

"I don't think they're connected," Sterling concluded. "The MOs are just too different—C4 explosives, a fucking EM pulse, some kind of freakin' heart attack–inducing weapon near DC, and now a goddamned football fan carrying enough ricin gas to exterminate thousands in Philly! It makes no sense!"

"But there is one quite disturbing thing they all do have in common," Clark remarked decidedly. "On the surface, they all appear to be normal, everyday citizens, yet each of them knew how to manufacture homemade killing devices, which tells me . . ."

Sterling cut in. "Any idiot can build a bomb these days with instructions off the Internet." He reached for the pack of smokes he'd laid on the table and tapped them hard.

". . . or they could have all had some specialized training," Clark concluded.

Sterling's expression darkened. Stress and lack of sleep were taking a toll—the bags beneath his eyes were swollen, his skin pallid. Grumpily, he lit a cigarette and took a deep drag to recalibrate his nerves. "Look, Jim," Sterling pressed, smoke escaping with his words. "Let's talk off the record. We've known each other a long time. What the hell's going on? You must know something."

"Wish I could share, Bill, but this case is classified need-to-know. Intel has to be compartmentalized."

"Need-to-know, my ass! How the hell do you expect me to do my job if you don't let me in the loop?" Not being the point man on the job was a bitter pill for Sterling to swallow. "Either we've got a bunch of crazies out there, or something big is going down!" He downed a hefty swig of black coffee and slammed his cup on the table with a thud. "You can't deny that six terrorist attacks within the last forty-eight hours is more than a bit coincidental!"

An uneasy silence fell between them.

Sterling nervously twisted the elastic wristband of his old Timex watch. He searched Clark's eyes for a sign. "Do you at least know who's behind this?" he asked quietly.

Clark had his suspicions, but instead of sharing, he ignored the question, opened the thick dossier, and flipped through the pages. Redirecting the conversation, he asked, "The football fan, Frank Davis, how's it going with his interrogation?"

"The usual shit is already done, but it all came back clean. Polygraph, infrared thermography, voice analysis—the whole nine yards. I've got Fleming on the case now."

Clark looked uncomfortable at that announcement. "Are you sure Davis is your perp?" he asked as he closed the report and began tapping the cover with his pen.

"His fingerprints were all over the gas cylinders," Sterling beamed. "Not to mention that we found a gas mask in his coat."

"Seems Mr. Davis intended on surviving," Clark replied in a measured tone. "Ricin gas has no antidote. The initial latent period of four to eight hours is followed by flu-like symptoms that progress within a day to gastrointestinal hemorrhage, as well as liver and kidney failure. A perfect crime, and ricin is easy to manufacture."

"I know al-Qaeda was experimenting with it," Sterling added nervously. "Do you think there's a link?"

Clark shook his head. "No, I'm afraid it may be more serious than that."

Sterling's face paled. "Fleming's sure he can crack him, but so far Frank Davis's claims of innocence are very earnest." He scratched his head and speculated, "Maybe the guy's just someone's patsy."

"Or, he's well trained in countermeasures and is an expert at appearing nondeceptive," Clark contended. "Are Frank Davis's parents still alive?"

"Both dead," Sterling groused, confused by the seemingly irrelevant question and irritated that Clark wasn't more forthcoming.

"Get me their birth certificates," Clark ordered, scanning the brief. "I don't see those here, or any passports. Can you make that happen—quickly?"

Sterling frowned and nodded. "Sure," he said as Clark made an intercom announcement. "Shortcut or Derek, will one of you bring Dr. Walker in?"

26

A brief knock announced Katrina's arrival. Clark opened the door and smiled, amused, when he saw that both Derek and Short-cut had escorted her. Leaving the two men outside, he closed the door and introduced her to Bill Sterling, who extended his mutton of a hand moist with perspiration. His crumpled shirt and ketchup-stained tie led Katrina to believe that Mr. Sterling hadn't been home all night. Offering him a thin smile that reflected her stress, Katrina returned his firm handshake, took a seat, and dried her hand on her pant leg.

"Dr. Walker," Clark began, "I'd like you and Bill to compare notes on Susan Bradford."

Sterling nodded and began his rundown. "Born in Bedford, Massachusetts, in 1984, good student, varsity softball player, graduated with a degree in electrical engineering from MIT, magna cum laude."

"Nice fit, considering the frequency weapon she built," Clark interjected.

Sterling's face brightened. "That's another thing the perps all have in common—they're all high achievers." Stopping short, not wanting to share information about the other suspects with Katrina, Sterling sealed his lips with a puff on his cigarette. Regrouping, he finished by adding, "Susan quit her job at a consulting firm about three months ago."

"That's when her son was born," Katrina informed. "Is he okay?"

"He's in protective custody. Ms. Bradford knew what she was doing," Sterling said. "The kill zone was tightly contained, the explosion that destroyed the evidence, localized. The area of the mall where she left him was completely unscathed."

Katrina breathed an audible sigh of relief and then gave Sterling a brief account of her session with Susan, including the alleged cult abuse.

"Cult?" Sterling's eyes lit up with hope. "That would explain a helluva lot."

"No. Not exactly," Katrina quickly countered. Thinking back to her dream, she added, "Don't get me wrong, Susan definitely suffered major traumas, but they had nothing to do with classic cult abuse."

"How do you know?" Sterling asked, eyeing her accusatorily over the rim of his coffee cup as he polished off the last drops.

"Dr. Walker is a sensitive," Clark replied matter-of-factly, as if it were everyday news.

"Oh," Sterling faltered. Confounded, he stared uncomfortably at Katrina and ventured derisively, "What does that mean—exactly? Do you see dead people and read minds?"

Clark shot him an exasperated look, but before he could say a word, Katrina spoke up. "It might help if we take it from a scientific perspective, Mr. Sterling," she replied.

"When you consider the multidimensional universe of string theory, field imprints, and principles of nonlocality, it's really fairly easy to comprehend."

"Did I mention she also teaches at Harvard?" Clark grinned at Sterling, who looked both annoyed and befuddled.

"I'm a skeptic," Sterling admitted. As far as he was concerned, Harvard was a liberal playground; her credentials meant little to him. "And, no, I'm not familiar with the science," he conceded, "but, I am aware of government research projects that claim to validate a broad range of paranormal abilities—spooky stuff like precognition, remote viewing, out-of-body experiences, and the like. But as far as I'm concerned—the verdict's out. My philosophy is—if you can't see it, then it doesn't exist."

"How about the air you're breathing, Bill?" Clark mocked. "Can't see it unless it's polluted, but it's still there. Catch up with the times! How do you think Newton felt trying to explain gravity? You can't see that either. But understanding it has sure proven useful."

Bill lit another cigarette and grumbled. "Okay . . . useful . . . I'm all ears," he replied dubiously. "What exactly is it that you sense, Dr. Walker? And what in the hell is it going to tell me that I don't already know about Susan?"

"Most likely a lot," Katrina replied with a small smile, and in light of Clark's support, which she found both curious and comforting, she explained, "Where most people see thin air, I perceive a broad bandwidth of information. Everything is energy vibrating at different speeds. The resonance of this vibration creates frequency patterns full of information. Even material objects have an energetic fingerprint," she added.

Sterling raised a curious eyebrow.

"My brain may process the data holographically or in parallel, like picture-in-picture mode on a television. Beyond that, the information can translate olfactory, auditory, and kinesthetic experiences, as well as direct knowings. Your cup on the table, for example, emits a composite frequency that reflects not only the core signature of the vessel itself, but also the added elements of color, size, and contents. The details are like toppings on ice cream. The coffee in your cup, for example, vibrates in a way that tells me it's a high-quality, mellow blend. Its energetic signature is more rounded, and its resonance more harmonious, than a lesser-quality brand."

Sterling picked up his mug and examined it quizzically before squinting back at Katrina. Jim Clark did have conspicuously good taste in coffee, but he chalked up her knowing to a lucky guess, or the fact that she must have had a cup. "This x-ray vision of yours," he quipped sarcastically, "can you turn it on and off?"

"It's not x-ray vision," she replied, somewhat annoyed by his condescension. "And no, not exactly. But with Susan, because she was seeking help, I was definitely on."

Hoping to ground the concepts into something Bill could appreciate, Clark added, "Think about hologram technology. It can generate 3D renditions because wave patterns of light contain the whole information from its original source, right?"

Bill nodded in reluctant agreement.

"That's basically what Katrina's brain does. Somehow she can access and translate information stored in wave patterns that most of us are oblivious to. It's kind of like being able to hear a dog whistle," Clark said, giving Katrina a small wink of apology for the oversimplification. Sterling squirmed uncomfortably in his chair. "Great, I get it, but how does all this relate to Susan?"

"Just like coffee has a resonance, so do life experiences," Katrina explained, and those experiences can imprint a person's field. The more intense an experience, the more likely it is to etch the field with a signature that is discernible and unique."

Sterling didn't know what to think, but one thing was certain—Katrina had his attention. "So how do you know it wasn't cult abuse?"

"Because her claims didn't match the imprints in her field. Don't get me wrong," Katrina assured him, "Susan definitely suffered severe traumas. The fracturing of her intrinsic, subtle anatomy was pronounced, and while I'm certain that her buried wounds directly contributed to her being able to carry out this act of violence, they didn't match the cult abuse story she told me."

"In short," Clark clarified, "the memories Susan was talking about were a fabrication of her mind, a self-defense mechanism shielding deeper, authentic memories—and that's why they didn't match what Katrina saw in her field."

Katrina nodded.

Sterling wiped his hand across his wrinkled forehead. "Well, if the deeper memories hold clues as to why she killed those people, then spill! What in the hell happened to her—really?"

"We didn't get that far in our session."

"Damn," Sterling grumbled. He pulled a small pad out of his shirt pocket and began scratching out illegible notes.

Before the pen fell quiet, Clark said, "In light of Dr. Walker's abilities, I'm going to take her to assess Frank Davis ASAP. There's a good chance we'll gain some insight that's not readily apparent."

Katrina looked at Clark, puzzled, "Who?"

Sterling ignored her question and protested, "Not a chance, Jim. It violates protocol. Besides, interrogation is Fleming's bailiwick, and he won't like it."

Sterling's comment ignited a heated exchange between the two men, allowing Katrina an opportunity to observe them at a deeper level.

Clark's interactive field left no doubt that he was the alpha and had the upper hand. Yet, with regard to his personal life, loves, passions, and traumas, those remained sequestered. Sterling's energy, on the other hand, was a veritable open book. He obviously liked the prestige his job gave him, but life felt out of control to him. He was doing his best to cover it up but was suffering from a variety of stressors. Honing in on a particular region of dissonance, Katrina noticed something curious. Beyond the crisis at hand, Sterling was suffering a personal crisis, the imprint of which was resonating betrayal and guilt. As if his biofield knew a therapist was listening, the troubled bubble of information popped, divulging itself like a parishioner at confession—Bill Sterling was having an affair.

Katrina snapped out of heightened sensory mode just in time to hear Clark tell Sterling in no uncertain terms, "It's not Fleming's call!"

Katrina stepped in to quash the debate. "Regardless of whose call it is," she informed them, "I have no intention of helping to interrogate anyone! That's not what my abilities are for," she added steadfastly. "I've told you about Susan, and now as far as I'm concerned, I'm done."

Sterling looked relieved. "That will certainly simplify things on my end."

Clark regrouped. "I would never ask you to do something you weren't comfortable with," he assured her, "but Frank Davis is a key suspect and we need help. I'm not asking you to grill him, I'm just asking you to read his field."

The veins on the side of Sterling's head bulged as he watched Clark try to convince Katrina.

Clark continued, "If we don't find out what's going on, more people are going to get hurt. Besides, I'm sure he could use some therapeutic help as well."

Katrina pressed her lips together, considering his earnest request.

"Damn it, Jim, she's got no clearance!" Sterling finally barked.

Clark turned to Bill. "I'm fully aware she needs clearance, especially considering the fact that Davis is at a black site and already officially dead!"

Sterling's eyes widened at Clark's brazen reveal of classified intel to a civilian, but before he could protest, Clark pulled a folder from under his legal pad and produced a stack of official-looking documents. He slid them in front of Katrina. "If you'll sign here," he said, pointing to the signature lines, "you'll have Top Secret clearance and can help us with Frank Davis."

"What the hell?" Sterling looked dazzled, as if he had just witnessed a magician's sleight of hand.

"I've already taken the liberty of arranging for Dr. Walker's clearance," Clark replied nonchalantly. He then slid Sterling a letter signed by the president, effectively silencing Sterling's curiosity as well as his inquisition.

Katrina stared, blinking in disbelief. She never had any intention of working for the government, and, as far as she was concerned, Clark's preparedness both with clearance and with rescue remained more than a little suspect. "Thanks, but no thanks," she replied resolutely and pushed the papers back across the table.

"I realize I haven't taken time to ask you how you feel about this," Clark backpedaled apologetically. "But we are in the middle of an escalating situation. If you can help navigate the interior landscape of Frank Davis's psyche, it might give us the edge we need."

Sterling realized he'd been outmaneuvered. Striving to save face, he repositioned his willingness to bring Katrina on board. "Since you worked with Susan," he began, "perhaps you can see if there's a connection between her and Frank, or if these are just isolated nut jobs."

Clark pushed the papers back toward her. "Please, reconsider," he said, offering visual assurances along with a smile as he held out a pen for her to sign.

Katrina wanted to reject the proposal out of hand, but her gut directed her otherwise. Torn, she picked up the stack of documents and began to scrutinize the legalese, leaving Clark holding the pen. To her great dismay, the documents disclosed egregious amounts of private information about her. After perusing the first few pages, she ranted at Clark, "Who in the hell do you think you are, running this kind of an investigation on me?"

"You have to understand," he sidestepped gingerly, "you were the last person on record to talk with Susan Bradford, so you can imagine we might run a background check on you." If he could only explain, she would understand that the report wasn't the result of a recent or random investigation but rather a compilation of her life—a life he'd been responsible for. But that information belonged in the Crypt. For the moment, he was going to have to let her be angry.

Katrina surveyed Clark skeptically. With stubborn reluctance, she turned the page and read on.

"When you have a moment, Jim," Sterling added sardonically, "I'd love to know how you managed to get her TS clearance so fast. It takes me six months to three years to get a Single Scope Background Investigation done . . ."

"This is a heck of a nondisclosure agreement," Katrina whispered after discovering that with clearance granted she would be subject to criminal, civil, and administrative sanctions if she failed to protect classified information from unauthorized disclosure. While she felt called to be of service, this wasn't what she had in mind as the way to do it. Yet, in the middle of her inner debate about whether to participate, Katrina's dream about Susan trickled back into her mind. She had wanted to help then, too, but couldn't get past the glass windowpane. Signing this would put her on the inside. She would not only be able to help Frank Davis, but potentially, she might also be able to help solve a bigger problem—a rampant epidemic of domestic terror. "I'll give it a try," she replied conditionally. "But I can quit whenever I want to, right?"

A gratified smile broke across Clark's face as she took the pen from his hand. He remained silent as ink flowed across signature lines, careful to not answer her question.

"Let's be clear," she added, in a steeled voice that masked her inner turmoil, "I'm not willing to violate my ethics, and I'm not interested in joining the CIA."

"Of course, Dr. Walker," Sterling confirmed. "You will remain a civilian and have Top Secret clearance relevant to this situation only. As for the CIA, you'll be working with Mr. Clark. He's not affiliated with Central Intelligence." Sterling shot an envious look at Clark who looked quite pleased to have a new asset on his team, and he couldn't help but wonder how connected Jim Clark really was. Documents signed, Katrina switched her focus to the problem at hand. "Now that I've got clearance, what can you tell me about Mr. Davis?"

Sterling gave her a brief overview and admitted, "We're just not getting anywhere with him. He's an average Joe and denies any knowledge of the ricin bomb he was carrying. Hell, after listening to the guy for a few minutes, you almost believe him." Sterling then remembered something and smiled slightly. He dipped his head to the side as he said, "There was one curious thing, however."

"And what might that be?" Clark asked.

"His shorts," Sterling replied.

"His undershorts?" Katrina asked in a baffled tone.

"Yeah. His underpants. There was no evacuation."

Katrina frowned, not following the interest in this man's underwear.

"When somebody gets hit by a car like that," Clark elaborated, "they go into shock—and more often than not, they release everything in their bowels and bladder spontaneously."

"Exactly," Sterling concurred. "They shit their pants. It's just a bodily reflex."

"So?" Clark prompted, turning back to Sterling. "He was unusual in what way? He held it in?"

"No," Sterling chuckled. "He ... uh ... had an orgasm and ejaculated instead. Sounds like a psych-case to me," he joked.

Katrina said, "That is curious."

Clark absorbed the information and nodded. The look in his eye indicated the detail clearly held some relevance. "Thanks, Bill," he said dismissively. "Notify Fleming that we're coming."

27

s soon as the door clicked shut behind Sterling, Katrina challenged Clark. "Do you keep that much information on everybody? Or am I an exception?"

"I can't speak for the government at large," Clark began, looking her straight in the eyes, "but with regard to my team, we gather no information on most people," he answered honestly, "and yes, you are an exception."

A cold stone of apprehension settled in the pit of her stomach. "That document practically contained my life story, including who I dated in high school. My gut tells me you didn't come up with all of that information in the last twenty-four hours," she pressed.

Clark's jaw muscle clenched, but his eyes didn't flinch. It was a good question directed at an excellent spy. He held his cover. "You've been on our radar for some time," he replied. "We're always scouting for exceptional talent, and when we find it, we run a thorough background check to prescreen. That's how I got your clearance done so fast. I've read your work and listened to most of your lectures. Frankly, I've been considering recruiting you for some time."

Katrina stared at him in silent disbelief.

"Any other questions?" Clark asked, hoping the answer would be no.

"I've agreed to help you. Now when can I go home?" she replied guardedly.

"You're not safe at home," he responded bluntly. "Besides, we'll need to employ your talents on site, full time, until this matter is resolved."

"I'm still a civilian!" she argued. "You can't keep me here against my will."

"But I can," he replied matter-of-factly. "You are a valuable asset, and I have the authority to put you in protective custody for national security. Even if you hadn't volunteered to help," he added, "you'd have to wait here in my facility until this is resolved." Clark continued, "In the meantime, I've seen to it that your clients and everyday life are taken care of. For the moment, the world thinks you have a bad case of the flu." He smiled ever so slightly, hoping this information would make her feel more comfortable, although from the looks of it he wasn't succeeding as well as he had hoped. Katrina was fuming. "The circumstances warrant our actions. I'm sure you understand," he added.

Katrina wasn't sure she understood at all. Standing up, she said, "Let me know when you're ready for me to see Mr. Davis. In the meantime, I'd like to wait in my room."

"Let's grab some food instead," Clark said. "We'll be heading out shortly, and the place we're going is not known for its culinary delights."

Katrina's stomach answered for her with a growl. She hadn't realized how hungry she was.

Silence fell between them as they walked to AWOL's mess hall, which sat deserted at this lonely hour of the night. Not large by army standards, the galley looked like an oversized kitchen, sporting state-of-the-art steel appliances, expansive countertops, stools at the bar to seat twenty, along with an assortment of tables and chairs.

Clark crossed behind the counter. "I am excited to see what you can do with Frank," he began, seeking to disarm her. Then, heading for the fridge, he asked, "Sandwich?"

"Vegetarian, please."

"I'm not surprised," he replied.

Sidling up to a barstool, she watched Clark pull out a veritable hoagie shop of options and could tell he was trying hard to make her feel comfortable.

"Have you always been able to perceive this way?" he asked as he slathered mustard across a slice of bread. "That's something your background check doesn't tell us."

"It's been an evolutionary process," Katrina explained. "I've always been quite intuitive and had a strong sense of precognition, but from a visual perspective, when I was young, I saw mostly clouds of color around people. As I grew older, I was able to recognize more specific patterns, but overall my abilities really ramped up after I had a near-death experience when I was twelve," she shared tentatively.

Clark's eyes rose to meet hers. Clearly the topic interested him. "What happened?" he asked.

"It was a drowning incident," she began. "I ended up on the other side for quite some time."

"Long tunnel? White light?"

She hesitated. "That plus more." Her mind drifted back to the experience that words proved sorely inadequate to capture. "I actually ended up in what I would call a celestial garden," she began. "When I arrived, I found myself standing in a small, grassy clearing. Light streamed in through ancient trees. Flowers were everywhere in the most vibrant colors I've ever seen, and as if to welcome me, they began unfolding their petals before my eyes, perfuming the air with a magical scent. It was as if each leaf and flower, even the air itself, was radiating what I can only describe as universal love. I felt immediately at peace, in deep joy, and with every breath I took, I found myself ever more filled with this omnipresent and quintessential love. It was like breathing super-oxygenated air that permeated my being from the inside out and transformed my very essence." She looked up and searched his eyes. Finding only inquiry, she continued, "Before long, I began to move into synch with my surroundings, and as I did, amazing knowings started to unfold within me. I realized that worldly matters often serve as deception points and that truly it is only the heart connections that any of us can take through time." Her eyes disengaged from his. "I didn't want to come back," she admitted. "I wanted to stay and explore that Golden World—a world without judgment, a world without pain. And then a group of guides appeared." She glanced at Clark, half-expecting a look of ridicule from him, but her authentic reverence left no question in his mind that she was sharing in earnest.

"Go on," he encouraged.

Sensing his genuine interest, she continued. "Two guides stepped forward and spoke with me for what seemed like half an hour, explaining that I had to return to my body, that I had some sort of purpose or mission to complete. I actually argued with them. But it was no use. The next thing I knew, I blipped through a membrane of sorts and found myself floating above a girl's body that resembled mine, although I felt completely detached from her. She was lying by the river. People circled around her working to breathe life back in. At the time, I wished they would just leave her alone. Then, suddenly, and without warning, it felt as if a giant hand grabbed me around my waist and slammed me back into the lifeless corpse. With a start, I became conscious, locked back in physical form. To be honest," she confessed with a pause, "I grieved the loss of that Golden World for years. At some level, I guess I still do, but the messages keep unfolding, and that," she smiled, "leaves me still feeling connected. After my experience, my perceptual abilities increased exponentially, as did my understanding of how people get fractured and how to help people heal."

The look in Clark's eyes had softened during the course of her tale. He, too, had had many brushes with death, and while he had no actual fear of dying, he found comfort in her experience. Seeking a point of connection, he confided, "I have some extrasensory abilities myself. I don't see things like you do," he explained. "For me, they are more like survival skills—sensing what's ahead and behind me—tapping into the web."

Katrina eyed him curiously. She wasn't sure if it was the conversation or glimpsing a behind-the-scenes, human side of Clark, but she'd started to relax. Intrigued by his revelation, she slipped into therapist mode and began gently running her own investigation. "When did it start for you?"

"As a child," Clark began. "My grandfather, Tsóyéé, was an Apache shaman, a medicine man of sorts. He taught me," he continued in a hushed tone. "I grew up with an intimate appreciation for nature and a sense of spirit outside of traditional dogma and religiosity."

Katrina studied the planes of his face. Yes, she could see his bloodline.

"Tsóyéé talked about a web of energy that connected all things through time. From the time I was a young boy until the day he died, he would take me into the wilderness and show me how to connect with animals and the environment in unconventional ways. He taught me how to hunt, not from a white man's perspective, but from a sense of oneness and gratitude. Although he also talked often about the healing arts, I focused on the ways of the hunter and warrior. Later, I adapted his teachings to survive in my line of work, to sense the surroundings, to anticipate what or who was around the corner or coming up from behind."

"That's an interesting application," Katrina granted.

Clark paused, deciding how much more to share. He closed the mayonnaise and mustard before continuing tentatively, "It gave me my edge. When I infiltrated behind enemy lines or went in undercover, I could blend in like a chameleon by matching the energy signatures of my surroundings and the people I was with."

As he talked, his field glowed brighter, as if a 100-watt lightbulb had been switched to 300 watts; and when it did, for a flash, Katrina caught a glimpse of him vibrating through time—a warrior holding a tenuous line in the fight between good and evil.

"The normal life expectancy of an undercover operative is eighteen months. I went in and out of deep cover for over a decade." And with that said, he inhaled half of his sandwich in two chomping bites.

Not wanting to interrupt, Katrina had been waiting to comment, but just as she opened her mouth to speak, Clark's cell phone buzzed.

Glancing at the incoming call, Clark swallowed what remained of his meal, chased it with a quick gulp of milk, and answered. He glanced at his watch and replied, "We'll be right there," and disconnected.

Katrina grabbed her sandwich and started scarfing it down as she followed Clark out the door.

28

The elevator rocketed skyward, and Katrina tried to calm her nervous anticipation at the prospect of working with a suspected terrorist. As they stepped out into a small, windowless waiting room, Derek's voice boomed from down a nearby hall. "ETD—two minutes, sir." He approached rapidly and handed Katrina a coat. "I understand you have your first assignment," he said, his face serious. "Where you're going is no cakewalk. Keep a stiff upper lip."

"Let's move out," Clark said, swinging open the door to the outside.

A gust of cold air flushed in and swept chills through Katrina's tired body. Struggling to pull on the jacket, she followed the two men out into the dark. The shivers found their way to her bones as she stepped out onto the roof of a high-rise.

"What are we doing up here?" she asked, trying to get her bearings. The morning sun had not yet peeked over the horizon. Small red lights punctuated the rooftop. The neighboring buildings were dark, except for a few lone offices. She surveyed the surrounding cityscape. And then it hit her. "Are we in Washington DC?"

"Where we are is irrelevant. Where we're going, that's what counts." With narrowing eyes, Clark surveyed the starlit, moonless sky. "Smells like rain," he noted, changing the subject.

Before she had time to press him further, a thump-thump-thump in the distance answered one of her questions. From the dark predawn skies, a helicopter dove into view. Plainly military, the war bird's bright xenon lights pierced the night. Hovering briefly, the Black Hawk's skids touched down. Rotor wash whipped Katrina's hair wildly about her face, and her stomach twisted into a knot that wound its way into her throat. Helicopters were not her idea of fun. Over the din, she shouted, "Can't we drive?"

"Hell no!" Clark replied, ignoring the tremble he heard behind her voice. "Keep your head down and stay close," he ordered, guiding her under the razor-sharp scything of the spinning rotors.

Katrina climbed into the back seat of the assault helicopter and cinched her seatbelt tight. Clark jumped in next to her with uncanny agility. With a nod to Derek, who was staying behind to manage operations, Clark secured the door and handed her a set of sound-dampening headphones along with a blindfold, which he pulled out of his coat pocket. "Put these on," he said bluntly.

"You've got to be kidding me—a blindfold? Don't I have clearance now?"

"Clearance doesn't mean you need to know where we're going," he remarked candidly. "You've got to understand—the more you know, the higher your risk. Now, please, put on the gear." Clark's tone left no room for negotiation. "We can talk on the way," he added, tapping the microphone in the headset.

Turning to the pilot, he said, "Take her up, Reg."

Through the speaker's headset, seasoned with a southern drawl, came an immediate, "Yes, sir."

Katrina fastened her blindfold in place. A whine ratcheted up and the blades spun faster. The pilot coaxed the helicopter off the ground, and Katrina swallowed a wave of nausea as the nose dipped and the bird lurched forward.

After the copter had leveled off, she asked, "With all the secrecy, I guess an agent's marital status is an out-of-bounds question?"

"Who, Derek?" Clark ventured.

"Not Derek," she replied quickly, a little embarrassed. "Bill Sterling. Derek is married to his country—if he has a wife, I'm sure she feels like a widow," Katrina thought out loud, and then admitted to Clark, "He is good-looking, though, in a chiseled jaw, hero sort of way."

Clark chuckled to himself, both at Katrina's analysis and the fact that her cheeks flushed slightly at the mention of Derek's name. "Bill Sterling is a matter of public record. And yes—he's married. But surely, he's not your type," he teased.

"No," she quickly guaranteed. "He is definitely not my type."

"Why? Did you see something in his field?" Clark's smile broadened. "You've piqued my curiosity. Is he the rogue I've always suspected?"

A small smile turned up the corners of her mouth. "I'm afraid information like that will have to be on a need-to-know basis."

"No, seriously, tell me," he said in a playful tone. "Was everything he said the truth?"

Katrina considered her response. "Pretty much," she replied, choosing not to disclose Sterling's personal information.

"You're going to be very handy to have around," Clark said, sincerely delighted, and he was glad that a blindfold stood between Katrina and the sentimental gleam in his eye.

Katrina, hearing only his businesslike remark, frowned in consternation. Her mind flashed back to his badge. "What's Cosmic Clearance?" she asked pointedly of the enigmatic man who was currently shepherding her expertise in the name of national security.

Clark paused for a breath before answering. "Cosmic Top Secret—CTS," he finally replied, "is above Top Secret—it extends my clearance to our allies. Only a handful of people have it."

Katrina noticed the joviality had disappeared from his voice. His tone indicated the topic was closed. "Get some shut-eye," he said finally. "You're going to need it."

Her body was tired, and in this moment, despite the extenuating circumstances, she felt oddly secure. Sleep overcame her in an instant.

Clark stared out the window and his face grew serious. He regretted that he'd have to expose Katrina to his world, yet he was thankful to have her on his team. Had Eliza survived, he was certain she would have chosen to serve by his side as well. Somehow, her daughter's presence completed an unfinished circle. He lost track of time, allowing his mind to drift in the early morning light. Before he knew it, the bird descended. The facility was in sight.

29

Clark escorted Katrina, still blindfolded, from the helicopter into a building. A door slammed behind her. The pervasive odor of stale urine crept into her nostrils, and she wrinkled her nose in disgust.

"Welcome to Black Hole One, Dr. Walker," he announced. "You can take your blindfold off now."

Squinting, Katrina shielded her eyes from the bright lights that studded the ceiling of the dismal gray corridor. "Where are we?" she asked.

"Let's just say, this is not a public facility—and what goes on here never happened," Clark replied. His own abhorrence for the location saturated his voice.

"Reminds me of Alcatraz," she quipped, eyeing her surroundings. "The only thing missing are the rats."

"Oh . . . they aren't," Clark replied disdainfully.

She hoped he was kidding, but she doubted it.

A clank down the hall announced Sterling. He had arrived before them and motioned for them to follow him.

The stench became increasingly pungent with every step as he guided them upstairs to a six-foot-wide corridor uniformly punctuated by metal doors with peeling green paint. Sterling stopped at an entryway barricaded by two stone-faced guards and announced, "Frank Davis is in here. Are you ready to do your thing?"

"Ready," Katrina replied hesitatingly.

"You take the lead, Dr. Walker," Clark said in a low tone. "I've got your back."

With a nod from Sterling, the sentries stepped aside in machine-like unison.

Katrina steeled herself.

Sterling turned the key and swung open the door. A malodorous cloud escaped from the semi-dark hole; the stench of human waste hung acridly in the air.

Katrina fought the urge to gag.

Clark grimaced visibly.

Sterling, apparently unfazed, switched on the light.

"Dear God!" Katrina gasped in disbelief. Nothing could have prepared her for what the windowless dark had concealed.

"Damn it, Sterling!" Clark exclaimed.

In the corner of a cramped eight-by-eight-foot concrete cell, Frank, the would-be terrorist, sat slumped, naked in a cold pool of his own urine with feces smeared over his thighs and groin. The splint on his broken leg was foully soiled. Slowly, he raised his head. A bloodied face, bruised and swollen, looked up at her.

Katrina took two steps backward, bumping into Clark, unable to mask her horror. She tasted acidic bile at the top of her throat and swallowed hard. Speechless, she stared in disbelief. "What article of the Geneva Conventions allows such treatment of prisoners?" she demanded of Sterling.

The cell's only lavatory appeared to be a clogged drain hole in the middle of the bare concrete floor that she assumed was for hosing off those who were interrogated in such an inhumane manner. A bloodstained wooden chair crouched in the far left corner. To the side, behind a locked wire mesh enclosure, a dirty table held pliers, dental instruments, and other grisly tools. A scene of torture and abuse—stored imprints of the cell's history that stretched long before Frank's arrival in this hellhole—flashed in Katrina's mind.

"So," Sterling said with false cheerfulness, ignoring her comment as he rubbed his palms together nervously, "I'll get you a chair."

Katrina grabbed Sterling by the forearm. "Forget the damned chair! I understand you've got a situation, but this is an inexcusable violation of human rights!" she ranted.

Clark glared vehemently at Sterling. It was far worse than he had anticipated. "Damn it, Sterling! You know better than this! What the hell has Fleming done?" he accused.

Sterling pointed at Frank. "This motherfucker was about to kill God knows how many people!" he snorted defensively. "That, in my book, is a deplorable violation of human rights! As far as I'm concerned, at this point, the end justifies the means. We have a nation of innocent people in need of protection, and after what's happened, you want me to treat this son of a bitch nicely?" He continued in a pained voice. "We have got to know what's going on . . . and fast! Hundreds of people—hundreds!—are already dead."

"If you want my help," Katrina declared in no uncertain terms, "this man needs to be cleaned up, given proper medical care, and brought out of here."

In Sterling's opinion, Clark was stupid to bring a civilian into the real-life world of counterterrorism. She had no idea of the compromises made in the name of freedom.

"Rein Fleming in," Clark ordered, "get Davis proper medical care, and bring him to G32. We'll reconvene there."

Sterling glared at Clark. "Fine," he reluctantly capitulated, fearing Clark would report him to the president if he refused. "We'll change venues. But first, Dr. Walker, how about a quick read?" he bartered. "I don't know how long until the next crazy blows, and any intel will help."

Katrina gave Sterling an icy, reproachful stare. She understood that his underlying motivation to protect innocent lives may have been well intentioned, but she found his manner of execution and demeanor

sorely appalling. Momentarily daring to gaze deeper into the hellhole, she turned back and glared at Sterling. "What I see in his field at the moment is your abuse, Mr. Sterling, and if you expect me to look deeper into his past or help you in figuring out what's going on, get him the hell out of here and give me some time."

"Time is one luxury we don't have," Sterling quipped, and turning to Clark, he added, "I vote for bringing Fleming back in. He can crack him."

"Damn it, Bill! Fleming's had his chance. I see how far it's gotten you," Clark charged, his expression unbending. "Bring Davis to G block. Dr. Walker and I will meet you there."

Sterling barked at the guards, "Get this son of a bitch cleaned up."

30

Katrina stormed at Clark as she walked down the corridor next to him on their way to the G block. "I thought black sites and interrogation like this had been outlawed!"

"They have been," Clark replied. "At least as far as the public is concerned."

"How can you support a government that treats people like this?" she demanded, her tone prosecutorial.

Clark remained silent for a moment, considering his reply. He had faced off with the CIA numerous times over their methods of interrogation, but he couldn't share details with her. He deemed tactics such as round-rooming and other psychosis-inducing strategies inhumane. Clark could do little to dissuade the CIA, but personally, he set firm boundaries—AWOL did not participate in such activities. But the brutal reality was inescapable—torture for the sake of information gathering was endemic at a global level.

Katrina misread his silence and said scathingly, "I assume by your lack of response that you approve of this."

"Although I am involved in this investigation," he replied quietly, holding back, "I definitely don't condone the treatment Mr. Davis is receiving. That's one of the reasons I brought you in to help. With the current crisis and the incriminating evidence against Frank Davis, I was afraid they might resort to this." Clark continued soberly, catching her eye, "I'm hoping you can find a clue or offer us some insight. If not, the powers that be will continue to look the other way. They're far more concerned with protecting citizens at large than the health and well being of a captive terrorist."

Katrina swallowed hard, putting the pieces together. "And because he's already been publicly pronounced dead, the quality of his life is irrelevant as far as they're concerned."

Clark nodded. "The president is open to what you do—I've bought us time for you to work. Besides, if my suspicions are correct, torturing Frank Davis is going to leave them empty-handed." Although Clark couldn't share classified information, he confided in a hushed tone, "You need to know I'm not callous about what Frank's going through. I've been on the other side of torture."

She looked at him quizzically.

"I did eighteen months as a POW and came out weighing 98 pounds," he began. "I dug my own grave and had to sleep in it more than once. I watched two of my friends, held captive in a filthy cage, kill each other fighting over a square inch of fat. Clark paused and averted his eyes. "Enemy officers stood by and laid bets on who would win." Brief flashes of posttraumatic imprints ignited in his field. "I managed to escape, but others weren't so lucky." Clark was telling the truth—and he had only scratched the surface. James Clark did understand, deeply.

"I can see it in your field," Katrina replied.

"I am painfully aware of what people are capable of when fueled by fear and a lust for power." As they reached the end of the dank hall and rounded the corner, Clark concluded, "I would never wish torture on anyone. There are ways to fight and win that still respect the humanity of your adversary—even when you have to extract information." Spirit laws echoed in his mind. Clark believed intelligence gathering was best accomplished by outsmarting adversaries. Anything less, in his opinion, reflected a lack of creative problem solving.

Katrina softened in light of his disclosure. She admired his seeking of alternatives to conventional interrogation techniques, and she didn't want to let him down. "I don't know what it is," she disclosed, "but there is something very odd about Frank's field."

"Did it look like Susan's?"

"I only had time to get a glimpse, but with the beating he took, I'm surprised I didn't see fractures all the way down to his core. In that sense, yes, his field was shielded similarly to Susan's."

"Listen," Clark said, stopping and turning to look at her, "the intel on this operation needs to stay highly compartmentalized."

Katrina searched his face for the underlying reasoning behind his warning.

"There are always leaks." Clark's expression grew hard. "Whatever you discover, share only with me, unless I tell you otherwise. No matter what any of them tell you."

"Who exactly is 'them'?"

"Sterling and everyone else."

31

Room G-32 was a vast improvement over Frank's previous dank cell and a testament to the minimalist appeal of well-used military furniture. An old army-green leather chair peeked out from behind a 1950s-era desk, across from which sat a worn couch, upholstered in olive green. The dull gray walls were bare. Without the faded floral rug that covered an eight-by-ten-foot patch of cold, gray concrete floor, the room might have been depressing.

Clark took a seat on the side of the desk, with one foot dangling, and watched as Katrina positioned the office chair near the couch in preparation for her soon-to-be client.

A moment later, the door to G-32 crashed open with a loud bang.

Caught off guard, Katrina's heart skipped a beat as a burly soldier in fatigues manhandled Frank into the room. Frank, now cleaned up and dressed in an orange jumpsuit, struggled futilely to stay on his crutches, which, despite his best efforts, fell and clattered on the floor as the soldier slammed Frank down onto the sofa without regard for his apparent willingness to cooperate.

"Stop it!" Katrina demanded furiously.

The guard ignored her and grabbed Frank's wrists in a vicelike grip, slapped handcuffs on, and squeezed tightly.

Clark cleared his throat, seconding her protest.

The soldier met Clark's warning eye and eased up. Pulling back a tattered corner of the rug, he shackled Frank's unbroken leg to a steel grommet in the floor and tromped outside to stand watch just as Sterling walked in.

"Satisfied, Dr. Walker?" Sterling mocked, not waiting for a reply. "Now let's see if you can persuade Mr. Innocent here to tell you what the fuck's going on!" Sterling smiled contemptuously at Frank, who blinked guiltlessly in response, and shut the door. In his heart, Sterling hoped Clark was right—perhaps Katrina would see something Fleming had missed. But his ego told him otherwise; he was, after all, a skeptic.

"Let's get started," Clark said, directing his attention to Katrina.

But Katrina had already begun sizing up Frank, who really did look like an average, clean-cut, homegrown citizen.

Frank welcomed her gaze. "Hello," he invited sheepishly, with a swollen, split lip that slightly impeded his speech.

Surprised by his cordiality, Katrina replied, "It's nice to meet you, Mr. Davis. My name is Dr. Walker, and I'd like to ask you a few questions."

"Of course, anything you like," he volunteered in trembling hope. "I keep telling them I'm innocent, but that's not what they want to hear." Tears welled up in his eyes and he continued desperately, "There's been a terrible mistake. I didn't do anything. I'm the victim here," he cried as an involuntary sob of relief escaped him.

"I understand," Katrina said comfortingly, all the while remaining fully cognizant that this was the same man who hours before had been carrying a weaponized chemical warfare agent in his attaché and a gas mask in his coat. She also noticed that although he pled innocence, his field was far from forthcoming. It revealed only a shallow and superficial layer. Frank Davis was hiding a storehouse of information beneath some sort of protective shield.

"Did you need money, Frank? Did someone pay you to do this?" she began, seeking to activate feedback from beneath his unusual barrier.

"I make good money," he stuttered earnestly. "I didn't do anything wrong." He started wringing his hands, apparently impervious to the pain inflicted by the handcuffs. "I'm a good husband and a loving father. I pay my bills and volunteer at a homeless shelter."

She watched his field with interest. Typically, when someone spoke of his or her family, a series of associated imprints—encrypted memories—would unlock, like a photo album unfolding. While Frank's statements about having a family registered as truth in his field, they failed to link to any deeper, related memories. Instead, they only skimmed the surface of his deeper truth.

"How did the gas mask end up in your coat, Frank?"

Chaos erupted in Frank's field, which was instantly silenced by a protective membrane that effectively encapsulated any further reveal. A split second later, a superficial layer reappeared, entirely sanitized. Frank took a deep breath and replied, "I don't know . . . I really don't."

Determined, Katrina changed strategies and asked Frank to recount his day backward, knowing that when people lied they generally couldn't retell their fabricated stories in reverse order.

"The last thing I remember is getting on the train, headed for the game," Frank replied. He then flawlessly recounted his morning all the way back to 7:52 a.m. when he got out of bed, omitting any mention of the bomb inside his briefcase. "They've got the wrong guy, I tell you. It's all a setup!" She had been effectively blocked again.

"Did your kids help you build the deployment device?" she asked suggestively, posing a catch-22 and hoping to find a parental tripwire like she had with Susan.

"My kids are at college," he remarked simply. His field registered truth. His children were at college. The balance of the leading question bounced off his protective shield without so much as a grimace registering on his face.

Katrina's heart sank. She was getting nowhere.

With a boom, Clark's deep voice cut in. "Damn it, Frank! You'd better tell us what's going on! Or you're going to find yourself back in that hellhole!"

Frank stared at Clark with confused and bewildered eyes.

Katrina motioned to Clark. "I need to talk with you in private, now."

Clark nodded, and they stepped into the hall. The sentry came in, and Frank shrank deeply into the couch and tucked his body into a tight ball at the sight of him.

32

Outside, in the corridor, Clark asked, "Are you stuck?"

"I want to try something different."

"We're short on time."

Katrina crossed her arms and tensed her shoulders. "Look, Mr. Clark," she began, "you asked me to come here. Now give me a *real* chance."

Clark exhaled audibly.

"When you interrupted, I noticed a few hot spots materialize in his field— interference patterns of significant intensity. I'd like to tag team him—you to distract him with questions, and I'll observe the hot spots that reveal themselves."

"You don't think he can defend two flanks simultaneously," Clark surmised, his eyes brightening.

"Exactly. Don't interrogate him too intensely," Katrina warned, "or he'll shield up tight, but mix it up enough to keep him focused solely on you. That way I can read his field."

Clark nodded and replied, "Let's take it one step further."

"What do you mean?"

"Once you see a hot spot, I want you to do more than observe. Take it up a notch and match the vibration of his hot spot. Experience it from the inside out."

Katrina frowned at his puzzling statement. "Establish an empathetic connection?"

Clark shook his head in negation. "More immersive than that—I need you to experience the stored information as if it's your own. Become *one* with it."

"But, I don't know how to do that," Katrina insisted.

Clark looked at her somberly. "Before my grandfather died, he told me how he engaged the spirit worlds. I know it's possible. Heightened sensory awareness is the first step. You've got that. Now you just need to learn to dance with the energy, rather than just watch from the sidelines."

"If you know so much, then why don't you merge with his hot spots and I'll ask the questions?"

"I'm not a healer," Clark replied sincerely. "But I believe you can do it. Or at least I'm hoping you can."

Katrina felt her chest tighten and stared at him in silent disbelief.

"I'm not asking you to spy. I'm asking you to stretch your abilities," he reassured with a small twinkle in his eye. "If Frank reveals hot spots, you're not invading his privacy by seeking to understand them fully, you're merely engaging with what he's putting on the table."

His face grew serious. "We've got to take our best shot, and we don't have much time."

Seeing no viable alternatives, Katrina nodded, still unconvinced of her ability to do what he suggested, and said, "In essence, you want me to slip between Frank's sheets and see how it feels to lie in his bed. That's a hell of a lot more than I signed up for."

Clark patted her gently on the shoulder and smiled as they turned to go back into the inquisition room. "You've got it."

Fear wormed its way into her stomach.

This is certainly a new twist on the term "undercover operative," she mused to herself as she walked back into G-32.

33

Frank, visibly relieved to see Katrina return, sat almost normally on the couch. His sallow eyes tracked her every move as she crossed in front of him.

"Frank," she began kindly, "my colleague is going to ask you a few questions." She nodded in Clark's direction and rolled her chair off to the side, out of his direct line of vision.

"But . . . I want to talk to you," Frank protested. "You're a doctor."

Clark started right in, changing the game. His voice sliced through the air. "You don't have a fucking choice!" Looming large, Clark stood in front of the desk. "Now, Mr. Davis, I expect your goddamned, undivided attention," he barked like a drill sergeant.

Frank gulped, looked up, and stared wide-eyed at Clark, who was getting a worried glance from Katrina.

"That's better," Clark growled, before smoothly shifting to a more benign tone. "Tell me more about your hobbies, your loves, and your lies," he began innocuously.

Frank's field shifted. Katrina began her assignment and quickly realized that to merge with a hot spot would require acute focus on her part. She had to relax. Current events had left her tense. Quietly drawing her legs up in the chair, she assumed a lotus position and took a few deep breaths. Within seconds, she started to relax.

"I like to play golf. I'm a pretty good bowler, too," Frank said in response to Clark's prompts. "I was in our company's league for four years."

Katrina closed her eyes and disengaged from the conversation. The two men's voices faded into a monotonous drone before slipping into the background and falling silently out of her awareness. A quiet stillness filled her mind.

Out of the corner of his eye, Clark continued to observe Katrina. Stress melted from her face. She almost seemed to glow with a soft, pale light. Meanwhile, Frank Davis, whom he was effortlessly keeping occupied with a steady cadence of inconsequential questions that were peppered with drill sergeant tactics, was a chatterbox.

Katrina quickly slowed her brainwaves, a biofeedback technique that came naturally to her, and reopened her eyes. Using a soft focus, she took in the gestalt of Frank's bioenergetics. Clark's method of distraction was working. Several hot spots had begun to percolate into view, one of which vibrated so erratically that the imprint promised to contain a significant peak or valley experience. Mottled and ruddy, the translucent mass hovered six inches in front of Frank's chest.

Match the frequency—experience it. Clark's words echoed in her mind. *But, how exactly?* she wondered to herself. Almost before she had finished posing the question, an answer popped into her head. *It's like matching paint.* Okay, she could do that. Like an artist, Katrina began combing through frequencies of color and emotional tones as she attempted to emulate the hot spot's color. But, no matter how hard she tried, an exact equivalent eluded her, and without a match, she could not immerse. It was then that she realized nuances beyond form and shade. Frank's beliefs and perceptions were also embedded within the complex imprint. *How was she going to match that?*

Her brain ran multiple scenarios before realizing she had to move beyond the mental aspect. Conventional approaches confined problem solving to the narrow scope of intellect and dramatically limited results.

Defying logic, she careened into the mystical and released the experience for service to the greater good. Her near-death experience had taught her that solutions to seemingly insoluble problems often came from where you least expected, but to access that potential you had to let go.

As soon as she let go, a bright pulse of light landed her smack in the middle of the concrete cubicle—Fleming's version of hell for Frank. A living hologram, the scene came to life around her. But rather than witnessing it as a third party, she was experiencing the world through Frank's eyes, as if she'd been beamed inside his body.

Leather straps bound her arms to a wooden chair. Fleming stood in front of her, smiling menacingly, a pair of pliers in his right hand.

Katrina's mind screamed.

Her heart pounded.

Fear penetrated her every cell.

Yet Frank's body, the one she consciously inhabited, was oddly calm, almost pleasured.

Her thoughts circled in her brain like caged animals. Imprisoned in the experience, incapable of moving Frank's body to action, she watched in horror as the pliers clamped down on her left thumbnail. She wanted to faint but couldn't.

Fleming, taunting, laughed a cruel laugh.

Overloaded with sensory input, Katrina rejected the scene, discarded the imprint, and focused on Clark as an anchor point to pull herself out. In her chest, her heart still hammered as she grounded back into real time. Her eyes flew open to see Clark relentlessly leading Frank down a variety of rabbit trails, holding space for her to work.

"Go on," Clark replied in an encouraging tone to a story of Frank leading a boy scout troop, "tell me more . . ."

Settling back into her body, Katrina realized that her fingers were locked in a death grip on the sides of her chair. Had she really become "one" with Frank's imprint? Desperately, her eyes sought Frank's thumb.

It was true! A dirty and tattered bandage covered the tip. In that instant she decided she had to go back in, no matter how unpleasant the experience might be.

Her ego argued that she was engaging in a new kind of espionage, but her heart was clear. Her intention sprang from her desire to help Frank and discover the information needed to solve the crisis at hand. Softening her gaze again, Katrina watched as intermittent anomalies floated in and out of view. Finally she noticed one, the resonance of which reminded her of Susan.

Her stomach tensed.

She targeted the new energetic signature and let go.

Instantly, the vibration swallowed her and she slipped into another reality-based hologram just in time to live through Fleming delivering a brutal blow to her midriff with a blackjack. She was back inside Frank's body.

Expecting Frank to be experiencing pain or fear, she was shocked when quivering warmth ran up through her core instead, accompanied by a deep yearning. Disbelievingly, she felt herself, albeit in Frank's body, becoming sexually aroused. Confused, she sought to understand Frank's perspective as intense ripples of pleasure cascaded through her.

Tingles ignited in her groin, coupled with a lust for more brutality.

Fleming struck another merciless blow—climax was now inevitable; an intense orgasm gushed through her.

"Katrina?"

In the distance she heard Clark's voice calling her. Following the thread of sanity, she pulled her consciousness out of the shocking imprint and popped back into the present moment. Her cheeks flushed both with afterglow and a tinge of embarrassment; she prayed her outward appearance hadn't evidenced her unwitting interlude into ecstasy. Trying to make sense of the situation, she assumed that Frank's outward appearance during interrogation never depicted his arousal at the pain inflicted by Fleming.

"Do you have something to add?" Clark asked, looking a bit concerned. "You seemed agitated. I thought you might have something to say."

"No," she replied, awkwardly rising from her chair. "But, if you'll excuse me."

Clark could see it in her face. She'd accomplished her task. She'd walked through the veils. "Let's take a break," he said and followed Katrina out the door.

"Are you all right?" he asked when they were alone in the hall.

Katrina struggled to compose herself. "Yes, but this guy is really messed up!" she said, somewhat befuddled and embarrassed to share.

"Go on," Clark pressed.

Katrina looked up at Clark, her eyes mirroring her confusion. "Frank loved Fleming's abuse."

"What do you mean?"

"I mean it was orgasmic. Frank enjoyed his torture. It's no wonder Fleming couldn't get anything out of him. He's impervious to pain. It feels amazing to him!" she expounded. "Somehow he is conditioned to believe that pain is pleasure."

"Shit!" Clark rubbed a hand across his forehead. "That's what I was afraid of." Then, looking back at her, he added matter-of-factly, "That explains his ejaculation when he was hit by the car. Nice work."

Katrina looked quizzical. "But, what does it mean?"

"It means you just uncovered a big piece of the puzzle, or perhaps I should say, confirmed one of my fears. But keep this particular bit of information to yourself."

"What should I do now?"

"Go back inside. Do what you would normally do with a client. I've got to make a call to the president," Clark said as he started down the hall. "And take the guard with you."

"I'd like to try hypnosis," she said, calling after him.

"Good idea. I'll be right back."

34

Katrina wheeled her chair closer to Frank, whose eyes reminded her of a caged and beaten dog. From a therapist's perspective, she was intensely curious what childhood traumas he may have suffered to end up in this state. "Mr. Davis," she began comfortingly, "I understand you believe you are being framed, and I'd like to help."

Frank nodded appreciatively.

"Would you mind if I put you into a state of deep relaxation to help you access your subconscious memories?"

"That would be great," Frank replied with a look of relief. "I certainly have nothing to hide." Lying down on the couch as best he could with one foot still shackled to the ground, Frank rested his cuffed hands on his stomach and closed his eyes.

"Frank, you are completely safe," she assured him, her voice as soft as a gentle breeze on a warm summer day, "safe to remember everything."

Clark, having finished his call, silently re-entered the room and watched with amazement as Katrina skillfully wielded her words, effortlessly guiding Frank Davis into a state of deep hypnosis. The water blue of her irises had turned misty, her demeanor Zen-like.

"Who do you work for?" Katrina prompted soothingly, all the while sketching impressions of Frank's interactive field on the pad of paper in her lap.

"Badelko Industries," came Frank's low, slumbered reply.

"Did you manufacture the ricin found in your briefcase?"

"No," he answered quietly, without deception.

Clark, seeking a clear view of the intricate markings and squiggles Katrina was recording, moved closer.

"Do you remember being beaten?"

"Yes," Frank replied, a half smile flickering across his lips.

Her brows knitting in concentration, Katrina noted a new anomaly and sketched it out.

"Were you beaten as a child?" Katrina continued in a steady voice.

Bam, bam, bam! The door slammed open with a loud crash.

"Sterling needs you both in the briefing room. Pronto!" the guard barked to Clark and Katrina.

Frank's eyelids flew open. He sat upright on the sofa. "How did it go? Did you find out who put that bomb in my briefcase?" he jabbered at Katrina.

"I'm working on it," she said reassuringly as she shot an angry look at the guard for the interruption.

35

Clark and Katrina entered the briefing room, and Sterling introduced Fleming to Katrina. Fleming acknowledged her arrival from his seat with a cold nod. His eyes were hard and glassy. Katrina recognized him immediately from her work with Frank, and haunting visions of Fleming's penchant for cruelty formed in her mind. She fought hard not to say anything.

Sterling started sputtering anxiously as Clark and Katrina sat down across the table from Fleming. "I just got a call from the president's chief of staff," he said, frazzled. "I need to know what you've got. There's a press conference in less than four hours!"

"Stall," Clark replied matter-of-factly. "Dr. Walker just got started." He lowered his chin and glared at Sterling. "Besides, Bill, you know damn well, even if we had something, they wouldn't tell the public the truth."

"I need to send Fleming back in," Sterling fidgeted, lighting up a smoke. "I can't risk not following protocol."

"The fucker was about to crack," Fleming boasted. "We can't waste any more time on this magic shit!"

Clark ignored Fleming and chose instead to speak directly to Sterling. "The president is well aware of Dr. Walker's involvement. We're under fire, but we have to keep our heads—play it smart."

"Seriously, Jim, you've gotta give me something!" Sterling ran his fingers through his thinning red hair. He stared at Clark with puffy, bloodshot eyes. "That key we found in Frank's pocket belonged to a storage unit that's housing a goddamned ricin manufacturing plant!"

"I'm aware," Clark informed him as Katrina's eyes grew large in shocked surprise. "I spoke with President Roberts a few moments ago. Shortcut is hacking the laptop found in the storage unit as we speak. In the meantime, let Dr. Walker do her job!"

"Hypnosis?" Fleming interjected, his lip curling derisively. "You've got to be kidding!"

"No, I'm not kidding," Katrina replied evenly, staring Fleming down, unable to mask her contempt. "I needed to get him into a different brain wave pattern so I could see past the beatings you gave him," she said accusingly.

"So you relaxed the bastard with new-age bullshit," Fleming criticized in a derisive tone. "Big fucking deal. What the hell did you find out?"

Clark barely held his tongue but let Katrina take the floor.

She flipped to the first page in her legal pad and turned it so both Sterling and Fleming could see. "I perceived markers in his field similar to Susan's," she said, pointing to a comprehensive sketch that contained multiple wavelike scribbles and fractals.

"Which means . . . ?" Fleming snorted cynically as Sterling lit another cigarette from the still smoldering butt of his previous one.

"Which means, even under hypnosis," Katrina reported tersely, "his words did not match his field, and . . ."

"Duh—no shit!" Fleming goaded. "The man is a pathological liar."

"Damn it, Fleming!" Clark slammed a fist on the table. "Let her finish."

Fleming sighed, exasperated. Momentarily backing off, he sank into his chair.

Katrina explained that although Frank wasn't suffering from false memories like Susan, he had suffered similar extreme fractures to his core.

A short knock at the door ushered in a young corporal with a tray of coffee, tea, and donuts for everyone.

"Thank God!" Sterling muttered, almost burning himself as he put a cup of the steaming coffee to his lips.

Flipping to her second drawing, Katrina pointed to a crosshatching. "This was also unusual. Both Susan and Frank had a walling-off of sorts, creating an almost impenetrable shell."

"That's great," Sterling grumbled, tobacco stick dangling from his lips, "but what the hell am I supposed to tell the Chief of Staff? Frank's coated in a virtual eggshell? I need relevant intel!"

Fleming made a face but this time kept his mouth shut.

"The answers are there, Mr. Sterling," Katrina insisted without explaining about Frank's penchant for abuse. "I had less than an hour. Give me more time."

Sterling nodded thoughtfully to himself for a moment before making the surprising announcement. "Fleming, you're a go!" Turning to Katrina, he apologized, "We just can't afford to spend any more time like this."

A broad smile cracked Fleming's thin face and he perked up, pleased to be back in the game. Smirking triumphantly at Katrina and Clark, he exited the room to begin his exploits.

"More trauma will complicate his field," Katrina warned, shocked that Sterling would unleash Fleming again so soon.

Clark had remained quiet, his eyes tracking the interplay, and then he said, "Bill, I hate to do it to you, but you and I are going to need to conference with the president."

"You've gotta understand," Sterling said, backpedaling, "I'm the one who has to face Congress. I'm the one who's going to get lynched by the press if we don't produce." Sterling addressed Katrina, "It's not that I don't value what you're doing," he said appeasingly, "and if Fleming doesn't break him in this next round, you can have another shot."

Clark, unmoved by Sterling's placations, glanced at his watch. "Now, Bill. Let's go."

Sterling rose somewhat reluctantly from his chair, grabbed his pack of cigarettes from the conference table, and preceded Clark out the door.

"I'll have someone escort you to the helicopter that will take you back to my facility," Clark said to Katrina as he stood to leave.

"I'd rather stay here and see if I get another chance," Katrina offered.

"Not an option," Clark concluded simply. "Go back to AWOL—get some rest. I have a feeling it's going to be a long day."

He hesitated at the door and looked back at Katrina. "Oh, and I was very impressed with the work you did with Frank," he said, pointing toward G-32, "and how you handled yourself in here just now."

She nodded her thanks, and before he turned to leave, they exchanged slight conspiratorial smiles.

36

The Black Hawk's skids hit the helipad with an unexpected thud, jostling Katrina awake from a catnap.

"Home sweet home," Reg's Texas twang boomed through her headphones.

Yanking off her blindfold, Katrina thanked Reg for a safe trip back and squinted out the copter's window. From the west, a fast-approaching squall line painted a charcoal streak across the sky. The helicopter had been outrunning the storm.

Lightning shattered the sky. A clap of thunder crashed close behind, its percussive force rattling the copter. Quarter-sized raindrops began to pelt the tarmac.

"Careful out there!" Reg cautioned. "Strong gusts." His forefinger pointed to the windsock snapping wildly on the rooftop.

Across the tarmac, Katrina could see Derek sprinting through the rain toward the helicopter, rain gear pulled over his head. Arriving at the copter, he yanked open the door, and a blast of cold, wet air hit Katrina like an ice wall. The temperature outside had dropped a full twenty degrees.

"Welcome back, Dr. Walker," Derek shouted over the still thrumming copter blades. "Let's get the hell out of here!"

She grabbed the copter's slippery metal doorway and stepped out as another deadly bolt of electricity ignited the sky. Simultaneously, a peal of thunder sent tremors rumbling through the rooftop beneath her feet. *That was too close.*

The air was alive with electricity.

The fine hairs on the back of her neck stood at attention. Making a run for it, Katrina ducked and headed for the rooftop door two steps in front of Derek. But, no sooner had she cleared the rotor wash than a gale force wind shoved her hard backward. Her feet slipped from the tarmac.

Derek reached out and caught her before she hit the ground.

Seconds after regaining her footing, a powerful gust moved Derek to envelop her shoulders in a strong, protective arm. "Come on!" he shouted over the howl of the wind, and they sprinted to close the distance. The last thing he needed today was to have to explain to Clark how the newest recruit had been swept off the roof.

The door to the helipad slammed loudly behind them, sealing out the volley of stinging rain.

Derek called the elevator while Katrina rubbed her hands together to warm up. Windblown and wet, she was a mess.

"Glad you made it in before the worst of the storm," he said, breaking the silence. "How did it go with Frank Davis?"

She frowned. "I can't believe the conditions they're keeping him in, much less the methods of interrogation they're using!"

"I understand, Dr. Walker, and you should know it's not something Clark condones."

"You can call me Katrina," she offered as they got on the lift. Water dripped from her hair, forming tiny droplets that caressed her skin. Her blue eyes captivated him, as did the soft curve of her lips, and her proud stubbornness stirred him deeply. The ping as the elevator reached AWOL's control room snapped his mind back to business.

"Clark's given you limited access to the facility—so you are under your own recognizance in the area between your room and the kitchen," Derek said. "Everywhere else is off limits."

"I understand," she replied. "I'm going to take a shower and get some rest."

As she walked away, Derek called, "Katrina, remember—you're on standby."

37

Inside Stingray's clandestine refuge, deep beneath the monuments of DC, Bill Sterling paced outside the heavy steel door of the president's emergency office and nervously rubbed his sweaty palms together. Moments before, Jim Clark had been called in to visit with the president privately.

A haggard-looking President Roberts stared at Clark from behind her desk. "Echelon intercepted a text about an hour ago," she said, holding up a piece of paper stamped classified. "NSA sent it to the boys at Langley, who, under the circumstances, then sent it to me."

Echelon, a highly secretive eavesdropping network, captured and screened data streams worldwide. Emails, texts, cell phone and landline calls, radio and satellite communications, as well as faxes were all analyzed. Key words considered sensitive were flagged and triggered a human review of any suspect communiqués.

"Our boys can't crack the code," she continued with frustration. "But, what's even more disturbing . . ." she added with a grave pause, her eyes carefully watching Clark, "is that it came addressed to a dead man—an operative named Silver Eagle."

Clark's eyes narrowed with suspicion. "I haven't used that code name for more than twenty years."

Unsmiling, she handed Clark the note. "Curious, isn't it?"

An uneasy feeling crept into Clark's belly as he scrutinized the encrypted text.

The president could see the gears in his mind turning. "Well, what the hell does it say?" she blurted out impatiently.

"That's a good question," Clark replied. "The code is based on a one-time pad I created years ago. The cipher is locked in the Crypt."

Roberts frowned. "Why didn't you use standard protocol?"

"When I created this encryption, we had moles inside our government and leaks everywhere." Clark leaned forward in his chair, his steely gray eyes meeting the president's in an unwavering gaze. "I was extracting high-level assets from the Eastern Bloc, so I created unique one-time pads for each asset." A concerned look of recognition broke across his face. He glanced down at the note and then back up at her. "This much I do know—it's signed Cobra."

"If memory serves me," the president replied, "wasn't that Nikolai Krueger's code name? The former Commissariat for State Security?"

"One and the same," Clark confirmed.

"I thought he was dead!"

"Twice over," Clark mused grimly. "KGB reported him dead after he didn't show up for his extraction. That was misinformation, because Krueger was later onsite at Himmelshaus moments before the strike. Reconnaissance reported no survivors."

The president's face grew ashen. "Dear God, Jim, if he survived the airstrike . . . maybe some of *them* did too."

"The sleepers?" Clark clarified, vocalizing the president's dread.

Roberts nodded, her troubled eyes growing dark. Sleepers were a nightmare to national security and a global threat. The U.S.'s annihilation of Himmelshaus to eradicate Blackheart's operation had been a drastic countermeasure. Named Project Clean Sweep, the covert initiative had received the tacit support of other world powers. The plan had been to eliminate sleepers in development, along with Blackheart's masterminds, and to destroy activation codes, thereby neutralizing any sleepers who had already been deployed, leaving them to lie dormant, blissfully unaware of their subliminal programming.

As if reading the president's mind, Clark added, "If Frank Davis is a sleeper, interrogation will never break him. Sleepers are highly programmed and have airtight cover stories. If we want to have a chance of finding out what's going on, I need Sterling and his henchmen to back off long enough for Dr. Walker to see through the veils and discover the truth behind Davis's programmed facade."

Roberts nodded grimly.

"I'll go back to AWOL and decode this message," he said, standing to leave. "After that, I'll take Dr. Walker back to Black Hole and see what she can find out." Clark folded the encrypted communiqué and tucked it inside his breast pocket. "In the meantime, Bill Sterling . . ."

"Bring him in," the president said, leaning back in her chair.

38

Katrina welcomed the warm water flowing over her body and would have taken an extended shower if it hadn't been for Derek's last words, "You're on standby." If the opportunity arose to work with Frank again, she wanted to be ready. Turning off the faucet, she toweled dry and put on the fresh set of clothes she'd found lying on her bed before flopping down and closing her eyes for a momentary reprieve. Intuitively she sensed it wouldn't be long before she was called back in, making pajamas a moot point.

As soon as her head hit the pillow, suddenly, out of nowhere, Frank's bloody, battered image materialized in her mind, like a lingering nightmare, and a shooting pain racked her body. At some level, she and Frank were still connected. Bolting upright, Katrina tried to shake the ghoulish images from her mind, uncertain whether she was tapping into a present moment of abuse by Fleming, a glimpse into the past, or a premonition of things yet to come. *And what was the root cause of Frank equating pleasure with pain?*

The bookshelf near the door beckoned with the promise of distraction.

Katrina walked over and examined its contents: *Mein Kampf, The Arms of Kruppe, The Spy Who Came in from the Cold*—not her idea of light reads, she mused as a loud grumbling from her stomach reminded her that she hadn't eaten in hours. Foregoing literary escape, she decided in favor of a snack and quietly slipped out of her room.

39

Back at AWOL, secluded in the privacy of the Crypt's reading room, Jim Clark was hard at work. The three original briefs from the president and an envelope Sterling had given him containing Frank Davis's mother's passport had been pushed to the side to make room for the riddle at hand. Before him lay the mysterious intercepted text, along with the encryption algorithm and cipher key for the one-time pad he had provided Krueger years before.

Nikolai Krueger had been smart. A high-ranking official with a nose for entrepreneurialism, he'd helped Clark infiltrate the Eastern Bloc to extract technology and human assets in exchange for handsome remuneration—he had served as a prostituted ally behind the scenes. Considering the sizeable cache the U.S. had offered him for defection, Clark had been surprised when Krueger had failed to show up for the rendezvous. In those days, a new identity, a home in the Caribbean, and a million dollars were nothing to discount.

Peering through reading glasses, Clark reached for his pen and set it to paper. In the golden wash of light from the antiquated desk lamp, he methodically decrypted the secret communiqué. It was no wonder that the NSA couldn't unscramble it—Clark's one-time pads were unbreakable. As part of the double encryption, he had jumbled in phonetic spellings from his grandfather's native tongue and, while the message wasn't long, each letter took a moment.

Finally, as if brushing cobwebs from a tomb, Clark resurrected the underlying dispatch. After adding spaces in the appropriate places, the unexpected message read:

RESCUE- ME

CELL-43

55.75222 N 37.632222 E

OLD-TREASURES- PROMISE-

LIBERTY- OR- DEATH

Clark's stomach churned. It seemed unlikely that Krueger had cheated death twice. *But if Krueger hadn't sent the message, then who had?* His mind reeled. Obviously, someone sought to lure Clark in. But how did this person even know he was still in the game? Like other closely guarded government secrets, Clark had been officially disposed of and buried at sea long ago. *A shot in the dark?* Not likely, considering the auspicious timing.

Clark read the deciphered note again. The promise of "old treasures" in exchange for rescue gnawed at him. Perhaps "treasures" referred to the sleepers. Maybe activation codes had surfaced on the black market after all these years and someone was trying to sell them, promising liberty from the problem at hand or death if the deal didn't go through.

Then, as if a ghost had touched his shoulder, he felt a tingle creep up his spine.

There was only one way to find out.

40

Quietly closing the door to her private quarters, Katrina tip-toed down the hall. She could hear a clamor of voices from the control room. Not in the mood for company, she padded softly toward the kitchen and, as she rounded a corner, the sounds of humanity dissolved, suddenly leaving her feeling oddly alone, as if in a museum after hours.

Under your own recognizance, she reminded herself as she wrestled with an overwhelming urge to explore an off-limits area of the complex. Curiosity winning out, she surreptitiously checked the door handles to a set of large double doors in the otherwise empty hallway.

Locked.

Continuing on toward the kitchen, Katrina stopped to peer down a darkened, nonsanctioned corridor. A mere twenty paces away, she could see light streaming out into the hall from a slightly open door. Daring to investigate rather than dine, Katrina furtively crept down the forbidden passage.

41

Quickly making his way up from the Crypt, Clark walked softly through AWOL and came to stand directly behind Shortcut, who sat in a cubicle, fully engrossed and hard at work hacking Frank's laptop. Clark tapped him on the shoulder.

"Ahhhhh!" Shortcut yelped, startled. "You scared the crap out of me!"

"Sorry about that," Clark chuckled softly. "How's it going?" he asked, motioning to the laptop. "I've got a couple of other urgent projects."

"Davis had set up some good defenses, but I'll be done soon. Guaranteed." Shortcut's eyes gleamed victoriously over his round, wire-rimmed glasses. "What's next?"

"For starters, this belonged to Frank Davis's mother," Clark replied, handing him the passport. "I need you to examine it inside and out. Use this," he added, passing him the State Department's official *International Passport Compendium: Production Specifications and Manufacturing.* "It expounds on chemicals, solvents, and the fiber content used in the creation of legitimate U.S. passports."

Shortcut's arm crumpled under the weight of the massive tome and the book hit the desktop. The resultant loud thud drew attention from nearby coworkers. Smiling awkwardly, he muttered, "Thank you, sir," somewhat embarrassed.

Clark smiled compassionately. What Shortcut lacked in physical strength he certainly made up for in mental prowess.

"What about Sprite? Can I call her to help?" he asked, his eyes darting from the passport to the voluminous read.

"Any excuse for a date," Clark teased.

Inept in the art of love, Shortcut blushed despite himself. The thought hadn't even crossed his mind.

"I also need you to look this up for me." He handed Shortcut a copy of the decoded text and pointed to the coordinates.

Shortcut's eyes flicked to the data and back up at Clark. "Russia?"

Clark smiled, impressed.

"Satellite photos?" Shortcut guessed.

"A full workup. And yes, call Sprite. We're gonna need her."

42

Nervously, Katrina peeked around the slightly opened door.

The small, well-appointed library was unoccupied.

Pushing the door open the rest of the way, she walked inside and found walls that were filled floor to ceiling with neatly ordered volumes. She had always loved books, but this was a dream come true. Rolling wooden ladders offered access to the highest shelves. To one side, a handsome yet comfortable-looking burgundy wingback chair, complete with ottoman and reading lamp, welcomed visitors; and nearby, a sleek, ergonomic chair sat behind a generous, hand-carved, antique mahogany desk that held an oversized state-of-the-art flat screen monitor. Aside from these, the small library was barren of personal effects.

Combing through the books, Katrina quickly noticed that they were divided into categories: strategy, criminology, new physics, philosophy, and the esoteric, including obscure works in Sanskrit. Impressed, she ran her fingers lightly across several spines to see which ones came to life under her touch. Even as a young girl this magnetic attraction acted as her literary barometer and had guided her to such childhood favorites as *The Incredible Journey* and *A Wrinkle in Time*.

But it was a *Scientific American* situated on the corner of the desk that drew her attention. Deciding to borrow it, she took a seat to leave a note and pulled open the top right desk drawer in search of paper and pen. Rummaging through office paraphernalia, she reached past a stapler, paper clips, and scissors, deep into the recesses.

Cold metal greeted her fingertips.

Curious, Katrina grasped the heavy object and pulled out a Parkerized 9mm handgun—a sobering reality check of her whereabouts. Turning the piece over in her hand, she studied its menacing design before carefully returning the deadly tool to its hiding place. Compelled to further investigate the facility Clark called home, she tugged on another drawer.

Locked.

Yet another.

Stuck but not locked.

She yanked harder.

Reluctantly, the overstuffed contents gave way and offered up stacks of letterhead bearing official insignia, including the Great Seal of the United States, the Official Seal of the CIA, and the Seal of the President of the United States.

Rooting behind the papers, Katrina discovered a framed black-and-white photo. Her heart skipped as she glanced down at the faded image. She stared in disbelief at the photo of a woman who looked disturbingly familiar—a blonde version of herself—the woman she had seen in her dream about Susan. The resemblance was uncanny.

Flicking on the desk lamp, Katrina examined the print more closely, not knowing how to separate dream from reality. A torrent of thoughts crashed through her mind, and she didn't notice when a towering, dark figure filled the doorway.

"I beg your pardon," stormed Clark, visibly perturbed. "Are you searching my desk?"

43

Bristling, Clark slammed the door shut behind him. "This area is strictly off limits!" he said in a gravelly voice. "What are you doing?"

Katrina locked eyes with him. Caught red-handed, she struggled to maintain a stalwart appearance as her trembling hand secreted the photo beneath the desk, out of sight. "I was just looking for something to read," she faltered, motioning to the magazine.

Clark tensed his neck muscles and squared his shoulders as he scanned the room, taking everything in. His penetrating gaze finally rested on Katrina, whose heart was pounding loudly in her throat. "There is no reading material in my desk!" he assured her sternly, motioning to the partially open drawer.

"I just wanted to leave a note saying I had borrowed the magazine," she replied, doing her best to look innocent.

Clark locked the door to the room and walked toward her. "You have no business in here! Let's go," he ordered.

She could not hide the photo any longer, nor could she put it back without him seeing. She countered pointedly, "First, tell me who this woman is!" and she lifted the picture into plain view.

Clark paused, a chess master calculating his next move.

Katrina held her ground, watching for a reaction, but Clark betrayed nothing.

Silence hung thick between them.

Seconds felt like minutes.

The nervous tension escalated.

And then, without a word, Clark closed the distance, decidedly turning the wingback chair to face the desk. "Sit here," he instructed, "and give me that damn picture!"

Despite his outward gruffness, Katrina noticed a flood of regret bleed through his field. She handed him the photo, and as she sat down in the wingback, for the briefest of seconds, she witnessed a sentimental man.

Clark laid the picture face down, as if ignoring it would solve the problem, and regrouped. Resurrecting his emotional cover, he took a seat behind the desk and silently cursed himself for having been careless enough to give her walkabout privileges. The more she knew, the less he could protect her. And now, she had the upper hand. Normally, he would have never given in to demands for production, but he needed her help. Taking a deep, almost resigned breath, he finally answered with reluctance, "That's a picture of your mother."

"My . . . mother?" Katrina said, glaring at him incredulously. "Give me a break!" she ranted. "I don't know what kind of a stunt you're trying to pull! My mother died in a—"

"Car crash," Clark finished and said, "and no, Hildegard wasn't your mother. I'm sure at some level you must have sensed that."

Katrina was stunned and disbelieving.

"You were adopted," he offered sparingly as he directed his attention to the computer monitor to hide his feelings.

Despite her disbelief, his words stirred an inkling of long-suppressed knowledge. Speechless, Katrina picked up the photo and looked deep into the woman's eyes. She found the woman's likeness to herself disturbingly familiar and the fact she had seen this woman in her dream about Susan even more perplexing. "I want to talk with her," she demanded in a tone that let Clark know she wasn't going to be easily dissuaded. "Where is she?"

Clark barricaded the personal history stored in his biofield before turning back to face her. "I'm sorry, Katrina," he replied in a professional, yet compassionate tone. "She died a few weeks after your birth."

Katrina noticed that he had guarded his field. She felt mistrust over his less than full disclosure, which added to her shock. "That's convenient," she replied curtly, with a narrowing of her eyes. "If, in fact, this is my mother, why exactly do you have a picture of her in your desk?"

Rather than answering, Clark glanced at his watch impatiently and stood to leave. "That's a long story, and now is not the appropriate time."

"Like hell it isn't!"

Clark opened his mouth to speak, but Katrina cut him off. "I'm not going anywhere until you explain why you—a complete stranger—know more about me than I do! Including what size clothes I wear and who my mother is!"

His gray-blue eyes grew stormy. He swallowed hard and revisited the image of Eliza in the frame. Resigning himself to the current topic, he sat back down. "Your mother was a gifted archaeologist with abilities similar to yours," he began, his tone growing grave. "She had been enlisted against her will to help decipher the treasure list of the Copper Scroll."

"Isn't that one of the Dead Sea Scrolls?"

Clark nodded. "It chronicles the alleged whereabouts of power relics such as the Ark of the Covenant and the Holy Grail, not to mention hoards of silver and gold."

"Sounds like the stuff movies are made of," she replied dubiously.

A small smile crossed Clark's earnest visage. "Ah, but the Copper Scroll's treasure list is real. Two of the lesser items have been already found. The trouble is that no one can decipher the rest of the hiding spots. They are riddled. That's why they brought your mother in."

Clark's field registered truth, and she felt her jaw drop slightly as imprints unfolded, adding depth to his words.

"Your mother wanted to defect from the Soviet Bloc," Clark continued soberly. "I ran the mission to extract her."

Katrina could hardly believe her ears. It explained so much but left many more questions unanswered. She struggled to put together the pieces.

"I'm sorry, Katrina, I did my best. But we lost her." Averting his eyes, he returned his gaze to the monitor. "She was really quite remarkable."

The reality of the story registered deep in her gut. Katrina slumped down in the chair and looked at the photo she now held in her hand. A single hot tear splashed on the surface of the dusty glass. Clark wanted to comfort her but did not know how. "It must be hard to have found and lost your biological mother in the same day," he finally managed.

She felt her stomach twist. "What happened?" Katrina asked, hesitantly.

Clark really wanted to slam the lid on the Pandora's box that had been opened, but he felt he owed it to Katrina to share a little more about her mother. Hopefully it would give her greater confidence in her innate abilities to work with Frank.

Hesitant to share, he warned, "This has to stay between you and me—it's beyond Top Secret." In response to Katrina's nod, he continued in a hushed tone, "Your mother decoded the Copper Scroll and found the greatest treasure of all—the map to the stone tablet of the Forbidden Text, an artifact that's fabled to harness the very power of creation."

Astonished, Katrina ventured half in jest, "Do you mean the Lost Stone of Hermes? That's been sought after for millennia."

Clark nodded. "It's gone by many names," he replied earnestly. "Either way, your mother was determined not to let the map fall into the wrong hands, and she refused to leave without it. At the last minute, she handed you to me and raced back for it. I never should have let her go . . ." his voice trailed off, and Clark's haunted face met Katrina's inquisitive gaze, a testament to the regret he still felt. "Alarms sounded," he continued, emotion choking his voice. "She came running out. There was a firefight. I did my best to protect her." Clark fell silent.

Tears spilled from Katrina's eyes despite her best efforts to keep them at bay; and while she felt grief, she also felt gratitude and a new sense of understanding. A deep, persistent, gnawing unease had been put to rest. The gulf of difference she had felt all those years with her adoptive mother finally made sense.

"I made a dying promise to your mother to get you out," he said, as he composed himself and returned the photo to the desk drawer, locking it. "And I did."

"You arranged for my adoption?"

"Hilde, the woman you knew as your mother, was a former, shall we say, acquaintance of mine in Germany," he explained. "We made a deal. She adopted you and was sworn to secrecy in exchange for American citizenship and new identities for you both."

Katrina's mind reeled.

"Your birth name . . . in case you were wondering, was Alexia." And with that, he pulled a thin folder boldly stamped Cosmic Clearance from the locked drawer of his desk. Flipping it open, he handed it to Katrina.

A small faded headshot of her mother accompanied a brief one-page dossier that outlined her mother's psi abilities that the CIA had deemed valuable: retro- and precognition, clairaudience, clairsentience, and astral travel. "So is this why you've been keeping tabs on me?"

"Your mother had been identified as a special asset. Considering her remarkable abilities," he continued, "it only made sense to keep track of you—just in case you had inherited her talents."

Glancing at him, she felt a tightness in her throat. Despite his apparent good intentions, she couldn't help but feel a little like a lab rat that had been watched its entire life. "What gives you the right . . ." she began.

"National security, in part," he conceded, revealing only a portion of the truth, "and my word to your mother to take care of you," he added.

Trying to make sense of it all and still dismayed by the fact that she had been shadowed, Katrina glowered and took a deep breath. "What about my father?" she asked.

"I don't know," he replied honestly.

"Is he alive?"

Clark's expression betrayed nothing. "Doubtful," he replied dismissively and stood to leave.

"I've had enough of this need-to-know bullshit," Katrina replied angrily.

His unbending gaze met hers. "The less you know, the safer you are," he said plainly.

From outside, an urgent knock at the door was accompanied by a bellow, "Sir, it's Derek! Sterling says he needs you both at Black Hole immediately. Frank is unconscious and has fallen into a coma."

"Damn it," Clark muttered as he turned to Katrina and motioned for her to close the top-secret folder. "You can finish reading that en route." Clark unlocked the door, and Derek glared angrily at Katrina, letting her know he wasn't happy that she had wandered into an off-limits area on his watch.

"Lock up my library," Clark ordered, "and take Katrina to the helipad. I'll be right there."

44

Derek was silent as he escorted Katrina to the helipad at a brisk military pace. She could tell he was upset with her for venturing "out of bounds," but she didn't regret having explored Clark's library. Things that hadn't made sense her whole life were finally falling into place.

"I'm sorry if I got you into trouble," she said, feeling bad for having put him into a difficult situation with Clark.

He shot her a stern look. "I told you to stay put!" Then grumbling, he accepted her apology, but added, "Just don't let it happen again."

Trying to ease the tension between them, Katrina started a new topic of conversation. "You already know so much about me," she began, "including private details of my personal life, how about sharing a little yourself? How did you end up working with Clark?"

After a long moment, during which she thought he might not answer at all, Derek's demeanor relaxed, his pace slowed, and he opened up, albeit cursorily. "Scholarship to Georgetown," he replied, "majored in poli-sci, did ROTC, then trained in special ops. One thing led to another . . ." His voice trailed off as they arrived at the elevator where both he and Katrina reached for the call button simultaneously, their hands colliding.

Derek smiled disarmingly, and they stepped inside the elevator through an awkward silence. Then, to Katrina's surprise, Derek breached the unwritten code of elevator etiquette—he stood directly in front of her and looked straight into her eyes.

She could feel the warmth of his breath against her face, and Katrina squirmed a bit inside.

Embracing her in his gaze, the flint in his eyes disappeared, and he continued divulging more personal information. "I was a prime candidate for Clark's team," he added. "No family—both my parents are dead. From a tactical standpoint—that's aces. If I get caught in a hostile situation, no one I love can be harmed to try and make me talk."

Katrina listened carefully and realized he was also trying to say he was single, but his biofield offered no reveals; it was entirely hidden behind service to country. It seemed only the sincerity of his eyes had pierced the veil of duty. The elevator doors slid open, and the intimacy of the moment evaporated.

Outside, a helicopter sat waiting, engine idling.

Her gaze met his in an unspoken good-bye, and she noticed the flint had returned to his hazel eyes—striking and strong. Perhaps someday he would allow her in. In the meantime, she would keep her distance. Katrina wasn't comfortable letting her guard down with a man she couldn't read, and she had a feeling there was more to this man than met the eye.

"Keep an eye on her, Reg," Derek said, turning to the pilot. "Clark will be right out."

45

Having successfully cracked the password on Frank's laptop and briefed Clark on the contents, Shortcut took a big swig of his sweetened coffee and began examining Frank's mother's passport. The large tome Clark had given him offered a very dry set of chapters devoted to passport construction and characteristics. He was on page 1058 when a slightly worn corner of the passport caught his eye—the blue cover had begun to delaminate from the interior paper by only the tiniest fraction of a millimeter, yet there it was—a break?

Almost knocking over his chair in excitement, he grabbed his phone. "Sprite, I need you up here."

Answering groggily, she mumbled, "At this hour? We're working in shifts, remember? It's my turn to sleep."

"Seriously. Come right away!" Shortcut insisted. "Meet me in the lab."

46

Deep in the heart of downtown Houston, a sleek, black BMW coupe zipped into a parking garage on Commerce Street near the courthouse, escaping the gray skies and chilly dribble of autumn's first cold front. Slipping effortlessly into an empty spot on the third floor, the driver's door popped open.

A tall, dark-haired man, dressed in a smartly cut blue pinstripe suit, wool coat, and gloves unfolded himself from the confines of the car. Walking to the rear of the automobile, he clicked a button on the key fob. The trunk's lid rose and he carefully extracted a piece of luggage. Small and black, the little suitcase had a long handle and wheels that clunked behind him as he strolled to the elevator.

Once on the ground floor, he emerged unnoticed onto the bustling, wet, downtown sidewalk and slipped into a sea of black umbrellas. Deftly maneuvering himself and his rolling bag through the foot traffic, he headed toward his ultimate destination—the First Metropolitan Bank Building, a fifty-six story high-rise a few blocks away on Louisiana Street. Clad in red Swedish granite, the gabled monolith was a gem in the Houston skyline.

Approaching the building from a block away, the man had stopped short to admire the tall structure when an alarm set on his cell phone sounded, grabbing his attention. After disabling the alarm, he dialed three digits with an agile finger.

"9-1-1," the operator's voice said. "What's your emergency?"

47

Katrina entered Black Hole's infirmary with Clark and Sterling by her side. The sharp odor of isopropyl alcohol and ammonia-based cleaning fluid assaulted her nostrils, bringing back memories of the veterinarian's office and her dog's euthanasia. Before her on a hospital bed lay Frank, limp, battered, and out cold.

"Shit," Clark remarked. His expression hardened as he eyed the octopus of plastic tubes and monitoring wires entangling the prisoner. "Fleming's out of control!"

Bill Sterling fidgeted and rubbed a palm worriedly across his forehead. "Lance just got a little carried away," he said defensively, trying to downplay the incident and reaching for the nearly empty pack of cigarettes tucked in the breast pocket of his shirt.

Next to Frank's bed, a nurse dressed in green scrubs looked up from where she stood, checking vital signs. Glaring at Sterling, she cleared her throat in warning and pointed animatedly at the clear plastic tube snaking into Frank's nostrils.

"Damn it! Oxygen! Can't smoke," Sterling complained. Disgruntled, he shoved the smokes back in their holding place and began pacing nervously. He was still wearing the same crinkled white business shirt from the day before, and now, despite the chill of the sterile infirmary,

Katrina noticed his stale unwashed odor and the sweat stains migrating out from his underarms. The situation wasn't good—an unconscious terrorist meant no answers.

"So, what's the prognosis?" Clark asked Sterling in a measured tone.

"Doc says it was probably a combination of stress . . ." Sterling looked down, avoiding Clark's gaze, "and injury," he reluctantly admitted. "Fleming thought Frank had passed out—but at this point even pain won't rouse him."

"You're trying to wake him with pain?" Katrina asked, eyeing Sterling dubiously. "Hasn't Fleming already tortured him enough?"

Sterling found no words to argue.

The woman in scrubs interjected, "Testing with pain is standard procedure," and as she crossed the room with Frank's chart in hand, her tennis-shoe-clad feet made odd little squishy noises on the linoleum floor.

Sterling made the introductions. "Major Sharon Brady, RN, I'd like you to meet Dr. Katrina Walker and Jim Clark."

Sharon Brady was an attractive woman, who wore an unnecessary amount of makeup. Her brown hair, sprinkled with gray, was tucked neatly in a French roll.

"Today is Major Brady's first day at the facility," Sterling informed them. "She's filling in for Major Blankenship, who was called out with a family emergency."

"Sounds like you've got your hands full," Clark commented.

"Yes, sir," Major Brady agreed, offering Clark a tight smile and nod, before dispensing a bone-crushing handshake to Katrina with her ice cube of a hand. She elaborated, "The pain we have administered is standard procedure: pressure on the fingernail bed, as well as supraorbital and sternal pressure," she continued clinically, "and the patient is not responding."

"Doc says he's slipped into a coma," Sterling added. "It could last a few days to a few weeks." His mouth turned down and deep frown lines etched his cheeks. "Shit, Jim, what are we going to do?"

"Are his pupils responsive?" Clark prompted the nurse.

"No," Brady replied flatly, shaking her head.

"Vitals?" Clark inquired unhopefully.

"Stable, at this point," she replied and flipped open Frank's chart to the third page. "X-Rays and CT scans show nothing beyond what we might expect." She shot a wary look at Katrina, not wanting to share too much.

"I've worked with someone in a coma before," Katrina offered, her voice quiet, yet filled with promise.

Brady cocked her head quizzically. "What kind of doctor are you?"

"A psychologist on steroids . . ." Sterling chortled.

Clark turned to Katrina and asked hopefully, "Were you able to help?"

Somewhat reluctant to tell them her story, Katrina nodded. "It was a motorcycle accident. An eleven-year-old boy and his father had hit an oil slick and spun out. An oncoming bus ran over the child, fracturing his pelvis in numerous places. By the time I was called, the child had been in a coma for three days. They'd already operated and inserted metal pins. There was no medical reason for his not waking."

"Go on," Sterling encouraged dryly.

Katrina paused before continuing, "When I arrived, he was unconscious and his interactive field was still. I didn't know what to do, so I placed the palms of my hands against the soles of his feet, closed my eyes, and connected with him. That's all it took."

"You're telling me that all you did was touch his feet?" Sterling scoffed. "Is that it in a nutshell?"

Brady frowned skeptically, while Clark listened intently and made mental notes.

"Not exactly," Katrina replied. "When I put my hands on him, I anticipated connecting with injured body parts in my mind's eye, but instead, I saw the boy standing in the dark. In his right hand he held a lighted candle, and the candle's flame illuminated his face."

Sterling narrowed his eyes and looked at her with wary disbelief.

"Like a dream?" Clark asked to clarify.

"No." Katrina explained, "It felt very different from a dream. Physically, I was standing in the ICU with my hands on him, then my mind went blank for a second, and the scene changed. In a flash, I found myself standing with the boy in the dark. It was as real and tangible as being here right now."

Major Brady stared incredulously at Katrina, and Sterling fought to stifle his cynicism.

With a nod of encouragement from Clark, Katrina continued. "The boy's eyes were shut tight. When I asked if he was all right, he told me he was too scared to look at what had happened. He was certain that both he and his father had been killed in the accident. As he spoke, the candle's flame grew ever shorter, threatening to go out. His life hung precariously in the balance, and by choosing not to look, he had locked himself in stasis."

"From a purely medical standpoint . . ." Major Brady interjected.

Clark, acutely aware of the resources offered by traditional approaches, cut her off. "And then?" he prompted.

Katrina went on to explain how she had given the boy a hug and promised that it was safe for him to look. "In that instant, he opened his eyes, and the accident scene came to life around us. Scared and shaking, the little boy watched it play out and, when he saw that he and his father had in fact survived, he looked up at me and smiled."

"That was it," Katrina concluded. "He disappeared—vaporized into thin air; and my awareness blipped back into the hospital room. Within four hours, he had regained consciousness."

"Four hours?" The number was an obvious disappointment to Sterling.

The twinkle in Clark's eye showed earnest surprise in her innate abilities. She had inadvertently navigated the intersection between ancient healing arts and the multidimensional perspectives supported by new physics. "Do you think you can bring Frank around?" he asked.

Brady glowered at Clark for usurping her domain, but she held her tongue.

"I don't know," Katrina replied, not wanting to offer false promises. "But I'm willing to try."

"Great, let's get this show on the road," Clark said, and exchanging glances with Sterling, he added, "Fleming can't do a damn thing with Frank until he regains consciousness anyway."

"I can't argue with that," Sterling agreed. "Anything's better than nothing at this point."

"Major Brady, if you'll excuse us," Clark prompted, "we'd like to get started."

"But sir . . ." Brady resisted, staring derisively at Katrina, "I think I should stay."

"Don't worry," Clark assured. "I'll call you if he flatlines."

Turning on her heel, Brady walked out without a word, her tennis shoes squeaking down the hall.

Sterling was about to leave too, when Clark stopped him. "Bill, before you go, I thought you should know that Frank's laptop did contain the manufacturing formula for the weaponized ricin."

Sterling's face darkened. "The formula for ricin was yanked off the Internet by the patent office back in 2004. That means Davis has either been cooking this a long time or he found a pirated version in cyberspace."

"More than that," Clark replied, "it's nonstandard. Frank was clever enough to soup it up and add a twist."

"Shit!" Sterling grimaced as he turned to Katrina and said, "All right, little lady, let's see what you're made of. Go wake this bastard up so we can find out who he was in cahoots with or if he's just a fucking lone ranger!"

Katrina nodded, a bit nervously, and in preparation, Clark summoned one of the ever-present guards who stood outside and ordered him to restrain Frank.

Katrina shot him a confused look.

"Just in case he wakes up while you're working on him," Clark explained, patting her protectively on the shoulder.

48

Standing next to Sprite in AWOL's underground lab, Shortcut peered anxiously over her shoulder. Nearby, a bank of computers ran programs that tapped research institutions, universities, and databanks around the world under autoscrambled mirrored servers with triple firewall variable flux encoding. Even if detected, no one would know who was tapping, effectively making AWOL's resources unlimited.

"Would you give me a little space?" Sprite said impatiently.

Shortcut reluctantly and marginally stepped back. He didn't take her grumpiness personally. They were both short on sleep.

Sprite's latex-gloved hand strengthened the magnification of the microscope. Close examination revealed a light tint of tan on the paper. Sprite knew U.S. passport paper contained white fibers and, producing a tiny scissor and specimen jar from a drawer, she snipped a sample into the jar. Carefully and in silence, she examined the fibers before rubbing her tired eyes. "The glue . . ." she began slowly, "it's not right. The residue left on these fibers matches a whiskey stain—scotch or rye."

Shortcut connected the dots and whipped open the research volume. "So the glue is potentially . . . ?"

"Exactly," she whispered cryptically. Her eyes remained intently focused on the task at hand. "Let's run a test on the passport cover."

With a nod, Shortcut's gloved hands excised one square centimeter from the corner of the passport. "Here," he said as he placed the cutting into a Petri dish.

Sprite applied three drops of her specially formulated solvent to the dish and then used tweezers to dampen the passport cutting. Carefully, she then placed the wet paper in a lab oven.

Pulling up two chairs, they waited with nervous anticipation for it to process.

49

In downtown Houston, his 9-1-1 call complete, the gloved man tossed the disposable cell phone down a three-foot-wide storm drain and continued walking nonchalantly toward his ultimate destination.

Sirens wailed, ever louder, closing in from all directions.

Confused, concerned people crowded the sidewalks, their mass bulging into the river of cars.

Escaping the commotion, the ordinary-looking man stepped out of the gray drizzle and into a welcoming coffee shop where the rich aroma of fresh brew greeted him. Ordering a triple tall Americano, he picked up a paper and took a seat near the window. Methodically sipping his black, unsweetened java, he read the *Chronicle*'s headline: "Fear Grips the Country, Despite Assurances and Arrests." Pausing, he looked up and gazed serenely across the street at the towering First Metropolitan Bank Building.

Reminiscent of a disorderly high school fire drill, fear-stricken people were pouring out of emergency exits and flooding the surrounding plaza, where evacuees, who had already escaped the building's staircases gathered, frantically speculating on what was happening.

A moment later, police arrived on the scene. Shouting in bullhorns and blowing whistles, they tried in vain to establish order.

50

In the infirmary, a guard cinched Frank's wrists to the cold metal bed frame with plastic cable ties. While Katrina understood Clark's reasoning behind the restraints, the reality of the situation made her cringe inside. Gingerly, she rested her hand on the extensive cast encasing Frank's shattered leg. Briefly studying his unconscious form, she asked, "Can we take off his socks?"

"Whatever you need," Clark replied, and he motioned for the sentry to remove Frank's penitentiary-issued footwear. Getting to work, Katrina laid her palms against the soles of Frank's bare feet, closed her eyes, and waited for something to happen.

Moments passed.

Frank's field sat idle and uncommunicative.

Katrina let out an audible sigh. "What's wrong?" Clark asked.

"I'm not getting anything," she replied. "He's not seeking help."

"But, his body definitely needs repair," Clark insisted. "Can't you connect with your mind, like you did with the boy from the motorcycle accident?"

"I'm not exactly sure how that happened," Katrina clarified. "Somehow the little boy let me in. Perhaps he wanted help. Frank's field simply isn't responding. It's as if there's no one home."

Clark realized he was going to have to stretch her abilities, even if it meant pushing her out of her comfort zone. "Lives are at stake," he began, soberly setting the stage. "I need you to imagine you're an operative infiltrating behind enemy lines. We need you to bring out as much information as you can."

"You want me to invade his field?" she clarified.

"Technically, yes . . ."

"I can't do that. The only reason I agreed to immerse with Frank's hot spots was because he offered them up. Right now, Frank's not sharing anything, and I am not about to start breaking and entering!"

Clark's serious look deepened, forcing crevices to form across his brow. "I understand your position on spying, but look at the bigger picture. This man may be so broken that he doesn't know he needs help. There are exceptions to every rule. Now, please."

In the sense that Frank's case fell more in the category of an intervention than traditional therapy, Clark's argument was right. Nonetheless, she offered only a conditional, "I'll try again, but I'll do it my way."

Clark sighed deeply and nodded. Her ethos as a healer was strong, and he admired that, but in his opinion, the current situation required more of a warrior's spirit.

Repositioning herself at Frank's feet, Katrina entered a deeper meditative trance. The clock on the wall ticked steady progress, but Katrina was not as fortunate. After eighteen minutes of repeated, failed attempts to get a response of any kind from Frank's biofield, she stopped. "Sorry. It's just not happening," she replied regretfully.

"Damn," Clark grumbled under his breath. He wished his grandfather could have been there to offer tutelage and help her unlock the latent abilities he was sure she possessed. As it was, all Clark could do was guide her based on secondhand information he learned as a child. "Let's regroup," he said. "If Frank was your patient in private practice, what would you do?"

"For starters, I'd be going in with love and compassion, rather than a sleuth-like intention," she contended. "Terrorist or not, at some level, he wants to be understood and heard."

Clark rubbed his forehead. Emotional engagement was certainly not a life-sustaining modus operandi for an intelligence agent. Finding the nexus point to engage Katrina's natural abilities was proving to be a bigger challenge than he had anticipated. "Fine," he replied, somewhat frustrated, "send the SOB some love."

Turning back to Frank, an inkling of trepidation crept through her bones as she laid her hands back on his feet. As soon as she shifted to a lens of deep compassion, a response rippled through her like the ping of a sonar signal. Intuitively she was guided to move her hands from Frank's feet to his right forearm. Once there, like a dowsing fork seeking water, her fingers were drawn to rest ever so lightly near his radius. Closing her eyes, she reached out with her heart.

A light hum, akin to a low voltage electrical current, began to vibrate through her hands. She'd found her connection point, and in a blink, she found herself standing before a dark wall, waiting for admittance.

The impenetrable barrier stretched as far and wide as she could see. There was no circumventing it. Although she had been granted access to Frank's subtle fields, his inner world remained sealed off.

Katrina pushed against the barricade. It was solid and dense. She shoved her shoulder against it like a firefighter breaking down a door to rescue people trapped in a burning room.

The wall stretched but did not give.

Marshalling her skills, she decided to take a roundabout approach. Rather than tackling the obstacle head on, she transmitted her thoughts through the barrier like ham radio waves in search of Frank's subconscious: *Please let me in. I'm here to help you.*

The wall responded by transforming into an inky-black, gelatinous goo.

She thrust her hand inside. It was cold and wet, like molded Jell-O.

Her perseverance did not go unnoticed. The barrier morphed once again—this time into a dense, pewter-colored fog.

Katrina inhaled quickly and then stuck her head inside, testing the air for toxicity.

Breathable but foul.

Logic dictated extreme caution, yet her desire to help Frank overruled prudence. Determined to venture out the other side, Katrina set out to walk through the malleable mass, only to discover that her shoes were stuck to the ground. Unwilling to give up, Katrina flung her body forward, prepared to land face down on her belly, hoping her five-foot seven-inch body would span the opaque miasma and give her a way out the other side.

As soon as she decided this, her feet broke free, and she stumbled forward, falling headlong into the misty vapor.

Scrambling to stand up, Katrina realized to her astonishment that not only had she fallen through the fog, but she had also fallen out of her physical body. No longer flesh and bone, the astral body in which she found herself still looked like her, yet was comprised solely of energy, although she could still feel, experience, and sense as if she were incarnate.

Above her, a fiery orb in the sky rapidly evaporated the nebulous curtain through which she had fallen, leaving her stranded in the middle of what appeared to be a flat, parched unending wasteland.

Blinded by the brightness, she squinted and shielded her eyes. A sudden gust of hot wind whipped her hair. Sand particles blasted her, stinging her skin.

She was surrounded by utter desolation—no creatures or life in sight, except for one lone tree in the distance. The sun beat down oppressively. Her astral body's bare feet burned hot against the scorched earth; the air temperature was blisteringly hot. Shade became requisite for survival, even if it was scant.

She set course for the solitary gnarled hardwood.

The deeply cracked soil crunched beneath her.

She hurried on searing feet across the bleak flats toward the aged grandfather of a tree, which jutted out against the horizon—a lighthouse in the desert sea. As she grew nearer, the tree revealed itself to be an almost lifeless shell; rotted branches clung to a charred trunk that bore lightning scars. It was dead, except for an almost imperceptible glimmer of green.

From behind the sun-dried branches, a sprig peeked out and hung on for dear life. The tree had not given up after all. The tiniest of leaves was daring to sprout. Below the modest offshoot, at the base of the trunk, a large cave-like hole promised shelter from the sun. Katrina dropped to her knees and cautiously stuck her head inside, nervous that she might find an animal hiding.

The musty hollow was larger than she anticipated. A cool draft wafted up from somewhere in the dark recesses, but she saw no creatures.

She crawled further inside to investigate.

The draft encircled her like wisps of wind, and then, without warning, became a vacuum force.

Sucked inside, she tumbled headlong down a hollow tube.

Nausea overwhelmed her. Her mind struggled to reconcile the inconceivability of it. She had entered a land where normal physics no longer ruled.

Fear racked her soul.

Exponentially worse than any roller coaster, with every second that she fell, the passageway narrowed, yet somehow her astral body had no problem adjusting as she plummeted down through the very tap root of the ancient tree.

Then, claustrophobia attacked her, and for an instant, Katrina felt she couldn't breathe.

Bam—she felt herself take a jog to the side.

She had entered one of the smaller branch roots.

Bam! Bam!—she felt two more jolts and the passageway continued to shrink.

Then plop. She was spat out, flat on her bottom, smack in the middle of a narrow trail deep within a dark forest.

51

Nestled between the skyscrapers of downtown Houston, tucked inside a coffee shop, the smartly dressed man drained the last drops of his coffee and dropped the paper cup into the trash. He headed out the door with his small black suitcase trailing close behind him and merged innocuously into the clamoring mayhem of restless humans. Good-naturedly, he slid through the crowd standing outside the First Metropolitan Bank Building until, near the center, he found a woman, whose wiry, blonde hair was as frazzled by the humidity as her nerves were by the crisis at hand.

"Excuse me, ma'am," he began politely, his earnest eyes gaining her attention. "I have an appointment at Malcolm Industries on the forty-eighth floor. What's going on?"

"There's been a bomb threat!"

"I see," he replied rather calmly. "I guess it's safe to assume my appointment can be rescheduled."

The middle-aged woman wrung her hands in front of her as she shifted on her feet. "I'm sure," she replied distractedly.

Surveying the tall skyscraper, he marveled at its elaborate architecture. *Truly an American monument—a testament to stolen power—false idols beckoning worship to a transaction economy, intoxicating the mindless and leading the world to demise,* he thought.

Friends, all in a similar state, gathered around the woman.

His eyes lit on her again. "I think I might have something that will help calm your nerves," he said as he maneuvered the small black suitcase in front of him with promise.

Her eyes brightened in response to his reassuring smile.

Bending over, the friendly man depressed the handle of the small black suitcase with a firm shove. And as he did, he looked up, catching her eye again, and grinned, a glint of hope shimmering in his eyes.

An instant later, he and twenty-three others vaporized into a misty cloud of mindless matter as the bomb in his suitcase exploded.

52

Desperate to rationalize her surreal experience, Katrina postulated that she might have fallen asleep while working on Frank. Perhaps this was just another bizarre, lifelike lucid dream. She reached down and pinched her arm hard to wake herself up. It hurt, but nothing happened. She was stuck where she was.

Not far away, a bloodcurdling howl stood the tiny hairs on the back of her neck on end.

She hunted for signs of life looking through the thick, shadowy woods. Nothing.

She turned to climb back up the root of the tree through which she had descended, but the opening had vanished.

Animalistic screams and more howling closed in.

She had to move.

Monstrous trees loomed overhead, tunneling the already dark, winding path. An eerie wind brought with it the smell of burning flesh and another evil howl.

Uncertain which direction to go, Katrina relied on the inward pull of her heart's magnetic north and followed the dirt trail as it snaked its way into uncharted territory. Less than a quarter mile up the path, she heard a low, throaty growl that rumbled in the shadows ahead. Instinct told her to turn and run, but there was nowhere to go.

Katrina froze.

Emerging through the dark, two gleaming yellow eyes fixed on her as a large, hungry black wolf, with its lips drawn back in a snarl, stepped from the shadows. At its flanks, two more sets of eyes appeared—the gatekeeper's pack.

A rolling mist began creeping rapidly through the underbrush, swallowing the path behind the wolf pack and obscuring any vision of what might lie beyond.

Its prey before it, the alpha wolf circled Katrina.

Fear threatened to strangle her.

Suddenly, the wolf laid its ears back and sprung fiercely for the kill, slamming Katrina hard against the ground. Its paws pressed heavy on her chest. Paralyzed with shock, Katrina wanted to scream but couldn't.

Strings of the animal's warm saliva drooled down on her face. Its fiery eyes pierced her soul, and in a bloodthirsty growl that somehow emerged as words in her mind, the carnivore promised, "I'm going to rip your heart out and eat it. My friends can have the rest—and with your heart, I'll own your soul."

The wolf pack yapped anxiously, pacing about, eager to participate, while overhead, a vulture swooped in to survey the impending carnage, anticipating the end. The scavenger's nonsensical message screeched in Katrina's mind: "Prophecy awaits; see with new vision or die that I might feast."

In this realm, Katrina realized animal communication transcended the limits of language.

From a tree branch to her right, a jaguar dropped to the ground, its spots shimmering through black fur, like stars in the night sky. With its ears back and teeth bared, the sleek beast crouched down and challenged the wolf pack for rights to the spoils, and as it did, its voice echoed in her head with guidance. "One must fight with the sword of the heart to survive a dark night of the soul."

At the moment, riddles were not what she needed! *Sword of the heart? New vision? Dark night of the soul?* Her mind struggled to decipher the clues.

Teeth gnashed. Katrina felt her death was only seconds away; the wolf's foul breath was hot against her face. Nauseatingly, it smelled of rotten flesh.

Her mind raced faster than her pounding heart. *Why did the wolf want her heart? What did her heart have to offer that made the beast believe it would own her soul?* Suddenly she remembered a cannibalistic tradition—to eat a fallen warrior's heart was to claim his power as your own. *What power lay in her heart that the wolf sought?* Then it hit her—the power of love.

The black wolf lunged for her throat with its jaws agape.

Summoning all her will, she pushed fear aside and gave the wolf the very thing it sought to take. She had to see the good around her. The wolf was a litmus test—a trial of faith.

With its incisors against her skin, the wolf stopped and pulled back unexpectedly, its yellow eyes questioning. Her new line of thinking had derailed it. Angrily, the wolf mustered an earth-shaking growl and attempted to launch Katrina back into her hellhole of fear—the place where it ruled.

Steadfast, Katrina wielded the broadsword of love, admiring the wolf's teeth and appreciating the role it played in her development as a healer. The stronger her convictions of love, the weaker the wolf became, until poof—the wolf pack vaporized before her eyes as if it had never existed. Stunned by what had just happened, Katrina sat up apprehensively and eyed the big cat sitting on its haunches only a few feet away.

The jaguar's silent jade eyes studied her. "Well done!" it commended her mentally rather than vocally. The magnificent beast rose. Black as the night, it padded softly down the path, its long tail curling upward just above the ground. "Come with me," it summoned.

Katrina fell in step beside her powerful companion and walked ever deeper into the mysterious woodland that seemed to be alive with a spirit of its own. Long, spooky shadows and gnarled silhouettes of bent and craggy trees resurrected memories of Sleepy Hollow in her mind. Trees shape-shifted into would-be forms, and blackness from nowhere filled the spaces between.

Something or someone was out there.

With her worst nightmares beginning to materialize, Katrina tumbled into fright.

Walking next to her, the jaguar growled. "Stop it! Keep your thoughts in the Light, or I promise, you shall manifest your darkest fears." The sea green of the animal's jade eyes grew stormy with concern. "I cannot protect you—I can only guide you. This war is yours."

Katrina was beginning to realize that she was her own worst enemy. Every horror show she had ever watched, every frightening Grimm's fairy tale she had ever read, had the power to come to life in this land of limitless possibilities. And once conjured, the dark forces were fueled by the very fear they produced—a deadly cycle for the soul.

Holding her mind in check, Katrina purged her negative thoughts, and the path immediately began to brighten. Soon she and her feline guide emerged from the woods into a clearing where a cluster of drab buildings sprawled before her.

Barbed wire encircled the perimeter. As Katrina approached the compound, thunderclouds formed in the sky, despite the fact that her thoughts had been reined in. She looked to her jaguar guide for answers, but it had disappeared.

A sudden feeling of aloneness swept over her.

Glancing back to the forest, she watched as the trail quickly obscured itself with rapidly growing underbrush. Her only option now was to go forward.

Reminiscent of a prison, the compound was studded with lifeless sentry towers. The unlocked gate had been left open, with its rusted chain dangling.

Katrina entered cautiously.

A stifled mewling met her ears, perhaps a hundred yards away. There was only a faint sound at first, which then grew louder.

Chills ran up her spine.

A small earthen oven wafted thick smoke into the evening air.

No one was in sight.

Walking farther, she heard whimpered sobbing. Her senses acute, she followed the cries, until suddenly, she saw him out of the corner of her eye—a little boy crouched against the exterior wall of a rundown, neglected structure. He was clothed in tatters and his body was ashen-hued, as if the color had been drained from his skin. With his chest racking from his stifled sobs, he didn't notice her approach.

Was he lost? Had he ventured down here and not found his way back? Katrina knelt beside him and sought his downturned face. "Can I help you?"

Recoiling, the young boy, who appeared to be no more than five, sobbed harder and hunkered down in fear.

"Please, let me help you," Katrina pleaded.

Hesitantly he lifted his sad, sullen face to meet hers.

She gazed into the sunken hollows of his eyes and gasped. It was young Frank!

"Have you come to take me home?" hazarded the weak voice, small and quiet.

She nodded a silent yes.

He placed his cold, pale hand in hers and struggled to his feet. "There are more," he whispered fearfully. "We can't leave them here." Pulling her by the hand, he guided her through the dilapidated building and down a deserted hall, until he finally came to stand before an unmarked wooden door.

A deep foreboding squeezed Katrina's chest. Bracing herself, she turned the handle.

Behind the portal, horror so unimaginable met her eyes that her knees threatened to crumple beneath her. Inside, decapitated and dismembered corpses were strewn across the floor; body parts rotted in piles. Grime-encased skeletons testified to the duration of atrocities witnessed by the barren walls.

Near the center of the room, a large, flat rock stood nearly four feet high. Ancient bloodstains trickled down its sides.

Young Frank, not uttering a word, stood somberly reverent of the scene. Then, tugging on her hand to gain attention, he pointed across the room to where several other young boys were huddled in a corner, trying to console themselves.

Katrina recognized each boy as a fractured piece of Frank. And although she yearned to understand how they had ended up here, she sensed she had to get them back to the land of the living now—to the world where Frank's comatose body was. *But how?*

Numbly, she felt the boy pulling her by the hand. Blood painted his bare feet crimson as he walked ahead, brushing without notice against fallen bodies, his eyes fixed only on the apparitions of his soul. Katrina wanted to go with him but, because she was not willing to defile the remains of human sacrifice, her feet were frozen.

Flies buzzed among the rotting flesh, and the stench gagged her. A message came on the flies' wings: "Judge not what ye see. Solutions exist with pure intent."

Tugging harder, the specter of Frank's five-year-old soul piece urged Katrina on. The group of boys had seen her. They were calling, hoping, waiting for her. Their desperation was more than she could bear.

Swallowing hard, she put the crippling scene before her out of her mind and focused on the mission at hand—to bring Frank's soul pieces home. Suddenly, a pair of galoshes materialized on her feet. This extra layer of desensitization gave her the ability to place one foot in front of the other. She was mobile once again.

Carefully stepping through the corpses, respectful not to disturb them in their rest, Katrina held tightly to the little hand that guided her and kept her mind trained solely on the stranded likenesses of Frank.

But midway across the room, her feet began to drag, as if she were walking through sludge.

Mortified, Katrina looked down to see that several ghostlike hands had taken firm hold of her ankles.

More and more hands appeared, latching on.

With each step, her feet became heavier. The hands morphed into arms and ultimately into full-bodied spirits.

Katrina's head swam as the ghosts clamored to tell her the shocking truths surrounding their deaths. They were trapped—stuck—unable to transition to the Light because their stories had gone unheard. Listening to their tales would set them free, but there were so many.

Pummeled by their screams, swallowed up in their pain, Katrina's attention became divided between the ghosts and the boys; her mind lost its singular focus.

Instantly, quicksand materialized beneath her feet.

With fear-filled eyes, Frank's soul shards watched from where they stood. She wouldn't reach them. Katrina was going under, drowning in a bottomless sea of phantasmal horror.

Tiny Frank gripped her hand and clung to her with all his might, trying to keep her from sinking, so that she might also bring back his brethren; but it was no use.

Somewhere, far in the distance, Katrina thought she heard her name being called.

There was a sucking sound, and she heard a loud boom!

Blackness was all around her.

The deep abyss swallowed her whole.

All she felt was the little boy's hand clenched tightly in hers.

"Katrina!" Derek's voice sounded closer now.

In a daze, she reentered the material world, and struggling to orient herself in her physical body, she groggily opened her eyes to find that her fingers still rested on Frank's arm. Inside her consciousness, she perceived an uncharacteristic feeling of delight at seeing Frank, a perspective that she immediately recognized as belonging to the little boy. By holding tightly to his hand, she had unwittingly brought him home. As soon as she had acknowledged his presence, a whooshing sensation passed through her hands and into Frank's arm. With the transfer complete, the connection that had hummed between her hands and Frank ceased.

Katrina felt more grounded after that and shook off her trance-like state. Looking for Clark in the chair where he'd been sitting, she was surprised to see Derek approaching instead.

"Are you okay?" he asked, obviously concerned. "You'd stopped breathing."

She was exhausted. "Where's Clark?"

53

In Black Hole's briefing room, smoke from Sterling's habit tinted the air—air that was already thick with apprehension, anticipation, and emergency. Clark and Sterling fell silent as Derek ushered Katrina in. Fleming was on his way but had yet to arrive.

"Done already?" Clark asked, glancing at the clock. Only thirty-two minutes had elapsed since Katrina had begun her last round with Frank.

"She stopped breathing," Derek scrambled to explain. "I had to snap her out of it."

Clark's eyes darkened with concern. "Katrina, are you all right?"

She nodded. "Just a little foggy still," she replied, and, pouring herself coffee rather than tea, she took a seat across from Sterling at the conference table. She felt as though she'd been gone for days and ached all over. Multitasking in the mystical realms had landed her in a death-defying tailspin, and she was grateful Derek had stepped in when he did.

Derek remained standing, and with an underlying sense of urgency apparent, he said to Clark, "If you don't need me . . ."

"Thanks, Derek. I've got it covered." Clark's terse response offered no clue that he and Derek were in the middle of orchestrating a covert op to Russia.

Turning to leave, Derek caught Katrina's eye before walking out the door, and he said, "Take care of yourself," with a worried smile.

Before Katrina could respond, Sterling began peppering her with questions as he smothered his cigarette. "Did you zap Frank? Is he awake?"

"No," she answered. "But maybe soon." Katrina hoped against all odds that the single soul piece she had recovered for Frank would be enough to tip the scales.

"Well, what happened?" Sterling asked in a tone that said he had expected results.

"I've never experienced anything like it," she began and then went on to describe the fluid, visceral world that morphed kaleidoscopically in response to emotion and intent—a surreal realm where animals had power and traumatized spirits hung in stasis, waiting to be unchained from earthly suffering.

Sterling stared at her dubiously.

In an effort to reconcile the unusual encounter, she leaned on science. "We live in a three-dimensional universe within what some physicists have dubbed the 'multiverse.' This multiverse is eleven-dimensional, and even though most of us are unaware of them, they certainly exist," she explained. "I think I might have opened an envelope of information stored in another dimension—a living tapestry of threads, bundles of energy fields—all somehow linked to Frank."

Sun-crinkles sprouted at the corners of Jim Clark's eyes as she concluded. "Nice work," he replied, proud of her determination. She had allowed adversity to push her abilities to new limits, yet a brief moment later when he considered where she had been, concerned frown lines replaced his smile. Gateways to dangerous realms had been opened, and he wasn't sure he had the knowledge to protect her.

During her report, although Sterling had kept a straight face, his ego had struggled with the merits of her participation. Baffled by her account, he looked back and forth between Clark and Katrina and groused, "Am I missing something here? Or are you putting me on? People are blowing themselves up left and right for no apparent reason, and you want me to about talk about boys that looked like Frank? Dead bodies and wolves! What kind of remote viewing is that?"

Clark corrected him. "It's not remote viewing at all."

"Oh," he grumbled, and crossing his arms, he leaned back in his chair and asked, "then what the hell was it?"

"In terms you'll be more familiar with, Bill," Clark began, "Katrina infiltrated behind enemy lines and extracted a valuable asset that may help us win the war."

Sterling looked at them doubtfully.

Intrigued by Clark's analogy, a small smile broke across Katrina's face. She hadn't thought of it like that, but in hindsight, he was right. In the inner realms she had accomplished what Clark had so often done in the outer world. He extracted assets out of oppressive darkness and transported them into what he saw as the light of personal freedoms. His intention, she imagined, was much the same as hers—a desire to serve humanity—although his originated from the idea his grandfather had given him of a warrior of light, and hers was sourced in healing others.

"If I'm not mistaken," Clark explained, "Dr. Walker stumbled into a shamanic journey. Her overriding desire to help Frank inadvertently led her to recover one of his missing soul pieces and reinstate it in his physical body." Although Clark had never personally experienced the realms into which Katrina had wandered, he likened her experience to stories his grandfather had told him.

"Soul pieces?" Sterling sputtered incredulously. Apparently the merit of what was happening was going over his head.

"Trauma causes soul loss," Clark replied, his patience with Sterling wearing thin. "Take a horse, for example," Clark began, nuggets of Native American wisdom echoing in his head. "A wild horse runs free, jumps over fences, and would never permit a rider on its back. A broken horse, on the other hand, forgets its true nature. Its spirit has been fractured and slips off into other realms, leaving behind a shell. The broken horse obeys a master who would have it do things unthinkable to a horse in its natural state."

"Who gives a fuck?" Sterling pushed himself out of his chair and started pacing. "Frank is not a horse!"

"But Frank *is* severely broken," Katrina confirmed, "as was Susan. Clinically speaking, what Clark is talking about is a type of dissociation. Under normal conditions, dissociation is a coping mechanism that allows the mind to distance itself from experiences too painful for the psyche to process. Severe trauma has the capacity to sever connections to a person's thoughts, memories, feelings, actions, or sense of identity."

Clark tied the concepts together. "The ancient tradition of shamanism holds that core essence can be lost, or flee to other dimensions, in an effort to escape harsh realities. Those pieces contain a person's willpower, passion in life, unique gifts, and the will to live. The person left behind is fractured, and this lack of being whole is attributed to being the root cause for illness, betrayal, bad luck, and numerous other forms of malaise. Of course, the degree of fracturing depends on life experiences."

An almost imperceptible nod marked Sterling's tacit understanding. He had seen friends come back from war as hollow-eyed, empty shells of their former selves. Some had even used substance abuse as an attempt to further dissociate from experiences that were too painful to remember.

Clark added, "Soul retrieval, like what Dr. Walker did with Frank, brings back the lost pieces, re-associating them, if you will, which in Frank's case, may help him remember or give him the will to change."

Sterling grumbled and took a drag on his cigarette.

Katrina elaborated, "In cases such as Susan's, people can dissociate to the point where multiple distinct identities known as alter egos or alters are created. Each has its own pattern of perceiving and interacting with the environment, and some alters may experience amnesia of what the other personas have done."

Sterling piped in. "That explains why the Susan who called you to set up an appointment was so different from the woman who showed up."

"Exactly," Katrina replied. "The intense emotions of motherhood debugged a layer of her programming, triggering a desire to heal. Apparently, her 'alter' personality did not want to heal, and I guarantee it was one of her alters that killed the people at the mall. The nightmares and panic attacks she was experiencing were partly symptoms of the internal struggle for dominance of one alter over another."

"Shit," Sterling replied. "If that's what's going on with Frank, we're screwed. How did these people get so fucked up?" Sterling's phone interrupted his diatribe. He fished it out and answered. "Sure," he muttered, and excusing himself, stepped outside to take the call.

In Sterling's absence, Clark asked Katrina with genuine interest, "Just out of curiosity, what made you enter the hollow in the tree?"

"There was nothing else there—just desert. It was the only hope of shelter."

"That took courage."

Puzzled and a little unsettled by his comment, Katrina didn't know how to respond. Courage wasn't what she had felt going in. Nevertheless, she appreciated the unexpected compliment.

His eyes still fixed on hers, a shadow passed across his face and his expression darkened. Opting for brevity to protect her from the details, he told Katrina how, while she had been working with Frank, Houston had become the latest strike zone.

Whatever positive emotions Katrina had momentarily been basking in evaporated.

With a bang, the door flew open and Sterling barged back in, accompanied by Fleming, who nodded a cold greeting to Clark and Katrina before taking a seat. Sterling, still on the phone, grumbled, "Yeah, hard to believe," into the mouthpiece and abruptly ended the call. Narrowing his eyes, he squinted cautiously at Katrina and took a swig of coffee before reporting somewhat disbelievingly, "Seems our boy, Frank, is awake."

Katrina smiled on the inside as Clark took a satisfied breath of relief. It seemed that the re-entry of Frank's soul piece into the present world had made a difference.

Fleming, visibly miffed at the assumption that Katrina's efforts had anything to do with Frank's regained state of consciousness, dismissed the event by ranting, "It's just a goddamned coincidence!"

Clark shot him a silencing glare and said, "So—here's the plan. Now that Frank's back with the living, we're going to wage a dual war. We've got to find out who the puppet master is if we're going to have any hopes of stopping this, and standard methods are getting us nowhere. Fleming, I want you to dope him with sodium pentothal and question him . . ."

Katrina protested. "Let me go back in. I can retrieve more lost soul pieces. Look at what bringing back just this one did."

Fleming chortled and Clark cut in before Sterling could react. "Absolutely not," he replied, without room for negotiation. "Shamanic journeying is dangerous—it gives new meaning to covert ops. It's not worth the risk. If I had known you might end up there, I never would have let you go in the first place."

"But . . ." she began.

"Subject's closed," Clark replied flatly.

"Problem is, truth serum's not reliable," Sterling countered. "People mix fact and fantasy so freely it's like friggin' Disney World."

"Even if Frank does confuse fact and fiction," Clark argued, "Katrina can watch how the answers resonate—congruent or incongruent with the imprints in his field. Sodium pentothal also makes subjects more talkative," he added, "depressing mechanisms of self-censorship and inhibition, and in that, Frank's shell might drop."

Katrina looked optimistic. "That's the opening I need."

The overeager glint in her eye told Clark his new recruit was going to need boundaries to keep her safe. In the hidden realms, only the strongest survived, and Katrina's inexperience left her vulnerable.

"I need you to revert back to observation only," Clark ordered Katrina. "I mean it—no immersion in Frank's field. The last thing I need is for you to go missing in action in another dimension."

Fleming clarified, "So I get to interrogate and she gets to watch?"

Clark nodded in reply.

"Hold on to your socks, little sister," Fleming smirked. "This is gonna be fun!"

Katrina shot him a drop-dead glare as he headed for the door.

54

In the infirmary, Frank, now quite conscious again, watched wide-eyed as Fleming pushed sodium pentothal from a syringe into the IV tube that penetrated his restrained forearm. Almost instantly, he stopped fighting against the bindings.

From the background, Clark supervised Fleming as he exuberantly began his new round of interrogation. Katrina sat nearby, observing from a chair. The strike in Houston, as well as her desire to help Frank, had redoubled her resolve. She was committed to taking the lid off of her abilities to get results, regardless of Clark's caution.

"Tell me about the ricin," Fleming demanded of Frank.

"I told you, I don't know . . ."

"Who put you up to it?"

Refusing to answer, Frank stared blankly.

Fleming inserted the needle again and boosted the dose, careful to leave him conscious.

Moments later, the drug—coupled with relentless questioning—had loosened Frank's tongue. His biofield followed suit and produced slurries of activity that mirrored his babbling. Blurry imprints failed to snap into focus—the interrogation was stirring up a response, just not a coherent one.

Fleming pushed harder, and Katrina began tracking discrete field encryptions that were playing peek-a-boo amid the quagmire of nonsensical data.

Cobra-like, Fleming struck again and again, trying to trip him up.

Stuttering and stammering in confusion, Frank's ego struggled to remain in control.

In his subtle energy body, the drug unexpectedly loosed a violent uprising of suppressed emotion visible to Katrina's naked eye. Innate goodness embroiled in mortal combat against deeply entrenched subliminal programming that fought fiercely for control of Frank's mouth, thoughts, and words. In the middle of the battle, Frank's recovered five-year-old emerged. Fueling Frank's will to live, the young child crusaded to unlock a suppressed, yet intrinsic, desire to be whole, only to witness glimmers of hope fall mercilessly before the demons of fear.

To lend the child a hand, Katrina needed to merge with Frank's interactive field, and fast. Reaching out with her heart, she engaged. Chaos instantly engulfed her as if a giant wave had crashed over her head, submerging her deep within Frank's multidimensional network of fields.

Fleming's voice vanished.

Katrina tried to come up for air, swimming with all her might, only to be swept away by a riptide. Apparitions flooded past like bodies in a burgeoning river. It was all too fast. She was flying through time.

Then suddenly everything stopped.

55

Stillness. Blackness everywhere.

Then, a time capsule of information—an imprint stored in Frank's field—came to life from the surrounding sea of nothingness. Ephemeral and granular at first, the scene rapidly turned into realistic solidity—a simply crafted, pine-planked, child-sized coffin materialized, but not before two male voices emerged, speaking Russian, which, to Katrina's surprise, she understood.

Stunned, Katrina grimaced as meaty hands gripped her forearms from behind. She looked down to find herself inside Frank's young body.

The scene continued to sharpen in focus as a man, who had at first appeared to be nothing more than an eerie apparition, solidified. Dressed in a white lab coat, he stood in front of her, his jet-black hair combed over to hide a balding head.

"You know I love you?" the strange man prodded, all the while one of his assistants continued to bind her arms tightly.

"Of course, Father," she heard herself reply. Frank still had control over the body she inhabited, although she felt everything as if it were her own.

"Things will become clearer after this," the man promised, with eyes icy and gray. "Soon you will understand what you need to do." He kissed the top of Frank's head, and from her insider's perspective, Katrina noticed Frank's body begin to tremble as he struggled to stay brave.

Menacingly, Father produced a syringe from the pocket of his lab coat. Smiling thinly and without warning, he suddenly pulled down Frank's pants and plunged the thick needle into his right buttock.

Searing liquid shot into muscle.

Katrina, and Frank, tried to fight back, but to no avail. A moment later the bruising embrace that constricted her arms became unnecessary. Although the urge to resist did not dissipate, an irrevocable paralysis overcame her.

Father and his assistant smiled as they observed with deep satisfaction the effectiveness of the drug she understood from their conversation to be curare, and to her shock, the terror had only begun. After being stripped naked, the body she inhabited was positioned face up in the coffin, where despite her being immobilized, she could still feel everything: the rough planking of the wooden box that scraped against her skin, the pounding of her heart in her ears and throat, and the unnatural fondling of the two men as they prepared her.

"It's time," Father announced.

"I'll get it," the other man replied eagerly. Walking briefly out of sight, he reappeared holding a large, bulging, brown burlap sack closed at the neck.

With eyelids frozen open, Katrina couldn't even blink to shield her eyes from what came next.

"Here you go, my love," Father cajoled as he poured a bag full of slithering snakes atop Frank's incapacitated body.

She couldn't breathe. Her heart felt like it was going to stop beating—but it didn't.

Snakes were everywhere—slipping down her arms, crawling between her legs and around her naked torso, sliding over her stomach and across her bare chest, slithering past her nostrils, around her neck and across her forehead. Katrina found herself hoping against all odds that this ghoulish reality was merely a horrifying, sodium pentothal-induced fantasy, rather than an authentic memory stored in time.

The men chuckled as they watched.

Imprisoned in an unresponsive body, the abuse was more than she could bear. She wanted out of this nightmare. *Now!*

Just then, a jolt wrenched her free of Frank's small form and she stood next to the man-made snake pit.

Before her, young Frank lay in the writhing serpent-filled box and she desperately wanted to help him, but in this astral plane she was not only invisible to others but also powerless to affect material change.

Then, she witnessed murder—soul murder. Frank's energy body fractured. To escape the brutality, ghost-like shards, one of which Katrina recognized as the five-year-old boy recovered on her shamanic journey, fled Frank's physical form and disappeared into other realms.

In that instant Katrina realized that, like the ghosts seeking to be heard, she had beamed into this memory because Frank's recovered soul piece had needed her to understand the root of his trauma. As soon as her heart moved to gratitude for the insight, her ears suddenly popped, as if on an airplane, and she could once again hear Fleming's gratingly annoying voice grinding out questions.

Her eyes flew open and she jumped up.

"What's up?" Clark asked.

"We need to talk." Running her hands over her arms, she shuddered inside. *Snakes.* She was glad to be back, fully, in her own skin.

56

At AWOL's underground lab, the oven's timer dinged.

After a long and painstaking wait, Sprite and Shortcut exchanged nervous looks.

"Moment of truth," Shortcut said anxiously, chewing two pieces of gum at once.

Sprite, who was not sentimental by nature, took a deep breath and opened the oven door.

Shortcut pulled out the paper.

The glue was dissolved, and the paper separated from the cover without prodding.

"Bingo," Sprite announced triumphantly, and with a smile, gave Shortcut a very rare and clandestine high five.

57

Clark's blood ran ice cold in his veins as Katrina relayed the disturbing experience to him and Sterling. The radical torture she detailed was a trademark of Invisible Warfare—a key element in brainwashing and mind control initiatives.

"Snakes and coffins! Another damned shamanic escapade?" Sterling slammed, his reaction predictable and blind to the underlying implications.

"This was different," she assured him with conviction.

"Damn it, Katrina. I told you to observe—not engage!" Clark chastised her, searching for patience. "You have more abilities than you know what to do with. Even during Project Stargate at the Stanford Research Institute, remote viewers were forbidden to astral project like that! Stop being so headstrong!"

"I don't think you understand. Frank can be saved. I can help him; and we need the answers that Frank's soul pieces want to share," she argued. "Besides, I can take care of myself!"

"Tick tock, boys and girls," Sterling prompted with frustration as he tapped the glass face on his Timex. "What now?"

Three excruciatingly long seconds of silence passed before Clark turned back to Katrina and asked, "Can you find your way back to the location where Frank was being tortured?"

Katrina shrugged and replied somewhat sarcastically, "I thought it was too dangerous?"

"Yes, but this time we do it my way."

"What's happening?" Sterling muttered, at a total loss. "Are we making progress? Are we stuck?"

Clark's demeanor hardened and he turned to Sterling. "We've learned one very significant thing, Bill, and you're not gonna like it. The brutality Frank suffered fractured his personality in such a way that he's immune to standard interrogation, as well as Fleming's version," he commented derisively.

Sterling's chest sank visibly. "What the hell are we supposed to do?"

"Mind control initiatives were pervasive during the Invisible War. We need to find out his make and model."

"How?—if he's never gonna talk?"

"He's said quite a bit already, Bill. You just haven't been listening."

Clark's phone chimed. He answered.

Shortcut didn't even wait for hello. "Sir, Frank Davis's mother's passport was forged!" he jabbered anxiously. "The flaw was in the cover glue—almost impossible to detect. Standard examination never would have discovered it."

Clark expressed his thanks and disconnected. "Let's go, Katrina," he ordered. "There's just one more thing I need to verify." And with that, Clark escorted her back toward G-32.

Sterling quibbled behind them, "And then what?"

58

With Frank left behind in Lance Fleming's questionable care, Clark dimmed the lights of room G-32 and prepared Katrina for remote viewing—a government-sanctioned, psi-based variety of intelligence gathering that defied time and space.

Katrina made herself comfortable on the couch where Frank had sat earlier that day.

Concerned for her safety, Clark set the ground rules. "Remote viewing requires you to be a detached observer. If you go in thinking it's your job to heal this man, you'll jeopardize the mission and put yourself in real danger that I can't get you out of," he warned, his tone firm. "This is not about saving one man's shattered soul; it's about saving thousands of innocent lives."

"But, what if . . ."

"No buts!" Clark reiterated. "Under no circumstances are you to get emotionally involved while you're out there. You are to follow my lead." The target to be described was the location where she had seen Frank with the snakes.

She exhaled heavily, leaned back, and tried to make herself comfortable for the jump to nonlocal reality that lay ahead.

A worried voice inside Clark encouraged him to take extra precaution. "Imagine you have a golden thread tied around your waist that's connected to me," he said, as she closed her eyes. "That will keep you from going too far," he continued in a soft tone, "and if you need to, it will help you find your way back home."

Katrina took a deep breath and, in her mind's eye, a thin glowing cord materialized around her midriff. Checking its tensile strength, she was relieved to find the thread unbreakable. Satisfied, she allowed herself to drift into a deep, peaceful state.

Nothingness rapidly enveloped her, and she felt as if she were flying through space toward the target destination without the benefit of sight or bearing. Her intention being her sole steering mechanism, she arrived seconds later.

The scene emerged in black and white, and she found herself floating high above what appeared to be the grounds of a giant estate. Heavily wooded forest stretched as far as she could see; a narrow cobblestone road offered ingress and egress. Around her middle, the golden strand still tethered her into the unseen, and experimenting from the safety of her new lifeline, Katrina discovered she could ascend and descend at will.

From a great distance she heard Clark's voice in the back of her mind, prompting, "What mental images are you getting?" and in a soft, hushed tone she described the buildings she saw below her. After a moment, the image went hazy, before it reinvented itself in color, and she discovered her vantage point had changed.

She had entered a building.

Clark's reassuring voice encouraged her to continue detailing her account.

"I see a long corridor . . . doors on each side," she murmured softly.

"What else?"

"I sense cold. The hallway looks sterile . . . feels devoid of compassion."

Clark reeled her back in. "Open your eyes for a moment, stay relaxed, and without analyzing what you've seen, sketch it out on the pad."

Somewhat groggily, she crafted a rudimentary drawing, and dropping back into her meditative state, slipped back into the site with ease. This time, she found herself inside an empty room that seemed vaguely familiar.

Her senses came online.

The colors intensified, transforming from pale watercolor to bright acrylic.

She could hear rain outside.

Turning, she noticed a window and, on feet as light as air, she walked over to look through the glass. Struck by an odd sort of déjà vu, a stone landed in the pit of her stomach when she realized this was the window from her dream, except this time, she was on the inside. Her heart thudded as she realized Susan and Frank had been abused at the same place. They were linked! *But who was behind it? And why?* The more her heart sought answers, the greater her sensory awareness became.

Behind her, she heard footsteps in the hall.

Instantly, she found herself standing once again in the corridor. Simply by shifting her focus from the window to the footsteps, she had relocated, and the scene filled in around her. Clark's voice faded into the distance as cold marble tiles materialized beneath her bare feet. She had fully immersed in the scene.

An involuntary tremble crept up her spine as a stern-looking woman with short black hair and a riding crop nestled beneath her arm approached. Behind her marched a group of youngsters whose uniforms matched Susan's in the dream. The schoolmistress spoke flawless English. "Today, children, we are going to watch a display of courage and solidarity."

Anxiety saturated the children's fields but was masked behind stoic faces.

Instinct pushed Katrina to follow, but the golden thread snapped taut and stopped her. Clark's orders flashed in her mind, but the "real" world felt distant and lackluster in this plane. Her soul told her she was on the right track. She reached down and untied the safety cord that bound her to Clark, freeing herself to infiltrate the ethers of the past. She caught up with the entourage as it passed through double swinging doors and entered a large gymnasium.

Each child, stone-faced and exceedingly well behaved, took a seat on the bleachers. In the middle of the gym's highly polished hardwood floor stood a lone wooden chair. Three people in white lab coats entered the gym, and Katrina's stomach cringed. Father was among them. His icy eyes made her skin crawl.

Across the gym another door opened. Through it stepped an adolescent Frank, reminiscent of one of the huddled boys in her journey; but now in flesh and blood, he was dressed in the same type of uniform as the others. With long strides, he crossed the gym floor and surveyed the attendees. Selecting one of the older children from the front row of the bleachers, Frank asked him to take a seat in the chair. Smiling, the two made small talk for the briefest of moments before Father walked over and greeted them with a smile. Patting each on the back, he reached into his vest pocket, pulled out a pistol, and handed it to Frank.

The training had been thorough. Emotionless and duty-driven, teenaged Frank accepted the firearm with a nod. The traumas he'd suffered had left him deeply broken and highly programmable.

Katrina was not prepared for what came next.

Wrapping his teenage fist around the butt of the gun, Frank leveled the barrel at his friend, who now sat motionless, staring blankly at the young spectators.

Running to his side, Katrina shouted for Frank to stop and desperately tried to pry the gun from his hand. No matter how hard she tried, she remained a helpless spectator, eyewitness to a travesty that had occurred decades before.

Frank pulled the trigger. Blood spattered, reaching even the children in the third row.

Frank's core energy shattered; more soul pieces that could no longer bear the reality at hand fled his body and ran for shelter in other dimensions.

Lightheaded and nauseous, Katrina felt faint.

Clapping and congratulations ensued. Frank had passed some sort of test—a rite of passage.

Darkness crept in. Then, a curtain of black dropped.

Clark's voice boomed. "Katrina, you're not responding to my prompts. What's going on?"

Her eyes flew open. Thank God she was back. Reflexively, she checked her clothing for blood. "It's worse than anything I could have ever imagined . . ." she stammered hoarsely.

Clark withheld comment as she solemnly shared what she had experienced. Still visibly shaken by the unnerving encounter, she asked pensively, "Things like that don't really happen, right?" She waited for Clark to respond, but by ignoring the question he told her that she had hit another need-to-know wall. Instead, he asked for her to finish rendering the sketch. Once she was done, Clark flipped on the light to get a better look. Squinting at two roughly drawn figures, he pointed and asked, "What are these?"

"Lion statues outside the stone-walled entrance," she answered simply.

Clark's eyes flashed in certain recognition. "Perfect," he said. "Now I know Frank's make and model."

59

President Lara Roberts was working feverishly with a handful of speechwriters to prepare an emergency address when the red phone rang. Roberts's expression darkened. It was Clark reporting from AWOL. Dismissing her staff, she took the call.

Clark tensely reported that Katrina had confirmed their worst fears. "Frank is a bona fide sleeper from Blackheart's program," he informed her, "as were Susan Bradford and the others, I'm sure."

"Shit, Jim! I thought this problem had been neutralized! How do we stop them?" the president asked worriedly.

"We can't, Lara," Clark replied, evenly and personally. "Not until we find out who or what's triggering them."

"So, let me get this straight," President Roberts said in exasperation, "activation sequences can be delivered by anyone, anytime, anywhere—by phone, email, or even by a waiter in a restaurant? We're sitting ducks!"

Clark's voice grew grim, "It's also possible that these sleepers were preprogrammed to detonate based on a date stamp or event. Currently we have no idea what's triggering them."

"If the public gets a whiff of this . . ." the president began with a controlled tremble in her voice. "We're already having a helluva time doing damage control. The electromagnetic pulse in Chicago got whitewashed as a weird power surge, but the blast in Houston and Susan Bradford's heart attack generator . . . those have been difficult to explain away."

"If we're lucky, we're dealing with a few remnant sleepers planted prior to Project Clean Sweep," Clark offered.

"And if we're not?" President Roberts ruminated, falling momentarily silent before asking about the intercepted text. "Do you think 'old treasures bring liberty or death' means someone's selling activation codes?"

"It could mean a lot of things," Clark replied. "Until I get to Russia and find out who sent it, we're stuck."

"I don't like it," President Roberts replied. "If it is Krueger, it's trouble. He's double-crossed you once and could do it again. If it's not Krueger . . ." the president paused before continuing ardently, "the stakes are too high—the note too convenient. I can't afford to lose you, Jim, and you need every edge you can get. I want you to take Dr. Walker along."

The line fell momentarily silent, and Clark was glad the president couldn't see his face pale. "Out of the question, Madame President," he replied finally.

"But, she can see what others can't; she demonstrated that with Frank."

"She has no tactical training," Clark rebutted firmly. "That's a risk I'm not willing to take."

The president, unaware of Katrina's past and Clark's promise to Eliza to protect her, didn't understand his reluctance. "We're at war, Jim," she concluded. "Ultimately, I'll leave it up to you, but as far as I'm concerned, conscript her if you have to. There's no time to waste."

60

Back at AWOL, a short eighteen minutes after concluding his call with the president, Clark hurried directly for Shortcut's desk.

Looking up from the stack of papers, Shortcut's worried eyes greeted him. He hadn't slept in two days and it showed. "Those coordinates," he reported, shaking his head, "it's going to be dicey." He handed Clark detailed satellite photos taken only hours before. "They land you smack in the middle of a bravta prison."

Clark didn't look surprised. Bravta was slang for brotherhood and referred to any number of organized crime syndicates that had sprouted in Russia since the fall of the USSR. The Russian mafia was prolific—countless displaced ex-KGB and ex-Soviet officers had morphed into mob bosses. To fund their new organizatsiyas, these power seekers stole state secrets, technology, munitions, and arms and sold them on the black market to the highest bidder.

Clark scrutinized the images. "Which group controls this facility?"

"A splinter cell—an arm that's gone dark. Not much intel on them," Shortcut replied as he rifled through his stack of paper and gave Clark a short report from British Intelligence. "MI6 had someone on the inside, but not for long."

"Dead?"

Shortcut nodded. "A confirmed kill," he said as he passed Clark a classified manila envelope containing relevant photographs. "The British Embassy in Moscow received an anonymous call directing them to the body." Shortcut grimaced as Clark pulled out the snapshots. He'd already seen them once, and that was more than enough.

Three-by-five glossies chronicled the scene. The former operative's mangled remains hung high in a tree to keep animals at bay. Intestines dangled from the eviscerated body cavity.

"Seems they don't like visitors," Clark conjectured, ignoring the bad sign. He slid the photos back in the envelope and prompted, "Anything on Nikolai Krueger?"

"Listed as dead for more than twenty years."

"How about unofficial channels? Cyber chatter? The underground? If he did manage to survive, he's likely operating under an alias."

"Yes, sir, I've done all of it. Interpol and facial-recognition databanks, too. Nothing."

Clark considered the implications. A bravta mafioso prison in Russia, and a rescue request from a dangerous, deceased KGB asset? It didn't bode well.

Shortcut pushed a thick stack of paper toward him. "Here are the details, including travel plans," he began. "But with all due respect, sir, considering what happened to the MI6 agent, the prospect of you and Derek infiltrating this place doesn't give me any warm fuzzies."

"It's all part of the game," Clark replied, hiding his own concerns behind a smile. He knew he was too close to be objective; this was personal. Picking up the goods, he thanked Shortcut and turned to leave.

"Be careful, sir."

61

Bright light startled Katrina out of a deep sleep.

"Sorry to wake you," Clark said. "But I didn't want to leave without saying good-bye."

Sitting up, Katrina rubbed her eyes. She had been so exhausted after working with Frank that she had fallen asleep fully dressed on top of the covers. "Where are you going?" she asked groggily.

Clark offered a superficial smile and didn't answer.

"Let me guess," she said. "This has something to do with the place I saw in remote viewing?"

Clark suddenly felt surprisingly uncomfortable to be on the other side of her keenly perceptive gaze. Somewhere during the last twenty-four hours in their work together, or perhaps because of her resemblance to Eliza, he had let her in, and she was reading his field. Rather than offering a cover story, he reached into his pocket and handed her Krueger's intercepted communiqué. "Tell me what you make of this?" he said.

Katrina held the paper and frowned. "Where are these coordinates?" she pressed, trying to get a full picture.

"Russia," Clark replied, handing her satellite imagery. Gently, he added, "Near Himmelshaus, the place where your mother died and where Frank was programmed."

Katrina paused to study the satellite photo and then locked gazes with Clark. "Take me with you," she said. "I can help you see through the person who sent you the note, and if you take me to Himmelshaus, I might be able to find my mother's map to the Forbidden Text."

"The map is burned and buried under rubble."

"That doesn't matter. Events from the past can unfold around me like a hologram. I've had it happen at battlegrounds and in the dungeons of old castles."

"Your mother would never forgive me," he replied. "It's too dangerous."

"If the map was worth her dying for, it's worth me trying to find it. Besides, who knows what I might see . . ." she argued.

Clark scrunched his forehead in concentration. If she could get a glimpse into the past, perhaps she could also see if anyone had survived the airstrike and, if so, that might shed some light on how the sleepers were being activated.

"So, can I come with you?" she pushed.

Clark could see Eliza's spirit in Katrina's eyes and knew she wouldn't be easily dissuaded. The president was right. Katrina would be a tremendous asset and a secret weapon. Krueger alone wasn't worth the risk of bringing her in, but if she could gain otherwise inaccessible intel, it made sense to bring her. He just had to keep her safe.

Reluctantly, he agreed and pulled an oversized envelope from underneath the stack of documents he was carrying. "I was going to give this to you to read while I was gone," he said, "but now you can consider these field notes. Some of your mother's journals," he said. "Read fast. We're leaving soon."

Katrina was speechless. Her stomach churned with anticipation and, as illogical as the proposition of going to Russia sounded, her internal compass confirmed the trajectory. She was on path.

He looked back at her as he exited. "You'll need a disguise. I don't want Krueger, or anyone else, recognizing you as Eliza's daughter. Well, then. For better or for worse," Clark's eyes glimmered, "welcome to the team."

62

The lights of Baltimore's inner harbor twinkled below him as Gregory Malchek leaned against his ebony cane and peered out of the Marriott's penthouse window. Tourists hurried along the neighboring walk, bundled up against the bone-chilling dampness. His trip from Washington DC, where he had met with Susan Bradford over coffee the previous day, had taken less than an hour by train and had been remarkably uneventful, affording him plenty of time to orchestrate other happenings that were sure to escalate things. Soon, America would be on its knees.

A short rapping knock sounded at the hotel room door.

Punctual. Excellent. Malchek turned and hobbled over to the chair by the desk and eased himself down with a murmur. "It's open," he called out.

Two identical male twins with dark brown hair entered, followed by a short, chubby, smiling blond man named Arthur Patterson. Nodding their greetings, the three men sat down opposite Malchek. Then, as if on cue, his phone chimed a shrill ring as the last man was seated.

Malchek answered in a soft, unremarkable voice, "Yes?"

The scrambled digital signal was mildly distorted, and through the crackling connection a male voice intoned, "Warm-ups are complete. How's the weather for the next round?"

Gregory Malchek's eyes narrowed as he answered, "Very much in our favor, I'd say."

"There's a storm coming," foretold the gruff voice.

"From the east?" Malchek verified. The glint of excitement in his eyes contradicted his habitually impassive face.

"Yes," came the answer with certainty. "Once this next phase is complete, they will welcome our hollow horse as salvation."

A satisfied smile deepened the crevices in Malchek's visage. "We're ready to play hard ball, Father," he confirmed. "Green-lit all the way."

"Excellent. Let the games begin."

Gregory Malchek hung up the receiver and fixed his stare on his three visitors. "Gentlemen," he began earnestly, "the critical moment has arrived. What we are about to do will please Father very much. You all understand your roles in this little performance?"

Malchek's three guests beamed proudly. Charged with enthusiasm, the blond man, Arthur, leaned forward and looked directly at Gregory Malchek. "Do I get to keep the million dollars?" he asked, nervous and hopeful.

A chuckle rumbled through Malchek's chest. "If the FBI actually gives it to you and lets you go, then yes, you can keep it."

Arthur inhaled exuberantly, a calculated smile crossing his lips as he looked at the brothers and nodded. "Either way, I will be content," he added, in a quiet and humble way. "This is what I have lived for. I feel absolutely prepared."

63

Katrina sat on the side of her bed and stared at the closed door with concern. Clark's final words, "Welcome to the team," still echoed in her mind. *What had she just volunteered for?*

"Cosmic Clearance" was stamped in bright red letters across the envelope she held in her hands. Inside, her mother's journals burned with secrets of the past. Knowing she had only a short time to familiarize herself with the contents, she opened the large envelope, pulled out a military-issue, green pressboard folder, and laid it open on the bed. Her mother's original journal entries were fastened on the left; the paper, like age-old newsprint, was crinkled and discolored. On the right was a typed translation.

Katrina ran her fingertips over her mother's ink, seeking connection with the woman she never knew. The handwriting implied stress and haste; the text was a jumble of Russian and German peppered with codes and symbols she could not understand.

She laid her hand flat across her mother's handwriting and felt a tingling in her palm. Her heart beat faster in anticipation. Latching on to the sensation, she immersed herself and suddenly found herself awash in her mother's emotions at the time of writing.

A sudden rush of fear closed her throat.

Yanking back her hand, she disengaged and scoured the translation for answers.

By my calculations, it is my fifth day of captivity. I've been repeatedly questioned about
my clairvoyance and have been subject to psy-
chological tests since my arrival. Today was
different—I was physically violated by a man
with the eyes of a shark.

Every inch of my body was measured and examined. My face is still swollen from where he
hit me when I refused to lie down. I don't
know what happened after they sedated me.
Even though I find no marks on my body, I feel
violated.

64

Faint footsteps motivated Frank Davis to open his eyes. Bit by bit, the sodium pentothal released its numbing death-grip on his mind. Still in a stupor, he gazed bleary-eyed at his aseptic surroundings.

Bright fluorescent lights glared down on Major Brady, whose back was turned to him as she stood replacing the IV bag that hung at his side.

Trying to connect brain impulses with muscles, Frank's hand quivered as he reached for her.

She didn't notice.

Mustering all his will, he struggled to choke out a croaky whisper, "I'd like to speak to Dr. Walker again."

"What?" She spun around, startled. "Did you say something?"

Frank cleared his throat. His voice came back stronger. "Dr. Walker . . ." he repeated, "I have something important to tell her."

65

Clark knocked at Katrina's door and stuck his head inside to find her reading. "Time to go," he said, motioning for her to follow. "Bring that with you. You can finish reading on the way."

She stuffed the file back into its envelope and raced to catch up with Clark, who was already walking double time down the hall. Based on the little she'd already read, Katrina had a lot of questions for him and didn't know where to begin. Just as she fell into step alongside Clark, Shortcut sprinted around a corner. "Frank Davis is asking to talk to Dr. Walker," he began breathlessly, his eyes flitting between Clark and Katrina. "He says he's starting to remember things."

Katrina's eyes brightened. "The recovered soul piece must be restoring his memories and his will to live."

Clark turned to catch her eye. "Would you rather stay?" he offered with hesitation.

"Do you think Frank knows who's behind this?" she asked.

"No," Clark replied in truth. "Even if you get inside his head, he won't know what his trigger was or who programmed him."

Katrina had to agree. With Frank's degree of fracturing, it would take time to reconstruct his psyche to a point where there could be any hope of glimpsing a coherent history. "Russia seems far more promising in the short term," she said. "I'll work with Frank when I get back."

Clark nodded and gave Shortcut last-minute instructions. Down the hall she could see Derek holding open a door for them; a tense, anticipatory half smile was etched across his lips. He had been informed that Katrina would be accompanying them and had mixed feelings despite Clark's explanation of the merits of her participation. Her inexperience complicated the op, and protecting her felt like a tall order.

Behind the door lay a storehouse chock-full of weaponry, high-tech gadgets, and tactical clothing. As Clark and Derek headed to procure gear, Sprite escorted Katrina to a dressing room and said, "Stay here. I'll be right back."

Seizing the moment, Katrina pulled out her mother's journal and continued reading.

```
I have been tasked with deciphering the rid-
dled locations of treasures listed on the Cop-
per Scroll. I first refused to assist, knowing
that any progress made will fuel my captors'
project and rise to power. I learned that
refusal is not an option when the man with
the shark eyes introduced me to six children—
three boys and three girls—selected to be my
"personal motivators." He promised that for
every day that I failed to make progress, one
of them would be tortured and killed. Then he
forced me to hug each one. I must find a way
to stop this monster.
```

66

As the hotel room door shut behind Arthur Patterson and the two brothers, Gregory Malchek used his cane for leverage and gained his feet with a wince. Walking stiffly across the now empty room, he locked the deadbolt and crossed to the dresser where he stooped and slid open the bottom left drawer.

Tucked inside lay a nondescript, brown paper bundle. Phase two, he thought with an involuntary feeling of duty. As if cradling a baby, he gingerly laid the parcel on the king-sized bed, and, using a scrimshawed pocketknife, he carefully sliced open the wrapper and peeked inside.

The first item he extracted was a folded, clear plastic tarp, which he laid across the silken duvet. Three 10" x 15" white plastic, airtight envelopes were next, as well as three identically prepared sets of legal documents. He arranged the papers neatly side-by-side on the protective tarp and placed the envelopes on the nearby nightstand. Completely focused on the task at hand, he took a careful breath before reaching back inside the bundle to pull out his protective gear.

Surgical latex gloves replaced black leather.

Snapping goggles snugly into place, he drew the elastic band of a respirator tight behind his graying head and began breathing through the mask. Now prepared, Gregory Malchek delved into the package once again, exhuming a small, locked plastic container with an airtight seal. Mouthing something under his breath, he entered the pass code and lifted the lid.

67

Engrossed in her reading, Katrina was thankful Sprite had not yet returned, and flipped the page.

Tonight, I snuck into the orphanage to check on the little girl Shark-Eyes had hurt. When I asked if she was all right, the girl told me that "Father" loves her. That she knows that he loves all of his children.

Upon hearing voices in the next room, I heard someone demand that Shark-Eyes—Dr. Steinhertz—produce something called the perfect "sleeper." I couldn't hear the entire conversation, but I did hear Shark-Eyes' superior remind him in condescending tones that previous attempts at mind-control initiatives had failed. It seems that with current operations, latent morality and compassion have cropped up at inopportune times and corrupted

directives, especially when sleepers have
been ordered to execute a kill.

I then heard Shark-Eyes explain the details
of his three-pronged approach to overcoming
previous obstacles: Selective breeding, coupled with the removal of his designer progeny
from their mothers at birth, allows him to
overcome nature-versus-nurture dilemmas. My
skin crawled as I realized that executing a
kill became far less of a problem when family
and society haven't conditioned a conscience.
Even more extreme, strategically directed
trauma ensures deep embedding of subliminal
programming within the fractured psyche that
makes carrying out unconscionable directives
mere tasks to be accomplished. I am astounded,
disgusted, and driven to action. Shark-Eyes'
children are the ultimate sleepers - making
an integral contribution to the success of
a greater plan for destruction. Suddenly my
recent visions of Armageddon make sense.

Sprite's quick footsteps snapped Katrina back to the present moment.
She tucked away the envelope a second before Sprite popped into the
dressing room carrying an armful of gear that she piled on a nearby chair.
Then, with a smile, she extracted a lens case from her pocket and handed
it to Katrina. "These are bionic lenses," she informed her proudly. "They
not only change your eye color, they enable maps and other data to be
superimposed in your field of vision in real time."

Intrigued yet somewhat apprehensive, Katrina picked up the
microcomputers between her fingertips and examined them. "How
do they work?" she asked.

"LEDs are embedded into the flexible plastic and flash up information," Sprite explained. "A built-in, wireless antenna beams information to the lens."

Katrina's forehead crinkled. "But I really need my vision to be unobstructed," she said, voicing her concern.

"That's not a problem," Sprite promised. "The microscopic circuits are built around the edge. And just to be safe, Clark insisted that only one of your lenses be bionic; the other is plain tint. Try them on," she encouraged, pointing Katrina to a mirror. "Shortcut hacked the records from your last eye exam, so they should be a good fit," Sprite offered as if it was nothing, and then went on to give Katrina a rundown of how to interface with the new gear while finishing her disguise. Within moments, Katrina's appearance had been transformed. Standing back to take a look at her handicraft, a gratified smile broke across Sprite's face. "Your best friend wouldn't recognize you," she said. "Come on. Clark's ready to go."

68

Katrina emerged from the back room, and Derek paused in his conversation with Clark at the sight of her. Dark, chocolate-colored hair danced against her fair skin, replacing her fox-auburn tresses and drawing attention to her now warm brown eyes. Katrina was striking, and as she approached in her snow-camo pants, Derek couldn't help but appreciate how her lightweight undershirt accentuated her breasts.

She joined the men, and Clark passed her some final gear. Cursorily examining the objects, she shot him a quizzical gaze to which he responded, "Part of your disguise . . . the fuzzy, ear-flapped hat will keep you warm, and the high-tech vest," he continued, "is the latest in liquid body armor—STF-treated Kevlar. It's lightweight and stays flexible until impacted. But remember, it's not foolproof, especially at close ranges or against rifles."

With those words, Katrina's face grew tense, and Clark could see that the potential danger of the journey ahead had hit home. "Still want to come?" he asked.

"Absolutely," she replied, putting on a brave face. Her insides trembled, despite her intrinsic sense of being on path. *What had she gotten herself into?*

Derek handed her a backpack, grabbed his gear, and called the elevator. One stop later, the trio stood on the helipad where a small helicopter sat waiting, blades thrumming.

Clark and Katrina climbed in the rear, and Derek buckled himself into the copilot's seat. The door slammed shut, the sound of the whining blades reached a higher pitch, and Katrina watched the tarmac disappear rapidly below. A knot formed in her stomach that tied together her mother's mysterious past, current events, and the covert op ahead. Twisting around to look at Clark, she pressed the button on her headset for a private in-flight conversation, her voice nothing more than a hushed whisper above the noise of the copter. "My mother had apocalyptic visions—I've been having them too," she confessed. "Fires and destruction in major U.S. cities. Catastrophic desolation."

Clark studied her face and digested her words.

"So, what exactly is a 'sleeper'?" Katrina hazarded, seeking to clarify some of the cryptic terminology in her mother's notes.

"Classic sleeper agents," Clark began in an ominous tone, "are operatives who are placed in target countries or organizations, not to undertake an immediate mission, but rather to lie in wait as assets for future activation. They have airtight identities, acquire jobs, and blend into everyday life as a normal citizen hidden in plain sight."

Katrina's eyes narrowed as she absorbed the implications. "Like Frank and Susan—and the others?"

Clark nodded. "But with a twist. The sleepers we're dealing with were developed under a program called Blackheart. It took the concept of sleepers to new heights. As you witnessed, extreme fracturing made it possible to create over- and under-personalities, alter egos that were conditioned to believe they were serving altruistic ends—martyrs with causes. This went far beyond brainwashing."

"So, in Frank's case, the over-personality was the perfect husband, and one of his under-personalities, the perfect terrorist. Neither knew what the other was doing," Katrina said.

"Right," Clark acknowledged. "Moreover, Father deprived his

seedling sleepers, the children he bred, of nurture and rigorously pro-grammed them with beliefs such as 'pain equals pleasure.' This created 'alters' that were capable of heinous crimes—alters who loved interroga-tion, rather than broke under it."

"Why didn't you share this with me sooner?" she asked, somewhat frustrated.

"He could have been programmed by any number of organizations. I couldn't afford to influence you," Clark explained. "I had my suspi-cions because of the nature of the incidents and the profiles of the per-petrators, but until you confirmed the target location of Frank's abuse as Blackheart's old headquarters, I couldn't be sure."

"It also helps explain why Susan's programming failed," Katrina replied. In response to Clark's inquisitive gaze, she added, "When Susan gave birth to her son, maternal instinct and love cracked her heart open. Those emotions violated core tenets of her subliminal programming. She began to destabilize—her alters went to war."

"Makes sense," Clark commented. "Love must have prevailed to some degree or she would have taken her child's life with her own."

"How many more Franks and Susans do you think there are?" Katrina dared to ask.

"I'm not sure. By the time Blackheart's operation was discovered, the threat to national security was deemed so great that the administration decided the only viable option was to wipe the slate clean." Katrina saw his eyes grow dark as he detailed Project Clean Sweep; the calculated morbidity of it all turned her stomach.

"I protested the mission as it was laid out. The collateral damage was too high," Clark explained. "I argued that at the very least the children could be rehabilitated and the researchers rescued. Needless to say, it fell on deaf ears. I tendered my resignation over it," he confided, "and shortly after that AWOL was born."

Katrina refocused on the problem at hand. "Since sleepers are both undetectable and unaware of their programming, how do we stop them?"

Before Clark could answer, the copter swooped down for a landing, cutting their conversation short.

Skids touched pavement.

The door flung open, and a stony-faced Secret Service agent in a black suit greeted them. "This way, please," he urged. "Watch your step."

69

In the privacy of his suite at the Marriott, Gregory Malchek peered through the protective goggles into the insulated container. On the left, housed in recessed foam cubicles, sat three clear plastic capsules, each containing different colored granules: green, violet, and black. Opposite, tucked in foam nests, rested three glass vials filled with clear fluid, and embedded in the center was a small metal misting bottle.

With great care, Malchek's nervous hands unscrewed the caps from the three vials one by one and meticulously emptied the contents of a capsule into each. He could hardly believe the day had finally come. When he had finished, he replaced the lids and gently shook the vessels. Holding his breath, he watched the liquid fizz and bubble, momentarily assuming the color of the granules, before returning to a clear state.

Satisfied that each reaction was complete, he proceeded to painstakingly pour the contents of each vial into the metal misting bottle. He cursed the almost imperceptible tremor in his hands, as he combined the lethal ingredients to make the diabolical concoction.

Tiny sweat beads brimmed above his goggles.

His breath came ragged through the respirator.

Quickly screwing the sprayer in place, he gently swirled the canister.

Now for the final touch: misting the documents that lay neatly on the protected bedspread.

The odorless, invisible compound dried almost instantaneously.

Gregory Malchek then slid each contract into its respective envelope, sealed the airtight enclosures, and stuffed them inside three pre-addressed FedEx envelopes. *Phase two has begun,* he thought as he smiled to himself with a deep sense of satisfaction. Setting the packages aside momentarily, he methodically gathered up his supplies. Fire would soon reduce all remaining evidence to ash, which would subsequently find its way to the bottom of Baltimore's harbor.

Pulling on his snug-fitting leather gloves, he gathered the packages and hobbled, cane in hand, out the door of the sanitized room and onto the streets of Baltimore.

70

At Andrews Air Force Base in Maryland, Clark and company climbed out of the copter and into an unmarked black sedan, which whisked them to a secured hangar nearby. Hidden inside, a sleek, droop-nosed, futuristic jet with delta-shaped wings sat waiting.

As the doors slid back, Katrina surveyed the winged bullet. "We're flying in that?" she asked dubiously.

"Yes, ma'am," affirmed the man clad in a blue zippered flight suit standing near the fuselage.

Clark and Derek greeted him with familiarity and introduced him to Katrina as Captain Harry Ingall. "Thanks for giving us a lift," Clark said, patting Ingall on the shoulder. "We're in a damn big hurry."

"So I heard," he replied, a tense smile breaking across his chiseled features. "I've got the bird for the job—the one and only XD-80," he added, introducing his aircraft with a nod. "She'll top Mach 4. We'll have you there in no time."

"You're kidding, right?" Katrina asked in amazement.

"No, ma'am," Ingall said with a small chuckle as he patted the side of the ship. "Her shell material is a classified ceramic-alloy blend. I don't have the authorization to reveal all of her technology, but I promise—she'll do the job," he said, and with that, he hopped into the pilot's seat.

Ducking inside the small interior compartment, Katrina was surprised to see how plush it was. Six wide leather chairs offered first-class seating that could be unlocked to swivel or recline. In the rear, a fully stocked bar accompanied refrigerated hors d'oeuvres and prepared meals, complete with compact Wedgwood crockery and short silver cutlery. From a business standpoint, the cabin was just as well appointed. A plasma monitor, satellite phone, and printer, along with a closet to hang coats, were all tucked away in convenient locations.

"It's a next-generation supersonic passenger jet," Clark explained as he and Katrina took a seat next to each other. Derek excused himself and headed to the back for food and shut-eye.

As Katrina cinched her seat belt, Ingall's voice came over the speakers saying, "Let's rock and roll!" The engines fired and Katrina's chest tightened as the XD-80 taxied onto the runway.

Clark noticed her unease. "Takeoff's the worst," he promised. "Her angle of attack is higher than conventional aircraft, then you'll feel a surge in acceleration as we pass through the sound barrier, but after that, it's smooth sailing. We won't even be in the air long enough for a movie," he smiled with assurance.

Her hands gripped the armrests tightly. The jet's engines whined and then screamed to life. G-forces slammed through her body and Katrina's stomach wedged against her spine as the plane roared off the runway. *Don't get sick . . . don't get sick . . . don't get sick!* Her knuckles were chalk-white from gripping the armrest. She took a cautious breath as the plane leveled out. The ground quickly disappeared below them as they blasted through the sound barrier and soared out over the Atlantic.

After leveling off, Clark rifled through his backpack and handed her another folder. "I brought you a little more light reading," he said. "I think you'll find this one intriguing."

Katrina glanced at the label, "The Forbidden Text," and offered him a brief smile before flipping the cover open.

Deciphering the Copper Scroll is challenging, but I am driven knowing that Shark-Eyes will make good on his promise to hurt the children should I not comply.

The task is hindered by the fact that portions of the scroll were destroyed when it was initially unrolled, and sectors of the remaining text are damaged or missing. The surviving portion inventories sixty-four treasures with vague descriptions of their secret locations. Additionally, I notice a number of seemingly innocuous anomalies—unrecognizable Hebrew vocabulary, conspicuous squiggle marks, and inexplicable half sentences. I sense that the purpose of this scroll exceeds what my captors expect of it.

Katrina paused and looked over at Clark, who was busily studying topographical maps of their destination. "Are people still looking for the treasures listed on the Copper Scroll?" she asked.

He looked at her earnestly. "Last I heard, two of the treasures had been found and a U.S. based research team is hunting for the Ark of the Covenant based on information deduced from clues in the Scroll. But that's not the real mother lode . . ."

Katrina looked at him skeptically and then kept reading.

I made great progress today—I was delivered a box that contained the crumpled remains of the clay that was once wound inside the Copper Scroll. The scientists initially charged with examining the scroll failed to account for the bas-relief pressed into the clay of

the scroll's entire text. In its current
state, the clay is nearly useless. But upon
sifting the remains through my fingers, an
image of the complete scroll with the entire
text came into my mind and I saw that there
are sixty-five, rather than the assumed sixty-
four, treasures outlined on the scroll. The
sixty-fifth treasure is Barad-Zed's map to the
Forbidden Text. The anomalies I'd noticed
within the list of sixty-four riches were
part of its encryption.

Documentation of the Forbidden Text first
appears in the age of Alexander of Macedon.
The mystical stone tablet is fabled to unlock
the powers of Creation itself, but time and
myth have obscured its location and existence. Legend holds that the tablet was broken into pieces and intentionally secreted
eons ago. The great sage Barad-Zed created
the map and placed it in the care of "secret
keepers," but it has not been seen since. My
vision of the Copper Scroll details the map's
location within a riddle: *Through the Valley
of Trouble Lies the Door of Hope.* Is this what
my captors are after?

Katrina nudged Clark and asked, "Who were the 'secret keepers'?"

"I'm not sure," Clark replied. "But one thing's for certain, the Copper
Scroll is different from all the other Dead Sea Scrolls. Whoever wrote it
was pretty smart to encrypt the information about the Forbidden Text
that way."

"It's almost as if they intended the other sixty-four power relics to
be decoys…"

Clark nodded. "And, with sections of the scroll destroyed, it required someone with your mother's talents to fill in the gaps."

"You believe the Forbidden Text actually exists?"

Clark cleared his throat and looked over his shoulder to make sure Derek was asleep, before answering in a low voice, "Before my grandfather died, he told me about a sacred stone tablet with some kind of writing that contained the keys to creation. He believed it came from the sky people."

Katrina's eyebrows raised curiously. "Go on," she encouraged.

"The ancients feared that man was not ready for this knowledge, so they broke the tablet and hid the fragments in all four corners of the world."

"Sounds like the stuff legends are made of."

"Myths are stories told to remind us of deep truths," Clark replied with a shrug. "Your mother never wanted the Forbidden Text to fall into Blackheart's hands. That's why she went back for the map."

Ingall's voice cut sharply through the aircraft's speakers, startling Katrina. "We've reached our cruising altitude of 56,000 feet. We'll be on the ground before you know it."

71

Frigid, damp wind sliced through Gregory Malchek's overcoat. After making his way out of the Marriott at Baltimore's Harbor, he limped as quickly as possible toward the FedEx drop box on Charles Street. He hadn't gone far before the wind robbed him of any lingering warmth, aggravating an old shrapnel wound that tortured his hip—a haunting reminder of his narrow escape from the inferno of Himmelshaus years before. America thought they had won that day, but they were wrong—dead wrong. Now, the time for payback was at hand.

Finally arriving at his destination, the drop box swallowed his three meticulously prepared packages and promised overnight delivery to unwitting accomplices in the game.

He pulled out his pocket watch: 5:46 p.m., plenty of time to finish cleaning up, make a phone call on Frank Davis's behalf, and get to the airport.

72

Katrina glanced up at the XD-80's plasma monitor. Flight stats indicated they were cruising high in the stratosphere at twice a normal airliner's altitude, racing toward Europe at a break-neck Mach 4.3. She peeked out the tiny window and wondered about her mother, and despite the awe-inspiring view of the earth below, she felt a sense of foreboding. Hopefully, the map to the Forbidden Text hadn't already fallen into the wrong hands. And even if it had, she was determined to retrieve it.

Clark sat next to her with his eyes closed, resting. Rather than disturb him with more questions, she continued investigating her mother's past.

```
It is 4 a.m., and I have just awoken from a
most lucid dream that has shown me the loca-
tion of the map to the Forbidden Text. I
found the riddled quote Through the Valley
of Trouble Lies the Door of Hope in biblical
texts; it's thought to refer to a deep ravine
in the vicinity of Jericho called the Valley
of Achor. I've been unable to find any other
```

references to the map's location, but tonight
I was informed in my sleep.

I found myself on the edge of a ravine in what
felt to be a sacred place. The air cooled
rapidly following the setting sun, and my
eyes honed in on a confrontation happening
between a man and two people in long white
robes, threshold guardians of some kind. The
guardians were denying the man's request to
descend into the canyon and explore its caves.
When he ignored their warnings and began his
descent, a lightning strike sprung from the
sentinels themselves racked his form, and he
fell hundreds of feet to the valley floor.

I, too, found that I was drawn to descend
the canyon. My fear that the gatekeepers
would strike me down was dispelled when one
directed me toward a narrow cave no more than
a meter wide in the canyon wall. I pressed on
through the narrowing cave until it opened to
a hollowed-out chamber. A hole in the ceiling allowed for a blue-hued stream of natural
light to illuminate a specific portion of the
chamber wall. Upon further investigation, I
found that the ancient runes within the band
of light were Barad Zed's map to the Forbidden Text, etched into the wall. I awoke with
the vision still in my mind and sketched it
before picking up my journal.

Katrina looked up to see Clark watching her, waiting patiently for her to finish.

"Does Derek know any of this?" she asked.

"About Himmelshaus and the map, yes. About your true identity, no," Clark whispered. "Your cover story must stay intact." His face grew serious in concern. "There's a chance that the mafia splinter cell running the prison we're headed to is linked to the people who tried to abduct you," he said as he reached into his pocket and pulled out a pair of military-issue, boxy, black-framed glasses with dummy lenses. "Wear your dog-eared cap and these when we go in," he ordered, "and, unless I say otherwise, you are not to utter a word."

Katrina accepted the spectacles, but pressed, "How am I supposed to function as a lie detector if I have to remain silent?"

"I'll give you a set of signals prior to landing so you can communicate with me surreptitiously," he explained, his voice growing grim. "Now for a little background on our target—the allegedly resurrected Nikolai Krueger." Clark paused solemnly before continuing, "Krueger was extremely clever and resourceful—but dangerous and not to be trusted. I find it hard to believe he survived, but . . ." Clark paused to pull out a dossier with a photo, "if it is him, double your guard."

Katrina took the folder and scrutinized the old photo carefully.

"Once we infiltrate the prison, I'll need you to pocket your heart," he said. "We may or may not rescue this person, depending on the deal."

"You can count on me for real-time feedback," she said. "I understand what's at stake."

"After the op is complete, I'll send Derek back with the goods and we'll make a quick stop at Himmelshaus to search the rubble," Clark said with a half smile. "In the meantime, before we land, I've got one more thing to share with you," he said and handed her a folder labeled "The Lover."

"Thank-you," she beamed.

73

After regaining consciousness, Frank Davis, wired with a set of electrodes that delivered a jolting electric shock each time his brain waves indicated he was falling asleep, had been returned to his small cell. Fleming's latest interrogation tactic was sleep deprivation.

Delirious, Frank lay with his arm across his eyes, desperately seeking respite from the fluorescent lights overhead. Teetering on the edge of fitful slumber, incessant electric jolts relentlessly teased his mind back to consciousness.

A loud echoing knock on the door mustered hope deep inside Frank's heart. *Maybe it is Dr. Walker coming to work with me again.* He lifted his head in expectation, but his smile fell as he saw his guest. It wasn't Katrina; in fact, to the best of his knowledge, he had never seen this man before. Average in height, with obsidian-colored eyes, this medical-clad caller sported a curiously fine moustache that made his upper lip seem oddly full.

Immediately, Frank suspected that this a hallucination. The sleeplessness had taken a heavy toll on his mind; earlier he had experienced an odd phantasm. A memory of witnessing a child being murdered had flashed before his eyes. A pistol had been in his hand. The hallucination had ended there, with a mind-rattling jolt from Fleming's merciless contraption.

"You requested Dr. Walker?" the visitor began as he closed the door.

Frank nodded and studied the man's face curiously, almost as if he recognized his effeminate features.

"Dr. Walker won't be joining you, I'm afraid," he said with a thin smile. "She is away at the moment." The stranger came to stand before Frank. No nametag was visible on his lab coat.

"Who are you?" Frank inquired of his mysterious visitor.

"That is not important, Mr. Davis." An unidentifiable European accent flavored his falsetto. "You will not be seeing me again. However," he continued, "Dr. Walker personally asked me to bring this to you."

Frank's eyes grew wide in anticipation.

From his lab coat pocket, the man produced a small, unlined white notepad and pen. "She would like you to write down your thoughts, your memories," the man explained, "anything that might be of interest."

Frank nodded eagerly as he reached for the writing instruments. "Thank-you," he murmured, turning the clean white pages awkwardly with cuffed hands.

"I imagine you have a lot to get off of your mind," the stranger said. Leaning forward to get closer to a nodding Frank, he lowered his voice. "As a prisoner, Frank, you were perfect," he continued in a calculated and deliberate whisper. "You have said nothing, and you should be commended for that."

Frank's expression brightened in a confused smile.

"However," the man went on, his dark eyes boring holes through Frank's frightened form, "as a loyal friend of our Father you were a miserable failure."

Averting his spellbound gaze, Frank stared instead at the man's curious moustache. He swallowed hard when he noticed a trace of lipstick in the cracks of the man's sinister lips.

"You *let* that woman into your soul," the snarling mouth continued. Foreboding drenched every word. "Father is deeply disappointed."

Instantly, Frank's confused smile melted. His face sagged, limp and vacant.

"Frank, you do remember Father, don't you?"

Looking down and away, Frank choked out, "Yes," before hanging his head and setting the paper on the floor.

"Then you know what needs to be done," the man said, finishing with a smile. Straightening, he walked out the door.

The padded steps of the man's white sneakers haunted Frank long after he was gone.

74

Katrina drank in her mother's words. "The Lover" held the promise of a glimpse into a deeply personal side of the woman she would never know.

Shark-Eyes is forcing me to participate in a selective breeding program. It would seem that my participation in this eugenics program is driven by his desire to enhance psi abilities and unlock parts of the brain largely untapped. His means are reprehensible. In addition to harvesting eggs and sperm and freezing them for later experimentation, he forces selected couples to mate. If a couple refuses, he harms the children. I don't know what I will do if I become pregnant, I would never allow him to enroll my child into his torturous program.

What Shark-Eyes did not account for is that the man I've been paired with may be my way out of captivity. I've known Kurt Schoenwald

for two months now, and though I was skep-
tical when he first told me that he was a
researcher like myself, conscripted against
his will, his energy and his contact led me to
trust him. And tonight I learned why—Kurt is
a U.S. counterintelligence agent. During our
session together tonight, Kurt confessed this
secret and his plan for escape, all concealed
beneath the sounds of our love making.

As our two bodies blended into one, for an
instant, I felt as if I had come home. To
where I cannot say, but my heart surrendered.
We lay there afterward, warm legs entangled,
glistening with perspiration, and I allowed
myself to float with him through a space of
timelessness, forgetting the circumstances.

I know this puts me in a compromising situation, but I sense that all is as it should
be. I find myself comforted by his presence,
and trusting of his intentions. Now I just
need to survive this place until the help he
promised to send arrives.

"Were you the help that got sent in to rescue her?" Katrina asked
Clark, prodding him out of a feigned catnap.

Clark, nervous about sharing, had been waiting for her to finish
reading. He was glad she finally knew at least part of the story. Nodding,
he added, "But your mother had to wait far longer than we expected.
Blackheart was tipped off by a mole inside our government. Schoenwald
barely survived his escape from Himmelshaus and was captured before
he made it out of the Eastern Bloc. It was months before he was able to
provide the CIA with the relevant data about your mother. Needless to
say, I didn't know she'd had a child when I arrived to extract her."

Katrina ventured hopefully, "Do you think Kurt Schoenwald is my father?"

"According to his debriefing, he had no knowledge of your mother conceiving during their time together," Clark replied truthfully. "For that matter, none of your mother's journals provide clues as to your father's identity." Painful though the reality was, Clark was aware that, in all likelihood, Eliza had been forced to couple with more men than just Kurt alone, and that she herself might not have known who Katrina's father was.

Katrina interrupted his thoughts, "This Schoenwald, can I talk with him?"

"I wish you could," Clark replied, "but he's dead." And that was the truth. Kurt Schoenwald, along with all of Clark's other former identities, *was* officially dead. Resurrecting a past that had been whitewashed could unravel AWOL.

Katrina's heart sank and tears welled in her eyes. Looking away, she stared silently out the window, not wanting Clark to see her cry.

He reached out and placed his hand on hers, offering silent comfort. He longed to tell her that he was the lover, but he had to protect her from a truth that could cost her her life. If there ever was going to be a time to explore this topic, now was not it.

Over the years, he'd toyed with the idea of doing a DNA test to confirm or deny his role in Katrina's paternity, but time and again he had decided against it. He didn't want to know, or for that matter, compromise Katrina's cover story by being a presence in her life. Instead, he cared for her from a distance, providing anonymous grants for schooling and seeing to her needs.

Ding. The pilot rescued Clark from brooding. "Time to buckle up and lock down your seats. I'm gonna drop this baby out of the sky."

Derek stirred and stretched, and Katrina inconspicuously wiped her eyes as she stuffed the journals into the large envelope. Clark checked his watch and mused—two hours, thirteen minutes. Not bad for a trans-Atlantic puddle jump.

75

At Denver International Airport, a uniformed driver opened the door to a white limousine. "Good day, gentlemen, madam," he greeted them, as he ushered the three waiting executives into the car.

Nearly unanimous nods answered.

Tucked inside the plush stretch limo sat Gregory Malchek. A new day had dawned, and smiling amiably, he greeted each of them, a twinkle in his eyes. His unsuspecting instruments had arrived. "I trust your flights were satisfactory?" he asked rhetorically. "I believe champagne is in order!" Pursing his lips beneath his gray mustache, he pulled a bottle of Dom Pérignon from a silver ice bucket and poured each of them a glass.

"Congratulations to all of you—we are embarking on an extremely profitable joint venture with global potential."

"Thank-you," beamed Denise, a twenty-six-year-old executive, as she accepted her drink. Her inherent beauty peeked through a somewhat reserved exterior and gave rise to fantasies among her male coworkers of what it might be like when she let her silky hair down. "I think it's safe to say that we're all ready to get started," she said confidently as she crossed her legs. Although professional, her black skirt-suit provided ample opportunity for the two male executives with whom she shared the ride to enjoy a view of her shapely bronze limbs.

76

fter landing at Rhein-Main Air Base near Frankfurt, Germany, the XD-80 immediately disappeared behind the closed, locked doors of a secluded hangar. Moments later Katrina found herself strapped into a three-point harness inside the modified cargo bay of their final transport—a Harrier Jump Jet with stealth technology that made it virtually undetectable to short-range tracking radar.

"I had to pull a few strings to get her," Clark explained in response to Katrina's confused looks. "She won't officially be in service for three more years, but between this bird and the XD-80, we're hours ahead of schedule, and that gives us the priceless advantage of surprise," he added with a glint in his eye.

In the dim light of the cargo bay, Clark looked as though he'd reverse-aged, and Katrina couldn't help but notice the electricity arcing between him and Derek. They were in their element, venturing into a dangerous situation. The plane taxied to the runway under the veil of darkness, and Katrina observed the unspoken exchange between the two agents. Their overt chitchat was only a cover for the deep concern and healthy respect they felt for the danger that lay ahead.

Suddenly, with a hair-raising vertical assault, the jet catapulted skyward and Katrina, white knuckled, clutched at her harness. Derek's reassuring hand found her knee. "At least we don't have to parachute in," he teased lightly. The straight white teeth of his broad smile stood out in stark contrast to the camo paint smeared across his face. Katrina took a deep breath. *Jumping in—I hadn't even thought of that.*

Pressing her into further conversation, Derek added, "I've been thinking about this sleeper programming; aren't we all actually programmed from birth by our parents, religion, culture, and dogma?"

"True," Katrina agreed. "We're all programmed to some degree . . . conditioned to stay in the box of approved norms. But Blackheart's protocols were extreme. They fractured the sleepers in a way that made them capable of being programmed to do the unthinkable without remembrance or remorse."

Derek leaned his head back and narrowed his eyes. "So, this programming acts like a computer operating system, running subconsciously in our mind. Bad coding can cause problems, like a computer virus? Seems reasonable enough. A Trojan virus for the human psyche?"

"Actually, yes," Katrina said. "That's a great comparison."

He sat frowning in silence and digested the implications.

🖥 🗨 ⑨

An hour and forty-six minutes later, Ingall slowed the jet's hellish speed to a mere 540 miles per hour, and Katrina awoke to find herself suddenly and acutely aware of the cold that permeated her feet.

The intercom crackled to life in her helmet. "ETA twelve minutes. Get ready to deploy. I'm in—and out."

As Ingall's words registered, her stomach flip-flopped. Certain she had misheard, she verified through the headset's mic, "You're not waiting for us?"

"That's an affirmative, ma'am," Ingall responded. "I've got to hightail it out of there."

Katrina gave Clark a concerned look, but he responded with, "No worries. I've got a helicopter on standby to pick us up on my signal when we're ready."

Instinct told her something wasn't going to go as planned.

77

Less than two hours after picking up the three executives from the airport, Gregory Malchek wiped his mouth carefully and concluded their lunch in a private booth at an upscale Japanese restaurant in downtown Denver. Phase two was progressing as scheduled. Father would be pleased and the investors satisfied.

Wincing a bit, Malchek leveraged himself with his cane and shifted positions on the cushion in the sunken dining area before beginning. "So, you all understand my offer regarding this joint venture?" he asked, eyes scanning his aspiring business associates. "I look forward to your answers within two days. All of your proposals were excellent and they deserve our support."

The three eager participants expressed their appreciation.

"I feel honored to be part of this group," Donald, the most obsequious of the trio, added, as he reached out to shake Malchek's hand. In his opinion, it had been a coup to land the deal.

"The contracts," Malchek said, "have been FedExed to your offices and will be waiting for you when you return. Half of the money is enclosed as promised, including expenses, and as soon as I receive the signed documents, the remainder will be wire transferred into your accounts. I would love to stay and chat," he continued as he checked his watch, "but we all have flights that leave shortly, so I think it best we depart for the airport."

As they rose from the table, Denise exchanged business cards with Tony, the better looking of the two male executives. Donald would have done the same, but he had run out. He promised to get their addresses from Malchek and be in touch. All in all, everyone seemed satisfied with the course of events and enthusiastically anticipated their future endeavors.

78

West of Moscow, deep in the Belarusian forest, the Harrier jet descended vertically to the ground, touching down in a small clearing.

Katrina's muscles tensed and she felt nervous adrenaline race through her body as Derek popped open the bay door. Without hesitation, he and Clark jumped out into the jarringly frigid night and in unison gave her a hand as the jet's engines idly churned. The trio jogged through the small clearing toward a stand of trees. As soon as Katrina ducked into the pines, the jet's turbines whirred. The aircraft lifted off, and a moment later, a sonic boom bade them farewell in the far distance.

In the darkness of the dense wood, the icy air and sounds of the night put Katrina's hearing on edge. Heavy clouds obscured the pale sliver of a crescent moon, and she jumped as Derek tapped her left shoulder from behind. "Here," he said in a hushed tone, pulling something from her pack and coming to stand face-to-face with her. "Let's get these on you." Katrina held awkwardly still as he dropped night-vision goggles over her eyes. She could feel the warmth of his body close to hers as he reached around to secure the head strap. "There you go," he whispered.

"It's pitch black," she objected. "I can see better without them."

Reaching around, he flipped the small power switch on the right side of her goggles. "Try them this way."

Suddenly, her surroundings sprang to life in crisp, green-hued detail, including the expression on Derek's face, in which she read apprehensive concern.

79

Frank sat hunched over in silence. Shivers racked his body. Twenty minutes after the unknown visitor had left his cell, he finally lifted his head. Slowly, a gleam of resolve formed in his eyes. *No more.*

Hands still cuffed, he used his teeth to hike up the left sleeve of his jumpsuit and took a deep breath before lifting his left bicep to his mouth. Buried inside his flesh, he knew, was the release—the way to sleep forever, the way to please Father. In search of the hidden death capsule, he bit down with all the force he could muster.

A wave of pleasure caressed his body, seducing him, as coppery-tasting blood gushed into his mouth.

Feverishly chomping down again, Frank stopped short, startled, as a young voice called, "Stop! Don't do that!"

Frank spun around. A young, translucent version of himself, that he recognized to be about six years old, stood staring straight at him. *Another hallucination?*

"Killing yourself isn't the answer," the guest insisted with calm resolve.

Programmed to self-destruct, Frank ignored the apparition and sought freedom. Biting down harder, he severed muscle with teeth and then spat to discharge the chunk of flesh.

Crimson remains flew through the gossamer figure that stood before him.

"You don't have to please Father anymore," his young self insisted.

Instantly, the effects of Frank's sleep deprivation faded. He was fully lucid and awake, with all his senses alert. This little boy was no hallucination. He was very real, a part of himself, even if there wasn't anything physical about him. Unsettled by the troubling presence of a younger self, Frank tried to regain control and stated firmly, "Pleasing Father *is* my duty."

"Your duty is to remember who you really are, not who they want you to be," the recovered soul piece challenged.

Deep inside, he knew his boy-self was right. Yet, in his mind, a war raged against the merciless conditioning that permeated his shattered core. Frank could see no way for both of the opposing forces to survive, and the pendulum swung to Father's deception points.

The boy's luminescence began to flicker and grow dim. He opened his mouth to speak, but Frank could not hear him.

Salty tears flowed down Frank's cheeks as he watched his young friend disappear from sight. Convinced that his soul piece had abandoned him, Frank pushed the turmoil of emotion from his mind and resumed tearing away bits of flesh, digging deeper.

Howls of pain and intense pleasure echoed beyond the empty recesses of Frank's cell as his animalistic screams and sighs of ecstasy gurgled and broke free. He didn't care if he was heard; screams and howling of all sorts were common in Black Hole.

Frank forced his tongue deeper, probing in and around the hole he had gnawed into his left bicep. Then he found it—a sleek red pellet of poison that resembled a bundle of muscle fibers embedded in the tissue.

Inner peace was only seconds away.

Whispering, Frank redeemed himself in the only way he knew how. "For you, Father," he toasted, "I am sorry. I will never disappoint you again."

As he sucked the bloodied encasement into his mouth, Frank once again heard the small, concerned voice.

"Stop, Frank. I'll stay here to help you."

With his face ghastly and smeared, Frank looked up to see his younger self now sitting directly before him.

"With both of us working together," the child began, his emanation growing denser, "it will be a whole lot easier to write stuff down for Dr. Walker. Besides, I like her," he said with a hopeful smile. "She reminds me of the nice woman who used to help us in the compound. Remember?"

Frank's mind groped through an open envelope in time, as his tongue played with the poisoned pellet inside his mouth. He tucked the capsule in his cheek and ventured nervously, "You mean Doctor Eliza?"

The boy nodded and extended his hand in a gesture of support.

Wide-eyed and shaken, Frank tentatively accepted the invitation and moved his bloodied, cuffed arms to meet the small diaphanous form. As soon as Frank's hand touched the lucent fingers, he felt a warm tenderness envelop him and he felt more whole. Still clasping the boy's hand, Frank felt infused by a newfound inner strength as the child's form merged with his own.

Feeling a sudden, intrinsic urge to live, Frank spit the suicide pill out of his mouth through his bloody lips and, smiling softly, he reached for the notepad and pen.

80

In the dark woods, a covert hand signal from Clark sent Derek out ahead. Turning to Katrina, Clark whispered, "Stay close," as a tactical tracking map superimposed itself onto her field of vision. Katrina struggled to assimilate the streaming data as they blazed an unmarked trail through the dark forest.

Clark picked up the pace, and Katrina tried to mimic their silent footfalls.

Wending around boulders and over the side of a hill, they crossed an icy brook. Surefooted on the slippery rocks, Derek guided her across, and after forty minutes at a brisk clip, the forest began to thin. In the distance, light from the bravta compound became visible.

Clark signaled a stop on a hillside, a hundred yards shy of the fence line. Crouching in the shadows, Clark and Derek traded their goggles for night-vision binoculars to study the complex below.

Double-rolled razor wire crowned a chain-link fence. Searchlights pierced the blackness and armed guards patrolled the perimeter. Inside the gates, a fleet of luxury automobiles littered a mansion's circular drive—Rolls Royces, Maybachs, Maseratis, and a lone, canary yellow

Lamborghini. Near the cars, three mink-clad vixens wearing a ransom's worth of diamonds could be seen flirting with various men, who encircled them in clusters, puffing at cigars with drinks in hand.

Raucous music shattered the still night air.

Clark took it all in with deliberate consideration. "If this is a trap," he smiled calculatedly, "I think we're early. That's one helluva party." Katrina leaned in to better hear him. Pointing to the outbuildings, he added in a hushed tone, "Based on the coordinates, that's the prison block to the north; adjacent are the living quarters for the militia."

Derek nodded. "Let's go crash a party."

81

Slender, manicured fingers folded a stick of gum and pressed it through ruby-painted lips. Knowing she was about to be called into action, she had moved into position inside Black Hole.

From behind a locked door, in a room adjacent to Frank's cell, she studied him from a surveillance monitor. He had started writing. Her dark eyes narrowed in puzzlement as she noticed him glance up to give a knowing smile to someone who wasn't there.

A second later the cell phone vibrated in her waiting hand.

Picking up the scrambled line, she listened intently to the initial silence.

After a predetermined pause, a deep voice that she recognized as Gregory Malchek's hissed, "Frank is late for his appointment."

"I'll see to it that he remembers," she said with a well-practiced American accent.

The line clicked dead.

Deftly, she opened the control box of Frank's sleep-depriving apparatus, which hung on the wall before her. Her trained hands maneuvered a pair of needle-nose pliers inside.

The machine redlined with a crackling zap.

A malevolent smile danced briefly across her beautiful lips as she watched Frank's body jump from the jolt. Eyes bulging, his back arched hard, and the pen and paper fell to the floor.

Mission accomplished.

Ceremoniously, she blotted her newly applied red lipstick with a Kleenex, and stuffing it in the pocket of her scrubs, she headed down the hall. A curious rubbery squeal from her tennis shoes cut through the silence, had anyone been there to hear it.

82

Katrina watched as Clark screwed a suppressor onto the threaded barrel of his 9mm SIG Sauer semi-automatic before clipping a well-cared-for Fairbairn-Sykes combat knife to his belt. The slender double-edged blade, designed exclusively for surprise attack and fighting, could pierce Kevlar and was long enough to penetrate both layered winter clothing and a ribcage. Reaching into his backpack, Clark retrieved two more items—a tranquilizer gun and a compact SIG of similar make to his own—which he matter-of-factly passed to Katrina.

"I'm not shooting anyone!" she said crisply, pushing the weapons back to him.

"Damn it, Katrina," Clark said, "you asked to come into the field, now take them," he insisted. "I understand you don't want to kill anyone," he added in a serious tone, "but you never know when you might need to defend yourself."

"I don't even know how to shoot!" Katrina retorted.

"At least take this one," he replied, pressing the tranquilizer gun into her hand. "If everything goes according to plan, you won't even have to aim it. Carry it for my comfort. It's non-negotiable."

Katrina sighed. Reluctantly accepting his logic, she clipped the holstered weapon to her belt, and Clark added gravely, "Sometimes it's kill or be killed."

Meanwhile, Derek checked his pistol and placed it in his left-handed holster. Armed with a plethora of paraphernalia, including a folding submachine gun, he signaled ready, and with a nod, Clark gave him the go-ahead to secure an entry point.

A searchlight scoured the fence line.

Derek crept closer.

A guard approached, patrolling the perimeter.

Katrina watched through binoculars and held her breath as Derek ducked behind a tree at the last minute to avoid being spotted. Timing his approach, he darted in, crouched low, and molded a plasticized thermite charge around the fence's heavy chain links.

From nearby towers, attentive eyes monitored the strobe light as it swept back, its bright orb hunting trespassers.

Hurriedly, Derek's fingers raced the approaching beam and attached a tiny magnesium remote ignition device. Securing the final wire, he fell back. The strobe's leading edge grazed only his breath, leaving the guard with nothing to see but a wisp of steam—fleeting vaporous evidence in the cold night air. Slinking back into the shadowed tree line, Derek delayed pressing the detonator until the beam reached the far end of the encampment.

Instantly, a white-hot flash ignited the fence, melting the steel links. The glowing metal cooled dark, and the severed mesh, in the outline of a body-sized flap, broke free and fell to the ground, seconds before the searchlight began its return path.

The perforation went unnoticed.

On Clark's command, perfectly timed between strobes and sentries, the trio crab-crawled through the opening in the fence as if it were a doggy door. Staying low, they scurried to the shadows that clung to the outside of the prison block.

In the distance, a perimeter guard approached, making his return pass along the fence line, while behind them, a door slammed at the end of the building. They could hear the footsteps of someone exiting the prison block only a hundred feet away, and Katrina's heart pounded as Derek, on Clark's signal, vanished furtively around a corner in silent pursuit.

The man, who had exited the prison, paused momentarily to pull out his gold-plated Zippo and light an unfiltered cigarette. Dressed in a tailored black suit, his eyes roamed the mansion before him as his puffs of smoke wafted into the dark night air. Ready to rejoin the party, he started back, his black, polished Italian leather shoes leaving no prints across the frozen ground.

Sneaking up behind him, Derek matched steps with the man for only a second before his weapon found its mark, smashing hard against the Mafioso's skull. Quickly dragging the limp body out of sight, Derek zip-tied the unconscious man's hands and feet before rolling him over and rifling through his designer suit. Relieving him of a pocket pistol, he confiscated a ring of keys and an access card from a wallet before condemning the man to a long slumber with a well-placed tranquilizer dart.

On the opposite side of the prison structure, a hacking cough stopped the approaching sentry less than fifty feet from where Katrina hid. Pulling a steel flask from his inner pocket, he took a swig of his self-prescribed medicine and wiped his mouth on his sleeve, pausing long enough to feel the firewater's warmth hit his belly. He wasn't sure whether it was vodka-soaked intuition or paranoia, but either way, a sense of danger crept through his skin.

From the shadows, Katrina could see him cock his head to listen. She swallowed hard and flattened her body against the building's wall.

With a loud click, the guard disabled the safety on his AK-74 and flipped on his flashlight.

Katrina looked around quickly for Clark, but he had disappeared. She now stood alone.

The sentry came closer, his flashlight illuminating patches of earth between the two buildings where she hid. Barely breathing, Katrina sent a silent telepathic call for help to Clark through the shadows, but dared not move.

The guard, now less than twenty paces away, jerked his flashlight hurriedly back and forth, until suddenly, the blinding light assaulted her retinas.

The beam had found is mark!

Her heart stood still.

83

Denise arrived back at her office in Atlanta to find the FedEx package from Gregory Malchek waiting on her desk. She sliced the envelope open and quickly rifled through its contents in search of the check she had been promised. "Shit," she swore, after combing through the papers twice. No check.

Plopping down in her chair, tired after a long day and a round-trip flight to Denver, she fished the cell phone out of her purse and dialed Malchek's number.

An answering machine responded.

In a sweet voice that concealed her displeasure, Denise recorded her message notifying him that while the contracts were in order, the check must have been inadvertently omitted, and that she looked forward to working with him. Hanging up, she put the cell phone down and noticed that her fingertips had begun to tingle. She wiped them across the fabric of her skirt, dismissed the annoyance, and began checking her email. Less than twenty minutes later, Denise felt flush.

A low-grade fever had set in.

She pushed through two more pieces of correspondence before stopping to examine her fingers again. They had become oddly numb against the keyboard. She rubbed them together, as if trying to remove a sticky substance. It didn't help, and deciding to wash her hands, Denise rose from her desk.

Her head swam.

She almost sat back down, but a wave of nausea urged her on and, unsteady, she trailed a hand along the wall in an effort to stop the room from spinning.

Surely it couldn't be the two glasses of wine I had on the plane. Maybe I've got food poisoning or the flu.

Not sick enough to vomit, Denise clung to the sink and splashed cold water on her cheeks, the mirror reflecting her ashen face. The whites of her eyes were bloodshot and her nose had started to run. As she reached for a tissue, her hand trembled uncontrollably.

84

In the bitter cold of the Russian night, Katrina's hands reached for the sky. Temporarily blinded and held captive by the guard's AK-74, she pleaded, "Don't shoot."

The sentry opened his mouth to shout alarm, but to her surprise, only a hushed garble escaped from his lips and his eyes went wide.

The weapon fell from his hand.

The flashlight dropped.

Clark had sneaked up behind him, and in a single deft strike to the man's exposed neck, his expertly trained fingers struck their mark. Hitting a highly sensitive pressure point, the man crumpled to the ground, unconscious.

Breathing a sigh of relief, Katrina, with adrenaline still rushing, lent Clark a hand as he tied, gagged, and hid the guard in the shadows. Just as they finished, Derek reappeared from around the corner and quickly passed Clark the pilfered access card and the set of keys he had retrieved. Pistol in hand, Clark led the way to the back door of the prison, where he swiped the card.

The light blinked green.

Silently, the three slipped inside and entered a dark foyer.

From down the hall, a television blared.

Derek stole down the corridor and crept up behind a guard who sat dozing off and on at his station as he watched an old Western rerun with subtitles. Neutralizing him with ease, Derek disarmed the man and set about disabling the bank of monitors that ran live feeds from strategically placed security cameras throughout the prison. With a few keystrokes, the images froze, providing cover for their operation, at least until a new guard took watch.

Receiving the all clear from Derek, Clark keyed open the inside doorway to expose a long, dark hall of dank, repugnant cells.

The reek of stale urine saturated the air, reminding her of Black Hole. Ignoring a surge of concern for Frank, Katrina began to breathe shallowly through her mouth to cope with the stench. Hurrying, she closed the distance with Clark as his flashlight probed through the small barred window of one cell after another in search of the dealmaker.

Derek, seemingly impervious to the rank odor, brought up the rear.

Most of the prisoners were asleep. A few hopeless souls with empty eyes stared back at Clark, but they remained silent, fearful of drawing attention.

Clark moved on. The cell numbers were climbing. A little more than halfway down the seemingly endless corridor, Clark paused at cell number 43. "This is it," he confirmed quietly.

Inside at the back of the cell lay a man curled in a fetal position.

Roused by Clark's intrusive light, the prisoner's troubled eyes anxiously sought out the identity of the visitors shadowed behind the beam. "Who's there?" he stuttered in Russian.

A stranger's face met Clark's gaze. Nonetheless, the prisoner's voice sounded familiar. Through bars of the window, Clark scrutinized the form before him and hazarded, "Krueger, is that you?"

85

A small mountain of used tissues filled Denise's wastebasket. Despite nausea, dizzy spells, and a nagging headache, she had opted to stay in her office and review Gregory Malchek's contracts. After blowing her nose yet again, she pulled out her compact mirror and glanced at her bright red nose. "Ugh," she complained to herself. "Airplanes!"

Hoping to nip the problem in the bud, she dragged her ailing body into her car and drove to St. Joseph's Hospital, grateful it was only four blocks away. Seeking after-hours care, she walked into the emergency room.

Inside, the waiting area was full. A young girl, scraped and bruised, cradled a broken arm against her chest. Nearby, an elderly woman in a wheelchair wheezed loudly, oxygen tanks by her side. Her family huddled around her. Not far from her, another man sat stooped over, vomiting into a pan.

Shakily, Denise made her way to the receptionist, who barely looked up to hand her a clipboard. "Fill these papers out and turn them back in," she instructed. "We'll call you when we're ready."

Spying an unoccupied chair in the corner, Denise wove her way through the infirm and came to sit under the television set, which blared: *With the country still reeling from catastrophic events in Chicago, Boston, Washington DC, and New York City, the explosion today in Houston at the First Metropolitan Bank Building looks to be the latest link in a chain of seemingly related events.*

Distressed by the breaking news and her deteriorating condition, Denise rubbed her burning eyes with one hand as the pen shook in her other; she scrawled nearly illegible letters across the forms. By the time she'd completed the seven pages and signed all the documents, chills had begun to alternate with hot flashes, and Denise was glad she'd come. After returning the paperwork to the preoccupied receptionist, she reclaimed her seat and collapsed with a thud. Wanting to let her new partners know that she'd be unavailable for meetings the following day, she rummaged through her purse, searched out the card Tony had given her at lunch, and dialed his number.

His secretary answered and told her that he wasn't feeling well either and had gone to see his doctor.

An exhausted sigh escaped her, and she laid her head back to rest.

86

"Eagle, is that you?" the cell's occupant said with a wash of relief from inside the cell. "I've never had my prayers answered so fast," the man faltered in surprise.

Katrina noticed that, regardless of the prisoner's warm welcome, Clark's field remained guarded and calculated, emotionally unmoved.

"Nikolai, I thought you were dead," Clark tested.

The man smiled as he struggled to stand. "Yes, that was quite an effective ploy, don't you think?" he asked with a groan. "My new life also required the handiwork of several gifted plastic surgeons," he added as he made his way toward the cell window.

Clark knew that war criminals frequently underwent major reconstructive surgery to assume new identities, but Krueger didn't fit that profile. Unconvinced the man before him was who he claimed to be, Clark ordered the prisoner closer, and shining the light directly in his eyes, searched for a telltale marker of Krueger's identity—heterochromia.

"So, it is you," Clark concluded coldly after confirming that the iris of one eye was brown and the other blue. Still distrusting, he continued, "You son of a bitch, I risked my ass to extract you! Why didn't you show up at the rendezvous? If the Cold War were still on, I'd gladly kill you for triple agency, you know."

"I got a better offer," Krueger admitted simply. "With the USSR on its deathbed, I joined a project that was being privatized—your people called it Blackheart. There I found something far greater than the piddly one million dollars your country offered me for defection."

"Looks like things turned out well for you, Nikolai," Clark replied with sarcasm. "Prison suits you."

Krueger glanced at his accommodations, his mouth turned down, and he closed his eyes tiredly. "The new boss thinks I betrayed him," he said with a weak smile.

Despite Katrina's best efforts to peek around Clark's head to get a glimpse of Krueger, she was unable to see. Clark's head blocked the small window in its entirety.

"How the hell did you get me that message?"

"I bribed a guard and prayed you'd come!"

"I'm not your 'get out jail free' card anymore! Those days are over," Clark replied flatly.

"You don't understand," Krueger begged. "Things have changed. The young one—Vladimir—he's the bastard in power now. Vladimir is crazy. Actually insane," he continued with visible contempt. "I need out. I thought we could partner like the old days. I've got a deal you can't refuse."

Katrina scanned the resonance of Krueger's voice, discerning what she could without a visual read, but he was shielded.

Playing hardball, Clark replied derisively, "What could you possibly have that would make it worth my while to risk breaking you out of here and getting these bastards on my case?"

Krueger smiled smugly, "How about a solution to your problem?" he taunted. "You are having a little issue with sleepers, aren't you?"

Clark's eyes narrowed. "What do you know about that? Have you got deactivation codes?" he snapped icily.

"Better than that," Krueger boasted. "I've got a list of all of the sleepers who survived the bombing of the research facility."

With hand signals, Katrina silently told Clark that there was something more at play; Krueger wasn't divulging the whole story.

"No deal, Nikolai," Clark replied. "I don't trust you as far as I can spit. Besides, we got it taken care of," Clark added, in a tone so confident that Krueger's plastic face twisted in confusion. Clark turned and walked away, motioning for Derek and Katrina to follow.

"Wait! Where are you going? There's more!" Krueger called after him.

"With you, there always is, Nikolai," Clark called back as he continued walking. "The pot would have to be damn sweet for me to play this time. You're just not worth it."

The negotiations had begun. Krueger scrambled for options. "Eagle, come back. I need you. I've got something you can't pass up. Don't be a fool."

Clark paused. "This better be good, Nikolai," he said as he slowly turned around, "or I may just put you out of your misery for dragging me back to Russia. I hate it here, remember?"

"It is," he said in an assuring tone, visibly relieved to have Clark return to the window. "It's a gem of a treasure—my life preserver, if you will," he added, "and if you want to stop Vladimir, you're going to need it."

Clark fixed his eyes on Krueger with a penetrating stare. "And just what might this crown jewel be?" Clark asked.

A smile cracked Krueger's falsely youthful face. "The map to the greatest treasure of all," he promised, "the Forbidden Text," and with that statement Katrina surreptitiously pushed against Clark's arm. She strained to see Krueger's field over Clark's shoulder so that she could confirm or deny his statements, but by the time she gained a glimpse of Krueger's field, it was too late.

Clark called his bluff. "Don't bullshit me," he said, as he leveled the barrel of his pistol at Krueger's head. "Trying to sell me goods that no longer exist will get you killed."

"I'll prove it! Just get me out of here," Krueger challenged with a crooked smile.

Clark sized Krueger up, considering the possibilities. Eliza's map had gone missing and Krueger would have been snake enough to take it. Without showing his hand, Clark cut the deal. "You've got both—the map and the list of sleepers?"

Krueger nodded.

"Where?"

"Not far from here ... less than twenty kilometers," Krueger explained anxiously, "in my hunting lodge."

Silent and resolved, Clark swiped the passkey to open the cell's lock.

The device blinked red—access denied.

Clark looked down and muttered, "The damn thing requires fingerprint ID!"

"I'll see what I can do," Derek replied, before disappearing down the corridor.

87

Illness and injury traipsed indiscriminately through St. Joseph's emergency room. Three hours had passed and Denise had fallen asleep in the waiting room with her head against the wall, when a gentleman sat down next to her and noticed a slight trickle of blood seeping from her nose.

Reaching out, he touched her arm and tried to rouse her.

She was burning up and unresponsive.

Hurriedly, he notified the receptionist, and, moments later, Denise was rushed into an examining room, where, stirring from the dark recesses of her mind, she awoke to find a disarmingly handsome young doctor shining a light in her eyes. "How do you feel?" he asked, flicking the bright beam in and out of her pupils, checking reflexes.

If at all possible, she felt worse. "What's wrong with me?" Denise croaked, her voice nothing more than a whisper. Touching her face self-consciously, she discovered a large welt had formed on her cheek.

"This is Dr. Marc Stevens," a petite, brown-haired nurse named Mariella volunteered.

"You passed out in the waiting room," the doctor explained in a comforting tone.

"Most likely, it's the flu," Mariella added as he continued his exam. "We've started an IV. You've got a fever and need fluids."

Marc Stevens warmed his stethoscope between his hands and placed it against Denise's aching chest. Closing his eyes, he focused intently and listened. "Let's get blood work done, stat," he ordered Mariella.

88

As Clark and Katrina waited for Derek's return, Clark studied the face of his old rival. For Clark, the mere sight of Krueger brought his long-buried anger to the surface, and he scowled through the rusting bars of the cell's window at the former KGB agent. Not only had Krueger been brazen enough to risk Clark's life by betraying him at the rendezvous, if he was in possession of Eliza's map, as far as Clark was concerned, Krueger was responsible for her death. Entangled in emotion, Clark didn't hear the minuscule click that sounded in the dim hallway.

By the time Katrina sensed the encroaching danger, it was too late. She had been preoccupied, trying to read Krueger's field for clues. Before she could scream, she felt the cold steel of a gun barrel pressed hard against her temple and a strong arm wrapped tight, like an anaconda, around her chest.

Clark looked up to see that a second guard had a firearm trained on his chest. The guard shouted angrily in Russian for him to disarm or watch Katrina die. As Clark raised his hands in surrender, Katrina's world decelerated into slow motion. Careful to comply, Clark answered the guard in fluent Russian and set his pistol on the floor, kicking it aside as instructed.

In the turmoil, from inside his cell, Krueger started barking orders in words Katrina couldn't understand. The guards' momentary hesitation and confused faces confirmed Krueger's power within the organization.

Seizing the opportunity of distraction, Clark liberated the sentry's gun and delivered a crushing blow with his elbow, dropping the man to the ground.

In the same instant, Katrina's captor collapsed. His face hit the concrete floor with a smack, and his arm fell across her feet. Derek's sharp shooting had sent a 9mm hollowpoint through his head.

Stunned, Katrina gently slid her foot out from under his limb as a faint whisper of luminosity separated from the man's body and passed before her as life drained out of the fallen man.

With no time to waste, Derek lifted the still-warm corpse and pressed the dead man's thumbprint against the lock's biosensor. The sensor's light flashed green and the lock clicked open.

Derek dropped the guard to the floor and took a relieved breath as he swung open the door. Inside, the aged KGB agent draped his arm over Derek's strong shoulder, making him a human crutch, and they headed out.

"Screw with me this time, Nikolai," Clark warned as they stepped over the fallen bodies, "and you'll wish Vladimir had had his way with you."

89

Denise ached all over. From the corner of her eye, she saw an elderly tree of a man looming ominously in the doorway. Keeping his distance, he scowled at her from beneath a shock of gray hair. Dr. Marc Stevens introduced the man as Dr. Abraham Roth, an infectious disease specialist.

Dr. Roth nodded in acknowledgment from a distance and squinted at the numerous little purplish, red spots that now flecked Denise's skin. "Petechiae—hemorrhaging capillaries," he confirmed, and, ever vigilant, he snapped on latex gloves prior to taking Denise's chart from Marc's hand. As he read through the notes, his owl-like eyes intermittently peered at Denise over round-rimmed spectacles. "Interesting," he finally judged. "Have you run a CBC?"

"Results aren't back yet. I just got her," Dr. Stevens explained.

"But this chart says she checked in over four hours ago," Roth challenged. "What the hell have you people been doing?"

"Standard triage protocol," Mariella defended. "She presented with flu-like symptoms. If we rushed everyone with that kind of presentation to the head of the line, we'd be overloaded."

Through her mental fog, Denise heard the interchange and opened her eyes. Her vision was a blur. She tried to tell them about her visit to Denver and her counterparts who may have contracted the same mysterious ailment, but she had no voice.

90

Silently retracing their steps, Clark and company quickly evacuated the bravta compound and disappeared into the shadowy edge of the forest. Krueger had been slowing them down, complaining, his stifled groans growing louder with each step. To keep up, Derek hoisted Krueger over his shoulders in a fireman's carry.

Scanning the trees for signs of life, Clark expertly navigated the group at breakneck speed around patches of snow, careful not to leave footprints. Under the cover of a stone ledge, wedged behind a thick stand of trees, he finally brought them to a brief halt and motioned for Derek to set down his burden. Katrina positioned herself to do reconnaissance innocuously from the background.

Shivers racked Krueger's body and he hunkered down in the cold. "Sons of bitches," he winced, holding his gut. "I think they fucked me up inside."

Katrina observed Krueger's morphic fields with suspicion. She didn't see any register of physical pain—drug addiction perhaps, but not damaged internal organs, as he claimed.

"Where's the lodge?" Clark demanded of Krueger impatiently. "I want that map and the list of sleepers."

Teeth chattering, eyes cast down, Krueger shook his head. "My life's not worth shit if I tell you. Once I'm out of the country, safe in America, I'll talk and you can come back to get it," he stalled.

"I'm not playing games," Clark snapped. Bidding Krueger a curt good-bye in his mother tongue, Clark turned and walked away, remarking coldly, "You made your bed, now lie in it. I'll leave you for Vladimir."

Krueger called after him. "Fine, I'll take you to the lodge. It's all there," he said reluctantly, "but my life is your compass. If you kill me, you'll never find the goods—they're too well hidden."

"Which way?" Clark demanded.

"About eight kilometers northwest of here," Krueger blurted, adding, "I'll need some morphine to make it that far."

Clark glanced briefly at Katrina for a clandestine signal before turning back to Krueger. As prearranged, she was leaning her weight on her right leg, indicating that Krueger was telling the truth about the goods, yet she longed to disclose that he was broadcasting multiple messages about his injuries. Unfortunately, no prearranged sign had been established for mixed information, and since she was banished to silence, she couldn't inform Clark of the nuanced data.

Nonetheless, Clark remained cautious, calculating options. "Get him some morphine," he ordered Derek, "enough to make him comfortable, but not enough to knock him out."

A smile of relief crossed Krueger's plastic-looking features as Derek extracted the medkit with a premeasured syrette from his backpack; but before Derek could inject the opiate, Clark stopped him. With a hefty advantage in hand, Clark pressured Krueger, asking, "Just how in the hell did you get the map?"

Yearning for the dope, Krueger stammered anxiously, "I found it."

Katrina now leaned her weight on her left leg, indicating that the statement was a lie, and Clark ordered, "Put it away, Derek. This bastard can't be trusted."

"Give me the fucking morphine!" Krueger exploded.

Clark's steely eyes sliced through Krueger, who hesitated before finally divulging, "We knew the strike on Himmelshaus was coming."

"How?"

"Moles deep within the CIA had given us all the information we needed, just in time," Krueger bragged. "We let the U.S. believe they had wiped us out so they wouldn't look for us anymore. It required sacrificing hours of work and many assets to complete the ruse." His mouth turned down and a shadow crossed his face as he remembered. "I had procured the map hours in advance of the strike. All went according to plan, except one thing," he paused, drawing his brows together contemplatively. "The woman who discovered the map got killed and, with her dead, no one's been able to decipher it."

Not by the flicker of a muscle or eyelid twitch did Clark betray what he felt.

Katrina, on the other hand, had been thrown into an emotional tailspin and fought to maintain a stoic exterior.

Clark kept his pistol trained on Krueger with one hand while he pressed speed dial on his satellite phone with the other. "This is Echo Fox to Kilo Base," he said. "We've got a change of plans—stand by for new coordinates and a revised ETD."

At the bravta compound, a few miles away, a klaxon drowned out the rock music, killing the wild party. The group's unauthorized entry had been discovered. Confused guests fled the mansion's harbor of illicit drugs and promiscuity as searchlights scoured the grounds. One beacon finally came to rest on the sagging section of fence.

A second alarm pealed in response, loud enough to be heard through the forest. Militia mobilized. Search dogs bayed in the distance.

Hearing the telltale signs of an impending posse, Clark gave Derek the go-ahead to inject the morphine, and they moved out with Krueger under Clark's gunpoint.

At the bravta compound, a small army of four-wheelers roared to life and fanned out, each taking different trails, attempting to weave a net of entrapment.

Krueger's morphine kicked in, and although his breath came raggedly in the cold night, he pushed himself to keep up under his own volition.

The motor of a single ATV buzzed closer, menacingly near.

Clark requested data regarding their pursuers, and an infrared satellite image displayed heat signatures on his bionic lens. Adjusting course accordingly, he spearheaded an escape route up a narrow game trail. Derek fell back and dropped out of sight, hiding behind a tree. The others proceeded without him.

A moment later, an all-terrain vehicle roared up the hill. Its armed riders never saw Derek, in camouflage, behind the spruce. Jumping out as the vehicle passed, Derek leveled his SIG and, in a single shot, dropped the rear passenger. The man toppled to the ground, and as he did, another well-placed round sent the driver crashing headfirst into a pine, destroying the vehicle.

"Damn," Derek muttered to himself, having hoped to capture one of the rugged machines. After field stripping the weapons, he threw them into the forest and jogged to catch up with Clark, Katrina, and Krueger, who were already making impressive progress climbing a particularly steep section of the hill.

91

Beep! The thermometer in Denise's mouth drew swift attention. "Fever's rising," Mariella, the nurse, announced with concern. "103.2 degrees."

Denise coughed. Phlegm rattled in her throat. Weakly, she spit it into a Kleenex.

"Doctors," whispered Mariella, audibly terrified, "she's bleeding!"

"Yes, I can see that, nurse," replied Dr. Roth, curtly, from the doorway. The infectious disease guru gestured toward the dribble of blood on Denise's upper lip that had begun to drip from her nostrils, and replied simply, "Clean it up."

"No, no, no . . ." Mariella said, backing away from Denise, "not that. She's coughing up blood," she said, holding up a sputum-filled Kleenex, "and the red welts are spreading."

The look on Dr. Marc Stevens's handsome face darkened as he walked over for a closer look.

Every muscle in Dr. Roth's stork-like form tensed as he took two steps back. Deep ravines crevassed his face. From outside the doorway, he barked. "Get her quarantined in an isolation unit. Now!"

A moment later, with a shaking hand, Dr. Roth dialed the CDC twelve miles away.

92

Derek rejoined the group as they rounded a yawing bend on a steep trail, and he overheard Clark fanning Krueger's ego to get more information. "So, that was quite a foil, Nikolai, knowing the airstrike was coming and convincing the U.S. that Blackheart was eradicated."

"As I said, we suffered some big losses to make it look convincing," Krueger confided, "but yes, most of the administrators escaped unharmed. The operation was relocated. We went dark, changing our identities and our appearances, which afforded us unparalleled opportunities both in our initiatives and in the forging of strategic global alliances," he said, smiling smugly.

Katrina confirmed the truth of his words with a predetermined cough.

"The original masterminds are all dead now: heart attack, cancer, diabetes, liver failure," he listed, "except Steinhertz, whom we fondly call Father."

The face of the man who condemned Frank to the snake pit flashed before Katrina's eyes, and she felt waves of disgust. *How could he still be alive? Where were the laws of karma?*

Krueger prattled on, "In his old age, Father put Vladimir, his favored elite prodigy, in charge. No sooner was that little son of a bitch in power than he immediately wanted to oust the old guard—people like me. He no longer saw our merit. We weren't pure enough—we weren't bred to be part of their elite. I was able to buy some time, with some information I had saved up, but when he started to do his housecleaning, I knew it wouldn't be long before he disposed of me . . . he wants to leave the past behind, so to speak. So I thought I'd better use the one-time pad I'd been saving all these years and partner with you, someone I could trust," Krueger smiled slyly. "If we can find the tablet of the Forbidden Text, that little shit will be history."

Katrina saw truth mixed with fabrication. She sensed a hidden agenda but couldn't quite put her finger it. The morphine wasn't helping. Not sure how to warn Clark, as their clandestine vocabulary of signals fell far short of conveying what Krueger's field revealed, Katrina coughed and sneezed.

Her signal didn't surprise Clark and he masterfully played along. "Interesting proposition, Nikolai," he replied. "I want to hear more, but first I'd better make sure we get out of here alive. What do you say?"

"Da," Krueger agreed.

93

From her home in Atlanta, a grave look of concern washed over CDC Director Dr. Barbara Ilsmith's face as she heard Dr. Roth's report, and she only had to listen for a moment before deciding to quarantine everyone who had had direct contact. Unspoken worry seeped through her tense voice as she added, "We'll send someone over right away to collect samples."

Hanging up the phone, her head fell back against her pillow, but only for an instant. Amid the rash of domestic terror that had plagued the country during the previous few days, she had worried that the CDC, too, might be tested. Nationwide fears of pandemic had risen due to recent outbreaks of swine and avian flu, but this sounded different.

In the dark, her husband grumbled as she slipped quietly out of bed and got dressed. The sleeping giant of a man was her rock. Stirring, he asked groggily, "What's up, honey? Will you be home for dinner?"

"I'll do my best," she replied and bent to kiss him good-bye, "but it's not likely."

Her cell phone chimed again. It was her assistant reporting that two men with similar symptoms had also been hospitalized less than an hour before—one in San Francisco, the other in St. Louis. "Damn," Barbara cursed under her breath, a deep sense of dread filling her chest.

"Notify the proper authorities and call Homeland Security. Based on the symptoms, tell them we have a possible Category A infection on our hands."

Hearing her words, her husband sat bolt upright in bed. "I'll drop you off some lunch," he replied, offering what little support he could.

Thirty-eight minutes later, at AWOL's command center, Shortcut's phone rang. It was Bill Sterling, who barked without a hello, "Get Clark on the line. Now!"

"Sorry, sir. Clark is currently unavailable," Shortcut sidestepped. Information about Clark's excursion into Russia had been compartmentalized to AWOL. Until further notice, Sterling was to remain unaware. "But I'll get your message to him as soon as possible," Shortcut assured him, his nervous voice making several choppy cuts.

"Damn it!" Sterling groused. "Tell him I just got a call from the CDC. We've got a problem—some kind of exotic pathogen is making people deathly ill."

"Bioterrorism?" Shortcut hesitated cautiously, "A two-pronged attack?"

The line fell silent for a moment. "Too early to tell," Sterling finally replied. "But the CDC is all over it. We'll have some test results by breakfast. I'll keep you posted."

94

They were almost halfway to the hunting lodge when instinct told Clark to circle back. He gave Derek the lead, leaving Krueger in his charge. Climbing up a steep outcropping of boulders, he peered through binoculars to scan the dense wood below. A hundred yards away, he saw a rustling, scurrying movement under the trees.

Clark sharpened the focus on his binoculars and zoomed in to see a massive, six-hundred-pound wild boar bolt from the shadows, its five-inch, knifelike tusks gleaming in the dark. Knowing something must have spooked it, Clark's eyes probed deeper.

Then, he saw them. Fifty yards upwind of the rooting boar, a small army of men with AK-74s slung over their shoulders were doing double time, darting in and out through a thicket of evergreens. Accompanying them, half a dozen hounds pulled hard on their leads, dragging their humans along.

More worrisome than the approaching threat in the distance, Clark sensed something off to his left. He felt it with his body rather than heard it with his ears.

Leaves crunched under weight.

A twig snapped.

Another boar? A point man? Whatever it was, it was causing him serious concern. Clark subvocalized into his throat mic, "Echo Fox returning. Make double time. We've got company approaching from the south and east. I'll catch up." He dropped softly from his perch in the rocks and sprinted through the trees. Taking a less direct path back, he ran up a narrow stream to break the trail of his scent before rejoining his party.

Changing the group's course, Clark picked up the pace to outmaneuver the posse behind them. Krueger grimaced and struggled to keep up. As they marched on, Katrina observed his biofield from behind. The news that Blackheart's men were closing in had left his aura vibrating with a paradoxical mix of fear and hope.

As the troop skirted a small field, keeping to the shadows of the trees, Clark used the possibility of their imminent capture to nail Krueger down. "Okay Nikolai, we'll partner," he smiled calculatedly, waving his gun in a less-than-friendly fashion toward the slippery operative as they ran. "But first, tell me why in the hell you've decided to start triggering sleepers, or the deal's off," he said threateningly.

"I'm no murderer!" Krueger said, defending himself heatedly. His voice coming in ragged puffs, he squawked, "It's all Vladimir's doing!"

Clark listened for Katrina's signal.

Clearing her throat, she signaled a lie, but wanted to say so much more. Not only did Krueger habitually speak in half-truths, but he was also clearly holding back. As they pushed their way through thick underbrush into a clearing, Katrina continued to give Clark the best feedback possible until, suddenly, a slice of the future materialized before her eyes, superseding not only her surroundings but also the feed from her bionic lens.

A millisecond before the event was to occur, the precognition of it crystallized in her mind.

Spinning around without warning, Katrina grabbed Derek and body-tackled him to the ground, shouting, "Sniper!"

Just then, a bullet pierced the air where Derek had stood, slamming instead into a tree.

Clark yanked Krueger down and ducked behind a boulder.

Derek quickly rolled out from under Katrina and shielded her with his body. Gun in hand, he faced the unseen assailant and ordered, "Go! I'll cover you!"

They heard another muffled crack.

Pine bark flew five feet away.

Belly crawling, Katrina scrambled across the damp forest floor toward Clark and the safety of the oversized rock. Another shot whizzed by, inches above her head. She couldn't get any lower.

Derek flattened himself to the ground and returned fire.

Some thirty yards away, another spark flashed.

Rocks exploded at Derek's heels, gouging up soil.

It was close. Someone had them pinned down.

Katrina felt an adrenaline rush as Clark's silenced weapon returned a hair-raising volley of fire. She crawled faster and was just twelve feet from the boulder's cover when a muffled thud in the woods confirmed that Clark's shot was good. Although relieved, Katrina felt a sickening jolt in her gut. Another fatality had been sustained on the mafia's side, but not before they hit Krueger.

95

At St. Joseph's Hospital in Atlanta, two nurses, Dr. Marc Stevens, and the man from the waiting room suddenly found themselves under mandatory quarantine with Denise. The triage nurse, wearing Mickey Mouse scrubs, who had first examined Denise, had already begun to feel achy and was lying down on a nearby stretcher.

Marc was tending to her, drawing blood samples, and starting an IV.

From the other side of the room, Mariella gasped, "Oh my God," as she worked to remove Denise's business attire and change her into a hospital gown. The welts that covered Denise's body had begun to ooze, and the purplish red spots were expanding.

Marc hurriedly finished what he was doing, changed gloves, and rushed over to take a look. He lifted Denise's eyelids. The whites of her eyes were hemorrhaging.

Groggily, Denise came to. Gasping a raspy, painful breath, she blindly groped for something to vomit into. Everyone in attendance watched, shocked, as blood-tinged bile splattered across the plastic tray clasped shakily between Denise's pale hands.

"Collect a sample," Dr. Stevens instructed Mariella. "It all needs to be cultured—her sputum, her blood, everything."

Denise tried to speak. Her voice croaked, and before she could form a coherent sentence, the room darkened as if a curtain had dropped before her eyes.

Unconsciousness released her blissfully from pain.

96

S hit!" Krueger hollered, grabbing his forearm where the sniper's bullet had found its mark. Blood oozed through his fingers and dripped on the ground. Clark had been careful not to leave footprints. A trail of blood was the last thing they needed.

With the sniper eradicated, Clark quickly slipped out his knife and sliced away Krueger's shirtsleeve to take a closer look. Shaken, Krueger winced and made small talk. "Judging by the voice of your soldier over there," Krueger said, dipping his head toward Katrina, "I see you brought a female into the field. How progressive of you," he jousted, "—and stupid, don't you think? They're weak, both physically and emotionally, when it comes to doing what needs to be done."

"If what needs doing is putting a bullet in your head, I am confident that she is capable and willing," Clark replied dispassionately as he examined and prodded the bullet wound.

Overhearing the conversation, Katrina stepped back a pace to distance herself from Krueger's studious eye. She knew she had broken cover to some degree by shouting "Sniper!" but she had no regrets. Derek would have been hit.

"You're not a stupid man or a sentimental fool," Krueger needled Clark, "so chances are you're not fucking her," he managed to grunt.

Clark applied pressure to the graze. "I wonder what special assets warranted you bringing her along."

Clark scowled and changed the subject. "Seems Vladimir thinks you're disposable," he noted, as he hastily applied a field dressing to avoid a trail of blood. "What makes him Father's golden child?"

Krueger's face contorted, but his eyes remained focused on the female soldier. "Vladimir's the best of the best," he began through gritted teeth, "but there are other Goldens as well," he admitted, "—all eugenically formulated to possess not only psi abilities but bloodlines that include Stalin and Mengele."

"Mengele?" Derek asked disbelieving. "The Nazi scientist who specialized in eugenics and wholesale murder?"

"That's just what the world needs right now," Clark grumbled sarcastically.

Nikolai continued pointedly, "Vladimir is the darkest and most powerful of all Father's children."

Bandaging complete, Clark grabbed Krueger's arm and yanked him to his feet. "Let's get the hell out of here," he said, and pushed Krueger ahead into the misty gray of the Russian forest. On edge for more snipers, they trekked at a harried pace, and Clark guided his company into the flowing creek he had crossed earlier. Ice gathered in patches around the stream's edge, but in the center, shallow clear water rushed over a rocky bottom. Walking a few kilometers in the brook would make their scent difficult, if not impossible, to track.

Frigid water rushed over the tops of, and into, Katrina's boots. The numbing cold sent an avalanche of shivers through her fatigued body. Krueger cursed beneath his breath—something about Siberia. They trudged faster, ice-cold splashes wetting their clothes. Derek and Clark kept a sharp eye on the shore, while Katrina engaged her senses with the surroundings at large, scanning for danger.

97

From outside the isolation unit, on the other side of the protective glass, Dr. Abraham Roth looked in, frowning. The inmates of the quarantine room stared back at him—fear in their doom-stricken eyes. In all his years as an infectious disease specialist he had never seen anything like this. Concern etched deep grooves in his face as he watched his friend, Marc Stevens, fully covered in latex gloves, goggles, and a mask, place specimen samples from those quarantined through the airlock.

Over the quarantine's single-line telephone, a hopeful Marc asked the CDC's representative who had come to collect the samples, "Have you got anything yet?"

The man shook his head as he put the vials in a biohazard container for transport. "All I know is that these need to be cultured—ASAP."

"When do you think you'll have the results?" Mariella pleaded, stepping up to the glass. "I have small children. I need to go home."

"Once we find out what's going on, we'll let you know," the anxious-looking CDC envoy assured them. "Just don't develop any symptoms," he added with a grim smile before walking away at a brisk pace.

Marc's eyes sought out Roth's. Pointing to the telephone, he motioned for him to pick up. In a low, conspiratorial whisper, he asked, "Seriously, what do you think we've got? Some kind of super-mutated smallpox?"

"I'm not sure, but whatever it is, it's not good," Roth admitted, shaking his head. "Denise was patient zero. Until we know more, there's nothing else that can be done."

"Damn." Marc Stevens frowned as he turned and looked at the lives he felt singularly responsible for but ill-equipped to diagnose.

Later at the CDC in Atlanta, dozens of doctors and researchers gathered, including representatives from the Special Pathogens Branch and the U.S. Army Medical Research Institute of Infectious Diseases (USAMRIID). A small ice chest labeled "Biological Hazard" held specimens of the infected fluids.

Teams were formed along familiar guidelines. One group was designated to isolate the pathogen; another was instructed to discover how it was transmitted and to try and build a molecular and biological model of the disease agent. The last team had the most vital job—find out how to destroy the disease and, beyond that, find a way to prevent it.

98

The water grew faster and shallower as Clark's group continued its march upstream. Clark, who had been silent for almost a kilometer, began to finagle Krueger into revealing more.

"Since we're all friends now," he began almost amicably, "here's a question that won't cost you anything. Who were the masterminds behind Blackheart?"

Amused, Krueger turned to Clark and smiled; the question had tapped into his youthful self, the high-powered Soviet official. "That was a well-kept secret, wasn't it?"

Katrina kept pace seven feet behind, barely out of their splashes, her senses on alert.

"When I'm settled in the U.S. and have my big fat book deal, you'll know it all, but I see no harm in sharing a bit of that now."

"You can trust me not to steal your ideas, Krueger," Clark replied. "I've got more important things to do than write a book about the past."

Krueger's eyes gleamed with pride. "The initial impetus behind the program was Stalin. He had tried unsuccessfully to breed apes with humans to create a supersoldier. He also invested heavily in brain research, including mind control. Combining these passions, he recruited former Nazis like Himmler and a protégé of Mengele to start a new initiative."

"Himmler and Stalin?" Derek cut in from the rear, sounding dubious.

"Yes," Krueger looked back and smiled. "Ah, you may be too young to know—Himmler faked his death and escaped into the Austrian countryside. In the end, through rat lines, he came to Himmelshaus and helped spearhead Stalin's well-funded breeding project. We had the privilege of many high-ranking sperm donors."

Derek seized the moment and probed, "Why did Blackheart target breeding candidates with extrasensory or psi abilities?"

"We weren't stupid," Nikolai said pompously. "We recognized the fact that these special gifts existed as potential in everyone and considered people who already possessed them advanced, and therefore, superior beings. Having those gifts along with high IQs, the men were then chosen for their leadership and cunning—and the women for their outstanding looks, ability to deceive, and sexual desirability." This last phrase gave birth to a deviantly crooked and lascivious smile. "The offspring were destined to become the übermensch of the future."

The sparkle in Krueger's eyes and his enthusiasm were not lost on Clark. "Yes, Krueger. Those were the days," he replied somewhat sarcastically.

"But, it wasn't just about eugenics. It was a tiered approach. Steinhertz created everything from expendable sleepers, to middlemen, to Goldens like Vladimir." Krueger's breath was coming in heavy puffs as he slogged onward, yet he continued boasting. "He knew how to program these little prodigies as well. Steinhertz could take a child and mold him or her into a brilliant, undetectable sleeper, who believed only what Steinhertz wanted them to believe and lusted for what he wanted them to lust for. Dedicated, loyal little puppets striving their whole lives to achieve the goals of their master and prepared, on a moment's notice, to sacrifice their lives for some secret, subjective ideal."

Katrina noted that Krueger's discourse matched his field encryptions until he insisted, "I, of course, didn't believe in all that. I found everything but the pay questionable—but Steinhertz was not to be crossed," which was when Krueger's field darkened, like a storm cloud brewing, before it cloaked completely.

"How long's it been since you were at your lodge?" Clark questioned.

"Six months at least."

Clark looked at Krueger skeptically and listened for Katrina's signal. She cleared her throat twice.

Just as he suspected. A lie.

Krueger continued. "And now—I'll give you the goods. Then you can stop the sleepers, and if you can find the Forbidden Text, more power to you. I'll be happy just to get out of the game and retire to my own private beach somewhere," he chuckled.

"Just keep moving," Clark ordered. Piecing things together, his sense of urgency increased. "We're almost there."

99

In Manhattan, the twin brothers who had met Gregory Malchek the day before in Baltimore were walking down Fourteenth Street with backpacks slung over their shoulders when a text pinged simultaneously on both their cell phones. It was from Malchek. The disease was at its proper stage for Phase Two to continue. He signaled the brothers to go ahead.

According to plan, they immediately descended into the nearest subway and rode to Penn Station, where they disembarked amid the throng of rush-hour commuters. Police officers stood by the turnstile, asking to inspect the purses and backpacks of random passersby. The woman behind the brothers was flagged; they continued their conversation about baseball without a second glance.

Making their way to the designated bathroom, they taped an out-of-order sign on the exterior door and slipped inside. After the last stall emptied, one brother pulled a cordless drill from his pack and secured the door from the inside. He then unscrewed the grill to the ventilation shaft while his likeness took electronic components, and two shiny steel containers, from his bag and assembled them on the bathroom floor.

Another text chimed. This one was from their partner, Arthur Patterson, confirming that he was on schedule and about to enter FBI headquarters in Washington DC.

The two brothers exchanged knowing smiles.

It was time.

With a latex-gloved finger, one of them tapped the red button on the timer. The digital LCD read 59:00, and then it started counting down.

His counterpart hoisted himself up and entered the vent's opening and was gingerly passed the canisters. The LCD screen now read 56:42.

Disappearing into the plenum, cradling the precious cargo, the twin crawled deep into the airshaft. Eight minutes and twenty-five seconds later he scuttled out, feet first. With haste, yet careful not to scratch the paint or leave other signs of entry, they reattached the grate and removed the screws from the door.

Inconspicuously, slipping back out of the bathroom, they removed the sign from the door's exterior and stuffed it in a backpack before exiting the station. As soon as their soles touched the sidewalk, they sparked victory cigarettes. Spying an abandoned copy of the *New York Times* lying on the sidewalk, one brother remarked to the other, "The headlines will be more interesting tomorrow."

"Indeed," replied his double, and turning south on Eighth Avenue, they disappeared, blending seamlessly in with the crowd.

100

Less than two kilometers from Krueger's hunting lodge, the group exited the stream, now a mere rivulet of water, and ducked into a patch of neighboring trees, where Clark unexpectedly called them to a halt. He closed his eyes and listened.

The brook trickled, breaking the silence.

Then, as if hearing something on the wind, Clark turned to Derek, his expression concerned. "Keep him covered," he ordered, motioning to Krueger, "and stay alert, both of you," he warned in a hushed tone to Derek and Katrina. "I'll be back shortly."

Derek trained his pistol on Krueger and instructed him to sit on a mossy rock.

Reticently, Krueger complied, cradling his blood-soaked arm. His worried eyes darted nervously about the woods.

Watching him, Katrina sensed that Krueger was hiding something big. Unsure what to think, she scoured the early morning shadows for danger and drew the tranquilizer pistol from its holster on her belt, disabled the safety, and laid it on her lap.

Meanwhile, Clark crept around the hillside's jutting rocks. Careful not to leave tracks, he avoided the dark evergreens with patches of snow under them, and soon, he came within visual range of the lodge.

Swinging himself up onto a low-hanging branch of a large hardwood, he climbed up to gain a better view and, leaning against the trunk, he lifted his binoculars. The world was magnified.

First, he searched for signs of the militia in pursuit, but they were nowhere in sight. Most likely, the water trek had thrown them off the trail and bought his crew some much-needed time. Then, he surveyed the lodge that Krueger had inherited as a payoff for services rendered somewhere along the way. The gray slate, two-story stone building appeared to have been built for aristocracy during the Czarist Era. As such, Clark guessed the building's construction included secret passageways and dead zones, offering numerous hiding places and escape hallways, making it impossible to find the hidden assets without Krueger's aid.

In front of the lodge, the grounds had been cleared. A deserted, narrow drive meandered from the forest to the entrance. The back of the structure nestled up into a hillside and, from the looks of it, offered no room for vehicles to park in the rear. The structure looked deserted and, with a posse tracking them, logic dictated that Clark make haste and return to his group, but his gut told him otherwise.

101

In Washington, Sterling and Fleming pushed through the doors of the FBI offices in response to an urgent call from FBI agent Ted Baker. An informant had turned himself in and wanted to trade information about two upcoming terrorist attacks in exchange for immunity and money. He was being held in "protective custody."

As they entered the lobby, the receptionist, who had been awaiting their arrival, sprang out of her chair and escorted them to their destination, her scant ninety-four-pound frame casting a toothpick-like shadow as she led them through the maze. "Agent Baker's expecting you," she said as she ushered Sterling and Fleming inside an observation room with a two-way mirror.

Baker sat at a table with a cell phone plastered to his ear. He was on hold and he cut right to the chase. Pointing at the man behind the two-way mirror, Baker reported, "His name is Arthur Patterson. We've run a background check. This guy's got a laundry list of minor offenses and may be a pedophile, but he doesn't fit the profile of the other perps. Most notably, he was arrested at O'Hare airport in 2006 with a straight razor in his carry-on. He was detained but later released."

"Did you offer him immunity?" Sterling asked.

"If his intel proves valid, but, you gotta know the son of a bitch wants more than immunity," Baker said in a tight, pressure-filled voice. "He wants a fresh identity and a million dollars in unmarked bills. I think he's running from something or someone big."

Sterling's eyes narrowed as he studied the blond man through the mirrored glass. Arthur Patterson's gelled hair drew attention to his red-hued skin and pale eyes and made him appear taller than five foot six. Calm and in control, he looked as though nothing odd was taking place.

Fleming piped in. "What's he got?"

"Says there's a bomb planted at New York's Penn Station—set to detonate in . . ." Baker glanced at his watch pensively, worry flooding his face, ". . . twenty-four minutes. I'm on hold with the bomb squad now," he said, motioning to the phone still against his ear. "National Guard and K-9 are already on the ground."

"Shit!" Sterling said and rubbed his brow.

"Did he say what kind of explosive?" Fleming probed.

Baker's eyes locked onto Sterling and Fleming, conveying a deep, unspoken fear before uttering the unthinkable. "Nerve gas."

102

A deep sense of foreboding still nagged Clark, who had been in surveillance of the lodge for almost seven minutes. The sun's edge was starting to peek over the horizon, shortening shadows and diminishing potential hiding places. He'd have to move out soon.

Just then, out of the corner of his eye, he caught sight of something. In one of the upper windows, a curtain parted and quickly closed. Someone was lying in wait. "Damn it," Clark whispered. Trading binoculars for a satellite phone, he cupped his hand over his mouth. "Kilo Base—this is Echo Fox. I'm uploading coordinates. There's a small clearing approximately four hundred meters to my east. Send the chopper in ASAP. Two to transport." Signing off, he dropped from his vantage point in the oak and ran unseen back through the forest.

Emerging from the trees, he returned to the group and without explanation handed Katrina the compact semi-automatic she'd refused earlier and ordered her to cover Krueger.

"But . . ." she began.

"I need to talk to Derek alone," he offered without explanation. "Kill him if he so much as moves."

Clark's demeanor left no doubt in her mind that she needed to follow orders. Taking the sidearm, she leveled the pistol directly at Krueger's chest, after which Clark moved off, out of earshot, and briefed Derek on the impending change of plan.

Unflinching, Nikolai Krueger stared down the barrel of her pistol and smiled as he studied her features hidden behind the disguise.

Katrina steadied the firearm, held its grip with two hands, and concentrated on looking like she meant business. She was not sure what circumstances could ever justify her taking someone's life, and she prayed she would never have to find out, but she didn't want Krueger to doubt her willingness to shoot.

Relentlessly, Krueger stared at her, scrutinizing. She could feel him peeling back the camo paint and military glasses. A master of deception himself, it took only a moment for cold, hard recognition to hit him. With a shrewd and knowing smile, he said, "Welcome to Russia, Dr. Walker. I was wondering where you'd disappeared to."

Katrina's eyes went wide. Fear ran cold through her veins, but she didn't utter a word to confirm or deny his observation, nor did she flinch as Derek sprung from behind and grabbed Krueger hard by the collar, shoving him to the ground on his knees. Pressing a pistol into the base of Krueger's skull, Derek yanked Nikolai's face skyward to meet Clark's.

"What do you know about Dr. Walker?" Clark demanded coldly, coming to stand in front of his adversary.

Cagily, Krueger stammered, "The sleeper, Susan, visited her. That's all."

Clark's icy cold and unwavering stare fixed on Krueger, and he smiled in amusement. "We've got a credibility problem with you, Cobra," he replied flatly. "You've been less than forthcoming, and if you tell me one more lie, Derek here is going to put you out of your misery."

Krueger winced, visibly shrinking back. "I don't know what you're talking about," he weaseled.

Clark had reached his limit and, bringing his face close to Krueger's, gritted out in a low and menacing tone, "For starters—there are people waiting for us at the lodge—it's a trap."

"I swear on my mother's grave," Krueger begged, his face twisting into a serious frown, and like an actor playing a role, Katrina watched as Krueger's biofield masked his core truth.

"Spare your poor mother, Krueger," Clark replied. "Dr. Walker is the ultimate lie detector."

"Yes, I'm well aware," he glowered, knowing his lies were largely useless in light of her abilities. "Clever of you to bring her along. I applaud your audacity," he replied, before adding bitterly, "—we almost had her ourselves, you know." Leering lecherously, he surveyed Katrina from top to bottom before quipping, "The clothes don't do you justice, my dear."

Katrina glared at him.

Their eyes locked and their fields connected.

Then a sudden realization hit him. The resemblance was unmistakable! She was Eliza's daughter. A calculated, cunning smile revealed his capped teeth. "You're as stunning as your mother," he gloated almost incredulously, "but even more desirable. It seems my friend Eagle has recruited exceptionally well."

Derek, confused, glanced up at Clark for answers, but none were offered.

Katrina's eyes narrowed as Krueger sat reveling in his discovery; his field swirled, sharing intimate details about his sexual relations with her mother. With her cover already blown, she dared to ask the obvious question. "Are you my father?"

Clark held his breath.

The sides of Krueger's mouth turned up in a slow smile, knowing he held a manipulative carrot, and simultaneously aware that she would detect a lie, he finally said, "I wish I could say it was me. But your mother was already pregnant when I joined Steinhertz's team." Pausing smugly in reminiscence, he added, "I did, however, find her pregnancy quite advantageous. I was able to leverage the promise of not taking you at birth for sexual favors," he snickered, "as well as for information about her discoveries."

Clark, barely keeping his anger in check, cracked his knuckles and allowed Katrina to press on.

"So, if you're not my father, who is?" she asked pointedly.

"Give Uncle Nikolai a kiss and I'll tell you," he leered.

Derek tightened his grip mercilessly and Krueger winced.

Katrina spat in Krueger's face, and she felt a true distaste for the man explode within her. "All it takes is a word from me," she bluffed, nodding to Derek and Clark, "and they'll kill you."

Nikolai sneered brazenly and then, deciding it wasn't worth risking his life, divulged, "Your mother was a fertile wench. Records showed she was bred with only one man, but his profile was excellent, which explains your exceptional talents, my dear. Unfortunately, I didn't have an opportunity to meet him. His name was Kurt Schoenwald."

Katrina took a deep breath and glanced at Clark, for whom the information had hit home. The question he'd never dared to ask had been answered. Luckily, Krueger had not ever known Clark by that name, and Katrina only knew Schoenwald as the lover in her mother's journal.

Krueger added, "If I had been aware that you were Eliza's daughter, Dr. Walker, I would have procured you much sooner, my dear. You would have been very useful. Bringing you to Vladimir would have put me permanently in his good graces."

"Vladimir knows Eliza had a daughter?" Clark ventured cautiously.

"She's part of his obsession, or should I say Father's," Krueger admitted, his eyes flicking briefly from Clark to Katrina. "It was assumed that whoever tried to extract Eliza got her daughter because the baby was missing when we evacuated," he continued, smiling creepily. "It seems the child was well hidden."

Derek understood the situation better with each passing moment, especially after Krueger directed his attention to Katrina and added, "They've been hunting you for years. They believe you may have inherited your mother's extraordinary abilities."

Clark's eyes burnt holes through Krueger. "Do they know about Eliza's map, too, or did you keep that little secret to yourself?" he asked unforgivingly.

Krueger laughed derisively. "They have a copy; although, it's a bit incomplete. I kept the original so I could find the stone fragments to the Forbidden Text myself, or sell it. Father still has a team working on his copy. He's on his deathbed and would like nothing more than to find the tablet and gain the elixir of life. But Vladimir isn't really interested in extending Father's life. He seeks the unbridled power that the stone's Forbidden Text would afford him. Short of finding the stone, his own plans for global domination are well under way."

Clark looked to Katrina for verification.

She nodded.

103

Inside Penn Station, twenty-three bomb squad technicians in bio-hazard suits combed the area as National Guard soldiers hurriedly evacuated panicked passengers. Sniffer dogs scoured trash cans, lockers, bathrooms, and ventilation units. Rail traffic citywide had screeched to a halt. On the street above, police had cordoned off a four-block radius, and nearby buildings were being evacuated.

With only minutes to spare, a shout was heard from deep inside the ventilation system where Arthur Patterson had directed them. "I've got something!" called an ambitious young lieutenant.

Ahead of him, in the dark airshaft, an eerie red glow emanated, faintly illuminating the otherwise pitch-black duct. Moving closer, Lieutenant Cassidy stared at the timer's digital readout: 04:32 and counting. *Crap!* He swallowed hard and let a faint shudder pass through him. Nerves of steel had always been his ally—he needed them now.

Propping his flashlight up, he gingerly unscrewed the bottom of the canister and fingered the tangle of wires that connected the detonator to the explosive. Too risky, he told himself, toying with the idea of playing hero and defusing the bomb on the spot. He needed to execute a Render Safe Procedure. "Where's that damn containment vessel?" he barked into the mic of his headset.

"It's coming, sir. Two minutes."

"Well, hurry the hell up!"

104

"Who's waiting at the lodge?" Clark pressured Krueger, who, knowing Katrina was monitoring his replies, admitted, "Vladimir's men."

"A double cross?" Clark confirmed.

"You know me," Krueger smiled nervously. "Vladimir thought I was planning a coup. To prove my loyalty I offered to use my one-time pad to lure you in." Then, trying to appear somewhat remorseful, he quickly justified his actions by adding, "You've been a thorn in Vladimir's side for quite some time, and the last thing he needed was you screwing up the execution of his current plan. Needless to say, Vladimir was quite intrigued by my offer and promised me a secure, high position if I succeeded in bringing you in," he said, pausing briefly before elaborating. "They beat me up a little and stuck me in prison for show. Once we knew the ruse had worked and that you were coming, he threw a party celebrating your impending demise. But somehow you got here a day early and fucked everything up! I had to improvise a new plan. My hope," Krueger finally disclosed, with an apparent high regard for his own cleverness, "was to deliver you to them at the lodge and . . ."

". . . keep the real map secreted for yourself," Clark said, completing his sentence.

"Exactly. That stone is far too valuable to leave it to them," he said.

"I'd guess that sharpshooter was really aiming to kill you?" Clark surmised.

"Unfortunately, yes. Vladimir likes to err on the safe side. No doubt, since you arrived ahead of schedule, he must believe I truly double-crossed him." Grimacing, he added, "Now he views me as a liability that knows too much."

"Which puts you between a rock and a very hard place."

With a shrug and a deep sigh, Krueger admitted, "I've been there before."

"The way I see it, Nikolai," Clark said, glaring at him unsympathetically, "You're about to be pronounced dead—again."

Krueger's mouth twisted unexpectedly into a deviant smile. "But I'm still worth more to you alive," he replied coolly for someone in his position. "You don't know the extent of their plan."

"I have a pretty good idea," Clark assured him.

"No, you don't!" Krueger insisted, groveling nervously. "In any case, you'll never find the map without me."

"You're consistent, Nikolai. I'll give you that," Clark replied.

Krueger shrugged. "You never know which way the wind will blow."

Clark sized up his prisoner. "So the snake might get to live a little longer," he finally said. And with Katrina in position to assess Krueger's field, he asked icily, "One more time, Nikolai. Who's activating the sleepers? And why?"

Krueger's momentary silence elicited a yank on his salt-and-pepper hair from Derek and a reminder of the pistol pressed against his neck. He hesitated only a breath longer before his desire to live overcame all other loyalties. "Vladimir. Fundraising," he finally blurted honestly. "These attacks were just a test—a proof to the big investors that Father's methodology was flawless and that the project is worth investing in."

Clark checked with Katrina, who nodded her head in affirmation. Krueger was finally speaking the truth.

105

Agent Baker looked as though he had aged ten years in the last five minutes. His face a virtual storyboard, he monitored the play-by-play situation on the ground at Penn Station from the cell phone glued to his ear while Fleming glared at Arthur Patterson through the one-way glass. "Give me a few minutes alone with this fink," Fleming said to Sterling, "and I'll find out what the fucker really knows."

"The FBI's already involved and negotiating with him. We'll go in together," Sterling responded flatly, not wanting a repeat of Frank's comatose state.

Suddenly, Baker exclaimed, "They've disarmed it!"

Sterling and Fleming shot each other a quick glance and waited for an update.

"Thank God!" Baker replied as he ended the call. "They got it contained nine seconds before the damn thing blew. We got lucky. That was too close!" he added, leaning back in his chair with a sigh of relief. "We never would have found it in time without Arthur's help."

"So he's for real . . ." Fleming said.

"So it would seem," Baker replied with a sigh of relief.

"Yeah, but you're not seriously going to give that son of a bitch immunity, are you?" Fleming challenged. "If he knew about the bomb, he's on the inside, and we don't negotiate with terrorists."

Baker exchanged a knowing glance with Sterling. "To begin with, he's not a terrorist, he's an informant. And second, his intel was good and saved our asses. He has also promised to tell us about one more imminent attack. If that pans out, I think the president will be happy to give him his price. Don't you think so, Bill?"

Sterling nodded and reluctantly agreed, "You betcha."

Baker added with a sly grin, "Keep in mind, Mr. Fleming, immunity is one thing. When and if I decide to let Mr. Patterson go out and enjoy his new life and his million dollars—that's another."

More at ease, Fleming chuckled, and as they stepped into the room to meet with Arthur, Baker led, saying, "Lucky for you, Mr. Patterson, it seems your tip about the bomb was valid."

"You found it in time?" Arthur asked, appearing genuinely relieved, to Fleming's mild surprise. "Now I get my immunity and my money. Right?"

"Just as we agreed," Baker said with a nod. Pulling a signed presidential pardon from his pocket, he set it on the table.

Arthur's eyes scanned the document briefly, noting the president's signature and seal. "Good," he announced finally. "And the money?"

"We've decided to wait on that," Fleming informed him, "until we see if your second piece of information is as good as your first."

"You can go fuck yourselves!" Arthur suddenly flared, leveling a vitriolic threat, "and you will have millions of deaths on your hands."

"Relax. I'll see to it that you get your money," Baker quickly assured him, playing the good guy.

Sterling was about to step in when his cell phone signaled a prioritized incoming text. Pausing to read it, his face grew grim and he asked Fleming to join him in the hall. "You've got to ship out ASAP," Sterling began, visibly shaken. "There's been an unexpected change of plans," he explained to Fleming. "You'll be briefed at the scramble site," and, pulling a well-used handkerchief from his pants pocket, he wiped his forehead adding, "I'll stay here and handle this."

"But sir, with all due respect . . ." Fleming protested.

"Now!" Sterling barked impatiently, exhaustion and frustration bleeding through. "Get your ass in gear! A car is waiting for you outside. Dress warm, you're going to need it."

106

The half-light of early morning illuminated Krueger's face as he said, "I've been kept outside the inner circle since Vladimir took over, so I don't know the details. But, what I can tell you is that the plan is already in the pipeline," Krueger asserted. "America is history, my dear friend. Time to liquefy your assets and evacuate."

Derek pushed his pistol forcefully against the base of Krueger's skull.

"How many sleepers did Blackheart breed?" Clark asked, dreading the answer.

Nikolai Krueger bowed his head and watched as wine-red droplets of blood from his injured arm marked the white snow in front of him. He understood what was at stake. If he told the truth and lived, Vladimir would surely kill him soon. If he lied, Derek would surely kill him now.

The tension-stretched time slowed, and holding her breath, Katrina waited, ready to weigh his answer.

Slowly lifting his eyes to meet Clark's, with his thick Russian accent drenched in a low and ominous tone, he began, "The program generated approximately eleven hundred assets. The airstrike that destroyed Himmelshaus killed almost half of them, but the greatest loss that night was the list of unique activation sequences for each asset. The earlier sleepers were already emplaced in America, but without the activation sequences, the assets will remain inert."

"If the activation codes were destroyed, how are sleepers being deployed now?"

Krueger grimaced uncomfortably. "Well, you see . . . not *all* of the codes were lost. Over the years, I occasionally took the opportunity to copy portions of the list and smuggle it out of the facility on microdots. It was risky, but I always make a point of securing insurance."

The blood drained from Clark's face. The full impact of Krueger's words cascaded through his field like a toppling stack of dominoes. Outwardly, Clark managed to remain cool, but inside his heart pounded. Swallowing hard, he pressured, "How many?"

"A few dozen," Krueger replied quietly, "maybe fifty. The exact number escapes me. But eventually I had to surrender them to Vladimir under . . . very unpleasant circumstances, along with the 'edited' copy of Eliza Freiberg's map. The recent attacks are from my lists. They are part of a fundraising effort—Vladimir believes the activation sequences for the remaining sleepers can be reverse engineered, but it is an expensive proposition. He needed funding, and now he has it. It is likely any surplus will be used to accelerate Father's hunt for the Forbidden Text."

The baying of bloodhounds cresting the hill drove home the urgency of the moment. The dogs had found their trail.

Katrina felt her chest tighten with fear and, for a second, it felt as though she couldn't breathe. She looked at Krueger and then back at Clark, whose eyes still glinted hard from the interrogation.

"What are we going to do?" she asked.

"You're going to get the hell out of here," Clark began matter-of-factly. "We can't afford to lose you. I've called in the chopper. Derek will take care of you," he added earnestly. "I'm going into the lodge with Krueger and will take another route home."

"I'm staying," she replied stubbornly. "You're going to need me to tell you when he's lying and, since there are men in the lodge, waiting in ambush, you're going to need Derek's firepower."

"Not an option," Clark said flatly. "Don't worry. I've been in worse spots. As soon as the chopper arrives, get out of here and don't look back!"

"You can't tell me what to do," she fired back.

"Like hell I can't!"

"I came all the way over here to help, now let me help!"

"You've got to see the bigger picture," he argued. Taking her by the shoulders, he pulled her aside and said, "Listen, you're the only hope we have of seeing through a sleeper's programming, much less trying to fix their fractures. And, if I do succeed in getting the map, you'd better be there to help us decipher it so we can find the Forbidden Text before they do."

"But—" she protested.

"No buts."

The look in his eyes told her that there was no chance of changing his mind. "All right," she agreed reluctantly, "I'll go." As she turned to leave, she added in warning, "Krueger's never going to stop scheming. Even he's telling the truth, it barely masks an intense network of lies and deceit."

She wasn't even five feet away when Clark called, "Wait," almost under his breath, and said, "there's one more thing you need to know."

He closed the distance between them, and despite his military demeanor and stoic face, Katrina noticed that his look had softened and, for the briefest moment, she thought she detected a glimmer of regret. Clearly he wanted to say something but was struggling with the words. "What?" she quipped, half-smiling, trying to lighten the moment. "Another secret? I think after this I'm ready to retire from your army."

Clark's eyes, now a stormy gray, met hers. Emotional turbulence erupted in his field. Katrina blinked and waited. She felt her stomach tensing, and she was troubled by the pained look in his eyes. She had grown fond of Clark in the short time they'd known each other. Somehow, through the adversity and ground they'd covered both in the physical world and in etheric realms, she felt as though she'd known him for years.

"I was deep undercover . . ." he began haltingly, ". . . in Blackheart's breeding facility."

"You were assigned to extract my mother . . ." she clarified.

Clark shook his head. "No, I'm afraid it's more complicated than that."

A crease knotted Katrina's brow.

"Kurt Schoenwald—that was one of my cover names," he finally admitted.

As his words struck home, Katrina's chest constricted heavily and her blood coursed with the thrill of adrenaline. "What?!" Her throat clenched and she looked at him with wide eyes, calming to vexation.

"So you mean to tell me . . ."

His field spilled open, generously revealing his past, and in an instant, her mind reeled with images of her mother and Jim Clark making love.

"All the things I told you earlier on the plane about Schoenwald were true," he hurried to explain. "I broke cover and was captured. It took me months to escape and get back to DC so I could brief them on Blackheart and request permission for your mother to defect. I was refused. Instead, the facility was ordered destroyed, along with all personnel."

Katrina watched as the fortress of duty that had locked away Clark's feelings crumbled and revealed his hidden truths.

"The reason Blackheart didn't know in advance about your mother's extraction was because I ran that as an independent mission. The bigwigs in Langley would have literally shot me if they had known."

"Why didn't you tell me you were my father?"

"I wasn't sure until Krueger's recent tirade," he replied. "I honestly didn't know she'd conceived during our time together," he smiled faintly. "You were a surprise."

Disbelieving, she grilled him. "You're a goddamned counterintelligence agent! Don't tell me with all the background checks you did that you never ran a paternity test!"

He explained. "It didn't matter. I cared for you as if you were my own. I loved your mother. I loved you."

Tears welled up in her eyes, and pieces of her missing past began to fit together as she realized that Clark, beneath it all, had a tender heart.

The muffled thump of copter blades sounded in the distance. "It's time for you to go," Clark said. Redirecting his attention to Derek, he snapped back to duty and called, "Get her the hell out of here!"

Swallowing hard, Katrina discreetly brushed away her tears. She'd just found her father and didn't want to lose him again.

"Good luck, sir," Derek replied, concern for his mentor etched on his face, and a second later, she and Derek were on the move. Breaking into a full run toward the designated clearing, they left Clark behind with Krueger.

107

Confidently leaning back in his chair, a pardon in one hand and two opened suitcases filled with neat stacks of money on the table before him, Arthur Patterson peered at Agent Baker through narrowed eyes and delivered his second piece of information. "You've got people—extremely sick people—quarantined in San Francisco, St. Louis, and Atlanta . . ." he began.

Baker, taken by surprise, glanced at Sterling for confirmation.

Sterling nodded. "That hasn't been made public. How do you know that?" he asked accusingly.

"Mysterious disease, isn't it?" Arthur said, pausing smugly, ignoring Sterling's menace. "No cure, either. And because of its unusually complex and enigmatic molecular structure, it's highly contagious and long-lived, even outside a host." Arthur paused and then continued. "I've got my pardon and my money. Now, after my new identity gets here, I'll tell you the rest."

Agent Baker shifted his weight in his chair and tapped his pen on the table. Patterson had them over a barrel. "It'll be here within the hour," he finally capitulated.

Arthur ran a finger over his chin as he contemplated his next move. "All right, then. We'll just have to wait."

108

With the private army to the rear closing the gap, time was Clark's enemy. Skirting around the back of the lodge, he pushed Krueger ahead of him at gunpoint. "How many men are inside?" Clark asked in a low whisper.

Krueger shrugged. "No telling. Give me a gun. I'll help you shoot them."

"Like hell I will," Clark quipped as he maneuvered the entrepreneurial Russian in front of him as a human shield. Then, just before reaching the back door, Clark drew his Fairbairn-Sykes dagger with his free hand and sliced the zip-tie binding Krueger's hands. "Open it," Clark ordered.

Nikolai Krueger's hand trembled visibly as he reached for the knob. Slowly and nervously, he checked the handle.

Left unlocked, it turned smoothly, yet Krueger hesitated.

"After you," Clark insisted, pressing his pistol into Krueger's back as the door swung open with a menacing creak.

Krueger, hands held high, inched along nervously, and they entered the dim interior in which the aroma of venison stew lingered.

Methodically, Clark canvassed the downstairs, room by room.

Suddenly, the kitchen door flew back and a startled gunman leveled his AK-74, firing a shot into the wall just to Clark's left.

"*Ni strelat!*" Krueger yelled. "Stop shooting!" He hoped against all odds that his rank within the organizatsiya warranted a cease-fire even though he was currently on thin ice with Vladimir.

The soldier, recognizing Krueger, looked momentarily puzzled, but then smirked at them before he opened fire.

Hitting the deck, Clark immediately squeezed the trigger of his silenced SIG.

Flesh gave way to lead, and the man crumpled in a heap.

With the downstairs secure, Clark prodded Krueger with his pistol. "Where to?"

"Library, second floor."

They crept up the stairs and Krueger motioned silently to an entryway on the right. Clark nudged the door open softly with the toe of his boot. No sounds came from inside, but he still pushed Krueger in first.

Gunshots cut through the library's musty air.

Krueger yowled and fell to the ground. A bullet had grazed his leg.

Four of Clark's casings hit the floor before the ambusher lay dead. He'd been hiding behind the loveseat.

Clark glanced out the window. The coast was still clear, but he could feel them coming. Hoisting Krueger to his feet, he pressured, "Now where's the map and the list of sleepers?"

Krueger nodded toward the back wall. "Right side, third shelf from the top. Past the porn books and drink-mixing guides, there's a Russian version of Dostoevsky's *Crime and Punishment*. That's the one."

Clark couldn't help but smile. "Show me," he said, steering the limping Krueger around the fallen soldier's growing pool of blood.

Pointing, Krueger motioned in the direction of the volume.

Clark reached up and pulled on the dusty tome. With a soft click, a security mechanism on an eighteenth-century painting unlocked and swung open to reveal a wall safe.

"What's the combination?" Clark urged with the wave of his gun.

"Left 47, double right 9, left 33."

Clark disengaged the bolts.

"Step over there." Clark motioned with the muzzle of his gun.

Krueger moved to lean against the mantle of the old stone fireplace. Blood stained his pant leg, and the soggy dressing on his arm had begun to come undone.

After taking another quick glance out the window, Clark depressed the handle and opened the safe. Inside, he found a small box and a loaded CZ 100 pistol, which he swiftly tucked into the back of his belt.

"Look inside the carton," Krueger encouraged him. "You'll see. Just as I promised. The map along with a few of Eliza's other artifacts."

Clark eyed him suspiciously and then, using his knife, quickly sliced open the tape that sealed the box.

109

octor," a hoarse whisper called from the corner of the isolation unit. "Look!" The triage nurse, who had first attended to Denise, had pulled up her sleeves and was staring down at her arms in stunned horror.

From across the room, Marc could see that her arms were dotted with welts and awash in a reddish purple rash. "I'll be right over," he assured her, grabbing supplies for an IV. He wasn't feeling well himself but prayed it was just fatigue.

Nearby, Denise began to wail, doubled over in pain. Judging by her symptoms, Marc suspected that she had begun to hemorrhage internally. There was nothing he could do except to ease her pain, and on the neighboring gurney, boils splotched Mariella's petite body.

Desperate to do more, Marc picked up the quarantine room's private phone and dialed Dr. Roth. "Have we heard anything from the CDC? Things are escalating in here," he said and his voice began to falter. "It's definitely contagious."

"Two more outbreaks are under quarantine," Roth's voice reported gravely, "but no luck yet on determining the pathogen."

Marc Stevens fell silent, muted by disbelief. The reality of the situation was starting to sink in.

Roth continued, "Hang in there. The CDC has teams working on it."
Marc was not reassured. "I'd like to make an outside call," he replied.
Roth nodded. "I'll see what I can do."

110

The Comanche helicopter did a daring bank turn and prepared for a touch-and-go landing in the small clearing below. Black and unmarked, it could have belonged to anyone with money and power.

"Come on!" Derek yelled to Katrina as gunshots sounded behind them. "We've got to go, now!" Bullets thwacked treetops, sending small snow showers down on them, while others zipped past and created tiny craters in nearby rocks. The enemy was fast approaching.

Katrina ran full sprint for the helicopter, which hovered a foot off the ground.

More bullets sailed past; one flew close enough to her right ear to send chills down her spine.

Derek, a few steps behind her, turned and opened a burst of cover-fire.

The copter door slid back and Katrina became conscious that no matter how fast she ran, everything appeared to be happening in slow motion. Her brain was functioning in primal overdrive, each footstep calculated perfectly to carry her closer to the copter, while maintaining as much cover from the trees as possible.

A hammering pain slammed into the back of her left shoulder.

She staggered and kept running. Sounds, smells, touch, and vision all suddenly became extra vibrant as fresh adrenaline surged through her veins. She'd been hit, but the Kevlar vest had intercepted the bullet.

Closing the distance, the welcoming hand of a soldier reached out, grabbed her forearm, and began hoisting her up into the copter. She wasn't sure if she saw it in the reflection of his pupils or if she sensed it, but by the time she turned around, it was too late.

Derek had crumpled to the ground fifteen feet behind her.

Wrenching her arm free, she dropped back down and ran to him. The soldier leapt out behind her, laying down a long volley of cover-fire with his M16. Together, they dragged Derek to the copter and were hoisting him inside when a grenade landed nearby. Rolling softly on the snow, it came to rest less than three feet from where Derek had been hit.

"Shit!" yelled the soldier and, shoving Derek inside, he yanked Katrina into the hovering copter.

"It's about time!" shouted the pilot, who spurred the Comanche skyward. A blink later, the grenade's shock wave sent Katrina careening against the door. Shrapnel pinged off the helicopter, which banked hard to starboard, nearly grazing treetops as it escaped.

Derek's body slid against Katrina's, his blood-drenched garb a brutal reminder that bullets had found their mark. The soldier who had helped them on board applied a tourniquet to Derek's leg and hastily field-dressed the wounds with QuikClot, all the while trying to keep his balance in the pitching helicopter that continued moving evasively to avoid fire. Applying pressure to another bleeder, the young soldier's fear-filled eyes met Katrina's.

Below, a gunfight raged as Blackheart's bravta attacked the lodge.

"Clark's pinned down," the pilot shouted above the din. "Hang on!" Pulling back on the stick, gaining just enough altitude, he rode the warbird hard, dipped her nose down, and strafed the bravta militia with the copter's machine gun.

Most of the men dove for cover in the trees; some fell, riddled with bullets.

One lone gunner stood in defiance and loaded a rocket-propelled grenade. Helplessly, Katrina looked on as he aimed at the broadside of the helicopter. She could almost see him smile as he fired.

The rocket roared past the copter, passing just inches below its skids.

Derek weakly turned his head to peer out the window. Mustering all his strength, he ordered the pilot to get Katrina out of the area, and as he spoke, a trickle of blood ran down the corner of his mouth.

The pilot clenched his jaw. He had his own orders. Ignoring Derek and dodging ground fire, he cut back and strafed the grounds around the lodge twice more.

Katrina thought of Clark. Even with the helicopter's assist, his odds of survival were not good. The lodge was surrounded, and more bravta were coming up the road en masse.

From deep within her, a desire to fight, which she had never experienced before, rumbled to the surface. Subconsciously, her hand touched the gun Clark had given her, and in that instant an unexpected jolt of precognition rattled through her. Again, the intuitive knowing came an instant before the event.

Seized with apprehension, Katrina watched as an explosion engulfed the lodge.

The helicopter free-fell a dozen feet as an orange glow ignited the sky and scorched the cold morning air.

The pilot struggled to recover and finally maneuvered out of range. Initiating a wide bank turn, he headed for safety.

Katrina's heart sank as she looked at the destruction below. The lodge was engulfed in flames. Bravta soldiers regrouped on the blackened earth nearby.

Silently, she and Derek surveyed the damage. Unspoken words hung heavily between them, and his hand reached for hers, offering her comfort, as a warm tear coursed its way down her cheek.

Acrid smoke billowed from the burning lodge.

Derek lost consciousness.

Her heart stretched out in search of Clark. She couldn't find him.

111

At CDC headquarters in Atlanta, more than one hundred doctors, biologists, and virologists sat restlessly packed into a small auditorium, all uneasy about the upcoming briefing, and all gruesomely fascinated with the bizarre new disease.

Dr. Barbara Ilsmith spoke first. "The good news," she said, "is that the disease seems to be contained. Everyone known to have been exposed is in quarantine and there have been no new outbreaks. The bad news," she continued gravely, "is that we're dealing with something incalculably dangerous."

Ilsmith then yielded the floor to three visibly fatigued doctors who were approaching the podium. A large projector snapped on and displayed a biochemical diagram.

A wave of chatter and concerned buzz ensued.

After the crowd finally quieted, the tallest of the three doctors stood at the microphone and solemnly addressed the gathered experts. "What you're looking at," he said, pointing to the display, "is a pathogen never seen before. We've named it Zeta-9." Popping up a new slide to reveal additional chemical formulas, he continued grimly, "As best we can tell, it's a weaponized adaptation of smallpox and Ebola."

An anxious audience member raised his hand and asked, "Where did it come from?"

"We don't know," the doctor answered somberly, "but this much we're sure of—it didn't evolve naturally. This is a designer disease. Someone with a great deal of skill and resources has synthesized it."

The second doctor came forward and added, "Due to this bioagent's total systemic penetration, we'd better come up with something fast, or we are all going to run out of body bags when this thing gets out there on a mass scale."

112

Deep beneath the Franklin Building, AWOL was on high alert. "What's going on?" Sprite asked breathlessly after sprinting through the facility.

"Derek's been hit," Shortcut answered.

"How bad?" she asked nervously, her lower lip trembling almost imperceptibly.

"Bad," he admitted. "What kind of medical facilities have they got at the new scramble site?"

"We didn't plan for that . . ." she stammered. "When I was notified that only Derek and Katrina were coming out, we changed to Plan C. I cut a deal with locals just outside Russia for a location where the helicopter could go in under radar. That's all. It's just an old industrial site where a little money bought us no questions and some time for Clark to get out."

"Damn," Shortcut replied tensely, squinting at an oversized monitor through dirty glasses. "I've got to get a field surgeon and some units of blood in there ASAP."

"I'll help," she offered.

Shortcut glanced up at her. The worry in his eyes spoke volumes. "Help us find Clark," he said. "He's MIA and his signal's gone dead."

Sprite's vivacious eyes turned grim. "I'm on it!" she said, rushing to activate a high-tech, interactive mapping system that integrated into a freestanding glass wall. "If he's out there, I'll find him," she promised. And with a touch, she began manipulating images of the lodge and the surrounding areas, toggling between topographical and aerial maps and satellite and infrared data. Dropping and dragging, she superimposed intel compiled from global sources, searching for clues, or any evidence that Clark may have been able to find an escape route prior to the explosion.

113

Everyone in the quarantine room was now symptomatic: Boils covered Marc Stevens's arms and torso; Mariella had begun to hemorrhage; pain racked the triage nurse who lay in a feverish delirium; and the male patient, the good Samaritan from the waiting room, was vomiting blood.

Denise thrashed about, convulsing on her makeshift hospital bed. Blood oozed from every orifice, and pools of infected, crusting seepage soaked the top half of her mattress. Her vital signs unstable, she arched her back violently and threw up a glob of blood with the most gruesome and pained expression anyone present had ever seen. Then, in a final gasp for air, she stiffened and died.

A flatline replaced her erratic heartbeat on the monitor, and Marc, fighting his own feverish condition, quickly applied a defibrillator. But she was gone.

Dr. Roth's voice came over the intercom and Marc looked up from Denise's corpse defeatedly, "Dr. Stevens, we've heard from the CDC."

He set down the paddles and picked up the private line.

Roth saw his pain and offered condolences. "There was nothing more you could have done. A patient in San Francisco was lost less than an hour ago as well."

Marc's mouth turned down in a frown as he eyed his counterpart through the glass. "What do they think it is?"

"It's not good, I'm afraid," Roth replied. "The CDC has an extremely high index of suspicion that the virus-like pathogen has been engineered. It's rapidly evolving, highly virulent, and they have no idea how to stop it. For the moment, containment is the only solution."

"There must be some experimental treatment?" A thread of hope hung in Marc's desperate words.

"Not yet. The predicted mortality rate is 98 percent."

A hopeless expression overtook Marc Stevens's face, despite his attempt at a brave facade.

"In short, it's the deadliest disease to infect mankind in centuries. If unleashed, it will dwarf all of the plagues that ever devastated Europe."

As he spoke, CDC employees wearing biohazard suits began sealing the room with mylar and duct tape. Dr. Roth stepped back to let them work and watched sadly as the windows were covered with this insulation.

Dr. Roth said, "I'm sorry, Marc."

"What about my outbound call?" Marc asked with fatalistic urgency.

Roth shook his head in negation. "Government's got this thing sealed up tighter than a drum. They've got spin-doctors whitewashing it so as not to cause panic. But I'll see what I can do about getting a message delivered for you."

Marc inhaled a painful breath and looked around the room. At this point, only he remained conscious. His eyes looked down for a moment, then back up at Roth. "Katrina Walker," he said finally. "Tell her I love her." He smiled lightly.

114

A few kilometers west of the Russian border, thanks to Shortcut's underground contacts, a gurney and two medical personnel stood waiting alongside a WWII-vintage ambulance.

The helicopter swooped in for a landing, and Derek was immediately placed on a stretcher and carried away. Determined to stay by his side, Katrina jumped out to catch up, when a stony-faced man with a crew cut stopped her. "Sorry, ma'am," he said, grabbing her by the arm. "You'll have to come with me."

"But . . ." she protested.

"You've got to be debriefed," said the man without equivocation. "Besides, there's nothing you can do for him. Let the doctors do their work."

Katrina's eyes followed Derek's litter as it was placed in the old ambulance. The doors slammed shut and it sped off toward a dismal gray cinderblock building, the color of which blended with the low-hanging clouds in monotone colors of despair. Throughout the abandoned industrial site, several structures proudly displayed their war scars and decay. Graffiti-emblazoned, the gutted buildings revealed bones of rusted steel.

Katrina barely noticed that she was shivering as her escort urgently shoved her out of sight and into the nearest building after cursorily introducing himself as Sergeant Smith. Taking off his jacket, he threw it over her shoulders and hurriedly led her through the frigid structure.

Inside, the air smelled stale and left a bad taste in her mouth. The plank floors clanked hollowly beneath her feet. Didn't they have heat in this place? Another wave of shivers overtook her. For no apparent reason, her thoughts suddenly drifted to Marc and her heart ached. Maybe it was seeing the ambulance that had reminded her of him.

"In here," Sgt. Smith said, directing her to an entryway at the end of the hall, above which a single light bulb dangled precariously from a stripped wire.

Behind the door in the vintage surroundings, a familiar face met Katrina's eyes. Fleming stood leaning over a well-worn conference table, punching buttons on a keyboard that looked sorely out of place. He was reviewing satellite imagery on his laptop.

"I see your computer is all set up," said Sgt. Smith to Fleming. "Can I get you anything else?"

"Keep me posted on Derek Gray's condition, some coffee, and . . ." pausing to take a quick glance at Katrina, he added, smiling wryly, "some donuts for the lady."

As her mouth opened to change the request, he cut her off and remarked disparagingly, "Oh, that's right. I'll bet you don't eat that crap." Waving his hand dismissively at Katrina's escort, who now looked confounded, he finished with, "Bring her something a vegetarian would eat—whatever the hell that is. And Sergeant, make it snappy!"

"Yes, sir," came the quick reply as the door closed behind him.

Fleming, not giving Katrina a second glance as she took a seat, returned his eyes to the screen, "Helluva mission!" he remarked sarcastically. "Agent Gray is half dead," he summarized coldly, "and as for Clark . . ." he paused haltingly as he switched to an infrared satellite feed, "there's no damned heat signature for him in this rubble!"

Katrina stared incredulously at Fleming's tall, lean figure. She wondered what kind of a childhood he must have endured to bring about such a capacity for vindictiveness and lack of regard for human emotion. And while she would have longed to glimpse his field for greater insight, her frazzled state rendered that impossible. Shock, trauma, and grief had knocked her off the grid. Until she could calm down and get some sleep, she was reduced to viewing the world without the added benefit of her broadband connection.

Fleming turned and leveled his gaze at her. His eyes narrowed. "Don't you think it's a little suspicious that you're the only one who's come out of this thing unscathed?"

His insinuation unexpectedly blindsided her. Steeling herself, she ignored his comment and countered, "Don't you think it's possible Clark got out?"

"Not a chance," he replied, his features evidencing only the tiniest glimmer of emotion, which Katrina quickly read to be frustration, rather than despair. "There was a tracking device inside his bionic lenses. The signal showed him inside the lodge when the explosion went off. A split second later, it terminated—he's gone."

Katrina stared numbly at the continuous live feed, watching as little red dots, the heat signatures of living bravta militia, gathered into groups. "Can't we zoom in and be sure he's not just captured?"

With a huff, Fleming replied, "Oh, trust me, I've looked—he's not there." Scanning backward through a series of real-time satellite photos, he continued, "Let me show you a snapshot of the only man that did get out of the lodge . . . and let's play twenty questions."

Katrina hoped against all odds that it might be Clark badly injured, or in disguise.

Stopping short, Fleming boxed the figure of a man and zoomed in, enlarging it again and again. Despite the graininess of the photo taken from a satellite miles up in the sky, the face was unmistakable and a wave of contempt crept up into Katrina's throat.

"Nikolai Krueger," she confirmed, before checking a second time. "Are you sure he's the only survivor?"

Fleming flipped the image back to live feed. "Yes," he replied. "I'm sure. Do you think for a second we would leave Clark in Blackheart's hands? We'd dispose of him ourselves first. The administration already has a full-time job denying involvement in this little escapade," he continued. "Best-case scenario—even if he had survived, he would have been captured and then would have had to terminate himself so as to not be compromised. Let's face it, Jim Clark is history, and we're sitting in a bucket of shit."

Steadying herself with a hand on the table, Katrina fought to sequester the wave of emotion that threatened to reveal her personal connection with Clark.

A knock at the door signaled the arrival of food and drink. Fleming barked his permission for Sgt. Smith to enter. Silence fell over the room as he laid everything out in the center of the table.

Grateful to see a pot of tea in addition to coffee, Katrina poured herself a cup, doing her best to hide her trembling hand.

"So, my little princess," Fleming continued mockingly, "what juicy tidbits have you got for me," he asked, as he poured himself a mug of black coffee. "Hopefully not more mumbo-jumbo, because real live people are dying," he jabbed.

Her heart felt like a cold stone, frozen in her chest. Normally she would have given Fleming a piece of her mind, but now, with Clark missing, his cheap shots were wasted on her. She had more important things to focus on. *Wouldn't I have felt him transition?*

Katrina looked at Sterling with pity. What could she share with him? Clark had told her to trust no one. Krueger had told them sleepers were planted everywhere. Bracing herself, she met his gaze. His dark, beady eyes pierced her soul, and she could sense that he was barely keeping his desire to use his "special" interrogation tactics in check.

115

FBI Agent Baker came back into the conference room and neatly arranged the new passport, birth certificate, and driver's license on the table in front of the informant.

Arthur Patterson examined his new papers meticulously. Satisfied, he leaned forward in his chair. "I will be concise," he began conspiratorially. "Ten days from now, this exquisitely engineered plague will be deployed simultaneously in every city, town, suburb, and hamlet throughout the entire United States."

Stunned, Baker and Sterling exchanged incredulous glances.

"I understand that your initial reaction may be one of denial or inconceivability, but I assure you, gentlemen, I am not exaggerating." Arthur's serious face revealed the truth of his grim forewarning.

Sterling reached for a cigarette.

Baker blinked in disbelief.

Witnessing the impact that his bold claim had on its unwitting recipients, Arthur's features twisted into a defiant grin. Before anyone could offer a reply, he added, "And, much to your humiliation, there will be a huge celebration throughout the world—by everyone who hates, envies, or fears America but would love to possess its rich and beautiful land."

116

Gregory Malchek's ebony cane lay against a private table in a restaurant overlooking the Pacific Ocean. Today found him orchestrating events from a Ritz-Carlton in sunny, southern California. The lion's head carved into the silver handle almost appeared to have a smile of satisfaction painted across its lips as Malchek dialed the secure line from a burner cell phone.

"Yes?" answered the man's cracked, raspy voice. A hand-rolled cigarette of the finest golden-leafed tobacco hung loosely from one hand, as blue smoke rings curled around his withered face.

"The stage is set," Malchek confirmed. "Are we ready to launch?"

"Change of plans," crooned the aged voice of the man who exhaled a lungful of smoke, which wafted through his yellowed teeth. "We've had an interesting turn of events," Steinhertz updated. "It turns out that Eliza Freiberg's daughter is alive," he smiled through intermittent wheezing and coughing. "And, an old adversary—Silver Eagle—has been eliminated."

"That is good news," Malchek smiled. "So what now?"

"Time to tidy up a bit. Patience has its benefits. I want to find the stone and initiate a termination sequence for Arthur. His job is complete."

117

In the makeshift conference room, Fleming's cell phone buzzed. It was Sterling asking to be put on speaker. He had news to share with both Katrina and Fleming. Pushing the speaker button, Fleming cranked up the volume and set the phone on the table.

Sterling began breathlessly, "I'm hightailing it from FBI headquarters over to the president now." Honking horns momentarily overtook the airwaves as Sterling jaywalked across a street, dodging a taxicab and a black limo. "Get set up to video conference with the president. There's been some breaking news!"

"What's the status on the disease? Any more cases?" Fleming prompted.

"The CDC is collaborating with USAMRIID," Sterling informed him.

Katrina knew that USAMRIID researched, among other things, defensive applications in biological warfare. Scrambling to get up to speed, she cut in, "What disease?"

"We've had three outbreaks while you've been gone," Sterling explained, panting as he hurried along. "It's an engineered, weaponized virus. The CDC has named it Zeta-9."

Fleming interjected, "Any luck treating it?"

"Not yet," Sterling panted as he walked. "Thought we'd caught a break when we learned there was a doctor in the Atlanta isolation unit named Stevens working hand in hand with the CDC to isolate the pathogen, but so far this thing's got a 100 percent mortality rate."

Katrina asked for clarification with a deep sense of apprehension, "Dr. Marc Stevens?"

"Yes," Sterling confirmed, averting his eyes from the camera.

"Is he all right?"

"I'm sorry, Katrina," Sterling replied. "I read your background check. I understand you two were close."

Katrina's heart sank and salty, silent tears ran down her cheeks as Sterling went on to briefly describe the situation and that Marc had been one of the last remaining survivors, fighting until the end to save the lives of those sharing his isolation unit. Sterling's voice emanated his genuine regret.

"Great, just what we need—tears," Fleming grumbled derisively under his breath as Katrina dried her eyes. He then asked Sterling, "Have there been any more cases?"

"No," he replied tensely. "But Arthur Patterson, our informant, claims that the biotoxin will be deployed throughout the U.S. in ten days."

"Maybe that's the big thing Krueger promised was in the pipeline," Katrina speculated.

Slicing through the thick silence that followed her words, Sterling replied, "You're going to be our only source of intel on that, Dr. Walker, now that Frank Davis is gone."

"What do you mean, 'gone'?" she asked.

"He was found dead in his cell," Sterling reported.

Katrina paused, stunned.

"From the looks of his remains, it appears that the sleep deprivation device might have malfunctioned," Sterling offered.

Katrina closed her eyes and pressed her fingertips into her temples. She took a deep breath and looking up, stared hard at Fleming, "That was one of your damned contraptions, wasn't it? It cost Frank his life! I could have helped him! Not to mention the fact that you've killed our only viable lead!" she railed.

Fleming's posture stiffened, but instead of a counterattack he carefully moved into a defensive position. Ignoring Katrina, Fleming told Sterling, "You can assure the president that the device was proven safe."

"Not everyone can be saved, Katrina. At the moment, it's a moot point," Sterling said dismissively. "We've got more pressing problems on our hands. Dr. Walker, what else can you tell me? Time is running short. I'll need to brief the president the second I walk in."

Taking a deep breath, Katrina suppressed her desire to reach out to Frank in spirit and said, "You don't understand. Frank's core fractures were healing. He was overcoming Blackheart's programming." Katrina exhaled and looked at the unmoved faces surrounding her. She knew they were beyond caring, but went on. "And to answer your question, the bombers—and I'm guessing this Arthur person—are sleepers developed by a group the U.S. thought extinct, codenamed Blackheart. Krueger alleged that hundreds of these selectively bred, deeply programmed operatives have been deliberately placed in high-powered positions not just in the U.S., but throughout the entire world."

"You mean plants?" Fleming clarified. "Like Karl Koecher or Aldrich Ames, double agents?"

"No," Katrina corrected. "Traditional sleeper agents know who they are. Blackheart's sleepers were different. His trauma-based programming created sleepers that had no conscious awareness of their programming. This is far beyond *The Manchurian Candidate*."

Fleming blanched; the blood drained from his skin. Disconnecting, he immediately hit speed dial for the FBI and ordered, "Move the snitch—Arthur Patterson—to Black Hole." The person on the other end of the line must have argued in return, because Fleming finished with, "I don't care what the fuck we promised him! Do it! Now!"

118

Mai Tais and visions of hula girls in scanty bikinis danced in Arthur's mind as he sat smugly in his cubicle, awaiting the return of FBI Agent Baker and his imminent release. With his mission accomplished, superbly, just as Father had wished, he deserved an extended vacation. After all, didn't all good students of the Order get sent on vacation after performing well?

Suddenly, out of nowhere, a high-pitched screech echoed in his head and rudely interrupted his fantasy. He'd heard sounds in his head before, even voices, but nothing like this.

Just then, the door to the interrogation room flew open and slammed against the wall.

Two armed guards stepped inside with Agent Baker. "Your ride is waiting," Baker announced, not revealing to Arthur that he had been fast-tracked to Black Hole.

Still on cloud nine, Arthur smiled, despite the piercing noise in his brain, pausing only briefly to cock his head and ask, "Do you hear that?"

"What?" Baker replied.

"That sound," he insisted. "Don't you hear it?"

The men shook their heads.

Arthur smacked the palm of his hand against his ear in an attempt to make it stop.

"Let's go," Baker ordered unsympathetically, and Arthur nervously began to bite his nails. The sound was unsettling and stirred deep emotions.

As soon as his fingers were in his mouth, the ringing probed his psyche in a tone he recognized from long ago. An eerie smile stained his face; before he even realized it, he had instinctively used his fingernail to pop out a small, hollowed-out dental bridge, releasing a hidden vial of cyanide. Compulsively, he chomped down. Nine seconds later, cheating Black Hole, Arthur fell to the ground, dead.

119

Fleming, clearly frustrated with the third-world accommodations, stretched his laptop's cord to reach the sole power outlet and plugged in a voltage adapter. The unit powered up, and the on-screen progress bar for video conferencing showed the spotty connection eking along, approaching 27 percent.

A loud knock on the conference room door demanded attention.

"Who is it?" Fleming barked.

Sticking his head in, Sgt. Smith announced matter-of-factly, "Derek Gray is out of surgery. He's in critical condition."

"Can I see him?" Katrina asked.

Before Fleming could deny her request, the crisp image of the president, with Sterling sitting at her left, suddenly appeared on the screen. Katrina's visit would have to wait. Unceremoniously and without warning, he pulled her chair uncomfortably close to his so that they could both be viewed through the webcam's lens.

President Lara Roberts appeared deathly calm, her hands folded neatly on the desk in front of her. Sterling's collar was damp with sweat, and Katrina saw the sheen of perspiration on his forehead.

"I'm glad to see you made it out in one piece, Dr. Walker," the president began with a somber nod. "I am aware of the losses suffered by the team and I offer my deepest sympathies. With time, we shall certainly grieve, but for now we have urgent business at hand."

Katrina noticed that, although the president was performing exceedingly well under pressure, her face told the story of exhaustion concealed by makeup. But more troubling than that, beneath her composed exterior, her morphic field reflected unmitigated fear.

Grimly, President Roberts continued, "It seems we have a situation on our hands . . ." She paused to take a drink of water and clear her throat before continuing.

Sterling fidgeted with his collar.

"A few moments ago I received a message from Nikolai Krueger claiming that Blackheart has sold the biotoxin, Zeta-9, to terrorists."

Fleming's entire body tensed next to hers and Katrina warned, "Krueger lies incessantly, but he did reveal that they were fundraising. Be careful. He is not to be trusted."

Fleming piped in, "Let's 'persuade' Arthur Patterson to tell us what the hell is going on."

Sterling's mouth turned down. "I guess you haven't checked your texts," he reported flatly. "Patterson's dead."

"What the fuck?" Fleming snapped. "I just ordered him sent to Black Hole!"

"Cyanide capsule hidden in a false tooth," Sterling elaborated. "Old school. Looks like some kind of microwave trigger set him off. He was complaining about hearing a high-pitched sound that no one else heard right before he offed himself."

"Damn it!" Fleming replied, slamming his hand down on the table with a bang.

"But that's not all—here's the kicker," President Roberts added solemnly. "Watch this."

On the monitor, a small, black-and-white video captured by a cell phone popped up to reveal the grainy image of a bandaged Krueger. "Hello, my dear friends of America," Krueger began in his thickly accented English.

The sound quality was poor and scratchy. Fleming raised the volume.

The video continued. "I am here to tell you that our organization has sold the biotoxin you call Zeta-9 to a long-standing enemy of the United States . . . whose name I cannot reveal. However, in the spirit of fair play," he paused with a small but intrepid smile, "we are willing to exchange a vaccine specifically designed to stop this threat for one Dr. Katrina Walker. You have two hours to decide your fate."

The video cut to streaks of gray and black. Then the screen switched back to the president and Sterling.

Fleming glowered. "Why the hell do they want *her*?" he asked suspiciously. "I'm telling you, it just doesn't add up. She's the only one who got out of Russia unharmed. Maybe she's one of them and they want her back," he ventured brazenly, before turning to scour Katrina from head to toe, as if looking for something that had eluded him.

"For Christ's sake!" Sterling said defensively. "She's a civilian and she's certainly no sleeper! If she was, she would never have helped us discover the truth behind Frank and we wouldn't know half of what we know today." Directing his comments to the president, Bill contended, "If they want a trade, we've got other people down in Black Hole and sites like Guantanamo Bay who could be more valuable to them than Dr. Walker. Hell, we don't even know if this vaccine is legitimate!"

The president cleared her throat, silencing the two men. "And we won't have a chance to test it before we make the swap." The president looked hard at Katrina, "Sometimes, there just aren't any good options. Dr. Walker, why don't you tell me why they are willing to trade you for this vaccine."

Katrina's breath caught in her throat. She hesitated.

President Roberts pressured, "We need to know . . ."

"They are after a bigger prize," she began. "They want to use my abilities to help them interpret a map that leads to the stone pieces containing the Forbidden Text," she began.

To her surprise, the president nodded knowingly. "I was hoping you and Clark would come back with the map."

"What map?" Fleming demanded, maddened at being out of the loop. "And what the hell is a forbidden text?"

Steeling herself, Katrina continued cautiously, "The Forbidden Text is fabled to contain secret codes for accessing what some might consider the alchemical powers of God. Steinhertz, the one they call Father, seeks the elixir of life. He is old and desperate to live. Vladimir, his young protégé, is power-hungry. He seeks the Forbidden Text like Hitler sought the Spear of Destiny—to rule the world."

Fleming snorted in disbelief and, holding her in his vice-like gaze, he relentlessly stared her down with unforgiving scorn. Sterling's face, on the other hand, emanated a pride that made it clear he had already been briefed on the ancient treasure.

Illuminating for Fleming's sake, the president explained the background of the Copper Scroll, and Fleming, although still cynical, relented. The president's corroboration had gone a long way to legitimizing the claim. "So this 65th treasure—the map to the Forbidden Text—is for real?" he prodded skeptically.

"Real enough to kill for," the president replied. "They're after the bigger prize."

"Okay, but why are they after Katrina? Don't they have psychics in Russia?" Fleming mocked.

Sterling interjected, "What's the viability of running a black-ops mission instead?"

"Not enough intel and not enough time," the president replied matter-of-factly. "Besides, it's more complicated than that. The woman who discovered the map and deciphered the Copper Scroll's encrypted 65th treasure was extraordinary. Her name was Dr. Eliza Freiberg, and Blackheart conscripted her against her will before we tried to wipe them out with Project Clean Sweep. She had keen extrasensory abilities. Clark ran the op to extract her." The president paused for a breath.

"Great, I get that. Clark was a hero . . . and he went down in a blaze of glory," Fleming said. "But again, what does that have to do with Dr. Walker?"

The president continued, her impatience with Fleming's attitude bleeding through in her tone. "When Clark attempted to extract Dr.

Freiberg, she was killed. All he successfully brought out was her newborn child and some journals."

Fleming and Sterling listened, still unsure what the president was driving at.

"Gentlemen, I'd like you to meet Alexia—Dr. Freiberg's daughter," the president announced, and motioning to Katrina, she tied the pieces together.

Stupified, Sterling gasped, "Katrina is a product of Blackheart's breeding program?"

"She was designed to be one of their elite," the president confirmed, "and although she wasn't raised in their program, it seems they have high hopes that she can decipher the map her mother left behind."

Fleming said, "Interesting," and turned to look at her once again, this time with an uncharacteristic smile. "So, it seems you are 'special' after all."

Katrina recoiled inside at his tone.

Sterling cut in, "With all due respect, Madame President, I've read Dr. Walker's file—each and every word. There was no mention of her being a product of the supposedly exterminated Blackheart operation! I never would have approved of her coming on board! The records show she's a U.S.-born citizen and the daughter of a woman named Hilde."

Nodding, President Roberts confirmed. "Need-to-know basis, Sterling—and at the time—you didn't need to know."

Sterling's blood pressure rose, painting his ears dull red.

"I was made aware of the circumstances of Dr. Walker's background when Clark arranged for her security clearance," the president continued.

Katrina tensed inside. Although the president thought she knew the whole truth, what she didn't know was that Clark was Katrina's father, and that was something she didn't plan to share. If Clark did manage to come out of this alive, the information would forever compromise him. She was Clark's Achilles heel—a daughter whose life anyone could use against him. Likewise, someone armed with that knowledge might believe she was privy to more about AWOL than she really was, and that would endanger her. No one could know.

"Madame President," Sterling began, "I still don't think sending Katrina is necessarily the best option. She's untrained. Wouldn't a look-alike or something fit the bill?"

"I'm afraid not," the president replied with resolve. "Katrina, under the circumstances, I have to ask you to go in."

Sterling leaned back in his chair, and a small smile cracked Fleming's face as the implications unfolded in his mind. "You will be our mole— our eyes and ears on the inside," he said.

Sterling added compassionately, "Once you get the map, we'll extract you."

"Then you can use your mumbo-jumbo powers to find the Forbidden Text for us," Fleming concluded.

"Actually, Katrina, I'm going to ask you to do more than that," the president interrupted. "For a chance at minimizing deaths, we need to understand Blackheart's organization from the inside out. We need a list of the sleepers that are lying in wait, planted around the world. We need to undo Blackheart's master plan. I'm going to ask you to undertake a very dangerous mission. You are untrained and unqualified, but you are the only person capable of helping us out in this situation."

"Don't worry, Katrina," Sterling said. "We'll get you out before it's too late," he promised, growing serious. "We'll even implant you with a tracking chip so we can monitor your every move."

It was all happening so fast; Katrina sat in stunned silence, feeling trapped. Out of nowhere, she felt a nurturing presence by her side. *Was it Clark?* As if in answer to her question, her mother's face flashed in her mind. Katrina swallowed hard as a surge of resolve exploded within her. *I will do this.*

"You're our only way into Blackheart at this point," the president pressured. "Your services are required not only for the good of this country, but for the world."

Katrina knew she had no choice. Maybe it was genetic, or maybe it was her soul's path, but she felt a strange call to duty. The opportunity to complete her mother's mission was right in front of her, and she was determined to see it through. Moreover, she knew that if Clark was alive he'd be targeting Krueger and Vladimir to get the information needed to stop the sleepers. If they were willing to trade the vaccine for her, she could get on the inside and help him—maybe even save him as he had saved her when she was a child. Besides, according to Derek, she was the perfect candidate—no family awaited her, at least not stateside. Even Marc Stevens had been eliminated. She nodded in acquiescence. "I'll go," she replied. "But, just for the record, where exactly are you going to install this tracking device and when?"

"A specialist can be sent immediately," Sterling assured her. "You won't even see a scar."

Stacking a set of papers on the table in front of her, the president concluded, "I'm glad you got out. At least now we know who we're dealing with. I'll contact Krueger and tell him he's got a deal."

Sterling added, "In the meantime, Katrina, get some rest."

"Yeah, you look like hell," Fleming joked, trying his hand at levity and failing miserably. "Camo paint doesn't hide those dark circles," he scoffed. Fleming didn't need any psi abilities to decipher the look that Katrina shot at him. Quickly regrouping, he bellowed for Sgt. Smith through the closed door.

Almost instantly Smith popped his head in. "Yes, sir," came his quick reply.

"Take Dr. Walker down to the infirmary. There's an extra gurney there where she can catch some shut-eye."

120

Katrina followed Sgt. Smith through the ramshackle structure to the infirmary in silence. Fleming stayed behind to coordinate her exchange for the vaccine with the president.

Inside the dispensary, a tall doctor with a brown ponytail stood hovering over Derek Gray's body. White gauze bandages oozed blood. A makeshift IV pole had been rigged with a hook on the wall. Katrina walked to the side of Derek's bed and gently laid a hand on his arm.

Despite her thick Ukrainian accent, the doctor's English was quite good. "Next twenty-four hours critical," she began. "Maybe he has no serious complication and pulls through," she continued with a grim smile.

"Dr. Walker needs to lie down," Sgt. Smith informed the doctor, pointing to the empty hospital bed next to Derek's. Apparently, the medical team had prepared for the possibility of two injured evacuees. "Someone will be coming to do a procedure on her shortly; but first, she needs some rest," he explained.

The doctor eyed Katrina and frowned. Dirty from head to toe, Katrina was an unhygienic addition to the post-op ward. Handing her a hospital gown and pointing to a washbasin, she said, "Wash self and change clothes. Then you sleep," she said. "I'll be outside. But do not disturb man. He need rest, too."

Katrina smiled and thanked her. Climbing out of her dirty clothes, she took off the Kevlar vest and reached back to touch her bruised shoulder. Her mind flashed back to when Clark had handed it to her back at AWOL, and a lump formed in her throat. Fighting back the tears, she hurriedly changed and pulled her bed closer to Derek's so that she could hear him breathe. If nothing else, she wanted him to know, at least subconsciously, that he wasn't alone.

The surge of adrenaline that had fueled her had finally worn off. Bone-tired, she was consumed by fatigue, and in that moment, the institutional gurney looked like the most luxurious bed she'd ever seen.

Exhausted, she pulled back the thin, blue blanket and lay down. Her head sank into the pillow and her body began to melt. Relaxing, she hovered in that blissful state between waking and sleeping where dimensions intermingled, creating an indistinguishable mesh between the worlds of particles and waves. Out of the corner of her eye, she thought she saw Derek stir. Or was it his energy body? She wasn't sure. Either way, intuitively she knew he was going to be all right.

She needed to recharge before embarking on the impending mission. *Time for a virtual vacation*, Katrina told herself as she closed her eyes. *Or would it be a real one?* she mused as she remembered that some indigenous peoples contended that dreamscape was actually reality, and that the world we believed to be reality was merely a reflection of the world we dreamt.

Momentarily setting aside thoughts of her impending assignment, Katrina began to drift. Although she was still awake, her body felt as if it was growing lighter, until before long, she felt as if she was floating two feet above the bed. Katrina had separated from her physical being and accessed the gate to astral travel and lucid dreaming.

A few hundred yards away, she saw a dim glow, and focusing on it, she suddenly found herself surrounded by ancient trees, whose long lives had given their gnarled roots time to shape the ground beneath them. The fresh smells of evergreen and soil mingled with pungent sap. As she walked down the path toward the light, she could hear the crunch of every twig and the rustle of every leaf.

An owl flew overhead, slowly circling, and way-showing to a ring of trees in which a Native American elder sat tending a fire. Flickering light danced across his angular face and a colorful, handcrafted blanket was wrapped around his shoulders like a shawl.

The spicy smoke of juniper greeted her. Not wanting to alarm him, she approached quietly and with reverence. His smiling eyes looked up as she neared, and he put down his fire-tending stick. "Welcome, my child. We have been waiting for you."

His ancient voice flowed through her like a gentle river. Resonating deeply to her core, it filled her with a warm sense of familiarity. She looked about, but saw only him and wondered at his response. "We?" she asked.

"Yes. We," he replied and, straightening his bent body to a surprising height, he directed her attention to a teenaged boy bundled in a sleeping bag, murmuring to himself softly in his slumber.

She studied the adolescent form and recognized Jim Clark, her father, as a young man.

The elder then turned to her and asked, "What name was chosen for you, Trueheart?"

Katrina stared at the man for a moment.

"My name is Katrina Walker. And who are you?" she asked of the man whose soulful eyes reflected timeless wisdom and whose weathered face celebrated life's journey.

"You may call me Tsóyéé," he replied. "I have come here, Katrina, to share ancient knowledge with you. This boy, my grandson," the man gestured with a hand, continuing, "will soon think that I have died. However, this is not true. I am simply departing from my physical body and journeying into a different realm of existence."

Katrina looked at him, confused. "I'm sorry, but I don't understand."

Tsóyéé smiled warmly, "Ah, but you do, my dear child. You understand much beyond even what I do. You are a seer. You have been on the other side yourself. You know that just because people are gone does not mean they are dead, and just because a body is dead does not mean a person is gone." He motioned for her to sit on a log nearby.

The fire warmed her as she sat. As Tsóyéé continued, his spirit body extended far beyond his physical form, creating a hazy, soft-edged ephemeral appearance.

"In my absence, my grandson will be tested. He will have to choose to walk forward in life as a leader, a warrior of light, or succumb to the temptations of darkness."

Katrina swallowed down the lump that had formed in her throat.

"You, too, will be tested," Tsóyéé warned. "The greatest war the world has ever known has begun. If there is to be any hope of restoring humanity and regenerating our earth, the broken pieces of Sacred Stone must be found and reunited, for the knowledge contained within it will awaken man's potential to heal. But, only one who can see beyond the veils can locate the missing pieces; and only one who is pure of heart can read the tablets of light." Tsóyéé looked at her gravely. "Trust the compass of your heart to guide you, and remember, the trials of darkness are but illusion if we awaken the light within."

An uncanny sense of hope flooded Katrina. Her feelings of loneliness and worry temporarily fell away and her field sang with purpose.

Intoxicated by her surroundings and the truth behind his gaze, Katrina almost didn't notice a faint noise building in intensity. She tried to ignore it so as not to disconnect from her astral meeting, but it kept pulsing in her mind, bringing her back to consciousness.

Opening her eyes, Katrina realized the persistent beeping was from nearby medical equipment. They were preparing to implant the tracking device.

121

Nikolai Krueger, bandaged and clean, sat in front of an ornate desk feeling vulnerable. The guard outside the sound-proofed office had relieved him of his pocket pistol, and the wounded spy felt an unnerving sense of déjà vu under the fierce blue-eyed gaze of Vladimir.

"So can you, or can you not, confirm the death of James Clark?" Vladimir asked, grilling him.

Krueger averted his eyes involuntarily before answering. "Sir, I can confirm that he was inside the lodge when it was destroyed."

Vladimir poured himself a cup of strongly aromatic tea from a silver service. He left the second cup empty. Lean and strong, his six-foot, four-inch frame overshadowed Krueger. "Don't dodge my questions, you ungrateful old bastard. Yes or no?" he demanded icily.

"No, sir. I lost track of him in my own escape. But may I remind you that infrared and thermal scans of the area showed only rubble . . . and two friendly casualties which were . . . neutralized for security reasons?"

"I should have had *you* neutralized for security reasons," Vladimir seethed.

Krueger didn't respond to the undisguised threat but glanced up, poker-faced. "I am still quite valuable to you, sir," he cajoled. "Katrina Walker will have confirmed my identity to her superiors and they will expect me to perform the transfer. Surely you don't expect them to make the trade with someone they cannot . . . hold accountable?"

"You overestimate your role in this, Nikolai. It's the vaccine they're interested in, not who they get it from. But, if there's any shooting to be done, I would prefer you to be on the receiving end of it," he responded without a trace of emotion. "So, yes, you shall go and perhaps save me a more valuable asset. The shipment of vaccine is staged and prepared; do not return without the girl."

Surreptitiously seeking to learn more about the plan, Krueger ventured, "Very clever of you to offer assurances that there will be no more sleeper incidents."

Vladimir smiled, his perfect teeth glinting, his handsome face hard. "The Americans are afraid and that's priceless. Why would I expend more assets?" he said and laughed and rocked back in his seat. "The sleepers have served us well in securing our necessary funding. It would be foolish to waste them."

"What will you do with the girl?" Krueger asked.

"I've got bigger plans, and Katrina Walker is part of them. See that she is unharmed. I want her voluntary cooperation."

Krueger tried to stare at him questioningly, but under Vladimir's crystal and unwavering gaze, he found himself squinting at the desk.

"Here are your orders. Consider yourself dismissed." Vladimir slid a red dossier across the polished desktop, and as he did, Krueger noticed the corner of black basaltic rock peeking out from a brown paper wrapping near the desk lamp. *Had Vladimir successfully procured a piece of the Forbidden Text's stone tablet? Impossible. His copy of the map is incomplete.* Ever-enterprising, Krueger motioned toward the rock and risked Vladimir's scorn by venturing, "Is that a gift for Father? Shall I bring it to him?"

Vladimir's contemptuous eyes locked on Krueger's, but Krueger quickly looked away. But before he did, he saw a lust for something that no man should dare dream of.

Krueger stood to leave and Vladimir said, "Oh, and Nikolai, I suppose you will correctly deduce that I have taken out some extra insurance against your unpredictable nature; someone by the name of Yemelyan Sidorov. Perhaps you've heard of my favorite assassin?"

Krueger swallowed dryly. "Yes, sir. Of course I have."

"Good. Then you know she will not miss. Make sure the Americans get their vaccine and that we get Dr. Walker. If you fail, you will not need to bother reporting back."

As he dared to glance at Vladimir's face, Krueger found himself once again caught by the odd sensation of familiarity. Was it Vladimir's nose, or his eyes? But then, such is common when dealing with the children of old acquaintances.

122

atrina hopped off the unmarked gray helicopter into a damp fog and fought back the trembling that ran through her core. The bright moon illuminated the dew-smattered field in an eerie grayscale, and the copter hovered a meter above the ground. She could feel the rotors cycling and she could sense the rifles of the soldiers on board, searching for hostiles or an ambush in the night. Her every quaking nerve screamed for retreat, but since her astral visit with Tsóyéé she felt an unshakable determination. Katrina knew what had to be done, and she knew the exchange was worth her freedom—or even her life. People needed the vaccine. The attacks had to stop, and more than that, she knew she had to keep her mother's map out of the hands of Vladimir.

A crackling noise filled her left ear. Touching her earpiece, she said, "Come again? Didn't read that." The voice came again, stronger this time. "I repeat, the vaccine has been loaded. We have the vaccine. Do you copy?"

"Roger," Katrina replied. She walked forward, waved her hand in a circle, and the helicopter's engine could be heard whining as it climbed into the sky, but she didn't look back. Telepathically, she reached out to Clark, hoping to access his field. She didn't find it, but nonetheless, deep inside she could not accept that the man she had so recently discovered to be an integral part of her life had gone. And here she was, about to reenter the place of her birth, of her mother's death, and of the genesis of this strange and dreadful saga. Perhaps this would be her opportunity to close the circle and—just maybe—she would find the Forbidden Text and rescue her father.

As instructed, Katrina dropped the earbud, kneeled on the ground, and put her hands on her head. After a moment, she could make out the beams of flashlights. Four armed silhouettes approached, flanking a trench-coat-clad man smoking a cigarette. Nausea overcame her when she heard Krueger's voice.

"Hello, Katrina," he said cheerfully, "how nice to see you again."

🗒 🗨 Ⓥ

Private First Class Enfield paused to wipe his forehead with his sleeve. The evening's chill had worn off quickly; it had been easy to work up a sweat offloading crate after unmarked crate of vaccine from the guarded truck and onto the small squadron of C-12 Huron airplanes. The pilots took off immediately, each escorted by an F-15 Eagle jet. They climbed to a cruising elevation and vanished in the safety of the dark sky.

🗒 🗨 Ⓥ

In Washington DC, a visibly relieved president televised an address to the public. "Ladies and gentlemen, I'm happy to report that the current threat to national security has been deterred and the nation's terror threat level has been lowered from red to orange. And thanks to the valor and swift action of the United States Armed Services, our efforts have led to a rapid procurement of vaccine for the Zeta-9 virus. The vaccine has already been tested by the CDC and found to be completely effective. It will be distributed by military transport to every major city by noon tomorrow. Be aware that convoys and roadblocks may occur in the early hours of the morning to make sure this vaccine gets where it needs to go. Please contact your local authorities or hospitals to learn where you can be inoculated."

Fact or Fiction?

Reality is the inspiration for the most extraordinary of stories, and *The Forbidden Text* is no exception.

The character James Clark has a real-life counterpart in the author's own father, who was an elite American counterintelligence agent. In the last years of his life, Dawn Clark became her father's "secret keeper" as she assisted him in writing novels that chronicled his adventures.

To discover more about the truth behind the fiction, as well as the inspiration for Dr. Katrina Walker's intrepid journey and the author's personal experiences in the hidden realms, visit: **www.DawnClark.net**.

Repairing Your Field With The Essential Upgrade

Dawn Clark has used her unique abilities to empower others to reshape their futures and the future of the planet. Her work incorporates the research of such notable physicists as William Tiller, Russell Targ, and Brian Greene, as well as biochemist Rupert Sheldrake. Dawn has counseled and advised people from all walks of life, including Nobel Prize and Emmy award winners, Fortune 100 executives, psychologists, teachers, parents, and teens. Working at the nexus of science and spirituality, she helps people repair core fractures, clear toxic emotions, and repattern themselves for longevity and success.

Learn how you can transform your life through Dawn Clark's Essential Upgrade at www.DawnClark.net.

ABOUT THE AUTHOR

An international best-selling author, Dawn Clark has spent her life creating works that empower others to reshape not only their future but also the future of the planet. Standing at the nexus of science and spirituality, she delivers a new vocabulary and insights and tools that help people repair core fractures, clear toxic emotions, and repattern themselves for longevity and success. Dawn has counseled and advised people from all walks of life, including Nobel Prize and Emmy award winners, Fortune 100 executives, psychologists, entertainers, teachers, parents, and teens.

A lifelong sensitive, her enhanced perceptual abilities provide her with an intimate understanding of the underlying mechanics that create our 4D experience. Her knowledge was deepened by a profound near-death experience, and her work incorporates the research of such notable physicists as William Tiller, Russell Targ, and Brian Greene; and biochemist Rupert Sheldrake.

Dawn delivers her message across multiple platforms and genres, including her interactive online adventure series, *The Essential Upgrade*. She has previously published a number of nonfiction books and, prior to her father's death, assisted him in writing novels that chronicled his adventures in American counterintelligence.